ST. PETER'S

MONSTERS

Best wishes!
NB
April 2009

ST. PETER'S
MONSTERS

Neva Bryan

NEVA BRYAN

Brighid Editions
Saint Paul, Virginia

Brighid Editions
P.O. Box 1428
Saint Paul, VA 24283

Published in the United States by Brighid Editions

Library of Congress Control Number: 2008910946

ISBN-13: 978-0-615-26391-5 (alk. paper)
ISBN-10: 0-615-26391-7 (alk. paper)

Printed in the United States of America.

10 9 8 7 6 5 4 3 2 1

First Edition

For my late uncles,
Roger Steffey and John R. Bryan, Jr.

On mountain soil I first drew life . . .

— Edgar Allen Poe, *Tamerlane*

One

Charlottesville, February 1991

Peter took his beating for the cracked ridges and deep valleys in her voice. He had started the fight because he was homesick and she sounded like home, but he blamed the bourbon. He had knocked back four shots of Maker's Mark before he ever met the girl.

He propped his elbows on the bar and ran his thumb around the rim of his fourth drink. The room was dim with smoke, heavy with heat. Images of Operation Desert Storm flashed across a television screen bolted to the wall behind the bar. Peter squinted at the flickering picture and wondered if his best friend was alive tonight. Matt thought military service was his ticket out of the coalfields. You really picked the wrong time to be all you can be, buddy.

The CNN anchor mouthed empty words behind the music that reverberated from wall to wall. Chris Isaak wailed from the speakers mounted near the ceiling. Peter sighed, dunked his thumb in the bourbon, and licked the liquid before it dripped on the bar.

"What are you doing in here on a weeknight, Hillbilly?"

Peter frowned at the nickname, but didn't correct the bartender. "Trying to get warm." He ran his hand through his shaggy hair and stared around the room.

He was the only student in a bar full of townies, and he liked it that way. Charlottesville was an uneasy blend of blue-collar locals, white-collar academics, and privileged college students. Peter thought himself a curiosity here, a working-class student, and he only enjoyed the town when most of the students disappeared in summer.

Two young men hunkered on stools next to him. He figured they were near his age, twenty-one or twenty-two. In another town, they might have been his friends. Not here.

The boy closest to Peter saw the girl at the pay phone and whispered something to his friend. The other moved down one space, so she might take a seat between them. Chicken hawks, Peter thought.

The girl perched on the padded seat without looking at the young men on either side of her. She laid her purse on the bar and rested her hands on it. When she requested a glass of Jack Daniels, Peter heard the gentle resonance of mountains in her words. He tilted his head to get a better look at her.

Auburn hair spilled down her back in ringlets. She wore a plain white T-shirt and ragged jeans. The rich scent of pure vanilla emanated from her. Leather braids adorned her neck and wrists, and Peter caught a glimpse of blue skin beneath the cords. Bruises?

She drank her Jack fast and ordered another. This time the timbre of her speech was unmistakable. Peter knew Southwest Virginia when he heard it. Homesick, he closed his eyes and saw winter hills layered across one another like felt, grey and black and brown, by turns. He pictured the peculiar sky, white clouds bursting through blue, hues sharper than those in a trendy pajama print. He shook his head and the clouds dissipated.

The two boys tried to flirt with the girl, but she stared at the television without responding to their advances. The young man on her right leaned around her and spoke to his friend. "Ricky, you ever seen a piece that nice?"

The blond next to Peter snickered. "Not in a long time, Bryce. Hey, sweetheart, wanna dance?"

The girl stirred, but she didn't answer him. The longer she ignored them, the cruder they grew. No, Peter decided, we wouldn't have been friends. He shot a sidewise glance at her. Why doesn't she just get up and walk away? She remained motionless, a silent shock absorber for the profanity of the two friends.

They had been at her for more than fifteen minutes when he finally decided to address the situation. He tapped Ricky on the shoulder. The boy whipped his head around and peered at Peter with glassy eyes. "Yeah?"

"Why don't you two give it a rest?" Peter suggested. "It's obvious she's not interested." The young man snorted and turned back to the girl.

Peter sighed and took a drink. He rolled its smooth heat across his tongue for a moment before swallowing it. The townie's elbow rammed into his arm. Bourbon splashed out of the glass and ran down his wrist. Peter narrowed his eyes and glared at the back of the boy's head. His hair was the color of banana flesh, his scalp very pink at the part. If Peter hadn't seen his brown eyes, he would have thought the boy was an albino.

"Hey." Peter poked his arm. "You're starting to get on my nerves. Why don't you take your show somewhere else?"

Both boys turned their attention to Peter. Bryce grinned; he reminded Peter of a shark. He ran a meaty hand through his thick brown hair and brought it down to the bar in a gentle fist. "Why don't you mind your own business, Hillbilly?" He looked over at the bartender and smirked.

The bartender polished mugs with a cotton towel, his eyes fixed on the three young men. Peter wrapped a tight fist around his empty shot glass. "I'm getting a little tired of that name. Now come on, give her a break."

The girl leaned back and stared at Peter across the blond boy's shoulders. Her eyes were as green as the first unfurling shoots in his mother's spring garden, but there was such despair in her expression that Peter shivered beneath her gaze. He was glad when she turned back to the pictures of war and death on the television.

Ricky looked around the room. "Did you guys hear that? He's getting a little 'tarred' of that name." Laughing, he placed his hand on the girl's knee. "You don't mind, do you, sweetheart?" She cringed at his touch.

Peter yanked on the boy's sleeve. He sized them up when they stood. Bryce, the brown-haired boy, was five or six inches taller than Peter, at least 6'5". Ricky was just as tall, though thinner than his friend. Might as well go for broke, Peter thought, and plowed into the blond.

A woman across the room screamed. Ricky wasn't soft, but he emitted a low oomph! when Peter hit him. He crashed into a table behind them. The girl jumped from her seat, knocking it over as she backed away from the men. Bryce stepped across her overturned stool and hammered Peter's jaw with three quick blows.

Peter was surprised to see stars. That only happens in cartoons. His knees buckled, forcing him to prop his elbows against his stool to stay upright. The bar's edge scraped his spine and he jerked forward. He rubbed his face and tried to ignore the eager eyes and pinched faces of onlookers.

Bryce waded in again with both fists raised above his head. He slammed the fleshy knobs down on Peter's shoulders, knocking him flat on his tailbone. Damn, that hurts! Seeing that the boy wasn't finished with him, Peter kicked with all the force he could muster. His feet connected with the young man's ankles and Bryce crashed forward on his face. He rolled over, wiping away blood and snot from his nose.

Peter slid backward, out of his reach. A man with a long grey beard reached down and helped him stand. "Thanks,"

Peter croaked. He waited for Bryce to rise. The young man grabbed the leg of a bar stool to stand. When he turned, Peter rammed his elbow into his forehead. Bryce dropped back to the floor and remained there, still as a side of beef.

Turning around, Peter stood nose-to-chin with Ricky, who raised a broken beer bottle in his hand and swiped the air in front of Peter's face. "Think you're tough, Hillbilly? Why don't you go back home?"

I plan on it. Peter laughed, and it surprised his opponent. When the boy glanced at the crowd around them, Peter knocked the bottle from his hand. They clutched each other in a bear hug and lurched across the room. Ricky mashed his fingers against Peter's throat. Sweet bourbon turned sour in his stomach and he gagged.

They stumbled across the unconscious friend; Ricky fell to his knees and Peter yanked his arm back. The boy expelled a high-pitched scream. Tendons stood in sharp relief on his injured arm and Peter, fascinated by the tight little knots, jerked the arm again. He felt a surge of adrenaline and a terrible satisfaction when Ricky screamed twice as loud. He intended to pull it back a third time, but the bartender's hand fell on his shoulder, so Peter released the young man.

The bartender jerked Ricky to his feet and pushed him across the room. He shoved him out the door. He pulled Bryce to his feet, shook him awake, and escorted him outside. Setting chairs in their proper places when the bartender returned, Peter said, "Hey, man, sorry about--"

"Forget it. Just pay up and take off. I don't want to see you back in here the rest of this month." The bartender grabbed glasses from the bar and dunked them in a sink full of soapy water.

Peter dropped some crumpled bills on the bar and mumbled another apology. He looked around the room for the girl with the green eyes. She had disappeared. "She didn't hang around long," he muttered to himself.

"She hit the door as soon as you guys started in on each other." A brunette with wild highlights smiled at Peter. She rested her manicured hand on his arm; the nail polish matched the blue streaks in her hair. "Didn't anybody ever tell you chivalry is dead?"

"Not where I come from."

The bartender cleared his throat as he began to sweep the floor. Peter sighed and pulled on his jacket. "I've got ice back at my apartment," the girl said. She tried to pat his jaw, but he pulled his chin away from her fingertips.

"No, thanks."

Stepping outside, Peter pulled his coat collar up around his neck and stared around the parking lot. He didn't see the two buddies. His jaw ached, his head throbbed, and his nose started to run. *This sucks.* He stumped across the parking lot hoping the alcohol and adrenaline lasted until he got home. *I need some more bourbon.*

He climbed in his truck, started it, and waited for the engine to warm. *Gonna have to start drinking closer to home. Dad'll jerk a knot in my ass if I get a DUI.*

He squinted at the road, trying to drive like he was sober, thankful that traffic was light. Too cold and too late to be out anyway. At the eastern end of town, the road crossed the Rivanna River. He concentrated on not hitting the side of the bridge, which spanned the black water. Halfway across the river, Peter noticed a still figure balanced on the edge of the bridge.

As he drew near, he recognized the redhead from the bar. She sat on the concrete lip outside the rails and stared up at the sky. Peter pulled close to the bridge, cursed when he heard the passenger side rasp against the wall. He cut the engine and tossed the keys on the seat. Climbing out of the truck, he fell and hit the cold ground. "Shit."

He pulled himself to his feet and looked across the truck bed at the girl. Her expression hadn't changed; she still wore that look of utter gloom. Peter walked around the truck, but froze when she finally saw him. "You okay?" he asked.

Without answering, she turned her face back to the stars. Peter placed his palms on the railing of the bridge, but the cold numbed them in seconds. He withdrew his hands and jammed them in his pockets. The girl wasn't wearing a coat. How can she stand the cold on her bare arms like that?

He looked up at the heavens and wondered if the girl was praying. I hope she's not going to do what I think she's going to do. He sidled closer, but stopped when she stirred and looked down at the river.

He struggled for something to say. "My mom helped me memorize the stars and constellations when I was a kid. Betelgeuse. Rigel. Castor and Pollux." Her silence unnerved him. He wanted her to say something, anything, to break the terrible spell that bound them to the bridge. "The Pleiades were my favorites. Seven Sisters. Makes me think there's a whole family up there. You like stars?"

Peter's heart bounced against his chest wall when she reached one arm up to the sky. He glanced side to side. Streetlights exposed the bridge's empty stretch of concrete. Any other night, I'd see cops everywhere I turned. Don't these guys know I'm drinking and driving? Where are they?

"When I was a little girl, Daddy told me stars were really angels. Angels looking out for me."

The soft cadence in her speech pulled him to her. He stood less than a yard from where she sat. "Maybe they are," Peter replied.

She laughed and pointed at the sky. A black stain smeared itself against the velvet night and the stars disappeared with quick little winks. The girl's laughter turned to sobs. Peter reached for her too late.

She fell hard.

Two

Southwest Virginia, 1969–1980

"Fell hard."

"What's that?" Liza asked without looking up from the biscuit dough she was placing on a worn baking sheet.

Edgar turned from the window and smiled at her. "Snow. It fell hard last night. Glad I got some extra coal in yesterday evening or I'd be wading through it now."

Liza placed the biscuits in the oven and layered strips of bacon in a cold skillet. She poured Edgar another cup of coffee and dropped down in her chair. "Least it's Saturday. You don't have to worry about sliding off the mountain to get to work."

Their house sat in a shady valley on top of Pawpaw Ridge, where the bony shoulders of Wise County and Dickenson County rubbed together. Snow lay longest on the mountains there, in the heart of the coalfields.

Bacon popped and Liza picked up a fork to turn it. When the fork clattered on the stove, Edgar looked up from his Bible. His wife was as white as the snow outside. "What's wrong, Liza?"

"Turn that bacon for me. I've got to run to the bathroom." She covered her mouth and dashed out of the kitchen. The bacon was crisp and brown when she returned.

"Y'all right?"

She nodded. "I must be coming down with something."

~~~

Liza stood in the kitchen one bleak morning a few weeks later and stared out the window. A knobby ridge rose above their home and arched its spine against the keen air. Morning dragged its ragged fog across barren mountains until they bled black mud. In the backyard, spongy moss nestled against stone outcrops and muffled the tap-tap of icy rain. Liza didn't move until the sun splattered itself against the sky and dripped golden down the naked trees.

She burst into tears when Edgar stomped mud from his boots and dropped his lunch bucket beside the kitchen door. "What's wrong, honey?"

"I've been coming down with something all right. A baby."

Edgar whooped and spun Liza around the kitchen. She hollered for him to put her down. He laughed and set her on the counter. "A baby! Who'd have thought it after all these years?"

She smoothed back the silver strands in her cinnamon hair. "That's just it, Ed. I'm forty-six. What are we gonna do with a baby at this late date?"

Edgar took her hands in his and kissed her chapped knuckles. "We're going to love it. God'll take care of the rest."

She worried through winter. When she cried at night, Edgar turned on the nightstand lamp and blue shadows fled to the corners of the bedroom. He gathered her in his arms and rocked her to sleep.

~~~

Spring's kind presence eased her mind and Liza put away her worries. A clean breeze encouraged her to open the windows. White cotton curtains flap-flapped against the windowsills. They tickled her cheek as she leaned out the window and called to her husband.

He brought sprays of lily-of-the-valley to the window and sang to her from the green shadows. Deep within the darkness of her mother, the baby girl heard her father's voice and danced inside the rounding mound of Liza's body.

Edgar wouldn't let his wife exert herself in the garden that summer. She wanted to feel the dirt beneath her fingers, the tomato vines that made her legs itch, and the soft corn tassels that brushed her head when she walked between the fluttering rows. "I'm about to lose my mind with nothing to do."

When she complained, he set her on the porch swing with needle, thread, and beans. "I don't guess preparing shuck beans'll hurt you."

By October, oaks and maples erupted into gaudy harvest colors. Black walnuts burst from their pungent hulls. The baby grew heavy and restless in her mother's womb. "I don't know what's wrong me," Liza said. "Nothing satisfies me."

One Sunday afternoon, they took a drive after church. Spying a field of pumpkins near Lebanon, she urged her husband to stop. They paid the farmer and piled the truck bed full of orange globes. For two weeks the dense, sweet scent of vanilla, ginger, and cinnamon wafted through the house. Liza made pumpkin pies each day, and every day she ate pumpkin pie.

No matter how many baths she took, her skin released rich spice into the air. One day, nuzzling her neck, Edgar named her Solomon's bride. She laughed, and quoted the Song of Songs, "Blow upon my garden so the spices there may flow out!"

That night her water broke. At the hospital, Liza suffered a punishing labor, but she bore the child the next day. She lay dying even as the nurse placed the baby in her arms. The tiny girl was perfect. Born on Halloween, her hair was golden-orange and her skin smelled like pure vanilla.

They called her Katherine Rose. Edgar thought she

looked like a baby bird nestled against her mother's chest, and so Katherine became Wren. Liza died with Wren still cradled in her arms.

~~~

"I sure do appreciate you taking care of Wren for me, Maryann. I don't know what I'd do without you to help me."

Maryann Trent smiled at him as she bounced Wren on her knee. "It's my pleasure, Edgar. She's no trouble. I just hate that you don't have any family to raise her up with."

Edgar sighed. "Well, neither one of us had any kin living down here. And don't have relatives in any other place that I'd be proud to claim."

"That's a shame." Maryann handed Wren to Edgar and draped a diaper bag across his arm. "I'm glad to take care of her."

Edgar raised Wren with a little help from all his neighbors up and down Pawpaw Ridge, but he relied on Maryann most of all. Every morning he dropped the baby off at her house and continued on to work at the mine. Each evening he returned for Wren, and painted her black with coal dust kisses before they got home.

~~~

By the time Wren was five, she looked forward to the drive home. On either side of the road, dark hollows hid clusters of houses. A few homes caught sunsets, gripping the mountainside with stubborn purpose. Wren liked to listen to Edgar's deep voice weave together the stories of their neighbors.

"That's Ival Mullins. He's never worked for anybody else. Seems to get along fine scratching out a garden in that little patch of dirt. Sells ginseng, too."

Wren nodded. Edgar had taken her "sanging" in the woods around their house. They didn't do it often because her father didn't want to kill it out. The herb and its roots were valuable and people had overharvested the plant.

Edgar jerked his chin at a bone-thin man with long brown hair. He sat on the steps of a trailer perched high above a rutted dirt road. "Hi, Nestor!" Wren stuck her head out the window and waved at him, "He blows his horn at me when his coal truck drives by Maryann's house."

They passed Jamie Hartsock's new brick home. Edgar shook his head at the paved driveway and two-car garage. "Should've got me a job with the railroad," he muttered.

The narrow hardtop zigzagged down Pawpaw Ridge and Wren began to fidget when they drew near home. Edgar turned the truck onto a dirt road and they descended into a lonely hollow where a burbling creek tumbled alongside the road. The water ran through their yard and behind their house into the woods.

As they pulled up to the house, Edgar looked at Wren and said, "Home again, home again, jiggety-jig!" She laughed, as she always did when he said it. Edgar smiled at her and tugged one of her auburn pigtails before they climbed out of the truck.

Wren set the table while her father cooked supper. From a cast iron skillet, he turned out a disk of corn bread onto a plate. He spooned fried potatoes into a bowl and set a jar of homemade chowchow on the table. He crumbled corn bread into their soup beans. Edgar laid some green onions next to Wren's plate. She ate them with gusto, although tears streamed down her cheeks while she chewed.

"I'll get the dishes later, Knothead." Edgar opened the screen door and beckoned her outside. They lay in the grass in the backyard. The little valley grew dim and Wren saw fireflies ascend into the falling darkness with intermittent flashes. They twinkled in the dark spaces between the stars.

"I wish I could spark and fly like a lightning bug," Wren said. "I would fly and fly until I landed on a star!"

"You know what stars really are, Knothead?"

"What, Daddy?"

"They're angels." Edgar waved his hand above them in

a sweeping gesture. "How many stars can you count? That's how many angels are looking out for you. Tonight we have lots of them watching over us."

Wren leaned on her elbows and counted to herself. Finally she sighed and reclined next to her father. "There's too many! I keep losing count. I bet there's a bazillion angels up there."

Edgar laughed and they both rested without speaking. Wren's skin itched where the cool grass tried to uncurl beneath her. She held her breath, willing away the tickling sensation running along her legs. When she could stand it no longer, she sat up and scratched her legs with violent pleasure.

"Come on." Edgar stood and picked up Wren. He carried her to the porch and they sat in the wooden swing. He pulled a string to turn on the porch light. Moths fluttered around the naked bulb and Wren heard the gentle *tat-tat* of their wings brushing the light

"I'd say it's time for you to take a bath. I'll wash up these dishes while you're getting ready for bed." Edgar hugged her and sent her inside.

After her bath, Wren waited for her father to come in and kiss her good night. He tucked her into bed. "Thought we'd go to the drive-in this weekend. If you want to."

"Yeah!"

"Sleep tight, honey." Edgar kissed her forehead. After he shut the door, she pulled back the covers and knelt by her bed.

"Dear Lord, please bless Daddy. Watch over all our neighbors. Please feed the birds and the squirrels. And the groundhogs, too, so they won't eat up our garden. And bless me too, Lord. I'm sorry I didn't eat my peas at lunch and made Maryann mad. It sure is hard to eat something I don't like, even if it is good for me. Amen."

Wren climbed back into bed and flipped her pillow over to the cool side. She closed her eyes and listened to the sounds of summer. The tinkle of the creek drifted into her bedroom, along with the throaty croak of a bullfrog and the inquiring call of an owl. The tin roof popped as it cooled; floors creaked under the weight of nothing. Wren covered her head with the blanket, but stuck her left foot behind the bed against the wall. Cold and smooth, the wallpaper soothed her to sleep.

Pawpaw Ridge called to her slumbering soul. Wren walked through the house, sure-footed in sleep. When she stepped outside, the wooden screen door whapped shut, but its sound didn't wake her. Although the dew covered her toes, she felt only warm turf beneath her feet.

Wren danced around the yard, arms stretched to the heavens. She lifted her face to the sun in her dreams and moonlight illuminated her fair skin. She whirled and twirled, spinning close to the stream. As she reached the creek bank, her father's strong hands gripped her shoulders with gentle restraint.

Edgar swept her up into his arms, careful not to wake her. He carried her back to the house. Upstairs he placed Wren back in her bed and watched her until he was sure she was settled in bed for the night.

~~~

Wren kicked the floorboard of the truck. "Why does Maryann have to come to the movie with us?"

"I don't know why all of sudden you don't want Maryann around. She's practically raised you. Now stop acting ugly and sit up." Edgar shifted gears, rolled down his window, and rested his elbow there.

I saw you holding her hand, she wanted to say. Instead she shrugged and muttered, "Maryann's an old maid."

Edgar whipped the truck over to the side of the road. Wren's head snapped forward and she extended her arms to brace herself against the glove compartment. "Little girl, do you even know what an old maid is?"

Wren hung her head. "I don't know."

"Where did you hear it?"

She swallowed to fight the tight feeling in her throat. "Some of the ladies at church." Her eyes filled with hot tears and she watched them drop onto the seat between them.

Edgar curled his fingers under her chin and lifted her face to look at him. Wren saw her own green eyes in his. "First of all, don't go around repeating things you hear grown-ups say, because they ain't always nice and they ain't always true. Second of all, Maryann's been real good to you. Better than she ought to, maybe. Now stop crying."

Maryann was standing in her driveway when they arrived. Her brown hair was plaited in a thick braid down her back. Although she usually wore dresses, today she had on blue jeans and a T-shirt. She carried a boxy purse draped across her arm. Maryann climbed in the truck and settled against the door.

Wren imagined herself expanding and filling the truck cab so Maryann and Edgar would be as far apart from each other as she could make them. He nudged her with his elbow when she flopped her arm out against Maryann. Wren deflated when they reached the drive-in at Castlewood.

She bounced with excitement as he parked in line with the other vehicles. They waited for dusk to fall. It never gets dark fast enough, Wren thought. Finally, the reluctant sun ducked behind the hills and pastures. Amber and pink clouds trailed behind it, sinking as slow as sweet syrup.

Edgar rolled down the window, grabbed a metal speaker from its pole, and hooked it to the window. Wren reached out and fiddled with a tiny knob on it.

"Don't do that, Knothead," Edgar said. "You'll tear it up."

Wren blew her breath against the windshield and drew pictures on the glass. Maryann pulled her fingers away from the window. "Wren, honey, you're smearing the glass. Don't do that."

"Why don't you take her to the concession stand before the movie starts?" Edgar suggested. He pulled some creased bills from his worn wallet and handed them to Maryann. She sighed when Edgar settled back in his seat and crossed his arms.

"You better not be asleep when we get back," she warned.

The air in the concession stand was heavy and sweet with the aroma of popcorn and cotton candy. She bought red-striped boxes of popcorn and drinks, admonishing Wren all the way back to the truck. "Please do not spill it everywhere! Do you hear me?"

Wren skipped back to the vehicle and slid in close to her father. Edgar grumbled and scooted into the corner. Maryann tapped him on the arm. "Wake up, Ed."

He snorted and sat up straight. Wren squinted at the milky screen in restless anticipation. Car horns punctuated the silence and snatches of laughter floated in the windows. Frogs began to call each other in their rhythmic language.

The speaker crackled to life and vibrated the window, so Edgar turned down the volume. Wren fidgeted with the dashboard instruments through the previews, but the movie, Escape to Witch Mountain, held her attention.

Wren chattered as they pulled away from the drive-in. "I felt sorry for those kids."

"Why?" Maryann tried to stroke Wren's hair, but she pulled away.

"All they wanted to do was go home, and they didn't even know where home was. They didn't have anybody." As the truck rolled across the dark hills, it rocked her into silence. The gentle mounds in Castlewood gave way to steeper ones past St. Paul. The road twisted and turned as it traveled beyond the little town into the mountains of Wise County. Wren leaned against her father and fell asleep.

~~~

Wren and Edgar lay in a pasture on the ridge above their little valley. Cow paths crisscrossed the field and the hills that flanked their house. Golden sage grass, perfect for cardboard box sledding, covered the hills. Flat on their backs, they waited for the Fourth of July celebrations to begin. Pawpaw Ridge offered a clear view of the fireworks in St. Paul and Coeburn.

"You eager to see the fireworks?" Edgar asked. He tugged one of her red curls and she swatted his hand.

"Yeah."

"Did you like the Bicentennial Parade this morning?"

"Yeah." Wren stared up at the sky, anxious to see the fireworks. "I liked the horses. What's bicentennial?"

"It's America's birthday. Our country is 200 years old."

"That's old." She scratched her knee. "I'm hot."

"Well, Maryann invited us up to her place for ice cream. She got your favorite, lemon."

"It makes my mouth juicy."

Edgar laughed. He rolled on his side and rubbed Wren's arm. "Listen. I wanted to talk to you about Maryann. What do you think about her?"

"Nothing." *Pop. Pop. Pop-pop.* "Listen!" They sat up and looked toward the scattered lights of St. Paul. Shooting stars launched into the air. Crazy corkscrews swirled and peaked, and spirals spilled across the hills. Green and silver droplets sprayed the sky like a million exploding fireflies. Fireworks froze in the night, briefly illuminating the black blanket above the town.

Peals and booms bounced across the mountains, and Wren jumped with each thunderous echo. The fireworks sound mad, she thought. She squeezed Edgar's hand.

When the sky was back to black, they remained prostrate in the grass. Wren searched for stars, but they hid behind smoke and clouds. Maybe they scared away the angels.

"Let's go get some ice cream, Knothead."

~~~

The next day Edgar and Wren walked through the woods and up the hill behind their house. He carried a bouquet of silk flowers for Liza's grave. Wren ran ahead of him and climbed across the barbed wire fence that enclosed the tiny graveyard.

Liza's was the only grave there. Honeysuckle fingered the fence, but it hadn't yet climbed through the wire to reach the grassy mound. Edgar placed the flowers in front of the headstone and laid his hand on the warm granite.

"Your baby's getting big, Liza-girl. There's things she's going to need, things she'll want to know, that I can't help her with."

Wren frowned at her father. She'd never heard him speak to her mother like this. She wondered if Liza could hear him. What's he talking about, anyway? She gazed at the mountains around them and decided this was the most beautiful place on earth.

As they walked back through the woods, Edgar held Wren's hand. "Wren, we didn't get to finish talking about Maryann last night. What would you think about having her as your mom?"

Wren jerked her hand from his and stared at her father. "My mommy is in heaven! I don't want another mommy."

"Well, sweetheart, of course, Maryann could never replace Liza as your real mom. But she's awful fond of you. And I'm right fond of her. You know, life's a lot easier when you have someone to share it with. Especially when you get to be my age."

Wren turned away from her father and rubbed the trunk of a poplar tree. The bark was smooth, but tiny shelves of fungus hung from it. She flicked them with her finger, breaking them into tiny brown shards. "You share everything with me. You don't need her."

Edgar shifted from one foot to the other and placed his hand on Wren's shoulder. "Think about it." They walked down the hill toward their house.

<center>~~~</center>

April lived up to its reputation for showers. The rain set
in with such vigor that Wren couldn't even see to the end
of their yard. She walked upstairs and stared at the creek
behind the house. It boiled and frothed like a crazy stew.

She ran back downstairs and looked out the kitchen
window. The water had crawled up the creek bank, and she
expected to see it at the back door any minute. Worried the
creek might reach the house, Edgar took the day off from
work. When Wren started her fifth trip up the stairs, he
called her back to the living room. "Why don't you sit still
for a minute? Git one of your books and read for a while."

Edgar was as restless as she was, though, and he rattled
the newspaper without reading it. "How about some hot
chocolate?"

"Yum!" Wren followed him to the kitchen and watched
him pour warm milk into cups of cocoa and sugar. They
drank the sweet milk without speaking. She enjoyed the
warm muddle in her stomach; it made her sleepy. When
her head began to droop, Edgar picked her up and carried
her to bed. "Take you a nap, Knothead. I'm gonna go call
Maryann and check on her."

She looked toward the window a moment. "The creek,"
she murmured.

"I'll be right downstairs." Edgar pulled the blanket up
to her chin. Wren wrapped both arms around her pillow
and curled on her side. Edgar stroked her hair until her
breathing matched the steady stream of rain on the roof.

He walked downstairs and called Maryann. Afterward,
he stretched out on the couch and fell asleep. The rain
continued to fall and the creek oozed over its banks and
crept into the yard. Edgar didn't hear Wren walk downstairs
and out the door.

She was sound asleep, even when brown water flowed
over her bare feet. She approached the bridge. Water rushed

19

through its wooden slats, but Wren managed to slosh across it. She slipped and the rushing water carried her off the bridge. The angry current rolled her over on her back and she wakened with a scream.

She sank beneath the creek's roiling surface. Slapping at the current, she reached for the sky but it disappeared behind the black water. She screamed again and water flowed into her lungs. A heavy weight filled her chest and she stopped struggling. Slipping into a dim world, she didn't feel the two hands grab her beneath her arms.

Edgar shouted as he pulled Wren from the creek. He dragged her up the bank and fell on top of her in the muddy water. She didn't move. He grabbed her by the shoulders and shook her, but she remained limp.

He turned her on her side and thumped her hard on the back. She didn't respond. He smacked her back again, flinching at the blow. Just as Edgar pulled back his hand a third time, Wren gagged and coughed up creek water. She heaved a deep breath and started to cry. "Thank God," Edgar said. "Thank God."

He gathered her up in his arms, carried her to the house, and bolted the door behind them. Setting her on the couch, he peered down at her. "Let me look at you, little girl."

Wren coughed again and muddy water spilled out of her nose. She sobbed. "What happened?"

"You just took a little swim in the creek and almost drownded! I fell asleep and the only thing that woke me up was wind blowing the door against the wall." He shook his head, spraying water on the floor. "Lord God Almighty."

Wren patted his arm. "I'm okay, Daddy."

"Well, let me get something to dry you off with. Stay right there."

Edgar retrieved a towel from the bathroom and dried her hair and her skin. Wren turned her face up to her father and smiled. She was pale, but her green eyes gleamed like a cat's. "Did you save my life, Daddy?"

Edgar sighed. "I wouldn't let anything happen to you if I could help it."

"Even if a monster tried to grab me and eat me, you wouldn't let it?"

"I would take that old monster and knock him down a rat hole!"

"Promise?"

"Promise. Now lay down there for a while." Edgar kissed her on the forehead. When he finished drying her, he covered her with an afghan. Leaning back in an armchair, he stared out the window at the bitter rain.

Wren shrugged beneath the cover. "Besides, Daddy, there's no such thing as monsters."

~~~

When the rain finally ended, Edgar, Maryann, and Wren ventured to St.. Paul. They made it as far as the railroad trestle at the western end of town. There the Clinch River blocked the road. In shock, they stood at the edge of town with several other people and watched the brown water churning around buildings in the distance.

"Look, Daddy!" Wren pointed a shaking finger at a Volkswagen floating down the river.

"Lord, Lord. Take a good look, baby. The flood of '77 is something you'll never forget as long as you live."

Maryann pursed her lips and twisted the ring on her finger. It had taken Edgar nine months to convince Wren they were really getting married. She took Wren's hand in her own. "There's no mistake about it. Some of these people'll be in a world of hurt."

~~~

"I love today." Wren skipped across the yard while her father raked leaves.

"Wouldn't have anything to do with it being your birthday, would it?" Edgar leaned on the rake, crossed his ankles, and tipped the toe of his boot against the ground.

21

"No! I mean today, this day." She struggled to explain, but ended up throwing her arms back to show her father what she meant. "This!"

The colors of the leaves were sharp enough to score the blue sky. The woods smelled of cinnamon and dark earth. Milkweed pods shed gossamer tears into the cold air. Fat squirrels sassed them from the safety of the treetops.

Edgar laughed. "Honey, I know what you mean. Now why don't you go play while I finish these leaves?"

Smelling winter in the air, Wren absorbed as much sunshine as she could stand. She lay on her back in a pile of crinkled leaves in the woods behind the house. She picked up a maple leaf and sniffed its musty scent. Sneezing, she examined it. It looked like one of the doilies on Maryann's dressing table.

"Maryann." Wren growled and rolled in the leaves. Maryann and her father were going to get married one day. She's always twisting that sapphire ring this way and that in the sun, like a crow with a bright and shiny! "Go away, Maryann," she sang. "Go away. Go away. Go away."

The distant slam of their screen door echoed through the valley. The searching voice of her father called her home. Wren leaped out of the leaves and ran through the woods.

Edgar leaned against the kitchen counter sipping a cup of coffee. "Maryann's upstairs. She brought your costume." He pulled Wren close and hugged her with one arm. "Hey, Knothead, which are you more excited about, Halloween or your birthday?"

She wrinkled her nose and scrunched her eyes. Taking a deep breath, she shrugged. "I don't know. They're both fun!"

Edgar pushed his cap back and scratched his head. "Now how old are you?"

"You know how old I am, Daddy."

"Let's see. I'd say . . . three?"

"I'm nine and you know it!"

"Nine? Surely not." He walked out of the kitchen with

Wren right behind him. "Got your birthday presents in here. Thought you might want to open them before we go trick-or-treating."

Maryann clattered down the stairs as they walked into the living room. "Happy Birthday, Wren."

"Thanks." Wren spied a big box resting on the coffee table. Yellow calico paper and a big white bow dressed the package. Edgar sat down on the couch and Wren climbed beside him to examine the gift. The tag was signed by Maryann.

Wren stuck her thumb in her mouth and chewed on it. Edgar pulled her hand away from her mouth with a gentle tug. "Well, are you going to open it or just look at it?"

She removed the bow and stuck it on Edgar's head. He rolled his eyes but left the bow. Wren tore the paper away from the box and unfolded the flaps on top. She cried with delight when she discovered its contents. "Oh! *Charlotte's Web*! And *The Wind in the Willows*! That's my favorite. No wait, *Little House in the Big Woods*, that's my favorite one."

"They can't all be your favorites," Edgar exclaimed.

"They can, too! They're my favorite when I'm reading them." She laid the books on the coffee table and offered Maryann a loose hug. "Thank you."

"You're welcome."

Edgar laughed as he slid a package from beneath the couch and handed it to her. It was wrapped in lavender tissue paper and tied with purple string. She admired the package a moment before ripping it open. The box contained all sorts of art supplies. Wren caressed the pastel crayons, charcoal sticks, and textured papers.

"I figured you could draw just about anything with the right tools." Edgar helped her dig through the items and lay them out on the table.

Wren flipped through the pages of a beginner's art manual. "Oh, Daddy. I love it!" She threw her arms around Edgar. "I'll draw the most beautiful pictures for you."

"Well, I guess since you're going trick-or-treating, you don't want no birthday cake." Edgar winked at Maryann.

"Yes I do," Wren shouted.

Edgar and Maryann finished their coffee and caramel cake while Wren got dressed. Maryann had sewn Wren a fairy costume, complete with a tiny bag of glitter for fairy dust. Wren tiptoed downstairs and flitted across the room to her father. "Guess what I am?" She twirled around to show off her diaphanous wings and sparkling skirt. Glitter glistened in her ginger hair.

Edgar crossed his arms and stroked his chin with one hand. He closed one eye and asked her to spin around again. "Hmmm. You look like an angel to me."

Wren sighed and shook her head. "No! Guess again."

"Oh, I don't know. A fairy, maybe?"

"Yes. You knew that, silly Daddy."

"Well, you still look like an angel to me. Are you ready to go?"

"Yes!"

He packed her and Maryann into the pickup and headed to St. Paul. They started in town and made their way back to Pawpaw Ridge. Foddershocks decorated yards, usually with pumpkins, squash, Indian corn, and chrysanthemums piled around them. Jack-o'-lanterns leered from the ledges of dark windows. Hoary sheets – makeshift ghosts – hung from eaves. Scarecrows guarded gates and sidewalks. When Wren started to drag her bag, bursting with candy and gum, Edgar called an end to the evening's hunt. She put up a half-hearted argument, ready to go home and count her bounty.

Edgar and Maryann examined the candy while Wren enjoyed popcorn balls, pumpkin cookies, and apple cider. She stuck candy corn in front of her teeth to make her father laugh; he tried on a pair of wax lips.

As the breeze tickled the wind chimes on the porch, Edgar entertained Wren with the tale of Rawhead and

Bloody Bones. When Wren began to peer wide-eyed at the dark corners of the room, he decided it was time to stop. Maryann made hot chocolate, and then Edgar accompanied Wren up to her room.

He brushed her hair and tucked her in bed. "You're not gonna be scared now, are you?"

"No."

"Good. Listen, Knothead. Maryann and I finally set a date to be married. We figured Christmas Day would be good. We'll end '78 right. What do you think?"

Wren shrugged. Edgar sighed and kissed her forehead. "I love you, baby."

"I love you, too, Daddy."

~~~

When Wren rose the next morning, Maryann and Edgar were in the kitchen drinking coffee. She stood between the living room and kitchen and rubbed her back against the doorframe. "How about some breakfast?" her father suggested. He patted his knee for her to sit, but Wren remained in the doorway.

Maryann placed her coffee cup in the kitchen sink, leaned against the counter, and crossed her arms. "Wren, how'd you like to be the maid of honor in our wedding?" She walked behind Edgar's chair and put her hands on his shoulders.

Wren walked around the kitchen, trailing her fingers along the appliances. She stared at her father out of the corner of her eye. When she reached the kitchen table, she placed her small hand in his calloused one and smiled at him. "I don't want you to get married, Daddy."

Maryann sighed and walked out of the kitchen into the living room. Edgar pulled Wren onto his lap and wrapped his arms around her. "Wren, we've already decided this. It'll be good for all of us. I want you two to get along. Will you do that for me?"

"No! I don't want her to be my mommy." Wren started

to cry. "You don't love me anymore."

"Katherine Rose Johnson. You know that's not true. I love you more than anything in the world."

"Then make her go away." Wren wrenched herself away from Edgar and ran outside. She sprinted through the back yard and climbed up the big oak that held her tree house. Edgar followed her and called her to come down, but she refused.

He shook his head and looked back at Maryann, who stood on the back porch with her hands on her hips. He walked to the base of the tree and climbed up the rope ladder dangling from a lower limb. Edgar grunted as he slid into the tree house on his belly.

He scooted across the floor and leaned against the plywood wall. Wren hugged her knees and narrowed her eyes at her father. "Go away."

"Wren, why are you making this so hard on your ole daddy?"

"I want it to be the way it's always been! She makes everything different," Wren said. She stood and looked toward the house. Maryann was sitting in the porch swing rubbing the nape of her neck.

"Give her a chance and you'll see it'll be better for all of us." Edgar reached out to Wren, but she jerked away from him. As she did, she stepped back and off the platform of the tree house.

Maryann's scream lasted longer than Wren's fall. A tree branch whipped her face as she fell. She landed hard and her wrists doubled up against the ground with a crunch! The force of the impact drove tiny rocks through her shirt into her skin.

She heard Edgar's voice, but it sounded so far away. I'm okay, she tried to say, but she couldn't breathe. Her hands were numb, so she couldn't turn over. She lay with her face smashed against the earth. She felt something wet run into her right eye. It stung and then her vision disappeared in that eye.

"Daddy," she wanted to shout, but it came out only as a groan.

"Wren! Oh God. My baby." Edgar bent over her and felt her legs and arms with trembling hands. "Wren," he shouted.

Maryann ran to Edgar's side and tried to turn Wren over, but he pushed her away. "Don't touch her," he yelled. "We've got to get her to the hospital."

Wren heard the shouts of her father. She felt an odd comfort in her father's cold hand as he caressed her temple. "I'm sleepy," she croaked. Darkness engulfed her.

~~~

"Wren? Can you hear me? You're not playing possum, are you?"

Edgar's voice was so thick with concern Wren didn't recognize it. She opened her eyes to see who was speaking. "Daddy?"

Edgar and Maryann leaned over her. Fluorescent light shined above their heads. For a moment, Wren thought they wore haloes. Behind them the walls were ugly green and white. The room seemed off-kilter; it took Wren a moment to realize she was looking through only one eye.

She raised her hand to her face and felt a soft bandage covering her right eye. Then she noticed a bandaged splint on her wrist. She looked down and saw her other wrist was packaged the same way. "Am I in the hospital?"

"Yes," Maryann said. "You're in the emergency room in Norton. The doctor says you'll be fine." Her voice hitched and she turned away from the girl.

Edgar patted Wren's arm. "You broke both wrists and a rib. You have a scratch on your eye. Got a deep cut on your eyebrow, too. Other than that you're in pretty good shape."

Maryann returned to the bed and leaned against the rail. "Do you know how bad you scared your father?"

Edgar twisted his cap in his hands. "Let's not worry

about that right now."

Maryann balled her hand into a fist and bounced it against the bed rail. "Stop making excuses for her, Ed. She could've been killed. You've spoiled her."

Edgar frowned. "She's not spoiled. And she's not killed." He patted Wren's arm again. "But you're gonna stay out of trees for a while, Knothead."

Maryann rolled her eyes and walked across the room. Wren struggled to sit up, but gasped at the pain. "Can't you wait a while to get married, Daddy? Please?"

Edgar unfolded his cap and jammed it down on his head in one quick motion. He sighed. "Yeah, we can wait a little longer, I guess."

Wren let her head sink back onto the pillow. "I want to go home, Daddy. Just you and me, okay?"

Edgar turned and looked at Maryann. She was speaking to a nurse. "Alright, baby. When the doctor says it's okay, we'll go home. Just you and me."

~~~

Wren was the first to rise, excited about her tenth Christmas. She ran to the bedroom window and wiped away the delicate lace of frost from the glass. She peered into the blue morning light, where the world was all sugar and cream. *It looks good enough to eat.*

At least a foot of snow had fallen overnight. Although she knew her father was still asleep, she couldn't restrain a gleeful shout. "We got a white Christmas after all, Daddy!"

Wren dressed quickly and pulled her parka from the closet. She rushed past Edgar as he stumbled from his bedroom. "I'm going outside to play in the snow!"

"Use your gloves and earmuffs!" Edgar's voice got lost in the clatter of her footsteps down the stairs.

Wren halted on the back porch and stared with reverence at the unblemished snow. She tiptoed off the porch with gentle cat steps, hesitant to mar the velvet perfection. Soon, however, she was frosted from head to boot with icy confection that turned her face pink and made her fingers stiff.

Edgar joined her after he bolstered his nerve with some toast and hot coffee. They built a castle with pine branches. He snapped off two long icicles from the eaves of the house and they dueled with the makeshift swords.

Soon Edgar fell back in the snow, his face slick with sweat. "I thought you were a princess," he panted. "I've never seen a princess who could handle a sword like you!"

Wren giggled. "I'd rather be a knight than a princess." She leaped across her father and kicked up a spray of snow. It frosted Edgar's beard and eyelashes. She flopped down beside him and flapped her arms and legs to make an angel.

They made an army of angels before the crunch of tires on snow interrupted their play. Maryann's truck crawled down the rutted road. She rolled down her window as she parked. "Come carry these presents for me, Ed!"

Edgar squeezed the gifts beneath the Christmas tree while Maryann made grilled cheese sandwiches and tomato soup. Wren drew winter pictures as they ate. "Here, Daddy, I made this for you."

He studied the picture. It was a realistic drawing of their house nestled in its tiny valley. "I swear, Knothead. You've got a way with a pencil or a crayon. A regular Picasso, you are."

Wren rubbed the small white scar that bisected her right eyebrow. A remnant of her fall from the tree house the year before, it was shaped almost like a question mark. When she cocked her eyebrow, she gave the odd impression of being twice as quizzical. "What's Spakisso?"

Edgar laughed. "Picasso. A famous artist. Maybe you'll grow up to be an artist some day."

"Did you tell her yet?" Maryann picked at the crust of her sandwich.

"Well, I was getting around to it." Ed stuck the picture on the refrigerator with magnets. Without turning to look at Wren, he spoke. "We set another wedding date. June first."

Wren jumped up from her chair. "Can't you wait a little while longer, Daddy?"

"No!" Maryann grabbed Wren's plate and set it in the sink with a clatter. "It's been more than a year since you fell out of that tree. I've tried to be patient with you--"

"Maryann! Don't fuss at her."

"I'm not fussing, Ed. But you're the parent and she's the child. She's dictating what you do and when you do it! Enough is enough."

Wren turned away when Ed pulled Maryann close and hugged her. He called to his daughter as she slid back into her coat. "Be careful outside."

She wandered around the yard the rest of the day, knocking icicles off trees and kicking clumps of snow. When the shadows grew long and weepy, her father plugged in the Christmas lights. Wren fluttered to their glow like a shivering moth.

Packages glimmered beneath the tree like a pirate's treasure trove. Plundering piles of boxes, Wren held each one to her ear and gave it a gentle shake. When Edgar nodded assent, she tore through layers of colorful paper and crackling tissue. She oohed over the toys and books, but shrugged at socks and panties.

By the time she finished opening her presents, wrapping paper, tissue, and cellophane littered the entire living room. Wren made her way through the bright trash and wedged herself between Maryann and Edgar on the sofa. She yawned behind her hand and laid her head against his arm.

"I really like the charm you got me for my bracelet." She dangled it in front them: shaped like a ten, the sterling silver charm reflected the blinking Christmas lights. "Thank you, Daddy."

"Did you like the present Maryann made you?"

Wren pulled a blue corduroy jumper from its box and

folded it in her lap. "Yeah. It's pretty."

"What do you say?"

She turned to Maryann and forced a smile. "Thank you."

"Did you get everything you wanted?" her father asked.

She glanced up at Maryann. She didn't smile this time. "Almost."

~~~

"I'm bored." Wren propped her elbows on the back of the couch and stared out the living room window. Rain stitched silver-threaded patterns down the glass. Through the mist, the hills looked like bundles of grey and blue wool. A dreary Sunday afternoon was more than Wren could bear. She sighed.

Edgar looked at his daughter over the top of the newspaper. "Have you done your homework for tomorrow?"

"Yeah."

Maryann sat in the rocking chair, hemming Wren's bridesmaid dress. "Why don't you draw something?"

"I'm sick of drawing."

"Well, sit on your fist and rear back on your thumb then." Maryann didn't look up from her stitch work.

Wren stuck her tongue out at her. She climbed off the couch and read the newspaper over her father's shoulder. She tapped her fingers on the edge of his chair. When Edgar didn't respond, she tugged on his sleeve. Why don't grown-ups understand BORED?

Edgar folded the newspaper and looked around the living room for a moment. Finally, he pushed the coffee table from the middle of the floor. Maryann looked up from her sewing. "What are you doing?"

"Finding something for this poor, bored child to do." He walked to the hallway closet and dug through some boxes in the back. He emerged a few minutes later with a stack of dusty albums. He stacked them next to the stereo and held each sleeve up to inspect it.

"What are those?" Wren blew dust from a record and read the label. "Nat King Cole. Who's that?"

"Your mother's favorite singer. Here's Dean Martin. Rosemary Clooney. Frank Sinatra. Myself, I've always been partial to Hank and Patsy and George. But she sure did like this stuff."

Edgar pulled a shiny black disk from its jacket and placed it on the turntable. He turned on the machine, lifted the arm, and set the needle in the record's groove. The smooth voice of Nat King Cole filled the room, singing about a boy who wanted nothing more than to love and be loved in return.

Edgar crooked his finger at Wren. "Come here, Knothead." He lifted her and set her feet on his own. She giggled when they began to dance around the room.

When the needle slid to the center, Edgar removed the record and replaced it with Frank Sinatra. He grabbed Wren's hand and twirled her in mad circles around the room. She threw back her head in gleeful abandon. They were a two-headed dervish enjoying the smoky tones of Sinatra.

After a few dances, Wren flopped down on the couch.

"Hot in here, ain't it?" Edgar said. He raised the living room window with a grunt. A cool draft of air wafted into the room.

Maryann shook her head. "You'll wear yourself out, Ed. Better take it easy."

Edgar sat down next to Wren and stretched his legs. They were both tapping their feet against the wooden floor when a dark blur whizzed between them. Maryann screamed and ducked.

A sparrow flew above them and around the room in great swooping whirligigs. Wren threw her hands over her head while Edgar chased the bird around the room.

"We've got to get it out. It's bad luck to have a bird fly in the house," he shouted.

They shooed the bird toward the window, but it was panicked and confused. It swooped into the kitchen, where it tried to fly out the window, ramming into the glass over and over. Wren screamed for Edgar to make it stop, but he couldn't get near it. Its attempts to escape grew feeble before it dropped into the kitchen sink.

Wren ran to the sink and stared at the bird. It was still now. She looked back at her father with tears in her eyes. "I think it's dead."

Edgar examined the bird and agreed. "It was scared. Its fear confused it." Maryann handed him a dish towel, which he wrapped around the bird. Wren started to follow him, but Edgar waved her back inside. He disappeared into the rain and came back a few minutes later empty-handed.

They returned to the living room. Maryann had closed the window. Wren sat on the couch in somber silence. The record had ended and the scritch-scritch-scritch of the needle punctuated the quiet. Edgar switched off the record player.

"Well, I think that's enough dance lessons for today. Why don't you go to your room and read for a while? I'm going to lay down here on the couch and rest my eyes for a few minutes."

Wren started upstairs, then turned and stared into the living room. Maryann hunched over the dress, her needle flashing in the lamplight. Edgar lay on the couch with his ankles crossed and his left arm thrown across his eyes.

~~~

Monday morning was as dreary as the previous Sunday afternoon. The children couldn't go out to the playground at recess, so they chased each other around the room with erasers or blew spitballs onto the ceiling. Wren sat with a book open in front of her, but she couldn't concentrate on the words.

The teacher had the heat turned up so high that Wren felt she could have rested her head on her desk and slept all day. Only the distant wail of sirens pierced the warm film that encased her. She jerked her head up and rested her chin in the palm of her hand.

"Katherine Johnson, did you hear me?" The teacher, hands on her hips, towered over Wren's desk.

"Ma'am?"

"I told the class to open your math books to page sixty-three. Why are you just sitting there?"

"I'm sorry, Miss Spencer." Wren grabbed the heavy book from beneath her desk and opened it to the appropriate place. The numbers looked as foreign to Wren as Chinese letters. She shook her head and inhaled to clear her mind.

The teacher called students to the blackboard to work out problems. The next hour they studied their geography lesson. Wren was examining a map of Africa when Principal Evans stuck his head in the door. "Miss Spencer, can I see you for a moment?"

She wagged her finger at the children before stepping into the hallway. The kids passed notes back and forth across the aisles; paper airplanes sailed over head. Wren rested her cheek against the desk, savoring its cool surface. She rubbed the graffiti carved into the top, reading it through her fingertips as if it were Braille.

"Katherine Johnson. Please gather your things and come to the principal's office." Miss Spencer stood at the doorway wearing an expression Wren couldn't read.

"Am I in trouble, Miss Spencer?" Wren asked as she grabbed her books and papers.

The teacher flushed and looked at an invisible point above Wren's head. "Just do as I say. Principal Evans will explain everything to you."

"Yes, ma'am." Boy, all I did was rest my head for a minute.

The principal motioned to Wren from the end of the hallway. She followed him inside his office. Maryann stood at the window, her back to the room. Wren's heart started to pound. "Is something wrong?"

Maryann turned and Wren saw tears streaming down her face. "Yes." Her mouth opened and closed in quick pops. She looks like a fish.

"What is it? Where's Daddy?"

The principal knelt down next to her. "Katherine, there's been an accident. The roof collapsed in the part of the mine where your father was working."

Wren let her books fall to the floor. "Is he okay? Where is he?"

Maryann crossed the room and squeezed her shoulder. "Sweetheart. Your daddy got killed." Sobbing, she blew her nose on an embroidered handkerchief.

Wren backed away from them and pressed herself against the wall. No, Daddy! You can't leave me! Don't be dead! Don't be dead! She felt a black monster rearing its head in her chest, crawling up her throat. It burst from her mouth in a scream.

The principal patted her on the head and rested his hands on her shoulders to calm her, but she continued to scream and cry. Maryann stood in the middle of the room, looking embarrassed. The secretary and the school nurse crowded into the room and tried to console Wren. She didn't hear or see them through her grief and rage.

The nurse called the doctor who worked at a clinic a few blocks away from the school. He arrived a few minutes later and pricked Wren's arm with a needle. She bit him and he cursed. The nurse wrapped both arms around her and held her tight. Soon Wren felt the monster climb back inside her chest. They both curled up and went to sleep in the dark.

Three

Charlottesville, February 1991

In the dark, in shock, Peter leaned over the edge of the bridge and watched her disappear into the black water. He gaped at the empty bridge, now wishing for traffic. "Shit!"

He climbed across the rail, leaped into the river, and hit the water fast. Unprepared for the cold current that engulfed him, his muscles tightened into hard bundles. Peter bobbed to the surface, sputtering and cursing his own stupidity.

I'll never find her in this, he thought, and then he turned and saw her pale hands disappear beneath the water. Please God, he prayed, and made a blind grab. Finding her fingers, he intertwined them with his own though his hands were numb. He pulled her up, grateful now that she hadn't worn a coat. His own leather jacket weighed them down, and he feared they would sink before he could make it to shore.

The girl neither fought nor assisted him in her rescue. I hope you're not dead, you crazy wench! He kicked and flailed his way toward the shore, though his legs and arms felt like chunks of ice. Just as he wondered if he could hold her much longer, they reached shallow water.

Peter dragged her up the bank and dropped her in the

stiff mud. He checked her pulse. It was weak, but she wasn't breathing. He turned her over and started mouth-to-mouth resuscitation. Please breathe. I don't think I can keep this up for very long! Please breathe.

Her chest hitched and she started to cough. Peter turned the girl on her side and she vomited ice water. As she retched, he became aware of a rattle in his head. It took a moment for him to realize he was shivering so hard his teeth chattered. The girl started to shiver, too. Hypothermia? He tried to remember if shivering was a symptom, but his mind was clouded with bourbon and ice water.

"Come on." He pulled the girl to her feet, now bare; the river had sucked off her shoes. He put his arm around her waist. She leaned against him and they staggered up the bank to the road. By now, they both twitched like marionettes beneath a mad puppeteer.

They stumbled onto the bridge. He wished he had left his truck running; they'd need the heat. I just wanna get warm. Then I'll get help.

By the time they reached the truck, Peter was dragging the girl. He stopped and stared at the door. For a moment, he couldn't remember how to open it. Man, you are really messed up! He grabbed the door handle, but his hands were so numb he couldn't mash the button hard enough to open it.

He leaned the girl against the truck, but she slid down the side and lay in a heap on the bridge. Peter pressed the door handle with both hands and it disengaged. He pulled open the door and climbed in to the cab. Then he remembered the girl.

He crawled back out of the truck and grabbed her beneath her arms. He huffed and grunted as he heaved her up into the truck. Her head hit the passenger side window and he winced at the cracking sound. Peter scrambled into the seat, slammed the door, and leaned against it with his arms wrapped tight around himself. His clothes were stiff with ice.

He patted the seat, feeling for his keys. They fell on the floor with a clink. Peter heard a car come across the bridge as he bent to retrieve the keys. He jerked upright to yell at the driver and banged his head on the steering wheel. His eyes watered as he stared at the receding taillights. Unbelievable!

He still shivered so hard he couldn't fit the key into the ignition. It made a *jig-a-jig-a-jig-a* sound against the metal casing. He grabbed his wrist with the other hand and shoved the key until it fit. The engine roared and Peter offered silent thanks to his father as he held his raw knuckles against the vent.

"It'd be a shame for you to have to hoof it everywhere your last year in school," his father had said when he tossed the keys to Peter. White with rusty spots, the old GMC was a company vehicle that his father had bought from a mining operation based in Buchanan County. His truck wasn't as nice as most of the cars he saw cruising around Grounds, but it got the job done.

And the heater works. Peter flipped the vents down to blow on the girl. Her bare feet were pressed against his thigh. He felt behind the seat for his old flannel shirt and wrapped it around her feet. When she didn't move, he checked her pulse again.

Steady, but I should still get her to the emergency room. My apartment's closer than the hospital, though. With that thought, he pulled away from the bridge and headed toward U.S. 29.

Peter ran the truck up on the sidewalk in the parking lot of his apartment complex. Shifting gears, he tried to park between the lines, but straddled two spaces instead. *Ah, the hell with it!* He jumped out of the truck, dragged the girl from the cab, and staggered to his apartment with her in his arms.

He opened the door and it banged against the living room wall. Half-dropping the unconscious girl on the floor, he shrugged off his coat and dropped it next to her. He trudged to the bedroom and removed his wet clothes. The bed looked inviting and he considered crawling between the covers to stop the shivering that jarred his skull. Can't do that. Gotta help that girl.

He pulled on the jeans and T-shirt he had tossed on the floor that morning. Grabbing the comforter from his bed, he spread it out on the floor next to the vent in the living room.

The girl was curled in a fetal position, shivering so hard he thought her head might split if it kept thumping the floor. He tried to pick her up but found he couldn't lift her, so he slid her limp figure across the floor and rolled her onto the comforter. He pulled the cover up around her, but then removed it.

"Can you hear me?" He gave her a few light taps on the cheek, but she didn't respond. "Miss? You need to get out of those wet clothes. Hello?"

Peter bit his lip and stared around the room for the solution to his dilemma. Finally, he shrugged and started removing her clothes. He caught a glimpse of a tattoo at the band of her underwear and averted his eyes. The leather cords around her wrists and neck had tightened as they dried, so he untied them. Green and blue bruises smudged her skin. What happened to you?

He left her underclothes intact. The tiny blue flowers that had faded to grey on her white cotton panties seemed pitiful to him. The girl curled into a ball, shivering in silence.

Peter pulled the comforter around her and grabbed the rest of the blankets from his bed to cover her. He emptied soda from a two-liter plastic bottle and filled the container with hot water. Rolling it in a towel, he placed it against the girl's feet.

After a few minutes, her shaking started to subside. Peter grabbed the cordless phone, but didn't dial. He knew he should call 911, but the situation didn't seem so life-threatening now. I'll call in a few minutes. He set the phone back on the coffee table.

I've got to get warm, too. He plodded to the kitchen and pulled a bottle of bourbon from the cabinet. He poured a fingered measurement in a glass and drank it. Warmth spread from his stomach to his chest to his muscles and he smiled.

Since he had used all his bed coverings on her, he wrapped a towel around his shoulders and put some thick socks on his now-tingling feet. Sitting on the couch, he still trembled. This ain't gonna cut it, he thought.

He stared at the figure bundled in the comforter. The blankets rose and fell around her steady breathing. She looks really warm. He stood and then sat down again. His muscles continued to spasm. Finally, he rose and walked to where she lay.

Peter stretched out next to her and slid under the blankets. He draped his arm across her and pulled the covers over both of them. He began to relax as his muscles yielded to her gentle warmth. I'll just stay here for a minute, he thought.

He inhaled her sweet scent. It reminded him of the vanilla sugar his mother used to make after a day of holiday baking. "Sugar and spice and everything nice," he mumbled. He drifted into sleep and dreamed he was in a bakery.

~~~

Peter woke up hot and sweaty. The pattern on the ceiling disoriented him. "Where am I?" he asked himself, and was surprised to hear little more than a croak. His throat was so sore it hurt to swallow and his head hurt. My whole body aches. I must be coming down with the flu.

Turning over, he realized there was a warm body next to his. The previous night's events slammed back into his memory. Oh, shit! Peter pulled the blanket down to reveal the face of the stranger he had saved.

Her ginger curls were matted against her cheek. He reached out and pushed her hair away from her face. Her fair skin and slender neck made him think of the swans that floated across the lake at the park. A milky scar, shaped like a question mark, ran through her right eyebrow. He moved his hand to touch it and she opened her eyes.

She whimpered and pulled away from Peter, taking the blankets with her. She wrapped them tight around herself and huddled with her forehead pressed against her knees.

"Wait a minute," he said. "It's okay. I'm not gonna hurt you." Sitting up with a groan, he thought, I couldn't hurt anything right now. The bar fight, the midnight dip in the Rivanna, and a night on the floor had taken their toll.

When Peter stood, blood rushed to his head and it began to thump in earnest. The girl slid across the floor until her back hit the wall. The look of fear on her face was so intense he felt guilty. He gestured to her, hands out, palms up, as he spoke. "Like I said, I'm not going to hurt you. I want to help. What's your name?"

She stared at him without responding. Peter sighed, sat down on the coffee table, and rubbed his forehead. He probed his face with his fingertips, grimacing at his swollen jaw. He lifted his eyes and saw the girl studying him. Leaning forward with his elbows on his knees, he said, "My name is Peter Sullivan. I'm an architecture student at U.Va."

Her face was a blank canvas. He tried again. "The University? Of Virginia . . . You know. Wah-hoo-wah. Thomas Jefferson and all that jazz?"

Silence.

He sat up and slapped his knees. "Well, I know you can talk because I heard you last night right before – uhm, you know. Remember? You were talking about stars and stuff?"

"Angels." Her voice was soft. He wondered if her throat was sore too.

"Yeah! Angels. I guess you had one looking out for you last night, huh?" Shut up, stupid. "So, uhm, don't you want to tell me your name?"

When she stuck her fingertips in her mouth and looked up at him from beneath long lashes, strange heat spread through his belly. Suddenly he understood why a man might kill or die for a woman. It's a wonder I didn't die last night. I must have lost my mind. He shook his head and ran his hand through his hair.

He sighed again. Looking around, he saw her clothes on the floor where he had dropped them. He picked them up, but they were still damp. "Your clothes are wet. That's why I undressed you last night." He felt his face grow hot. "I mean, you know, to get you warm. I thought we were both going to freeze to death. You lost your shoes out there in the river, too. Anyway, I think I might have something you can wear temporarily."

He escaped to the bedroom, where he flopped down on the bare mattress and pondered the situation. I guess I should call the police or somebody. Geez, for all I know, she's an escaped mental patient. Peter looked at the clock on the nightstand. 9:37.

Great. I'm late for class. What am I gonna do with her? I can't leave her here in my apartment. Then again, why not? What's she going to do? Steal my valuable collection of Pink Floyd T-shirts? Peter snorted.

He got up and went to the bathroom, thinking a shower might clear his head. Removing his clothes, he caught sight of bruises on his shoulders and chest. Examining himself in the mirror, he winced at the image. A purple bruise underscored his jaw and he had bruises of his own around his throat. Bloodshot, weary brown eyes and matted black hair completed the pitiful portrait. He savored the shower, although he caught himself listening for sounds of the girl leaving the apartment.

He dressed in jeans and a thick sweater before

retrieving clean sweat pants and a T-shirt from the floor of his closet. He returned to the living room and dropped them in front of the girl. "I'm sorry I don't have any shoes to fit you. I can grab some on my way home from class this afternoon. I hope these clothes will do until yours dry. You're pretty tiny."

Downright thin, now that I've got a good look at you. "Are you hungry?" Her green eyes gleamed at the mention of food. He gestured toward the tiny kitchen. "I've got some leftover pizza in the fridge. And cereal. Oh, I've got a whole cabinet full of ramen noodles. You're welcome to whatever you can find."

"Thank you."

Her soft reply moved him. He stooped in front of her, and she dropped her head. "Look, is there someone I can call for you? A relative? Or a friend?" She shook her head. "Do you need to see a doctor?" Again she shook her head. "Would you like me to call the police?"

"No." She reached out from beneath the blanket and clutched his wrist. "Don't! Please?"

Peter peered into her face. Are you running from the law? Or just a mental case? He found it difficult to think when he looked in her eyes. Don't be a sucker, man. Call the police. Do it now.

"I've got to get to class. I'll be back in a few hours."

He grabbed his keys and a brown corduroy jacket. At the door, he turned back, hesitant to leave this stranger in his apartment. She hadn't moved from her spot on the floor. He closed the door on her sloe-eyed stare, thinking she looked very much like an abandoned cat.

~~~

Peter sat in class doodling in his notebook. Every few minutes he picked up the thread of the lecture and wrote down the professor's comments in neat script. When the session ended, he looked down at his sparse notes and shook his head. I should've just stayed home, he thought.

He weaved his way through clusters of students in the hall and headed for the door. *I wonder if I'll have anything left in my apartment when I get back.* Racing out of Campbell Hall, he double-timed his way down Rugby Road toward the dining hall, ignoring the shouts of students – flower children wannabes – protesting Operation Desert Storm. The cold wind drew him up short and his muscles knotted beneath his clothes. At Newcomb Hall, he stuffed some cookies in his jacket pocket and trotted down to the bookstore.

He grabbed small sweatpants and a hooded jacket embroidered with an orange Cavaliers logo. The cashier rang them up and Peter cringed at the total. *I should've gone to a regular store,* he thought. *Actually, I'll have to do that anyway. She needs socks and shoes and I don't even know what size.*

He found sneakers and socks at a shopping center. At one store, he contemplated panties and bras a long time before he realized the sales ladies were staring at him. He felt himself blush and left that store without making a purchase.

By the time he reached his apartment building, it was a few minutes past three o'clock. He killed the engine and listened to it *tick-tick-tick* away the seconds. Looking down at the bags in the seat, he felt foolish. *Did I dream last night?*

He looked at his apartment window. A pale hand pulled back the living room curtains then disappeared. His heart started to thump. *Well, I guess that answers that question.*

Peter grabbed his mail from the box next to the door and entered the apartment. The living room was empty, but the faint scent of vanilla lingered in the air. He shut the door behind him and dropped the shopping bags on the couch. The apartment looked different, and it took him a few seconds to realize it had been cleaned. The scarred coffee table gleamed, as did the wooden floor. Books stood at attention on their shelves. Dust bunnies, candy wrappers, and beer bottles had been cleared from sight. This wasn't exactly what I had in mind when I figured she'd clean me out, he thought.

"Hello?" he called, but it came out in a whisper. He cleared his throat and tried again. "Hello?"

He stuck his head in the kitchen. The shiny appliances and empty sink impressed him. This place looks better now than it did when I moved in.

He walked into the bedroom. The bed was made, the covers turned down on one side. He looked toward the bathroom, the only room left in the apartment. "Hello? Are you there?"

Peter heard the distinctive *snickety-whisk* of a plastic shower curtain being drawn or pulled back. He waited for the sound of water but heard nothing. Finally, he walked to the door and peered into the bathroom.

The girl sat in the dry tub, still clothed in his sweats. She pulled her knees to her chest, wrapped her arms around her legs, and shrank into the corner. She didn't look at Peter when he sat down on the edge of the tub.

"Looks like you've been busy," he said. His words sounded hollow as they bounced off the tile.

She pushed stray curls back behind her ear, but didn't say anything. When Peter reached out to touch her sleeve, she grunted and pressed herself against the shower wall. He decided to try a different tactic.

"Hey, if you don't talk to me, I'm going to turn on the water and get your feet all wet." She gaped at him as he reached out and spun the crystal handle marked C. When a stream of water rushed from the faucet, she drew her feet closer in to her body.

Peter reached down and flicked some water across her feet. She squealed and tried to stand, but lost her balance. He steadied her, and then lifted her from the tub, surprised at how light she seemed now that she was dry.

He turned off the water and turned to see her staring at him. She leaned against the sink. Peter ran his hands through his hair and rested his shoulder against the doorjamb. "Are you going to tell me your name?"

She stuck her fingertips in her mouth for a moment and stared at an invisible spot near Peter's left foot. "Wren," she said, finally. "Like the bird."

When she spoke, she hollowed out her name into two syllables, so it sounded like "Ree-un."

"Wren. That's pretty. You know, you kinda talk like I do. Where are you from?"

She shrugged her shoulders. Peter tried again.

"I live near St. Paul. Ever been there?"

Wren's head shot up and she stared at Peter as if seeing him for the first time. Goose bumps popped across his skin and he shivered. "Well, anyway, I brought you some clothes. Warm ones."

He leaned back from the door and held out his arm toward the bedroom. Wren hesitated before walking past him, through the bedroom, and into the living room. There she stood with the ragged armchair between herself and Peter. He sat on the couch and pulled his purchases from the bags. He laid the clothes and shoes on the chair. "I hope they fit."

Wren stared at the folded clothes like a bird charmed by a snake. When Peter shifted with impatience, she snatched them from the chair and ran to the bathroom. She returned a few minutes later dressed from head to toe. Not too bad, Peter thought. Even the shoes fit.

Wren perched on the edge of the armchair and stared at the toes of her new shoes. Watching her chew on the edge of her thumb, Peter wondered what she was thinking. He struggled for something to say. "Uh, did you eat while I was gone?"

She nodded.

"Oh, well, that's good. I brought you some cookies." He

pulled the sweets from his jacket pocket and held them out to her. Pulling her thumb from her mouth, Wren smiled and took the cookies from Peter.

"Thank you." She nibbled the edge of one and held out the remaining cookies to him. He shook his head and leaned back into the couch.

Might as well get it over with, he thought. "Why did you jump off that bridge last night?"

Wren paused in mid-nibble. She bowed her head and auburn curls fell across her face. She finished the mouthful of food with a loud swallow and laid the remainder of the cookie on the coffee table. Looking up at Peter, she said, "I couldn't think of a reason not to."

"Oh." Peter picked up a throw pillow and hugged it to his chest. He didn't like the blue waves of helplessness washing over him.

Wren cocked her eyebrow and the white scar jumped into her forehead. "Why did you pull me out?"

Your eyes haunted me. He shrugged. "Couldn't think of a reason not to," he said.

She laughed, and the full-bodied sound surprised Peter, but he was more shocked to hear himself laugh. Their peculiar mirth rebounded off the walls of the sparse little apartment.

~~~

They sat in silence after that. Conscious of her scrutiny, Peter poked through his mail. A crisp envelope caught his eye and he noted the return address was that of Bryan and Greene Associates. The firm was an architectural company in Central Virginia, one of the most prestigious in the state. Peter had applied for an internship with them. I probably didn't get it, he thought as he ripped open the letter.

After scanning the letter, Peter tossed it in the air with a shout. Wren jumped, and then smiled at him. "Did you win the lottery or something?"

"You could say that!" He picked up the letter and waved

it in her face. "I just got my foot in the door of a very prominent architecture firm. I'm interning with them this summer." Grinning, he reread the letter. "Excuse me. I have to call my mom and tell her."

He ran to the bedroom and picked up the extension there. His mother sounded flustered when she picked up the phone. "Pshew. Hello?"

He shook his head at her greeting. He pictured her standing in the kitchen with her hand on her hip, blowing stray hair out of her eyes. "You sound tired. Dad must be giving you a hard time."

"Oh, Lord. He'd worry the knots off a wooden man. He's been down in his back the last couple of days, and didn't go to work. Lord God Almighty, he's run me to death." Peter heard the scrape of a chair, and then his mother sighed into the phone. "Well, how's my big'un?"

He smiled at his mother's pet name. He was the oldest of three -- the only boy -- and he stood tall beside his petite sisters and mother. "Uhm, I guess you could say it's been an interesting week. Oh, guess what? I got an internship with Bryan and Greene Associates here in Charlottesville. Dr. Malcolm putting in a good word for me must have helped. I start right after graduation."

"Well, I'm proud to hear that, baby. I was hoping you'd get to come home for a few months after you graduated, though."

Peter heaved a mental sigh to deflect the guilt. "I know, Mom. But this is an opportunity I can't pass up. I'll be home eventually, anyway."

A voice spoke in the background. "Your daddy is hollering at me. Hold on." She offered a muffled reply to the voice, but Peter couldn't understand what she said. He weaved the phone cord between his fingers as he waited for her to come back on the line.

What do I say about Wren? Hey Mom, I pulled this suicidal girl from the river last night and she's here in my apartment. Oh, by the way, I undressed her and fell asleep with her. Yeah, that'll go over real well.

He decided to appeal to her spiritual nature. Mom, you remember how you're always telling me to be a Good Samaritan? He was formulating his approach when she returned to the line.

"Listen, baby, I've got to get off here. Your daddy wants to take a bath and see if it helps his back any. I'll have to help him in the tub. He told me to tell you he was real proud of you for getting that job."

Pshew. Safe. "Okay, Mom. I'll talk to you tomorrow or Sunday."

"I love you."

"Love you, too."

~~~

Peter cooked a simple dinner for Wren. He made a big omelet, cut it in half, and slid the golden crescents onto two chipped plates. He toasted bread and smeared it with his mother's homemade blackberry jam, scraping the sides of the jar to get the very last bit of sweet fruit. He and his father had picked the berries behind their house last summer.

As he cooked, Wren stood with her back against the wall and watched him with wary tension. He didn't try to talk to her. He poured two glasses of milk, set the drinks on the table, and motioned for her to sit.

Wren hunched over her eggs and toast. She drained the milk from her glass in one long draught and sat with her arms folded in front of her plate. A pale white moustache covered her upper lip. Peter chuckled and reached across the table to brush her mouth with a paper towel. She cringed, so he withdrew his hand.

"I'm sorry. I was just going to wipe away that milk moustache." He offered her the paper towel, which she took and wiped her mouth.

They both leaned back in their chairs and examined

everything but each other. The apartment was quiet except for the hum of the refrigerator. Finally, Wren looked at Peter and said, "I appreciate what you did for me."

"Well." He didn't know what to say.

Wren carried her plate and glass to the sink. "I have to go."

"Now?"

"Yes. Thank you for the food and the clothes. You didn't have to do that. You're real nice."

Peter blushed. "Well, where will you go?" He envisioned her trotting back down to the bridge to finish last night's job.

"I don't know," Wren said. "I'll figure something out." She walked to the living room with Peter close behind.

He circled around her and stood with his back against the door. "Well, wait a minute. You don't even have a coat! You'll freeze to death. It's colder now than it was last night."

Wren bit her lip and shivered. "There's a shelter somewhere in this town, I bet. I don't want to put you out any more than I already have."

Peter pictured her lying in the dark in one of the homeless shelters across town. He had never been in one, but he imagined it wouldn't be very pleasant. "You haven't put me out," he said. "I think you should stay here tonight. You can have my bed and I'll sleep on the couch."

"Oh, no, I can't do that. I'm already beholden to you for everything else you done for me." Wren tried to sidestep Peter, but he stood firm with his hands wrapped around the doorknob.

"Wren. Please stay. It's not any trouble at all. In fact, I'd be glad to have the company. Anyway, it's nice to hear somebody who talks like me. Feels like home." He paused and stared at her. "You are from down my way, aren't you?"

She offered him a reluctant nod. He smiled and held his hand out toward the couch. Wren stroked the scar on her eyebrow as she took a seat in the living room. She pulled her knees up to her chest and Peter wondered if she always cocooned herself like that when she was around strangers.

"Where?" he asked.

"Pawpaw Ridge."

Peter leaned forward in excitement. "Hey, that's only about twenty minutes away from our house. Where did you go to school?"

"Oh, it was a long time ago I lived there. I lived in Bristol since I was twelve. I got adopted after my daddy died."

"Oh. What's your last name?"

"Why?"

"Just curious." He leaned back in the armchair and stretched his legs beneath the coffee table.

Wren watched Peter cross and re-cross his legs. She leaned forward and picked up one of his books from the coffee table. "You must be real smart, huh? Do you like college?"

Peter laughed. "Sometimes I like it a lot. Sometimes I hate it. I was valedictorian in high school. Then I got here and realized I'd just been a big fish in a little pond, you know?" *I've never told anybody that.* "And it seems like everybody here's from northern Virginia or on up the east coast. The way they act, you'd think Southwest Virginia's in a whole other country."

"I guess they don't like it cause they never seen it. Nothing's prettier than my mountains," Wren said.

Peter smiled at the proprietary tone in her voice. "I went through fraternity rush and this one guy asked me what my father did for a living. I told him he's in mining and he wanted to know how many mines my dad owned. Of course, I laughed and told him Dad doesn't own coal mines – he mines coal. Well, as soon as I said that, the guy just smirked and walked away."

Wren's mouth turned down at the corners. "My daddy got killed in the mines when I was a little girl."

He wanted to fold her in his arms and rock her. "I'm sorry." He hesitated to pry into her personal life; it felt like he was picking at a scab. But I need to find out if she has a family. "What about your mom?"

"She died when I was born."

"Oh. Then you got adopted and moved to Bristol?"

Wren shifted in her seat and blew a soft breath against her fingertips. Peter could see her push away another time and place to answer him. "Yeah, that's pretty much it." She yawned, covering her mouth with the back of her forearm.

"It's getting late. I want you to take my bed tonight. I'll crash on the couch."

"I can sleep on the couch."

Peter frowned. "Are you sure? It doesn't seem right for a guest to sleep on the couch."

She giggled, but it sounded like a fork scraping a pot. "I didn't know I was a guest. I feel more like a stray cat."

Peter shivered, wondering if she had read his mind that morning.

~~~

He made up the couch while Wren showered. Peter smacked a sheet against the air and watched it float down across the couch. The clean scent of fabric softener wafted to the ceiling. He held a naked pillow under his chin and snaked a pillowcase up over it with both hands. He laid the pillow on a stack of blankets on the coffee table.

Leaning back in the armchair, he waited for Wren to return from the bathroom. He cracked his knuckles and listened to the footsteps thudding in the apartment overhead. A door slammed on the strident voice of a child. Peter shifted in his seat and tapped his fingers against his knee. The thought of warm water beading on smooth skin swooped into his mind.

He jumped up and hurried to the kitchen. He poured Jim Beam in a glass and carried it to the living room. Resting in the chair, he held the liquor to the lamp and grinned at the gilded light in the glass.

"You like to drink?" Wren leaned against the doorway between the bedroom and the living room. She stroked the dark ring of bruises around her neck. His clothes, a clean T-shirt and pair of shorts, swallowed her thin frame.

Peter blushed and set the glass on his knee. "No more than the average guy." She remained in the doorway. Self-conscious beneath her gaze, he gulped the bourbon without tasting it. "Well, I guess you're all set. I wish you'd take the bed, though."

"The couch is fine." She padded to the couch and stood behind it.

You always put a piece of furniture between yourself and me. I'm not going to hurt you. Peter ran his hands through his hair and looked around the apartment. He walked to the door and locked it. Flicking off the light in the kitchen, he looked at Wren. "Do you want me to leave a light on?"

Wren shook her head. She remained behind the sofa as Peter walked into his bedroom. He turned back and saw she still hadn't moved. He snapped off the lamp in his bedroom and amber light from the street filled the apartment. "Holler at me if you need anything, okay?" he called from the doorway.

"Okay." Her voice was as soft as the flutter of moth wings in the dark.

Lying in bed, Peter grew hypersensitive to everything around him. He could hear the tiniest sounds: the slow drip of the kitchen faucet . . . the pop of gravel when a car pulled into the parking lot . . . the rustle of cotton as Wren turned over on the couch. That sounded loudest of all. Each time she moved, he felt all the hairs on his body stand on end.

All at once, Peter's bed felt gigantic. He imagined he would have to crawl a long distance just to reach the edge of the mattress. Extending his arm, he was shocked to feel his hand hang over the side of the bed. He sighed and flopped around like a fish on dry land. Didn't have any trouble going to sleep last night. Of course, I was half-dead and curled up next to a semi-warm body.

The thought of a warm body didn't make him any sleepier. He lay flat on his back and laced his hands together against his bare chest. Staring into the dark, he thought about their conversation. I can't believe you grew up so close to where I live. Pawpaw Ridge.

It was one of his favorite back roads. He closed his eyes and pictured the mountain in high summer. He and Matt would roll down the windows on Matt's Chevelle and let the warm wind sting their skin as they rode around the mountain. Blind vines of kudzu groped the ditch, hiding nearsighted groundhogs in its thick mat. As the car navigated the switchbacks, fine dust settled across the bright blue cornflowers and peppery weeds that grew beside the road.

Peter grew warm as he pictured the summer air wiggling and wavering above the black hardtop. Sometimes the car seemed to glide across the mounds and dips in the road until he thought it might float above the neat little houses nestled in the folds of hills.

They usually drove around late into night. Peter liked to watch the evening haze descend with dusk and cover summer's sassy colors with blue shadows. It made him feel strange, like he might laugh and cry all at the same time. He smiled at the memory and felt himself tumble into dreams of lazy summer days.

~~~

Peter awoke the next morning to the sound of the shower. He opened one eye and saw a diagonal of light slash the carpet in front of the bathroom door. Didn't even hear her come through here. He glanced over at the clock and saw it was just a little past seven. He groaned and covered his face with the blanket.

A few minutes later the bathroom door opened and Wren tiptoed past him. Steam and the refreshing scent of soap trailed behind her.

Peter sat up and stretched, enjoying the crackling sensation in his spine. By the time he showered, shaved, and dressed, he could hear her working in the kitchen. He ambled into the living room, surprised at how fat and lazy he felt.

Wren was washing the dishes from last night's dinner. Peter joined her at the sink and dried plates and utensils. He knew it should feel odd to be doing such a mundane chore with a total stranger, not even making small talk, yet it seemed natural. *I wonder if she feels the same way.* He gave her a sidelong glance and thought she looked as comfortable now as she had since he'd met her.

She started when he finally spoke. "I was thinking we should go have some breakfast. Then we could go to the mall and get you a coat and some other things you might need."

She paused from wiping the stove with a dishcloth and looked up at him. Tears filled her eyes. "I can't take anything else from you." She twisted the wet rag in her hands and draped it across the faucet. "It wouldn't be right."

"Why not? My mom taught me to do for other people when they can't do for themselves. And I have a feeling you can't do for yourself right now. Am I right?"

Wren wiped her eyes with the back of her hand. She nodded.

"Okay, then," Peter said. "Let's go eat. I'm starving!"

After he warmed up his truck, they hopped in and headed to a pancake house.

The dining room was packed with truck drivers, harried families, and students. Three men in suits sat at a table next to Wren and Peter, exchanging business cards and friendly banter over waffles. Their laughter was so loud Peter had to strain to hear the waitress and Wren.

She drowned tall stacks of golden disks with syrup and licked the tips of her sticky fingers in between bites and then leaned back in the booth while he finished eating. She cocked her head and studied him. Her expression mystified Peter. He wiped his mouth and curled his lips in a self-conscious smile. "What?"

She reached across the table and brushed his jaw with her knuckles. Peter shivered, but he didn't pull away from her. The bruises had started to fade to shades of green and yellow. "Doesn't look too bad now, huh?" he asked. She withdrew her hand and he felt the skin tingle where she had touched him. He pointed to the bruises on her neck and wrists. "Wanna tell me about yours?"

She crossed her arms and averted her eyes. "No." Fat teardrops fell into her plate.

"Please don't cry. Forget I asked. I'm sorry."

"I'm sorry, too." Wren scoured her eyes with a rumpled napkin. "It's my fault those guys hurt you."

"I'm the one who started the fight. I come a hair getting my butt kicked, too. I'm no knight in shining armor, but I guess I didn't do too bad."

Wren laughed as loud as she had the night before. It intrigued Peter to hear such a carefree sound coming from someone who seemed so worn with care. Her laugh was rich and throaty, and he sensed it drawing the attention of the men in the dining room. They sat straighter or stood taller when they noticed her.

She doesn't even realize it, Peter thought. The business men at the next table had grown quiet. They stared at Wren over cups of coffee and whispered to each other. Peter narrowed his eyes at them. He finished his milk and slammed the plastic glass down on the table. It rocked back and forth: *clunka-clunka-clunka.*

"Let's go."

~~~

He took her to a nearby mall. They wandered in and out of stores until he found a rack of winter coats. Peter dug through them, ignoring the sales people who watched them with suspicious eyes. He yanked a red coat from the rack; a puffy down-filled thing that he thought looked like it would be warm. "Here, try this on."

He held it for her as she slid her arms backwards into it. Peter spun her around and zipped it up to her neck. He jerked the waist down to straighten it, as he had seen his mother do to his sisters when they tried on clothes for her. "How does it feel?"

"Warm." Beads of perspiration popped out on Wren's forehead. She flapped her arms. "I can't get my arms down to my sides."

Peter laughed. "You sorta look like a big red marshmallow, but that's okay. It has lots of insulation."

Wren removed the coat and Peter put it back on the hanger. He started to walk away with it, but she grabbed his arm. Blushing, she pointed to another coat on the rack. It was the same style, but dark purple. "What about that one?"

Peter tried not to smile. "You like purple, huh?" He stuck the red one back on the rack and found a purple one in her size. "Okay, let's see. What else? What else?" he asked himself. "Jeans, I think."

He put two pairs of jeans and three T-shirts into her arms. They walked to the lingerie department, but Peter stopped short, as if he had reached an invisible barrier. "Uhm, you go on and find – things. I'll wait here."

Wren smiled at the high red spots on his cheeks and thrust the jeans and T-shirts into his arms. While he was waiting, Peter found purple gloves and a scarf that matched the coat. She came back in less than three minutes with plain white panties, bras, and socks. They carried the clothes to the nearest sales counter. The sales girl smiled at Peter and flipped her blonde hair as she rang up the items, but she ignored Wren.

Peter pulled a credit card from his wallet and stared at it a moment. His father had given it to him for emergencies. He had only used it twice in four years, most recently to repair the alternator on his truck. He glanced at Wren, who stood off to the side with her arms crossed, staring at her feet. I guess this qualifies as an emergency, he thought.

Strolling through the mall, they passed two police officers talking to a security guard. As they drew close, Wren turned her head and examined the window display of a bookstore with great interest. She let her hair fall in her face. White spots bloomed on her knuckles as she clutched the bags and hurried toward the exit.

"Hey, wait up." Peter pushed through the door behind her. Wren's breath decorated the air with quick little white wisps. She dropped her bags and clutched the cold pole at the bus stop. She trembled with such violence that the sign clanked on its pole.

She mewled when he touched her shoulder. "Wren? Are you okay?"

She took a deep breath and held it several beats. "Yes. Yes, I'm fine." She glanced back at the mall entrance. "Can we go?"

"Is there something you want to tell me?"

"No."

"What kind of trouble are you in?"

"Let's just go. Please?" Her wide eyes pleaded with him to stop asking questions.

Peter grabbed her bags, muttering to himself as they walked through the parking lot. What have I gotten myself into?

~~~

Back at the apartment, Wren sat near the window and cut the price tags from the clothes. She folded them with such care that Peter felt guilty. He tried not to stare at her, but he couldn't seem to look at anything else when she was in the room. Late morning sun streamed through the window, igniting the light in her auburn hair.

Peter remembered a line from an old movie, *The Philadelphia Story*. Jimmy Stewart, in love with Katherine

Hepburn, tells her "You're lit from within, bright, bright, bright. There are fires banked down in you, hearth fires and holocausts."

He didn't realize he had said it aloud until he saw Wren gaping at him. "That's beautiful," she said. "Is it a poem?"

Peter shook his head, unable to speak. He felt like his entire body was full of air, an expanding shell that might burst at the slightest touch. He clutched the couch, wondering if he had lost his mind.

Wren frowned. "Are you okay?"

"Fine," he gasped. He lay back with his head on the couch arm and closed his eyes.

A moment later her cool hand touched his forehead. He looked up and saw her springtime eyes searching his own. It was simple, then, for him to say, "Stay."

Four

Southwest Virginia, 1980-1985

"Stay here? I don't think so." Maryann's voice carried from her kitchen to the back porch. Wren sat in the porch swing and listened to Maryann and Regina Mullins talk over coffee.

Wren thought Regina's voice sounded very much like the bark of the little Chihuahua she sometimes hauled around with her in her big Lincoln. "She's got no family. Don't you feel obligated to take her in?"

"Obligated?" Maryann snorted. "Why should I?"

There was a long silence before Regina answered. "God Almighty, Maryann, you were going to be her stepmother anyway."

Wren heard a coffee cup clatter against its saucer. Maryann sounded puzzled. "I wonder." She paused. "I wonder if Ed would have really gone through with it. He put off our wedding date every time she jerked her chin at him. Sometimes I wonder if she didn't fall out of that tree on purpose."

"She's just a little girl! What child wants its mother replaced?"

"I wasn't trying to replace Liza." Wren heard anger in Maryann's voice. "But I would've been good to Wren if she'd let me. She didn't want me to." Maryann sighed. "She tried me. That's all there is to it. And I put up with it for Ed. But he's not here now."

Wren rubbed the tip of her sneaker against the wooden floor and wiggled her toes inside her shoes. She was glad to be out of her church clothes, which Maryann had made her wear to the funeral home and the graveyard.

The graveyard. Wren didn't want to think about it, but the image of Edgar's grave came to her unbidden. She imagined her father closed up in his shiny box deep beneath the earth and decided it didn't seem much different from him being underground in a coal mine. Except he's never coming back home. The black monster awakened and stretched inside her, so she stuck her fingertips in her mouth to keep it at bay.

"I don't know what Liza was thinking, letting herself get pregnant at her age anyway," Maryann said. Her mother's name caught Wren's attention and she eased back against the wall of the kitchen so she could hear better.

"From what I understand, they didn't think they could have a baby. Wren was just a happy accident," Regina said.

"Happy. Well, nobody's happy now. She's got no family. Ed told me one time the only family him and Liza had left was just distant cousins, and he didn't lay claim to none of them. Said they were all whoremongers, gamblers, or drunkards."

Regina clicked her tongue. "Surely all of them can't be that bad."

"Well, I've never known him to visit any of them or even call one." Maryann cleared her throat. "Anyway, Wren's never wanted to be around me. That's not going to change. I can't take responsibility. The woman from social services is supposed to be here anytime now to pick her up. They'll get her in a foster home and that'll be that."

"Well," Regina said, "I better go. I don't want to be here for that. It's not my place to tell you what to do, Maryann, but she's just a pitiful little girl."

"Then you take her, Regina. At least you've got a husband who could help you. I don't have anybody. Walk a mile in my shoes before you judge me."

Their voices faded as Maryann accompanied Regina to the front door. Wren heard the Lincoln pull out of the driveway. She pulled her knees close to her chest and wrapped her arms around her legs. Listening to the sound of the television coming to life, she thought, Maryann doesn't miss *Days of Our Lives* for nothing.

A car pulled into the driveway around 2:30. Wren jumped when a knock resounded through the house. Maryann answered the door and the low murmur of female voices drifted through the house for several minutes before she called to her. "Wren! Come inside, please."

She walked into the house and found Maryann and another woman sitting in the living room. The woman was tall and thin, with long white hands and watery blue eyes. She reminded Wren of a vampire. She stood and held out her hand. "Hello, Wren. I'm Sharon O'Neil."

Wren lingered in the doorway between the kitchen and the living room, staring at her feet. Maryann frowned. "Wren, don't be rude. Say hello."

"Hello."

"Miss O'Neil is with social services. She's gonna help you find a new home and a nice family to live with."

"I have a home," Wren said. Maryann glanced at Sharon and shrugged.

Sharon patted the couch cushion. "Come sit with me for a minute." Wren shuffled to the sofa and perched on the edge.

"I know this may be hard for you to understand, sweetheart, but the house where you lived with your daddy is not going to be your home anymore. It'll be sold at auction and the proceeds will be used to pay off the bills he owed and to pay for his – his funeral. Whatever is left over will go into an account for you, although it probably won't be much."

Maryann stirred. "There's also a small account at the bank in St. Paul. Our neighbors and some of the men Edgar worked with took up a little money for her. I've got the information written down for you."

Sharon nodded. "Good. We've got a nice foster family that you're going to stay with for a while, Wren. Have you got your clothes packed?"

Wren jumped up, ran to Maryann, and threw herself into the woman's arms. "Please don't make me go. I'll be good if you let me stay. I promise!" Sobs wracked her body until she felt like she might fly apart.

Maryann closed her eyes and pursed her lips. "Wren. This is the best way. Now be good and stop crying." She pushed Wren away. "You're just making this harder on yourself. Sharon will make sure you git taken care of real good."

"That's right, Wren. I know this is hard, but you'll get used to it. I promise." Sharon knelt next to Wren and wiped her tears with a handkerchief. "Now, dry your eyes and we'll get your things. It's time for us to go."

Maryann had gathered Wren's clothes, toys, and pictures in boxes and stacked them next to the front door. She draped a ragged brown sweater across Wren's shoulders and put a Barbie in her hands. She and Sharon carried the boxes to the rusty Buick Skylark sitting in the driveway. Wren leaned against the car while they packed the trunk. When they were done, Sharon ushered her inside the car and buckled her in the front seat.

Maryann leaned through the window and patted her arm. Wren laid her head against the door and cried. As they pulled away from the house, she looked back, but Maryann had already walked back inside and shut the door.

~~~

The Landolls, Wren's first foster family, lived in Coeburn.

They ignored her sighs and sobs, although she cried so much the first two weeks her eyes swelled shut. Mrs. Landoll spent most of her attention on herself.

She was very particular about her things. "If you want something in this house, you must ask permission to use it." Including soap, shampoo, towels, and toilet paper, Wren discovered. And Mrs. Landoll's personal toiletries.

She allowed Wren to sit with her each evening as she prepared for bed. The first time, Wren poked through the bottles and jars on the vanity. The woman frowned, but didn't say anything until Wren squirted Chanel No. 5 on her wrist.

"I told you not to touch my perfume or anything else unless you ask first. That is very expensive! Now put it back."

Wren learned to sit still, although her fingers twitched when she looked at the baubles and potions and lotions. The woman's bedtime rituals fascinated her. Each night Mrs. Landoll rolled her blonde hair and secured it with bobby pins. Wren thought it a neat trick that the woman could hold the tiny metal pieces between her pursed lips as she maneuvered her hair with both hands.

When she slathered cold cream on her face, Wren caught the faint scent of honeysuckle. "What's that for?"

"It keeps the skin young, Wren." The woman sounded bored as she rubbed cold cream on her face.

"How old are you?"

The woman stopped rubbing her face and narrowed her eyes at Wren's reflection. "I do believe you are the most unmannerly child I've ever seen. Don't you know it's rude to ask a lady her age?"

"I'm sorry," Wren said. "I just figured if you wanted to look young, it meant you were old."

Mrs. Landoll glared at her a moment before resuming her facial massage with vigor. When she finished, she wiped her hands with a tissue. Turning, she placed her hands on

Wren's shoulders and looked into her eyes. "Go brush your teeth and get in bed."

Wren dreaded going to bed. She went to bed hungry every night. Even after five months, Mrs. Landoll required her to ask permission to snack. But when Wren asked, her foster mother always said no. Wren felt there was never enough food on the table for her and three other foster children. But they always have their fair share, she thought, as she watched Mr. and Mrs. Landoll heap food on their own plates.

Pangs of hunger gnawed at her especially hard at night. She knew this evening would be no different. In bed, she thought of the meals her father used to fix for the two of them. Golden-brown potato cakes spiced with sage and black pepper . . . pickled corn . . . fried green tomatoes . . . macaroni and tomatoes . . . biscuits and gravy and pickled beets. She covered her head with a pillow and cried. Please, God, help me not think about food.

Wren tossed in bed until the sheets wrapped around her legs. She couldn't ignore the hollow feeling in her stomach anymore. Sliding out of bed, she crept downstairs to the kitchen. A streetlight shined through the kitchen window, guiding her to the cabinets.

She climbed onto a chair and retrieved a pack of crackers from the cabinet. She ate the saltines with sweet deliberation, savoring the crisp snap of each one, licking the salt from her fingers. When she finished, she drank a glass of water. She might not be full, but she could feel full.

Wren was washing the glass when Mrs. Landoll laid her hand on her shoulder. She dropped the glass into the sink and cried out as it shattered in the stainless steel bowl.

"Katherine Rose! You're supposed to be in bed. What are you doing down here?" Mrs. Landoll squeezed her shoulder to turn her around.

The woman's face was shiny with complexion cream. Rollers clung to her head like pink link sausages. She tightened the belt on her terry cloth robe as she glared at Wren.

Mr. Landoll stood behind her. He sat down at the kitchen table and rubbed a hammy hand through his thinning hair. Wren looked from him to Mrs. Landoll and licked her lips.

"I was thirsty. I wanted to get a glass of water. I'm sorry I broke the glass."

Mrs. Landoll raised her eyebrows and searched Wren's face. She walked to the cabinet and began searching through cans and boxes, homing in on the saltines like a bloodhound. She pulled down the box and drew out the open pack of crackers. She tossed the package onto the kitchen table with a triumphant "Hhmmph!"

"Look at this, Ernest! Katherine came down here to get a drink of water. So who ate these crackers? The mouse in her pocket?" She turned to Wren. "You know the rules. You're supposed to ask before you touch anything in this house."

"I'm sorry. I was hungry. I didn't want to wake you up." Wren backed up to the refrigerator and grabbed the door handle with her sweaty hands. She rocked from side to side, pulling on the handle.

"Well," Mrs. Landoll said, "I guess we have to show you what happens to people who don't obey the rules, isn't that right, Ernest?" Mr. Landoll nodded in weary agreement.

Mrs. Landoll grabbed Wren by the shoulders and pulled her away from the refrigerator. The door came open and a bottle of ketchup fell to the floor and shattered. Red sauce splattered their bare feet.

"Now look what you've done! Wasteful! You'll clean that up after we're done and that's a fact! Now come over here with me." She grunted as she pulled Wren over to her husband.

Wren tried to slither from her grip, but Ernest reached out and grasped her by the elbows. He sat her down hard in a chair. Mrs. Landoll returned to the cabinet and began rifling through it.

Ernest pulled Wren's arms onto the table and clasped her hands with his own, as if greeting a good friend. He rubbed the tops of her hands with his thumbs and turned up her palms. He was gentle as he uncurled her fingers and caressed them. Tears rolled down Wren's face and dribbled into her upturned hands.

Mrs. Landoll retrieved a 28-ounce can of green beans and returned to the kitchen table. She smiled at Wren as she hefted the can with both hands. "This is what we do to little girls who steal our food."

The woman brought the can down onto Wren's fingers with all the force she could muster. The black monster reared its head and roared.

~~~

Wren lived with two other foster families in 1981. Her hands took six months to heal. Nightmares replaced her bouts of sleepwalking. Every night she woke up screaming that she was drowning. The third family called social services to take her back because Wren threw her plate on the floor three days in a row. Miss O'Neil forgot to tell the foster mother she shouldn't serve green beans.

Toni and Mark were Wren's fourth set of foster parents. She moved in with them in 1982. They lived in a ragged house, one of many in a stretch of houses that had been part of an old coal camp. All the houses, painted in dirty pastels, were tall and narrow and set close together. I bet I could stick my hand through the window next door, Wren thought, when she looked out her bedroom window. She missed her room overlooking the musical creek on Pawpaw Ridge.

She liked their backyard, though. They sat in the yard and listened to a symphony of birds in the trees while they ate breakfast. Toni taught Wren how to identify birds by their songs. Wren loved the birds; so did the old cat,

Cyclops.

The cat, an old stray Toni brought home from the dumpster, was the color of marmalade. He had ragged ears and only one eye. He streaked up the steps one day as Toni and Wren played checkers on the porch. He dropped a glistening package on the floor and proceeded to bat the red and black disks off the board. While Toni shooed him away, Wren went to inspect what Cyclops had discarded.

It was a baby bird, but it was so undeveloped Wren couldn't identify what kind. If it had possessed any down, the cat had worn it off. One of its legs dangled by a tendon, and its right wing was missing. Its tiny beak opened and closed. When Wren gagged, Toni ran to see what was wrong. She sent Wren to the bathroom while she disposed of the pitiful creature. When she told Mark about it, he took the cat back to the dumpster. They never saw Cyclops again.

Mark brought Wren treasures from his job. A bulldozer operator at a strip mine, he often found fossils embedded in the earth he moved. She lined the rocks up along her windowsill, fascinated by the perfect imprint of tiny ferns, veined leaves, and strange insects in the stone.

After more than a year with Toni and Mark, Wren still dreamed of drowning and screamed herself awake. "Daddy pulled me out of the creek," she cried one night as Toni rocked her. Her eyes followed a silver light sliding across her bedroom ceiling. "Mark's home," she murmured.

"You're getting sleepy, aren't you?" Toni brushed her hair away from her face and leaned her back in the bed. "I bet Mark is, too. I wish he could get off the hoot owl shift."

"Hoot owl," Wren repeated. She closed her eyes, fell asleep, and dreamed of owls with angry eyes and hard beaks.

The next morning Wren raised her head and squinted at the sun warming the roses on the wallpaper. The light's different, she thought. She looked over at her clock and realized she had slept past ten o'clock. Something's wrong.

Toni let me miss school!

She hopped out of bed and pulled on her robe and slippers. Trotting downstairs, she called to Toni in a loud whisper. Mark would be in bed and she didn't want to wake him. She pulled up short in the empty kitchen. Where is she?

"Toni? Where are you?" Wren stuck her head out the back door, but the yard was deserted. Opening the basement door, she stood on the top step, peered into the dim light, and called out a tentative "Hello?"

She walked down the hall trailing one finger along the wall. The wall was paneled and her finger bumped over ridges every few inches. Wren counted them as she walked toward the living room. "One, two, three, four . . . ." She counted thirteen before she reached the living room. Sunlight slashed the dim air and dust motes floated in the sharp yellow beams.

A shadow crossed the window and Wren realized Toni and Mark were on the front porch. Why is he still up? She chewed on her thumb for a moment and stared at the front door's brass doorknob. It had tiny dents in it like dimples. Wren laid her head against the door and tried to listen to their conversation.

Hearing Toni sniffle, she pushed open the door in one furious fling and stood stiff-legged in the threshold. Toni sat in a rocking chair with Mark crouched down next to her. They both looked up at Wren, but neither spoke. Toni tugged on her runny nose before finally wiping it on her pajama sleeve.

Wren walked to her and placed her tender fingers on Toni's knee. "What's wrong?"

"Oh, honey. We --" She stopped and looked at her husband.

Mark sighed, sat down on the porch, and crossed his legs. "Come here a second, Wren."

She shuffled to Mark. Since he was sitting, they were

face to face. She ran her fingers along his black moustache and curled the ends up. He placed his calloused hands on her arms and rubbed his nose against hers in an Eskimo kiss. She giggled, but his solemn expression made her stomach tingle.

"Wren, I got laid off last night."

"Oh." She stuck her fingertips in her mouth and stared at him. When he didn't say anything else, she asked, "What are we going to do?"

Toni reached out and stroked Wren's curls. "Mark talked to his brother this morning and he said there are a lot of jobs up in Manassas. He said we could come stay with him until Mark finds a job up there."

"I've never been to Manassas," Wren said. "When will we move there?"

Mark rolled his head back and forth on his shoulders to stretch the muscles. Frowning, he pulled Wren into his lap. "We won't be able to take you with us, sweetheart. My brother has three kids and they live in a small house. There wouldn't be room for all of us."

"But I wouldn't take up much room," Wren replied. Toni started to cry, but Mark squeezed her knee to stop her.

"Look, baby," Mark said, "I know it's hard for you to understand, but sometimes we have to do things we don't want to do. We don't want to leave you, but we have to."

"Everybody leaves me," Wren cried. She pulled away from Mark and stumbled back into the house. Nobody cares what happens to me. Nobody loves me. What's wrong with me?

~~~

Her final foster family adopted her when she was fourteen. In 1982, Cindy and Don Palmer had adopted a son, Thomas. They finalized Wren's paperwork a year later. "Now our family is complete." Cindy clapped her hands and showed Wren the papers.

Cindy was an office manager for a manufacturing

company in Bristol. Don had retired from the Detroit police department years before they moved to Virginia. He piddled around the house while Cindy worked.

Cindy encouraged Wren to pursue art classes in school. "You have natural talent. With a little guidance, you'll make a real artist." Ignoring the protests of Don and Thomas, Cindy set up a studio for Wren in their garage.

"You play favorites, Cindy." Thomas pushed away his plate and tossed his fork on the table after dinner one night.

"Thomas, that's not true. If you'd stay out of trouble and express an interest in something meaningful, I'd be happy to work with you." Cindy scraped food from his plate into a bowl.

"I'm an artist, too."

She rolled her eyes. "Covering your friends in tattoos, homemade tattoos, does not make you an artist."

"He's good enough to be an apprentice. Miller said so." Wren smiled at her stepbrother.

Don frowned. "Tom, I thought we told you to stay away from that tattoo place."

Thomas shifted his eyes from Don to Cindy to Wren. He licked his lips and scowled at his sister. "Thanks a lot, big mouth."

"I'm sorry, Thomas." Wren touched her lips with her fingertips.

Don stood and slipped his belt from his pants. He jerked his head toward the back of the house. "Let's go."

Thomas clutched the edge of the table and pleaded with his mother. "Cindy?"

Cindy laid her hand on her husband's arm. "Don, he's really getting too big for that. He's almost sixteen years old."

Don slapped the belt against his pant leg. "When he's eighteen, he'll be too big. Until then, he's got to learn discipline."

Thomas climbed to his feet, his eyes watery pools in his ashen face. Wren pulled at his shirttail, but let go when

Don glared at her. "You want some, too?"

"No, sir." She dropped her head.

Cindy escaped to the kitchen, leaving Wren to listen to the repeated *thwops* of the leather belt on her stepbrother's skin. Wren squeezed her silverware with each blow. She looked down when Don returned to the table and saw she'd bent her fork double.

Thomas hadn't uttered a sound, but Wren knew he would cry that night after Don turned off the lights. I'm sorry, Thomas. I'm sorry.

~~~

"Happy Birthday, Wren." Cindy snapped her picture as she blew out the candles on the cake.

"Fifteen. Looks like you've got a ways to go before you get to can this place," Thomas whispered in Wren's ear. "Two more years and I'm outta here." They both laughed, pretending he had made a joke.

Later, Cindy joined them as they gathered crumpled paper and twisted ribbon into a garbage bag. "Hey, you two. Sit down here a minute. I need to talk to you."

Wren and Thomas flopped on the couch with the green plastic bag slumped between them. Don eased himself into a nearby recliner. Cindy seated herself on the edge of the coffee table and, for the first time, Wren noticed blue circles beneath her bright eyes.

Cindy blew air from her lips. "Well, where to start?" Don cleared his throat, but she didn't look at him. "I've been feeling pretty bad lately. I went to the doctor a few weeks ago and they ran some tests on me. I found out this morning – well it turns out -- it turns out I have cancer." She laughed and Wren shivered at the gulping sounds.

Thomas leaned forward and clasped Cindy's hand. "What's going to happen to you?"

"Well, I'm going to take the standard treatments. Chemo and radiation. But I wanted you both to know that, uhm--" She rolled her lips together until they formed a white knot.

"It doesn't look good," Don said as he stared at the wall on the other side of the room.

Wren pressed herself into the couch cushions. She watched Cindy's teardrops fall onto the back of Thomas's hands. Some landed on the hairs on his wrist, enlarging them as a magnifying glass might. Wren concentrated on the down on his arms, golden threads stitched into her stepbrother's bronze skin.

She mashed her mouth with her fist, afraid her thoughts might escape, afraid the black monster might slide out of her mouth. You're not fair, God.

~~~

Wren swiped the canvas with black paint. After Cindy died, the world seemed shades of grey and black. Wren withdrew from her classmates. Before and after school, she cooked meals and cleaned the house. At night, she went to the garage and painted. Now she stood before a canvas and slapped murky oils against a white square.

She paused and tugged at the braided leather cords around her wrists and neck. Thomas had given them to her for her sixteenth birthday. It's hard to believe Cindy hasn't even been dead a year. It seems like a million, sometimes.

She stared at the canvas and shook her head. I wish Thomas would come home early tonight, she thought. He'd been working at the tattoo shop as an apprentice. Their stepfather didn't even respond when he found out. Thomas had ceased to exist for Don when Cindy died.

At least he doesn't have to worry about getting beat all the time. Don's got other things on his mind now. The paintbrush skittered off the canvas and Wren cursed under her breath.

She glanced at her watch. After eleven. Where are you, Thomas? Wren cleaned her brushes and put away her supplies with measured deliberation. By the time she finished, it was almost midnight. She sighed and turned out the lights in the garage. Maybe Don will be in bed.

He wasn't. Dressed in striped pajamas, he stretched out in the recliner and stared at the television. Wren stuck her head in the living room and mumbled "Good night."

"Here, wait up. Fix me some toast, will ya?"

She turned her head away from him to frown. "Oh, okay. Just stay right there." Please.

In the kitchen, Wren slapped pats of butter on bread and stuck it under the broiler. She retrieved a jar of grape jelly from the refrigerator and spooned some on to a plate. Bent down to check the toast, she didn't hear Don come up behind her. When he laid his hand against the small of her back, she screamed and dropped the pan of toast on the floor.

"You scared me, Don."

"I wasn't trying to scare you, Wren. Now why would I want to do that?"

She threw the toast in the trash can and started over. Don leaned against the counter and watched her. She had to restrain herself from scratching her skin in the places she felt his eyes. She squatted to remove the toast from the oven, careful to position her backside away from her stepfather. Don thanked her for the meal before she fled to her bedroom.

~~~

"Can't you come home earlier, Thomas?" Wren sat with him on the steps behind the school, hugging her books to her chest.

"You know I can't. What's wrong with you, anyway? You look like shit." Thomas grabbed her chin between his thumb and forefinger and examined her face.

"I haven't been sleeping very well."

"You still having nightmares?"

"Not exactly." Wren brushed a speck of dirt from her sneaker.

"What then?" She stuck her fingers in her mouth, but

Thomas pulled them to his jeans and wiped them dry. "Stop that."

"I don't like being alone in the house with Don."

"Has he been hitting you?"

"No." Wren peered into her stepbrother's face, willing him to understand so she wouldn't have to voice the truth.

After a moment, his blue eyes darkened and the freckles stood out on his pointy face. "Son of a bitch! Did he touch you?"

"Shh. Somebody will hear you." Wren clapped her hand over Thomas's mouth and stared around the school grounds. Walking across the parking lot, two football players approached a group of cheerleaders and the girls giggled behind their pompoms.

"What did he do, Wren?"

"Nothing. Well, mostly he just stares at me. It makes my skin crawl. But last night, he touched me on the back while I was fixing some toast for him. And another time he pushed up against me while I was washing dishes." She folded her hands on the stack of books and half-smiled at Thomas. "I'd just feel better if you were home at night."

Thomas jumped up and slammed his hand down on the stair railing. "I'll kill him. I swear I will, Wren."

"Thomas, don't say that." She started to cry. "I miss Cindy. And I miss my daddy. I miss home."

Thomas pulled Wren to her feet and snatched the books from her hands. "Come on. From now on, you'll go to the shop with me."

"But what about my chores at home? What about my homework?"

"Screw your chores. And you can do your homework at the shop."

Wren ran after Thomas. "What'll I tell Don?"

"You won't have to tell him anything. He'll know why you're not there."

~~~

Thomas twisted the cap off a beer and handed the bottle to Wren. She took a long pull on it and wiped her mouth with the back of her hand.

He yanked the bottle from her grasp and took a quick sip. Smacking his lips, he handed it back to her. "That's all I can have or my hand won't be steady." He turned to get a better look at her. "You don't have to do this, you know."

"But I want to. I've seen your tattoos. You really are good. It would be an honor for me."

"Then why do you need this?" He pulled another beer from the carton and tipped it at her.

Wren shrugged and looked out the window. They sat in Thomas's Honda in a shopping center parking lot. Most of the stores were dark, but his workplace was brightly lit. Its neon TATTOO sign flashed through the rain. "Since I'm only sixteen, can you get in trouble for tattooing me?"

Thomas laughed. "No more trouble than I would for buying you beer. Miller wouldn't let me do it, but he's out of town. And Bailey won't say anything because he's got a crush on you."

Wren blushed. She had joined Thomas at work for the last three weeks. She stayed in the back room and studied until the shop closed. Each night, Bailey wandered into the room every few minutes and made small talk with her. He always stood close to the door, warned by Thomas to keep his distance.

Wren burped and pulled another bottle from the carton. She stroked away condensation from the brown glass. "I wonder why Don hasn't said anything to me."

Thomas shrugged. "Maybe he got to thinking about what he did and got scared."

"Maybe." Twisting off the bottle cap, Wren rolled it between her fingers and flipped it into the back seat. Thomas rolled his eyes and snorted, so she chugged the beer. "Okay, I'm ready."

The shop was empty tonight. Bailey looked up from a

magazine and smiled at Wren. He flipped his long blond hair out of his eyes. "Hi, there."

"Hey." She stuck her hands in her pockets and gazed around the room. Photos of customers and sample tattoos lined the walls. She sat down behind Miller's desk while Thomas pulled together his equipment and supplies.

Bailey leaned on the desk and crossed his arms. "So Tom's going to give you a tattoo, huh? What are you getting?" A white puckered scar that originated below his right eye ran down his face, along his neck, and disappeared beneath his T-shirt. He had been in a motorcycle accident when he was in high school. Wren tried not to stare at the scar.

"An angel."

"Nothing fancy, but I designed it just for her," Thomas said. "Okay, Sis. Let's get this show on the road."

Thomas cleaned and shaved a spot on her abdomen, just above her panty line on the right side. He transferred the angel stencil to her skin and began the outline. Wren clenched her teeth throughout the process, wishing she had drunk another beer.

Thomas clicked off the machine a few minutes later. "I've got to change needles so I can shade and color it. You doing okay?"

Wren nodded and closed her eyes. She jumped when Thomas laid his gloved hand against her stomach. "You ready? Here we go."

Once, Bailey patted her foot. "You're doing good, Wren."

When Thomas was done, Wren looked at the result in the mirror. Through the bloody ink, she saw the delicate image of an angel. "She's beautiful, Thomas."

Bailey grinned. "An angel for an angel. You've got a way with a needle, Tom."

Thomas assured Wren it would look perfect after it had healed. He cleaned it, applied some ointment to the area, and bandaged it. "You look a little pale. Why don't you go on out to the car while I clean up? I'll be out in a little bit."

"Okay. See you later, Bailey."

"Bye."

Wren returned to the car and drank another beer. Her stomach throbbed, but she resisted the temptation to rub it. Fat raindrops spattered the windshield. She rested her cheek against the cold door and stared into the shop. Their faces looked like melting wax behind the rain-streaked windows. She closed her eyes and fell asleep to the sound of rain pelting the car's roof.

She dreamed the same dream as always. She stood in the middle of a yard. Floodwaters trickled around her feet, drawing closer each second. She walked between two houses, but the water had overtaken the backyards. She turned back and crossed a street, but water rolled through the trees and uprooted them.

Wren teetered on a shrinking chunk of sidewalk and looked around for an avenue of escape. Brown water rushed around her and began to lick her ankles. Angry storm clouds gripped the night sky. One velvet blue patch managed to clear its way between the clouds and in its midst a bright star shined. Wren reached up with both arms and screamed, "Help me!"

"I've got you," Thomas said. He had opened the door and caught Wren as she fell out of the car. "You shouldn't lean against the car door like that. You'll bust your head on the sidewalk."

Wren shuddered and scooted across the seat. Thomas let her drive while he finished the rest of the beer. The pale blue numbers on the car's clock registered 1:30 when they arrived home.

Wren was glad to see the house was dark. Thomas leaned into the door and pointed his key in the vicinity of the doorknob. After three tries, he got it to fit and opened the door. She locked the door behind them and whispered good night to her stepbrother. He headed for the finished basement, where he'd moved his bedroom after Cindy died.

Wren removed her shoes, tiptoed across the living room, and padded up the stairs. She entered her bedroom and turned on the light. She jumped when she saw her stepfather sitting on her bed.

He sat ramrod straight with his palms flat against his thighs. He wore boxer shorts and a sleeveless T-shirt. A thick mat of grey hair covered his arms, legs, and chest. He looked over at the clock and back to Wren.

"Look, I know it's late. I'm sorry."

"You will be when I get done with you. Get your tail over here." He didn't raise his voice, but Wren still flinched. When she hesitated, he snapped his fingers. Her knees wobbled when she walked to the bed.

His belt curled on the bed like a dark snake. "Don, please don't." She hated the pleading tone in her voice, but she couldn't control it.

"Drop your pants." His voice remained low.

Her hands shook as she unzipped her pants, but before she could get them pulled down, her stepfather grabbed her wrists. He pointed to the bandage that peeked out of the top of her panties. "What is that?"

"A tattoo."

"Well, well. Painting pretty pictures on your skin, huh? Let's see it." He reached down and yanked the bandage loose. Wren shrieked and clutched her panties with white-knuckled fists. Don leaned in and stared at the angel.

She shivered at the glint in his eye. "Where's that angel flying to, sweetheart?"

Wren pushed at his hands when he rubbed his fingers across the artwork. "Please, don't!"

"Who gave you this?"

She pursed her lips and shook her head. Don clutched her hip and shook her. "Thomas."

Don shook her again. "Thomas, huh? You let your

brother touch you all the way down there? I never knew you were such a nasty girl. You going to show it off? That's what you were going to do, right? Show it off to boys you like? Seems to me this is just an excuse for you to drop your drawers!"

Don stood up, twisted Wren around, and pushed her onto the bed. She tried to roll away, but he pulled her onto her back. She started to cry and he slapped her. He stuck his forefinger between her eyes, then to his lips. He dragged Wren's jeans down her hips to her knees.

When he climbed on top of her, she turned her head to the wall. The black monster uncurled and crawled out her mouth, making her gag. Don placed his fist against her lips to silence her. "Beautiful," he whispered. "You're so beautiful. Beautiful." His whispers turn to grunts and groans.

After he was done, he pulled up his pants. "Don't move." He left the room, but returned a minute later and stood in the doorway. He had retrieved his revolver from his bedroom. "Don't get any bright ideas about telling Thomas," he said. "If you do, I'll kill him. And I know you wouldn't want that."

After he left, Wren pulled a pillow to her face and released a long, silent scream into it. She lay in bed in a daze. When she looked at the clock again, it was six-thirty. She rose from the bed and crept down the hallway to the bathroom.

She showered, using a washcloth on herself until her privates were raw. She toweled off in the blinding steam. Wiping film from the mirror, she saw a strange girl staring back at her. The girl looked pale and hard, but she knew she would break like a porcelain doll.

She leaned over the commode and expelled an explosive stream of vomit. When she was done, she brushed her teeth and padded back to her room. Wren re-bandaged the tattoo and pulled her robe tight around her. She dragged the sheets from the bed, climbed on the bare mattress, and stared at the ceiling.

He'll kill Thomas if I tell him. But I can't stay here. Wren rested her elbows on her knees and gripped her skull. *What do I do, Daddy? I'm scared. What do I do?*

After a few minutes, Wren dressed. Then she dug through the closet until she found her gym bag. She crammed panties, jeans, and T-shirts in it. She placed pictures of Edgar, Liza, and Thomas on top of the clothes and zipped the bag. Sticking her head out the door, Wren listened for signs of her stepfather moving around the house.

Satisfied he was still asleep, she walked down the hallway with her shoes in one hand and her bag in the other. In the kitchen, she put on her shoes, opened the freezer door with care, and reached into the back for a frozen bundle of money Don kept stashed for emergencies. It was wrapped in butcher paper and he had written $782 on it with a grease pencil.

She filled a plastic grocery bag with cans of pop, snack cakes, and peanut butter crackers. Her heart did a little jig when the bag crackled, but the house remained quiet. Wren surveyed the kitchen one last time and considered leaving Thomas a note. But the thought of the oily black revolver convinced her that was a bad idea. She took a deep breath and walked out the back door.

Creeping through backyards and alleys, Wren walked for almost an hour before she reached the bus station. It was deserted this Saturday morning. Hard plastic seats, orange and yellow, filled the center of the room. She approached the ticket counter, where a girl wearing a bored expression sat flipping through a fashion magazine. The girl blew a bubble and the scent of green apples floated into Wren's face. "Help ya?" she muttered without looking up from the magazine.

"I'd like to buy a ticket to uhm–"

The girl rolled her eyes. "Well?"

Wren thought about the farthest place away she could go. "How much is a ticket to Virginia Beach?"

"Eighty dollars." The girl looked at Wren as if she doubted she could come up with that much money, but Wren surprised her by counting out the sum on the counter. The thawed money was damp and the girl crinkled her nose as she stuffed it into the cash register. She handed Wren a ticket and directed her to the chairs. "Bus won't leave for another 40 minutes."

Wren sat down and stared out the window at the parkway. A steady stream of traffic flowed between Tennessee and Virginia, and she wondered where everybody was going so early in the morning on a Saturday. She checked the clock on the wall above the door. Thirty-five more minutes. I wonder if he's up yet. She shivered.

She picked up a People magazine from a nearby chair and thumbed through it. When she glanced at the clock again, only twenty minutes had passed. She sighed and tossed the magazine on the seat next to her. Her stomach started to cramp.

She went to the restroom and discovered blood in her panties. She slipped a quarter into a dispenser for a sanitary napkin. Remembering Don crawling across her, she had to fight a wave of nausea. After she cleaned herself, she returned to the lobby.

Wren sat in a chair, crossed her arms, and closed her eyes. She didn't realize she had dozed off until she felt herself being shaken awake. A police officer leaned over her and she panicked. She looked at the exit, wondering if she could run fast enough to get away from him.

"Miss," he said. "The girl at the counter said your bus was getting ready to leave." He smiled at her.

"Oh, thank you." Despite her relief, her heart continued to pound against her rib cage. She exhaled, grabbed her bag, and stood. The policeman had returned to the counter and leaned against it, allowing the ticket attendant to pull invisible threads from his uniform. The girl was giggling as Wren walked out the door.

The bus smelled stale. Wren walked past the seven other passengers to the very back. She slid down in the seat and stared out the window as the bus rolled out of the parking lot. It lumbered out of Bristol and gained speed when it reached I-81.

Wren pulled out a map she had picked up at the bus station. She had never been beyond Smyth County. The bus would travel north on 81 past Wytheville, Blacksburg, and Roanoke. At Staunton, it would leave 81 and travel along I-64. Wren didn't know if the driver would take them through Charlottesville and Richmond, or if he would choose a smaller road to get to Virginia Beach. She hoped she didn't have to change buses.

She folded the map and stuffed it in her back pocket. She twisted in her seat to ease the pain between her legs. Her stomach started to cramp again. She clenched her fists and felt beads of sweat pop out on her forehead. Please, God. It hurts. Make it stop.

The gentle vibration of the bus rocked her in her seat and she closed her eyes to absorb the motion. I'm sorry I didn't say goodbye, Thomas. Get away from him. Get away as fast as you can.

She thought of her house on Pawpaw Ridge. The little valley grew smaller in her mind as she drew farther and farther away from the mountains. Wren pictured mounds of honeysuckle and cried at the thought of her parents wrapped in its sweet scent.

Five

Charlottesville, March–April 1991

The sweet scent of vanilla pervaded Peter's sleep. He dreamed he was home in his mother's kitchen. The room was dusty with sugar and so hot Peter's skin felt sticky. Ginny piled pies, cakes, and cookies high on the counters and the table. "Here." She handed him a bowl coated with thick cake batter. "I know it's your favorite part."

"I really shouldn't," Peter answered. He ran his finger around the inside of the bowl until it was covered with cake batter. He licked the batter from his finger and nodded at his mother. "It's good." He scraped all his fingers through the cake batter. Cupping it in his hand, he devoured messy fistfuls of it.

"You're going to make yourself sick. You'd better be careful." Ginny slapped his hand. He dropped the bowl and it clattered on the floor.

Peter awoke with a start. His heart hammered against his rib cage. He thought he had heard a door bang. He jumped from bed and lurched through the apartment, clicking on lights in each room. Wren's blanket lay on the floor in front of the empty couch and the apartment door stood wide open. Peter shivered when a cold breeze swept into the living room. He stepped outside to investigate.

Wren pirouetted around the parking lot with her arms lifted to the sky, cooing at the stars. Her eyes were open, but Peter knew she was seeing something other than the sky over Charlottesville. She had been living with him for more than two weeks, but this was the first time he had seen her sleepwalk.

I guess I don't need to worry about waking you. If you can walk around this gravelly, glassy parking lot barefoot in your sleep, you can sleep through anything. When Wren swept past him, he grabbed her hand and restrained her with gentle pressure. She crumpled into a boneless heap, but Peter caught her before she hit the ground.

He carried her inside to the couch and covered her with a blanket. She turned on her side and fell into the even rhythm of deep sleep. Peter grabbed a beer from the refrigerator, flicked off the living room lights, and sank down in an armchair. He studied Wren's face while he drank.

Backlit by the glow of the kitchen, her hair was the color of pumpkin, her skin like cream. Freckles sprinkled the bridge of her nose. Peter wanted to sweep his tongue across them, convinced they would taste like cinnamon sugar. He crept to the edge of the couch. Leaning over her, he inhaled her heady essence, the perfume in his sweet dream.

He rested on the edge of the coffee table and admired her serene features. You never look that relaxed when you're awake. Even after this long, Wren was jumpy. As nervous as a long-tailed cat in a room full of rocking chairs, his mother would have proclaimed. If he brushed against her or tried to take her hand in his, she flinched. She recoiled when the phone rang.

Peter didn't know why she was the way she was. She had revealed few personal details about her life. She hadn't answered any direct questions about herself, except one. One morning at breakfast, he noticed her rubbing the question mark in her eyebrow.

"How did you get that scar?"

"Daddy built a tree house for me in a big oak in our yard. I fell out of it one time."

"Ouch. And all you got was one little scar?"

"I broke both my wrists and a rib. A branch just about put my eye out."

"What made you fall?"

"I was mad at Daddy." She stroked the scar, her expression unreadable. "Didn't pay attention to where I was going and stepped right off the edge."

Some things he learned about her firsthand. Like her weird green bean thing. She hadn't ventured out of the apartment until he invited her grocery shopping. "I pretty much live off of junk. Why don't you come with me and pick out food you like."

Walking through Food Lion, he was surprised at the provisions she dropped into their shopping cart. Mustard greens. Soup beans. Canned salmon. Cornmeal. "You shop like my mother. If you can cook like her, you'll make my day."

"I'm a good cook." She threw a package of salted bacon into the buggy. When they rounded the corner of the next aisle, she slowed until her feet were almost dragging behind the cart.

She stopped at the green bean section and scanned the cans. At first, he thought she was looking for a particular brand or kind of bean, but she just stood there wringing her hands. Another shopper, an elegant woman in a sari, had to reach around Wren to retrieve a can of beans.

Peter waved his hand in front of her glazed eyes. He snapped his fingers, but she didn't move. Finally, he grasped her twisting hands, but she yelped and pulled away from him. He knew there had to be a story behind it, but he was afraid to ask. *I hope she didn't escape from the psych ward,* he told himself as they finished shopping.

Now, sleeping in the warm light of the kitchen, she looked normal. Peter grazed her chin with his thumb. She murmured and pulled the blanket up across her face. He sighed, finished his beer, and went back to bed.

~~~

Beep. Beep. Beep. Peter slammed his hand against the snooze button and snuggled back under the covers, but the aroma of bacon and eggs pulled him from bed before the alarm sounded a second time. He found Wren humming as she made breakfast. She handed him a glass of orange juice and turned her attention back to the food sizzling in a skillet.

He slumped down in a chair and rested his head on the table. "You're awfully perky this morning," he mumbled against the plastic tablecloth.

"You're not. What's wrong? Have another hangover?"

Peter lifted his head and frowned at her back. "I didn't drink that much last night. No more than the average guy."

"This average guy you keep talking about . . . I'd hate to see his liver." She slid bacon and eggs onto a plate and set it in front of him.

"What are you, a card-carrying member of the Virginia temperance society?"

Wren sat across from him and dug into her food. "Nope. Just seems like you drink every night."

"If I recall correctly, you were swigging Jack Daniels the night I met you!"

Wren's fork clattered against her plate. She hung her head and tears dribbled down her face into her food. Peter gritted his teeth. "Don't do that. You're ruining your breakfast." She continued to sniffle. "Come on. You're ruining *my* breakfast."

He sighed and handed her a napkin. She wiped her eyes and forked some eggs into her mouth. Peter finished his food and cleared his plate off the table. "I didn't sleep well last night. You woke me up," he said to her back.

She laughed. "What, was I snoring?"

"Sleepwalking."

Wren turned and stared at him. "Oh."

"I guess it's the first time you've done it since you've been here. Either that or I've slept through the other times."

She scraped the rest of her breakfast into the trash. "I'm sorry about that. It could be worse, I guess. I used to have screaming nightmares."

"Yeah? What about?"

Wren stacked plates and glasses in the dishpan and squirted dish detergent on them. Without thinking, Peter grabbed a dish towel, ready to dry the dishes she handed him. She turned on the spigot and watched hot water rise to the rim of the pan. "Drowning."

Peter raised his eyebrows. "Any particular symbolism there?"

Wren snorted as she swiped congealed egg from a plate. "I almost drowned once." She glanced up at Peter. "I mean, once before. As a matter of fact, it happened while I was sleepwalking."

"Great. Falling out of trees. Falling in water. Nightmares and sleepwalking. You're an accident waiting to happen. Anything else I should know about you?"

Wren's spring-green eyes darkened into hemlock shadows. She shook her head. "No. Nothing at all."

~~~

Later that week, he returned from class and found her at his drafting table. "What are you doing?"

"Just passing time." She crumpled a sheet of paper and tossed it at the trash can.

Peter caught it in his right hand and smoothed the creased page. She had penciled flowers across the paper. Even in shades of grey, they looked alive. He recognized many of the plants as his mother's favorites: bleeding hearts and bluebells, morning glories and moonflowers, snapdragons and sweet peas. "Wow. This is good. Better than good, actually."

"I could do better if I had my paints."

"Is that what you do? You're an artist?"

Wren ran her fingertips across her mouth and walked across the room to stare out the window. Flowering cherries bowed beneath their fat buds in the parking lot. Two men in khaki uniforms loosened soil in barren flower beds. A third man sat on the tailgate of their truck and gestured with a cigarette. The smoke coiled into an S and slithered into the air. Wren looked up at the sky. "I've never seen a robin's egg as blue as the sky is today."

"I hate it when you do that." Peter jerked the curtains together.

"What?"

"What? When I ask you a question, you either change the subject or act like I didn't speak at all!"

"The less you know about me, the better." Wren stalked to the kitchen and drew a glass of water.

Peter followed her. "I think I've earned your trust. If you're in trouble, maybe I can help."

"I don't want your help."

"What do you want??"

"I want you to leave me alone!!" Wren slammed the glass into the sink bowl and water and crystalline splinters flew across the counter. Peter flinched and rubbed his cheek. Examining his hand, he saw blood smeared across his fingertips.

Ashen-faced, Wren pushed him into a chair. "Don't touch it." She yanked paper towels from the roll and wet them. "Let me see." Stooping in front of him, she dabbed his cheek, peered at the cut, and dabbed again. "Doesn't look like there's any glass in it. Here, hold this against it for a minute."

Peter pressed the makeshift bandage against the cut and watched Wren dig through the cabinet. She retrieved a bottle of rubbing alcohol and tipped it into a clean paper towel. Crouching in front of him again, she pushed aside his hand and patted the cut. The cool liquid burned his skin.

He turned his head. "Ouch!"

"Hold still." She twisted his head so she could apply more alcohol to the cut. "There."

Peter reached up to touch it and she smacked his hand. "Ow. Well, you're definitely not a nurse."

Wren leaned forward and pressed her nose against his for a brief second. The gesture was so unexpected he didn't know how to respond. He felt as firm and as flexible as a water balloon.

"Yes, I was an artist," she said before she stood and walked out of the room.

~~~

Despite her reluctance to talk about herself, she was eager to learn about Peter. Thumbing through his photo album one night, she pointed to different pictures and asked him about his family.

"This one's from homecoming my senior year." Dressed in muddied football uniforms, a long-haired Peter and another boy leaned against the hood of a blue Chevelle. A cheerleader stood between them. The girl had yanked Peter's ponytail just as the picture was snapped. His head was thrown back, his dark eyes as warm as a cup of cocoa.

Wren leaned over the photo album. "Is that your girlfriend?"

"No, that's my youngest sister, Rachel. The guy is my best friend, Matt. They've dated off and on for years. He's over in Iraq right now."

Peter flipped the page. "That's Drew standing in my yard." A young woman leaned against a fence in front of a two-story house. A steep hill was visible in the distance. Drew's blonde hair fell over one shoulder of her peach silk blouse. Full-bosomed, round-faced, she offered a wide smile to the photographer. "She was my steady the last few years of high school but we broke up before I left for college."

Wren studied the picture of Drew. "Girls are always

leaving messages on the answering machine, but you never call them back."

"No use calling them back when I see them in class every day."

"No steady girlfriend now?" Wren asked without looking up from the pictures.

"I date, but I haven't had a really serious relationship in a couple of years."

"Why not?"

Scratching his jaw, Peter squinted at the ceiling. "Ahh, I don't know. Just waiting for the right girl to come along, I guess." He cleared his throat as she turned the page. "That's Mom and Dad."

The black and white picture showed a heavyset woman and a tall man sitting on a metal glider beneath a tree. A baby crawled on a blanket at their feet. His naked butt arched, his left foot extended behind him, he reached for a toy lamb the woman held out to him. His downy hair stood up in tufts all over his head like ruffled crow feathers. Wren giggled. "Is that you?"

Peter blushed and rolled his eyes. "Yes. I keep meaning to take that picture out. And there's my other sister, Theresa. She's a hairstylist." He pointed to a picture of a girl with hair and eyes as dark as his. She slumped on a couch with her arms crossed, her tongue stuck out at the camera.

Wren sighed and shut the album. "All of my pictures are in the river. They were in my purse."

"Who did you have pictures of?"

"My parents and my brother."

"Your brother?"

"My stepbrother. Thomas."

"Where is he now?"

"I--" *Braatttt.*

Peter flung a silent curse at the phone as he picked up the receiver. "Hello?"

"Hey, man, it's Ike. Where've you been? I haven't seen

you in weeks." Peter held the receiver away from his ear
when he heard the caller's braying voice.

"Ike, I've been tied up lately. What's up?" Peter eyed
Wren as she wandered into the kitchen and grabbed some
cookies from a cabinet.

"Tied up, huh? Well, untie yourself, man. I'm having a
St. Patty's party Friday. I guess this'll be my last big bash
before graduation."

Wren folded her legs beneath her in the armchair and
munched on cookies while Peter talked. He turned his head
and lowered his voice. "Oh, I don't know if I can make it."

"Come on, Sullivan. You're gonna say no to free beer?"

Peter licked his lips and cut his eyes to Wren. She
plucked a chocolate chip from a cookie and tossed it into
her mouth. "Well. I might drop by with a friend for a few
minutes."

"A friend, eh? Great! See you Friday." *Click.*

~~~

"I don't think this is such a good idea." Wren hurried to
catch up with Peter as he walked down 14th Street.

"We won't stay long." He paused and pulled her scarf up
around her neck. "But it is St. Patrick's Day, after all. We've
got to celebrate the green!"

They arrived at a ragged brick house a few minutes later.
All the doors and windows were thrown open. Speakers
blasted Little Feat from the second floor windows. Irish
flags dangled from the eaves. The porch was packed with
partygoers. Wren didn't protest when Peter grabbed her
hand to lead her through the crowd.

He headed to the kitchen where two thick-necked
young men pumped beer from a keg into plastic cups. Peter
grabbed a cup and followed suit. "You want one?"

Wren shook her head. Peter downed the beer and
licked the froth from his lips while Wren stared at their
surroundings. The kitchen floor was covered in black
footprints. It was sticky and their feet made sucking noises

when they walked across the room. Peter threw his hand up at three girls standing at the back door smoking. "Where's Ike?"

One of the girls blew smoke into the cold air and ran her tongue across her teeth. "I think he's upstairs, Pete. Haven't seen you around lately." She cocked her eyebrow at Wren and half-smiled.

Peter shrugged without answering the girl. He pulled Wren back into the living room and up the stairs. The hallway was narrow and dark. Wren ducked her head as they passed two people clamped together in the hot shadows. A girl's giggle trailed them down the hall.

They stopped at the only room with an open door. The stereo expelled music from the room with such force the door bounced against the wall in steady taps. In the bedroom, a young man pushed his long orange hair back behind his ears as he bent over a stack of CDs. He didn't turn when Peter yelled at him from the doorway.

Peter moved in and grabbed his shoulder. "Ike! Shit, man, I think my ears are bleeding!"

"Sullivan! Hang on! Let me change the music." He held an iridescent disc to the light and squinted at the title. Shoving it into the stereo, he smiled. "Stevie Ray Vaughn." The music blasted behind them as Ike followed them down the hall.

Perspiration dropped into Wren's eyes and she ran the back of her hand across her forehead. Ike flung open a door. "Hey, toss your coats in here. My heat messed up and I had to open all the windows." Peter threw their jackets on an unmade bed and they followed Ike to the kitchen.

Ike drew a beer for himself and drained it in one long swallow, then he refilled Peter's cup. He eyed Wren over black horn-rims. "You gonna introduce me to your friend, Pete?"

"Ike, this is Wren. Wren – Ike."

Ike wiped his hand on his Bob Marley T-shirt and

extended it to Wren. "Nice to meet you."

"You, too." She crossed her arms, leaned against the sink, and stared at Peter. He downed a third cup of beer, spilling some of it on his sweatshirt.

Ike laughed. "Sullivan, how did a slob like you end up with such a gorgeous girlfriend? Where's the justice?"

"She's not my girlfriend."

"Oh?" Ike propped himself against the sink and grinned at Wren. She leaned away from him, a smile fixed on her face. "It just so happens I'm not seeing anyone right now. What do you say? I've always been partial to redheads."

Back off, Peter thought. He tossed his cup in the trash and stepped between Ike and Wren. "Forget it, man. She's not interested in a loser like you."

"Loser? Sullivan, you're an--"

"Ike!" One of the thick-necked boys stuck his head in to the kitchen. "Bram's got the punch ready."

Ike flapped his hand at him. "Yeah, okay." He turned to Peter. "Come on."

A group of students were lined up around a large plastic trash can in the living room. The air was poisoned with the smell of Hawaiian Punch and grain alcohol. Bram, a dark young man with close-cropped brown hair and light blue eyes, scooped cups through the trash can and passed them through the crowd. He nodded at them. "Sullivan. Thought you'd disappeared off the face of the earth."

Ike held his hand over Wren's head and pointed his index finger at her. "He's been busy."

Bram shoved a cup into Wren's hand. She raised it to her lips, but Peter jerked it out of her hands before she could take a sip. "Ever do any drugs?" he whispered in her ear.

"No, why?"

"Now's not the time to start." He pointed at a piece of paper floating in the cup. "Bram dumped acid in the punch."

"Acid?"

"LSD. Drink this and you'll go on a trip you never wanted to take." Peter emptied the punch back into the trash can, tossed the cup in the floor, and glared at Bram. "Where've you got the good stuff stashed, Ike?"

Ike tilted his head and stared at the ceiling. "Upstairs."

They joined Ike in his bedroom. Peter and Wren sat on the bed, while Bram pulled a chair close to Wren and rested his arms across the back of it. Ike poured bourbon in four cups and passed them around. "Maker's Mark. You've got rich taste for a redneck, Sullivan."

Peter sniggered and tossed back his drink. Ike stared into his bourbon and wrinkled his nose. Bram tilted his cup at Wren and winked at her. "What's your name, babe?"

She blushed behind her cup. "Wren."

"I haven't seen you around before. What's your major?"

"I'm not a student."

"Oh, where are you from? Wait, let me guess. You're from down there where Pete lives, I bet. You sound like it." He turned to Peter. "She sounds like it. Her father a coal miner, too?"

Peter rubbed his eyes with the palm of his hand. "Yeah." Pouring more bourbon in his cup, he didn't see Wren's mouth turn down at the corners.

Bram grinned at her. "A genuine coal miner's daughter, eh?" He started crooning the lyrics to the Loretta Lynn song, off-key.

Flushing red, Wren leaned against Peter and whispered in his ear. "Can we go now?"

"Yeah, in a minute. Let me get one more drink." He passed his empty cup to Ike for a refill.

Bram's leg brushed Wren's and she scooted closer to Peter. "You've had enough," she whispered.

"No, I haven't," he slurred. His tongue felt thick and he smacked his mouth. "I'll decide when I've had enough."

Ike jumped up. "I almost forgot! I got paint! I thought

we'd do Beta Bridge for St. Patty's."

Beta Bridge was a University landmark. Every few nights a different group of students – drunken Greeks, idealistic protestors, academic clubs – painted bright graffiti across the bridge.

Peter chugged his drink. "Paint," he muttered. "Did I tell you Wren is an artist?"

Ike smacked his hands together. "Perfect. It's late enough now. Let's go."

They stumbled toward Rugby Road with paintbrushes, buckets of paint, spray paint cans, and bourbon bottle in hand. A few students were scattered in the yards of fraternity and sorority houses, but the bridge was deserted. Peter sat down hard on the sidewalk and thrust his legs into the road.

Ike and Bram sprayed the side of the bridge bright white. Wren stood to the side and watched Ike pop open cans of paint. Bram tossed a brush to Wren and shined a light on the bridge. "Here ya go, artist. Let's see how good you are. Paint us something!"

Wren glanced at the bottle in Peter's hand. He looked down at the Maker's Mark as if seeing it for the first time. Not much left. Might as well finish it. He winked at her. Tipping the bourbon to his mouth, he finished it in three loud swallows. Wren shook her head and dipped the brush in the paint.

She slapped the brush across Ike's shirt and then threw it over the bridge. Ike and Bram stared open-mouthed at her. Wren looked at Peter. "Can we go home now?"

He sighed. "Yeah." He tried to stand, but wobbled and sat back down on the sidewalk. "Whoops."

Bram and Ike pulled his arms around their shoulders and lifted him. Peter offered Wren a sheepish grin. "Had a little bit too much of the good stuff."

Ike kicked a paint bucket into the road. "We'll help you get him home."

The walk back to the apartment took a half hour longer than it had earlier in the evening. Peter felt himself spiral into unconsciousness once and awoke to the sting of Ike slapping him in the face. "Stop already," he mumbled.

When they reached the apartment, Wren pulled his keys from his coat pocket and let them inside. Bram eyed the folded blankets and pillows in the floor as they lowered Peter to the couch. Wren yanked his coat off and tossed it in the corner. Ike rolled him over on his side and his knuckle hit the carpet.

Right away the room began to spin. Peter groaned. Please, God, don't let me puke. I hate to puke. He listened to Wren thank his friends as she herded them to the door. Always so polite. He giggled at the thought. The door closed with a *snick* and the chain rattled against it as she locked it.

A moment later he felt his eyelids being pulled open. Frowning, Wren peered into his face. Peter turned his head. "What?"

"Nothing." She eased into the chair and draped her legs across its overstuffed arm. Peter closed his eyes against her disapproval.

Feeling the room twirl around him again, he rested one foot on the floor, willing himself not to vomit. When the room continued to spin, he sat up and wiped the sweat from his face. He started to salivate. He lurched across the room, trying to make it to the bathroom in time. He heard a faint knock on the apartment door as he stumbled through the bedroom.

His stomach heaved in violent spasms just as he fell in front of the toilet. He threw up and the sour smell of it made him vomit again. He cursed the bourbon. Gagging, he cursed Ike. Peter heaved into the toilet a third time and cursed himself. He stayed in the bathroom until he felt his stomach was nothing more than an empty, angry pouch.

He rinsed his mouth, brushed his teeth, and washed his

face. His haggard image eyeballed him from the mirror, so he laid his hand across the glass and smeared it. *I've got to stop doing this to myself.* He heard voices when he walked out of the bathroom.

Peter froze in the doorway between his bedroom and the living room. Bram stood with his back to him, pressing Wren against the door with his body. He whispered in her ear and ran his hands through her hair. Wren's face was the color of cold oatmeal. She shook her head at whatever Bram said and shoved her fists against his chest.

Bram didn't budge. He tried to kiss her, but she turned her head. Her eyes were closed, so she didn't see Peter behind them. Bram plucked at the waistband of her jeans, trying to slide them down her hips. Peter saw the tattoo he'd spied the first night he met Wren; it was an angel.

"What the hell do you think you're doing, Bram?"

The young man jumped like a sprinter at the sound of the starting gun. Turning, he blinked several times and tried to smile at Peter. "Pete! Uhm, I lost my ID. I thought maybe I dropped it."

"In her pants?"

"Come on, Sullivan. We were just having a little fun." He shot a pleading look at Wren.

"Is that right, Wren?" Peter turned to her. She hung her head and her hair shaded her eyes. She stuck her trembling fingers in her mouth and rocked against the wall. *She's freaking out,* he thought.

His anger was not red, nor even black. Instead, it washed across his eyes in amethyst waves. Clenching his fists, he looked down at his arms and saw his veins knotted in purple relief against his fair skin. Peter felt his heart expanding and contracting within his chest with such violence he wondered how it could still beat.

Bram seemed to sense the ferocity in Peter. Whey-faced, he tugged at the doorknob. The door shuddered open and he stumbled outside. Following, Peter fell on top of him and kidney-punched him. Bram grunted and tried to crawl across the parking lot. Cursing him, Peter scraped his face against the asphalt. Bram elbowed him and he rolled off.

"You're crazy, Pete! You've lost your mind." Bram shouted at him from a safe distance. He darted into the dark shadows between two buildings. Peter spit and returned to the apartment.

Wren had curled up into a ball on the floor. She almost had her whole hand crammed into her mouth. She stiffened when Peter touched her. A staccato sound escaped around her fist: *unh-unh-unh-unh.*

Peter stretched out behind her and spooned himself around her quivering figure. What happened to you? Trying to absorb her anguish, he whispered to her. "It's okay. I won't let anybody else hurt you. It's okay. Shhh."

~~~

They still rested in the same position the next morning when the phone rang. Peter opened his eyes and sunlight pierced them with yellow daggers. Clydesdales clopped through his head as he staggered to the phone. "Hello?"

"Hello?"

He pressed his fist against his forehead. "Hello?"

"Peter, is that you?" His mother's voice sounded tinny.

"Yeah, Mom."

"You sound funny. What's wrong?"

"Nothing. What time is it?" He squinted at the clock across the room, but couldn't make out the numbers.

"Were you still in bed? Good Lord, Peter, it's after one o'clock! Are you sick?"

You have no idea. Acid climbed into his throat and he coughed. "I'm fine, Mom. Just had a late night. Can I call you back later?"

"Wait. I was calling to see if somebody stole your credit card?"

"No. It's right here in my wallet. Why?"

She breathed into the phone and Peter clenched his jaw. "Well, then you tell me why you bought women's clothes, son."

"Women's clothes?"

"Yes. And panties and bras! Lord have mercy, what is going on up there?"

He looked across the room at Wren. The sunlight picked up the fire in her hair. The flickering flame kindled a peculiar passion in him. I'm burning, he thought. Ashes and dust.

"Are you there, Peter?"

"Yeah. Uhm, it was for the homeless." Not exactly the truth, not exactly a lie.

"The homeless?"

"Yeah, I donated clothes to a homeless person."

His mother was silent for a moment. "Well, that was a nice thing for you to do, Peter. I'm right proud of you."

You are scum. Don't lie to your mother. "Well, I've got to go, Mom. I'll talk to you later."

After he hung up, he drank a soda to wash away the bad taste in his mouth.

The phone rang many times that weekend, but Peter let the answering machine pick up the calls. "I don't want to talk to Ike or Bram or anyone else," he told Wren. She nodded and laid her head against the table while he cooked supper.

~~~

Wren wouldn't talk to him about what happened that night. Convinced she would run away if he forced her to talk to him, he didn't push. He wanted to keep her with him. He had seen crows hoard shiny objects for their nests; sometimes Peter thought he might look down and see his body covered in glossy black feathers.

He bought art supplies for her so she wouldn't be bored when he was in class. Wandering around Charlottesville and the University, Wren sketched the buildings, the landscape, and the people. She was fascinated by the Rotunda, the serpentine walls, and the Colonnades. Behind Lambeth apartments, the Colonnades curved above an amphitheater that hugged Lambeth Field. The architecture school was nearby, across the railroad tracks. Sometimes Peter met Wren at the Colonnades for lunch.

He greeted her with a bouquet of daffodils one bright afternoon in early April. They walked to the amphitheater and shared lunch. When they finished eating, Wren leaned back against the steps and smiled at the sky.

"You look like one of those daffodils, turning your face to the sun like that," Peter said.

Wren laughed. She plucked a flower from the bouquet and, closing her eyes, twirled it against her lips. Peter felt butterflies batting his insides with tattered wings. Without thinking, he reached out and stroked her chin with his fingertips. Wren shivered. He slid his hand up and caressed her cheek. Leaning forward, he inhaled her vanilla skin and brushed his lips against hers. She stiffened against him and pushed him away.

"Don't. Please." She looked down at her hands clenched in her lap. She had crushed the daffodil. Tears slid down her cheeks and fell onto her fists. She rubbed them into her skin with her thumbs.

"I'm sorry, Wren. Please don't be upset with me. You're so beautiful--"

Wren covered her mouth with one hand and jumped up. She ran up the stairs toward Beta Bridge. Peter followed, his voice dogging her steps, pleading with her to stop. Catching her at the bridge, he grabbed her arm, but she jerked away and stumbled off the curb in front of a University bus.

Tires squealed, brakes screamed, and Peter squeezed his eyes shut. He waited for the sound of a thump, but all he heard was the whoosh of the bus door and a male voice asking Wren if she was okay.

Peter opened his eyes and saw a uniformed young man with dreadlocks and very pale skin help Wren to her feet. When he approached them, the boy placed himself between Wren and Peter.

"Hey, man! You just chased her out into traffic. I almost hit her." Wren wobbled a moment and clutched the young man's arm. "Are you okay?" he asked.

"Just a little shaky," she said.

He looked at Peter with suspicion. "Is this guy bothering you? You want me to call the cops?"

Wren laughed and it sounded like fingernails against a chalkboard. Peter felt himself flush red. "I wouldn't hurt her."

"I'm alright," Wren told the boy. She moved to Peter's side. "He's my friend. It's fine, really."

The driver shrugged and returned to the bus. Moon-faced students peered out the bus windows at Peter and Wren. The doors folded shut and the bus headed down Rugby Road toward the Rotunda.

Peter turned to Wren and placed his hands on her shoulders. This time she didn't pull away from him. "Let's take a walk."

They walked down Rugby Road, past Mad Bowl, and crossed the street to the Rotunda. Neither of them spoke until they reached the Lawn. Peter guided Wren to a shady spot and she sat with her back against a tree. For a moment they watched tourists take pictures on the steps of the Rotunda. Students glided past them on their way to classes. Others played Frisbee or hackeysack on the clipped grass.

Finally, Peter turned to Wren and spoke. "Tell me."

The two simple words had the force of a release valve. Wren burst into tears and sagged against the tree. Peter dug his fingers into the grass. Letting her cry without comforting her was difficult, but he sensed it was the right thing to do. Her sobs slowed and she wiped her eyes with her fists, like a child would. After she composed herself, she looked up at him and said, "My stepfather raped me when I was sixteen."

He felt his mouth turning words over his tongue, not sure which ones to spit out and which ones to swallow. Finally, he said, "I'm sorry."

He touched her sneaker. She focused on his hand as he rubbed the shoelace between thumb and forefinger with a gentle motion. "Daddy was crushed to death in the mines. We didn't have any other family, so I got sent to a foster home."

Wren put her fingers to her mouth, and then let them trail down her chin to the hollow of her neck. She related to him how hungry she was in her new home and how her foster mother punished her for eating the crackers. He learned about the other foster families, and Toni and Mark. She described her stepbrother, Thomas. Then she told him about her last night in Don's house and her flight to Virginia Beach.

"That was six years ago." Wren gathered her hair behind her and piled it on top of her head. She rested that way for a moment, her elbows forming wings. She chewed on her bottom lip and sighed. "I don't want to talk about it anymore, okay?"

"Well, your stepdad--"

"What?"

"He shouldn't get away with it."

"Drop it, Peter. Please! Promise me."

I should call the police. Or the newspaper. Or my dad. I could get in my truck right now and drive to Bristol and—

"Peter?"

"What?"

"Promise me you'll drop it." Wren reached out and placed her hand over his, a gesture so foreign to her that she trembled when she did it. Her hands were sticky with moisture, but soft.

Under her gossamer pressure, Peter knew he would do

whatever she wanted. "I promise." For now. "I wish I could change what happened."

"Well, you can't, Peter. Life is not all bluebirds and rainbows. Bad things happen and some people get more than their fair share."

He disliked the sarcasm and self-pity that crept into her words. "You're right. But it doesn't mean you stop living." He closed his eyes before he spoke again. "You didn't jump off the bridge that night for this thing that happened six years ago. There's something else you're not telling me."

"Yeah, there's a lot of things I haven't told you." She started to cry again, but she laughed through her tears. "When you look at me, Peter, your eyes are like melted chocolate. I don't think I could stand to see them change. And they would if you knew all about me."

Peter opened his eyes and leaned forward to peer into her face. "Try me."

She let go of his hand and reached up to touch the tiny scar on his cheek, a reminder of shattered glass. "I'll just hurt you."

Peter cupped his hands around hers. He leaned forward and rested his forehead against hers. He gazed into her eyes. "Say it."

She held her breath for a beat. "I got pregnant."

Six

Virginia Beach, 1985-1988

"Pregnant?" Wren stared at the doctor.

"Yes." The doctor, a grey-haired man in blue scrubs, closed the green curtain around them. He tilted his head at Wren. "And your blood sugar was low. You look undernourished. What have you been eating lately?"

Wren averted her eyes. At the bottom of the curtain, she saw clunky white nursing shoes, surgeon's clogs, and loafers pass back and forth through the emergency room. Antiseptics and cleaning fluids didn't quite cover the smell of human misery in the hospital, and she covered her nose. Nausea uncoiled itself in her stomach and throat, and she let her head fall back on the thin pillow. The sick feeling passed gradually, and she raised her head again.

The doctor laid his clipboard at the foot of the bed and pulled a stethoscope from around his neck. "Can you sit up for me?" He guided Wren's elbow as she leaned forward, then he listened to her heart. He draped the medical instrument back around his neck and scratched notes on her chart. A nurse joined them and the doctor asked her to take Wren's blood pressure. After a gentle examination, he allowed her to lie back on the bed.

He held the clipboard to his chest and crossed his arms

over it. "You didn't have any I.D. on you when they brought you in."

"I'm homeless."

"How old are you?"

Wren bit her lip as she lied. "I'm nineteen."

The doctor lifted his head and looked at her down his nose. "I wouldn't have figured you much older than sixteen."

Barely two months, she thought.

When she didn't reply, he continued. "Are you married?"

She shook her head.

"Where's the father of the baby?"

She shrugged. The doctor shifted from one foot to the other. "Is there a parent we can call for you?"

"No!" She hadn't meant to shout, but she shuddered at the thought of some well-meaning nurse calling Don to tell him she was here. She shook her head and looked at the floor.

The doctor sighed and tried to touch her shoulder, but she cringed. "We have a lot of resources here to help people in trouble."

"I'm sorry," she said in a lower voice. "I don't need any help. Really. I just need to go now. Can I go?"

He looked concerned. "I don't feel comfortable releasing you on your own. I'd feel a lot better if I could call someone to pick you up."

"No. I'll be fine. Please, just let me go, okay?" She clasped his wrist and looked at him with pleading eyes. He rubbed his brow and, after a moment, nodded.

"I'll go get the release papers signed. I want you to finish that juice the nurse brought you." He pulled a wad of bills and a business card from his shirt pocket. Tossing them on the bed, he said, "Eat a good dinner tonight. And think about using that card. It's a place that can help you make some decisions about this pregnancy." He disappeared through the curtain.

Wren threw back the sheet and sat up in the bed.

Rubbing her stomach, she shuddered. Pregnant! What am I going to do?

It had been six weeks since she fled her stepfather and made her way to the coast of Virginia. She had spent most of the stolen money at cheap motels. With less than a hundred dollars left, she began to ration her food to one meal a day. She thought the nausea and fatigue was from hunger and the stress of panhandling. She was begging for money on a busy street when she fainted.

And woke up here. If I could just talk to Thomas, maybe he could tell me what to do. But remembering the gun in her stepfather's hand, she pushed that thought away.

The nurse returned with some written instructions from the doctor. She asked Wren to sign some paperwork. "Since you're uninsured, you need to see someone in the finance department to make billing arrangements." Wren nodded, although she had no intention of talking to anyone about the bill. She signed a fake name on the papers.

~~~

She ran out of money before the calendar rolled over into 1986. Wren went to a shelter a few days after Christmas, and then on New Year's Day, she called the tattoo shop from a pay phone in the dining hall. She was surprised when Bailey answered the phone.

"Is Thomas there?"

"Wren? Yeah, he's here. He moved in to the apartment over the shop a couple of weeks ago. Where are you? The guy's been worried to death about you!"

"I just need to talk to Thomas. Please, Bailey."

"Hang on." She heard him place his hand over the receiver and shout at Thomas, but she couldn't understand what he said.

"Hello?" Thomas's breath was heavy in the phone.

"Thomas, it's me." Her throat contracted and she sobbed.

"Where are you? I've been all over four counties looking

for you! Don said he didn't know where you were. All he could talk about was how you stole his stupid money."

Her chest hitched and she slid down the wall with the phone pressed to her ear. She took a few deep breaths to gain her composure. "I don't know what to do, Thomas."

"What is it? What's wrong?"

"I'm pregnant!"

She heard Thomas mutter under his breath and then, "What happened?"

She hesitated. "Don."

"Don?" His voice rose and Wren heard Bailey's muffled response in the background. "Don got you pregnant?"

"The night I got my tattoo. He was waiting for me when I got upstairs." She wailed in response to Thomas and the ragged residents who were eating turned to stare at Wren. Cupping her hand around the phone, she whispered. "He raped me."

Thomas fired a fusillade of curses. The phone seemed to explode in her ear: *thwack-thwack-thwack*!! Wren pictured him slamming the phone against the counter.

Bailey came on the line. "Are you there?"

"Yes." Wren heard something crash in the background. "Put Thomas back on. Is he okay?"

"He's flipping out, Wren. He just took off out the door. What did you tell him? And where are you? I'll come get you."

"I'm too far away. Bailey, please go get Thomas before he does something bad! He'll get in trouble. I'll call back!" She hung up without waiting for his response.

~~~

She called back the next day and Bailey picked up the phone on the first ring. "Boy am I glad to hear your voice."

"Where's Thomas?"

"He's in jail, Wren. He beat the hell out of your stepfather. He almost killed him! Put him in the ICU."

"Oh my God." Oh, Thomas, I should have never called

you.

"I think Miller's going to try to post his bail." Bailey cleared his throat. "Listen, he wanted me to find out where you are so I can come get you."

"Forget it, Bailey. I'll never come back down there. Don -- he hurt me. Bad. I'm afraid he'll try to hurt me again. Or Thomas."

Bailey sighed. "Sweetheart, Don's not in any condition to hurt anyone right now. Miller said for you to come to the shop and stay in Thomas's apartment. We won't let anybody hurt you. Just tell me where you are."

"I can't," Wren croaked. She slammed the phone into its cradle. I can't. I can't. I can't.

~~~

Wren knew she should call Bailey again, but she didn't have the heart to hear how much trouble Thomas faced. At the shelter, she curled up on her bunk, rolled her blanket tight around her body, and ignored the other residents who paused by her bed. Covering her head, she tried to remember her real father and her true home. In this grimy room, Edgar's face was indistinct. She feared he and Pawpaw Ridge would fade in her memory.

She thought of the cool spring days they had spent together in their little valley. While her father plowed the garden, she walked between the furrows to examine the treasures he unearthed: old glass bottles, arrowheads, headless dolls, and iridescent beetles that shined in sunlight. Spiders bristled in the glistening grass along the edge of the garden.

Her father dropped tiny seeds that would transform into tender stalks. They would grow tall in the summer heat. When he finished, they would sit on the hill and breathe deep the sweet scent of apple blossoms and grass clippings. Sometimes they sat like that all day, watching the light wash green knolls and mossy undulations into the blue and purple gloaming.

Remembering brought grief. Each morning salty tears streaked her cheeks. She walked through the streets of Virginia Beach from daybreak until dark, chewing on her thumb, sucking her fingers.

~~~

In late January, she called the number on the card the doctor gave her and made an appointment at a local clinic. After some preliminary questions and an examination, a nurse left her in the procedure room. She pulled her knees up to her chest and drew the paper gown down to her ankles. Wrapping her arms around her legs, she rocked on the cold table. Sighing, she laid her head against her knees. She heard muffled weeping in the next room and rocked faster. The mewling noise grew louder, until it sounded like the cry of a cat.

It reminded her of that old tomcat, Cyclops. She could see his ragged ears and scarred face; he always seemed to be winking at her. *That SOB is a real cat's cat*, Mark had told Wren. *He'll kill anything that crosses his path.*

She thought of the baby bird he had dropped on the porch. Squeezing her eyes shut, she saw the little creature again. Looking more alien than bird, its tiny beak opened and closed. Wren felt sick to her stomach.

Footsteps paused outside the door and she tensed. The steps continued down the hallway and Wren deflated. She jumped when the nurse finally popped her head in the door. "How are we doing? Are you cold?"

Although she was shivering, Wren shook her head no. The woman patted her on the back. "The doctor will be here in just a minute."

Suddenly, the black monster inside Wren hammered her gut. It wanted out. Gagging, she jumped from the table and ran to the bathroom. She dry heaved for several minutes and when she finished, she gathered her clothes and began to dress.

"What are you doing? The procedure--"

"I can't do it. I'm sorry. I changed my mind," she said. She stumbled down the hallway and out the door.

Wren pressed a fist into her abdomen and clenched her teeth. The cold air was tinged with salt and she pulled her jacket close around her. She headed for the beach, her feet growing heavier with each step.

A few brave souls plodded along the sandy strip and gathered seashells the somber ocean had spit onto the beach. Two children bundled in heavy jackets built a castle of sand. Wren walked to the ocean's edge and contemplated its dark depths. I might crumble like the shore if the ocean washed over me long enough.

She sat on the beach and waited for night to fall. Light blue sky morphed into the ocean's dark blue until it was difficult to distinguish between water and sky. Persistent waves gripped the gritty shore. Sandcastles tumbled. Footprints faded. The water washed away evidence of human activity and gave the sand a semblance of purity.

Her teeth chattered and her ears ached. She pinched her cheeks to draw warm blood into her face. Wren lay flat on her back and lifted her numb hands to the silver stars that seemed to dangle just out of her reach. She clasped cold air with her fingers and drew it down to her brow. She rubbed her eyes, forcing tears to spill down her face. Sand clung to her glazed cheeks.

"I hate you," Wren said. The being growing in her dark womb was unmoved by its mother's passion. It remained silent and still.

Wren stretched her arms and legs out to form an X with her body. She moved them back and forth, then turned on her side and curled up inside the angel she had made in the sand. She would have slept there, breathing winter's poison wind, if a police officer hadn't roused her and escorted her off the beach.

~~~

She contacted Bailey in March and discovered that Thomas

had been sentenced to a year in prison. When she refused to tell him where she was, he gave her the prison address. "At least write to Tom. He's really pathetic right now."

"Do you know what happened to Don?"

"He's out of the hospital, but I think he has to go through physical therapy. I'm telling you, Wren, Thomas messed him up bad." She thought Bailey didn't sound too broken up about it.

He offered to wire her some money. "Can you spare it, Bailey?"

"Sure. I'm independently wealthy," he joked.

For the first time in months, Wren laughed. The rusty sound scratched her throat and she coughed. "I'll pay you back one of these days. Thank you."

After they made arrangements to wire the money, Wren made Bailey promise not to tell anyone she was in Virginia Beach. They hung up and she returned to her bunk.

~~~

Wren carried a tray of hamburgers and fries across the restaurant and plopped it down on the table at booth five. Six men with a telephone company logo stitched on their shirts beamed at her. Wren smiled back and unloaded their food.

"Here you go. Enjoy." She smiled at each man. A big smile and eye contact, she had learned, meant a bigger tip. The men thanked her and watched her walk back to the kitchen. They didn't see her smile disappear when she turned away from them.

She leaned against the wall in the kitchen and blew wisps of hair away from her face. Her hand moved to her stomach. Sixteen, pregnant, and homeless. She rubbed her belly and reminded herself at least she wasn't jobless.

The director of the shelter had secured a job for Wren at a diner. Wren had lied to the administrator about her age and her name. She also lied by omission, neglecting to mention her pregnancy.

Even though she was more than five months pregnant, she had gained little weight. If her uniform was a little tighter in April, her coworkers chalked it up to regular meals. The cook knew she lived at the shelter, and he made it a point to have a plate of food ready for her when her shift ended. She didn't have the energy to eat after she walked back to the shelter.

The baby drained her. The baby. Always, her thoughts returned to the lump in her stomach. Some nights she pulled the pillow over her face to smother her hatred for the baby. She hated herself for hating it. *I know you didn't ask to be here. But you're part of him, so now he's in me. I don't want him in me -- ever again.*

When she thought of Don inside her, sharp pain cut through her abdomen, her back, and eventually, her anger. She placed her hands together as if in prayer and squeezed them between her thighs until the pain receded. She didn't sleep on those nights.

Last night had been a sleepless one. And this time the pain didn't go away. *Why are you hurting me?* she asked the baby as she took orders and waited on tables. She tossed her head and smiled at the telephone workers, all while red hot pincers tore at her insides.

She was glad to see them rise from their table, leaving the restaurant in a noisy knot. The last man, tall and very thin, turned and winked at Wren before he walked outside. Ricki, the other waitress, rolled her eyes and twisted her ponytail around her index finger. "I bet you got another good haul today." She looked over Wren's shoulder as she counted her tip. "How much?"

"Never enough, Ricki." Wren pocketed the money before she gathered dirty plates and glasses. When she leaned across the table to retrieve crumpled napkins, beads of sweat popped out on her forehead. Pain hammered her below the waist before relief came, as abrupt as the released cork of a champagne bottle. Wren imagined she could almost hear *pop!* right before the pain stopped. She started to laugh until she saw Ricki's face.

"Wren! What's wrong with you?" Ricki pointed to the floor.

Wren glanced down and saw blood streaming along her legs. She looked around the restaurant and was horrified to see everyone in the room staring at her. Covering her face, she ran to the bathroom.

Wren hunched down in a stall and tried to stem the flow of blood with paper towels. Ricki and Valerie, the other waitress, called to her from outside the bathroom door. She heard Ricki ask the other girl to call 911. No! she tried to scream, but she couldn't open her mouth because the pain had returned with a vengeance. She collapsed on the floor and watched the light grow dim.

~~~

Wren pulled a sheet of paper from a drawer and sat at her kitchen table to write Thomas a letter.

July 1986. Dear Thomas. She chewed on the end of her pen and stared at the ceiling.

Dear Thomas. I'm sorry it's been so long since I've written. I lost the baby. I've been really sick for a couple of months and am just now getting back on my feet. It's strange – I thought I'd be happy to get rid of that baby, but I felt really bad when I had the miscarriage. I hated it sometimes, being part of Don. But I loved it too, being part of me. I know that doesn't make sense.

I miss you. I wish I could do something to help you. Bailey said Don's been coming by the shop, trying to find out where I am. I don't know what he would do if he found me. Thomas, stay away from him when you get out. Please! I couldn't stand it if something happened to you.

I'm working again, still at the diner. And I'm out of the shelter! My boss made a deal with me. He's letting me stay in the efficiency above the diner cheap. In return, I do the opening and closing cleaning in addition to my regular duties. It's hard, but I don't mind. Anything's better than living at the shelter.

I've saved a lot of the money Bailey's been sending me – bless his heart.

Wren sketched a picture of Bailey at the bottom of the page and drew a halo over his head. *Anyway, I'd better go. Time to open the diner. Be good, brother. I love you. Wren*

~~~

"Promise me it won't disrupt our business." Gordon stacked chairs upside down on tables as he talked to Wren.

"It won't," she told her employer as she swept the floor beneath the tables. "I promise."

He shook his head and sighed. "I don't know. You know me, Wren. I'm a plain guy. The thought of murals all over the diner walls makes me a little nervous."

Wren laughed. "You liked the sketches I showed you. When I get them on the walls, they'll be even better. Trust me, it'll give this place some real character."

Gordon snorted. "I don't need character. I need customers."

In the end, he let Wren paint the walls. She based the murals on famous artwork. She transformed Salvador Dali's melting watches into melting pancakes. The Mona Lisa held a bag of French fries in her hands. A Jackson Pollock wall paid tribute to the table condiments. Andy Warhol's silk-screened Marilyn Monroe became cheeseburgers.

Regular customers brought friends to show them the revamped diner. Each day the lunch crowd expanded. "Not a bad problem to have," Gordon told Wren. He gave her a raise.

Visiting business owners offered Wren opportunities to paint their offices. Her sideline career as an artist reduced her downtime; sometimes she only slept two or three hours a night. *I may be sleep deprived, but I'm not starving*, she wrote Thomas. *I've made enough money to repay Bailey and even have a little extra put away.*

~~~

One late May afternoon, during her break, she flopped

down in an empty booth and rested her head on the table. Sun streaming through the diner window warmed her skin and she pressed a sleepy smile against her arms.

"Man, all this talk about how hard you've been working was a crock. Here you are sleeping on the job!" Thomas's voice pierced her syrupy consciousness and she jerked upright.

He had slid into the other seat in the booth. His hair stood in little blond spikes and his blue eyes twinkled. He had more tattoos on his caramel skin than she remembered, including a brown wren on his forearm.

"Thomas!"

They reached across the table and hugged each other for a solid minute. Wren slid into the seat next to Thomas and leaned against his shoulder. He put his arm around her and rocked her. After a minute, she wiped her eyes with a napkin and laughed. "I can't believe you're here."

"I got out a few weeks ago. This is the first chance I've had to get away from the shop. Let me look at you." He pulled back from her and examined her face. "You're a little thin, but I guess you could look worse, all things considered."

"You, too. Was it bad?"

Thomas scratched his nose and stared over her head. "Let's just say my goal in life is to never go back."

"I'm sorry. It's my fault. I shouldn't have--"

"Stop it. I made my own choice and I accept the consequences. If I had to do it over again, I'd do the same thing. Except I would finish the job. I hate the thought of that SOB still pulling a breath."

Wren folded the damp napkin into a fan. "Have you seen him since you got out?"

"Well, when I was still in, he kept stopping by and hassling Bailey about you. Miller finally ran him off. But I've seen him driving past the shop a few times since I got out."

"I'm afraid for you, Thomas. He had a gun." She squeezed the napkin in her fist.

"I can take care of myself, Sis. It's you I couldn't take care of. I should have walked you to your room that night."

Wren shook her head. "It's not your fault." She lifted her fingers to her mouth, but Thomas yanked her hands to the table.

"Look at us. You blame yourself for my troubles and I blame myself for yours. Aren't we a messed-up pair?" Laughing, he looked around the diner. "Wow. You did all this? Cindy was right. You really are talented." He grabbed a menu from its placeholder. "Now, let's see how you are as a waitress. How about some lunch?"

~~~

Thomas spent the weekend with Wren. Monday morning he shoved his clothes in a duffel bag and tossed it in his car. She leaned on the fender and shaded her eyes against the bright sun. "I still think you should move up here, Thomas."

"I'd like to be closer to you, Sis, but I really owe Miller. Besides, it's easier to work for him than it would be to explain my criminal record to a new employer."

"I'm sorry." Wren hung her head and let her hair fall into her face.

Thomas crooked his forefinger under her chin and lifted her head. "You have nothing to be sorry about. Let's not get into this again. I'll be back up as soon as I can." He reached into his pocket and pulled out a roll of money. "In the meantime, take this."

Wren shook her head and shoved the money against his chest. "I don't want that."

"Take it! It's from Miller, Bailey, and me. It's not a lot, but I know you can use it." He slapped it into her palm and closed her fingers around it.

She hugged him. "You're all I've got, Thomas. I love you."

"I love you, too. Take care of yourself. Eat." He climbed

into the car and leaned out the open window. "And call me."

~~~

Loneliness overwhelmed Wren after Thomas left. She worked as many hours as she could, less for the money than for something to occupy her time. Thomas's visit made her realize how isolated she had become. She craved company like she might crave salt or chocolate, yet she thrust away potential friends and prospective romances. She wanted companionship, but the thought of physical intimacy made her stomach roll.

She tried to cultivate a touch-me-not cool, but men read it as a come-hither vulnerability. Customers -- teenagers, old men, business men, all types of men -- lingered at the counter long after their plates were empty. Wren discovered flowers, tiny gift-wrapped boxes, or cryptic sticky notes beside her tips. She gave away the flowers, returned the boxes with a polite shake of her head, and tossed the notes into the garbage.

Some men engaged her in conversation just to hear her talk. In Virginia Beach, her accent was distinct. "You sound just like a Southern belle," she heard more than once, and she always rolled her eyes. She had never thought of herself as Southern. I'm a mountain girl, she told herself. Can't people tell the difference?

Her suitors weren't limited to customers. One night, after the diner closed, Gordon came up behind her as she wiped down the counter. "I was wondering if you wanted to go see a movie this weekend?"

"Oh, Gordon, thank you, but I can't." She didn't look up from her work.

"You never go out." He reached up and twisted one of her curls around his finger. When his knuckle brushed her neck, she shuddered. "Don't you get lonely?"

"No, not really," she lied.

She rebuffed his advances, but he didn't seem to mind. He continued to hover around her despite her obvious lack of interest. She didn't feel threatened by Gordon. His admiration reminded her of Bailey's – respectful – so she tolerated his crush because he maintained a courteous demeanor.

~~~

On New Year's Eve, Wren propped herself in front of the television and watched people celebrate in New York City's Times Square. Depressed, she drank half a bottle of Jack Daniels and spent the first day of 1988 with her head in the commode. When she was able to think again, she decided she needed to get out of the diner and the apartment. This is not living, she told herself. It's existing.

Wren attended free park concerts when the weather warmed. When summer days boiled, she hung out in the air conditioned library or went to a movie. Her favorite pastime, though, was visiting art galleries. She spent long evenings admiring local artwork and observing the people who attended gallery openings.

She turned nineteen on Halloween and decided to treat herself with a visit to a new gallery. People crowded the room, and their voices buzzed all around her. Weaving herself between clusters of animated artists and supporters, she felt cold perspiration cover her back.

She managed to block out the crowd long enough to enjoy the glass pieces that dangled from the ceiling. She thought their unique beauty a wonderful birthday present. The artist had contorted striated glass – damson, apricot, indigo – into nebulous shapes that reminded Wren of outer space.

She admired an iridescent globule and exclaimed to herself, "That looks like the aurora borealis! How lovely."

"Most people just see globs of colored glass." A male voice behind her sounded pleased.

She turned to see a young man with his arms crossed over his purple and blue rugby shirt. He was solid and trim beneath his shirt and jeans. His black hair was cropped close and shot through with silver, though he looked no older than Wren. He reached up and twirled the glass so the light caught it with dramatic effect.

Turning to Wren, he gazed at her with eyes the color and shape of almonds. "Hi. I'm Michael. I'm the artist."

Black panic flowed up out of her chest and she swallowed hard. Then she realized Michael had spoken again.

"I'm sorry, what?"

"What's your name?"

"Wren."

"Wren. May I escort you through the gallery?"

"Oh. Uhm, I--"

"Would be thrilled? Great!" He placed his hand against the small of her back and guided her from piece to piece.

Wren sucked in a deep breath at his touch. Before long, however, she forgot his hand as she gazed at the rich swirls of glass. "They're exquisite."

She took a surreptitious peek at the price tag on the piece nearest her and covered her mouth with both hands. Wow! I wonder if I could get that much for my paintings!

"I have to talk to that man standing over there. He's a potential buyer. Please don't go anywhere." Michael excused himself.

She watched other women watch Michael as he walked across the room and shook the hand of a man wearing a turban. A woman in a red strapless dress and a pearl choker draped her arm across Michael's when he started back across the room. Sipping a glass of wine, she whispered in his ear and they both laughed at what she said.

Wren wondered what it was like to be so confident and relaxed in the midst of all those people. Even as a child, she had been happiest in solitude. Just Daddy and me.

Michael disengaged himself from the woman and walked through the room, shaking hands and nodding to his patrons. She saw he was working his way back to her and braced herself as he greeted one last admirer.

He wiped his brow in pantomime exhaustion and laughed. "I hate this stuff. It's a lot easier to create the art than it is to sell it. I like the tangible part of it, you know?" When Wren nodded, he continued.

"There's something really pleasing about having an idea come alive in my hands. Glass is a great medium. It's very satisfying to feel the finished curves and lines beneath my fingers."

His comment made heat rush through her body. She felt her face grow red and peered up at Michael as if he knew what was happening to her. He frowned, and she jumped when he touched her sleeve. "Are you okay?" he asked.

"I'm not good in crowds," she whispered.

He looked over her head and scanned the room a moment. "Come on," he said and guided her through the back of the gallery, outside to the alley.

They sat on the stoop of the back door. Wren bowed her head, afraid to look at Michael, but sensing his stare, she blushed.

He leaned his elbows on his thighs, and clasped his hands together between his legs. "Are you shy? Or just quiet?"

"Tonight, I don't know what I am."

"Well, let's see. I would say radiant as the sun and cool as the moon."

"That's the prettiest thing anyone ever said to me," she managed to say. Her heart crashed against her rib cage. I wonder if this is how a rabbit feels right before the hawk grabs her from the ground.

"I guess I should get back in there." He rubbed his fingers and thumbs together. "Some of those people have money to burn." When she didn't respond, he pulled her face to his. "You know you have beguiling eyes? They're every shade of green I've ever seen, and some I haven't. I wonder how they look in the morning light."

His words hung in the cold air, waiting for her to pluck them from darkness and do something with them. She opened her mouth to reprove him and heard herself say the unthinkable. "Come home with me."

~~~

Wren stood at the window and peered between the curtains. The street light dazzled her. She closed her eyes and pressed her forehead against the glass. Behind her, she heard Michael sit up in bed.

"What's wrong?"

She clenched the curtains in her fists. "Nothing."

She wondered how something that seemed so adversarial could be called lovemaking. Sparring in the dark, it seemed to her. When she had struggled against his weight, he misinterpreted and moved deeper into her. She felt sick and thought she might vomit. Let it be over soon, she had thought then, and it became her mantra.

Now he padded to the window and touched her shoulder. She stiffened and he dropped his hand. "Did I do something wrong?" he asked.

"No." She twisted away from him. Grabbing her clothes from the floor, she began to dress. Out of the corner of her eye, she saw him shrug. He followed her lead, dressing with quiet efficiency.

Wren drew a glass of water and concentrated on drinking it with slow, loud swallows. Michael walked up behind her again, but he didn't touch her. Without turning around, she set the glass on the counter and squeezed it. "Goodbye."

He didn't move or speak for a solid minute and Wren wondered how long she would have to stand there listening to her jaw muscles work. Finally, he mumbled a quiet "Bye." She waited until she heard the door close with a snick before she turned to face her empty apartment.

She locked the door and threw the deadbolt. Stripping

the bed and herself, she left the laundry in a pile in the bathroom floor. She retreated to the tub and took the hottest shower she could stand. She emerged from the steam, her skin bright red from the heat and the scrubbing, and pulled on a robe.

In the kitchen, she drank another glass of water, then another. I hope the monster drowns. She laughed then and slid down the front of the sink and curled up on the floor. She felt ancient.

Michael knocked on her apartment door the next day. She stood on the other side of the door and listened to his voice calling to her, soft and puzzled, hurt, then angry. She was relieved when he finally left.

~~~

Thomas phoned her right before Christmas. As soon as he said hello, Wren began to babble. "I hope you're coming up here. I really miss you. Bring Bailey with you. I don't want to spend Christmas alone, Thomas!"

"Wren! Shut up for a minute." Thomas cleared his throat. "I don't want you to panic, but you need to know, Don found out where you are."

Terror wrapped its rubber fingers around her throat. For a moment, she could neither swallow nor breathe.

"Wren, are you there?"

She uttered a choked cough. "How did he find out?"

Thomas sighed. "He broke into my apartment while we were out. Took a bunch of my letters, which have your return address on them."

"When?"

"Some time last night. I just got home a few hours ago and found the place wrecked."

"He'll come here, Thomas." Her voice cracked. "What do I do? What do I do?"

"Hey, first of all, don't freak out. Are you listening to me? Wren?"

"I've got to get out of here, Thomas."

"Well, I think that might be a good idea. Get your clothes together and take off for a while. Don't tell Gordon or anybody else where you're going. Then call me back when you've found a place to stay."

Perspiration beaded on her face. Without thinking, she rubbed the tattoo on her belly. Her skin felt clammy. Wren chewed on her thumb and wondered where she could go. The black monster whispered in her ear, echoing Don's voice: Beautiful.

Thomas was still speaking when she hung up the phone. She ignored its ring as she stuffed her things into a backpack. Slamming the door behind her, she hurried down the stairs. She tripped and tumbled to the ground. She jumped up and ran down the street.

It took her twenty minutes to get to the bus station. She bought a ticket and boarded the next bus leaving Virginia Beach. Sitting in the front seat, she leaned her cheek against the dark glass. It felt cool and smooth against her skin. The bus pulled away in a hiccup of diesel smoke while she crouched inside its rumbling belly.

The monster continued to chant to her. Beautiful. You're so beautiful. Beautiful. Beautiful. Beautiful. She pressed her palms against her temples to squeeze it out of her head, but it just laughed and gibbered. All the way to Richmond.

Seven

Charlottesville, April–May 1991

"Richmond? Is that where you've been living the last two years?" Peter leaned back in the grass and tried to absorb Wren's story.

She crossed her arms and scratched her shoulders. "Yes."

"So what happened when you got to Richmond?"

Wren pulled herself into a tighter knot. "Shouldn't you be getting back to class? I thought you were working on your final project."

"Don't change the subject." Peter sat up and clutched her shoe. "What happened?"

"Nothing! It doesn't matter. But now you know why I'm--" She struggled for words, but finally just shook her head and shrugged. "I don't want to talk about it anymore. I'm tired. I think I'll go home and take a nap." Wren used the tree trunk to pull herself to her feet. She eyed Peter with a wary expression when he rose.

He pulled her into his arms, squeezed her against his chest, and kissed the top of her head. Releasing her before she could protest, he stepped backward a few feet. "Be careful. I'll see you later." He turned and trudged toward the Rotunda.

~~~

Wren didn't volunteer the rest of her story and Peter didn't have time to pursue it. Work on his final project intensified. He spent long hours at the architecture school and less time drinking. Wren sketched and painted while he was away from the apartment.

One night he returned to find her working on the last in a series of landscapes. Greeting him when he walked through the door, she held up the picture. "What do you think?"

Gentle hills and terrible ridges stretched across the landscape. A foamy creek tumbled in a cleft between two hills and ran through the yard behind a plain white house. "I like it. Is that your house on Pawpaw Ridge?"

"Yes. At least, that's what I remember." She scratched her nose, smudging it with white paint.

Peter offered her a brief grin before he sank down in the armchair. He closed his eyes and rubbed his temples. "I can't wait for this project to be done. I've got a massive headache. I think I need a drink."

"That'll just make your head hurt worse." Her voice was stern.

He opened one eye and peeked at her. "In case you hadn't noticed, I haven't been drinking much lately."

She lifted her shoulders without answering. Placing the painting back on its easel, she pushed the coffee table away from the couch and gestured for him to sit on the sofa. "Come here."

"Why?"

"Just come here."

Groaning, he moved to the sofa. Wren perched herself on the back of the couch and placed her legs on either side of him, her bare feet flat on the brown cushions. He squinted at her slender toes and smiled; she had painted her toenails purple. He closed his eyes and bowed his head when Wren placed her cool hands on the back of his neck.

She rubbed the taut muscles there with firm

movements. He exhaled quiet delight. A few minutes later, she laid her palms against his forehead and eased his head back until it rested against her abdomen. Using her fingertips, she massaged his temples.

Her fingers glided down his skin, and she rubbed the tiny scar on his left cheek. The tiny alabaster pit was discernible only when he pressed his nose against the mirror. Wren cupped his face and ran her thumb pads along his jaw line.

His headache had disappeared, but now the rest of his body ached in a whole new way. Blood rushed through him and thrummed in his ears, fed his heart, warmed his center. Suddenly he was granite, flint, diamond. *I could pull you down on this couch right now and love you.*

Instead, he kept his eyes and his mouth shut. This was the longest period of time Wren had ever voluntarily touched him. *I'm not going to do anything to make her stop.*

She bowed her head and her hair fell around him. "Does it still hurt?"

You have no idea, he thought. "Feels a little better." His voice was hoarse. *Don't stop. Please.*

She stroked his shoulders and he felt himself relax again. She pressed her knee into his side and he sank into the cushions, into sleep.

~~~

The general malaise of winter disappeared after Easter. April heralded May with a flourish of pastel blossoms and vibrant leaves. Fresh air drew students, teachers, and Charlottesville's residents out of classrooms, offices, and homes. Wren and Peter succumbed to spring's temptations one Saturday morning with a trip to the park.

They stood at the edge of the lake and tossed breadcrumbs to the birds. Ducks flanked the downy banks of the water. Some swam, single file, with their tail feathers erect as they cut military-precise lines through the water. In unison, they paused to trawl for dainties.

Wren laughed at the moochers that waddled behind them. She cast more breadcrumbs to appease them. Peter found a grassy spot on the bank and motioned for her to join him. Waving away the ducks – for fear of being nibbled to death – they sat on the ground and enjoyed the view.

"Look," Peter said. He pointed to a mallard walking through the mud. Its bill was misshapen. "Poor guy's got a bad kisser. I bet he has a hard time catching his dinner. We better feed him." He tossed a large amount of bread in the bird's direction and shooed away the other ducks until he was sure it had eaten.

Wren smiled at him when he returned to her side. "Have you always been this way?"

"What way?"

"Rescuer of all creatures great and small."

Peter thought about all the unfortunate animals he had brought home as a child. He had spent many evenings explaining to his mother why a rail-thin dog was tied to the porch or why an abused cat was hidden in his closet. Although she fussed about the animals, Peter knew the inevitable bowl of food and water would be forthcoming after the lecture.

He shrugged and bounced his shoulder against Wren's. "I guess so." She didn't lean away from him.

Peter stared at the water and wondered what he would do when his family came up for his graduation. He still hadn't told them about Wren.

Wren. Wren. Wren. Her name was the sound of windshield wipers during rain. It whispered to him from behind the music on the radio. It soothed him to sleep at night.

"What?" She looked at him with a raised eyebrow.

"What?"

"You said my name." She distributed the last of the bread to the ducks and clapped her hands together to release crumbs from her palms.

"Oh. I was just thinking about graduation next month. My family will be here."

She pulled her legs close to her chest. Resting her elbows on her knees, she shaded her eyes with one hand and looked at Peter. "So you're wondering what to do about me."

Peter sighed. "Yes. No. I mean, you make it sound as though you're a problem I have to resolve."

"Well, in a way, that's exactly what I am." She stretched her legs out in front of her and picked at the grass between them. "It's okay. I've been thinking about it, too." She turned her head away from Peter and stared across the lake. "I think I should go pretty soon."

"No. I don't want you to go." He couldn't restrain himself from touching her leg. She looked down at his hand but didn't withdraw.

"Peter, I can't stay with you forever. I've already been here too long. And my daddy would be so ashamed of me for sitting on my butt the last two months while you paid for my food and clothes. And I know your family wouldn't appreciate it. This is as bad as being on the draw. It ain't right."

"What's not right about it? You didn't force me to do anything I didn't want to do. I want to help you."

"You're getting ready to graduate. You're going to have a great life as a successful architect. You can't do that if I'm dragging you down."

"You're not dragging me down! Don't you get it?" He tugged at a strand of her auburn hair and rubbed it between his fingers. "I love you."

She moved away from him then. "Don't say that."

"Why not? It's the truth."

"Look, you treat me so sweet. But I don't deserve it."

"What are you talking about?"

She stood and dusted off the seat of her jeans. "You've

got a paper to finish, remember? We should head back to the apartment."

Peter continued to sit and stare across the water. Finally, she reached down and brushed his shoulder. "You coming?"

~~~

Peter was annotating his research paper when a knock sounded on the door. A pot clattered in the kitchen and Wren stuck her head in the doorway. "Who's that?" she whispered.

He peered through the peephole and saw Ike standing in the glow of the amber streetlight. He wore a Baja pullover and had twisted his hair up in little braids all over his head. He held up a bottle of Absolut in front of the peephole.

Peter sighed and opened the door. "Shouldn't you be studying?"

"I needed a break. Can I come in?"

Peter looked back to see what Wren would say, but she had retreated to the kitchen. "For a few minutes. But I can't party tonight, man. I'm working on a paper."

"I won't stay long. Hey, got any OJ?" Without waiting for permission, Ike walked straight to the refrigerator and dug through the shelves until he found juice. Wren folded her arms and leaned against the kitchen counter. Ike grinned at her. "Screwdriver?"

Peter ran his hand through his hair and bounced from foot to foot. "I don't think tonight's a good night for any hard stuff, Ike."

"Just one drink, Sullivan. Come on."

Wren frowned at Peter when he pulled two glasses from the cabinet. Avoiding her eyes, he followed Ike into the living room and watched him mix the drinks. Ike spilled vodka on the coffee table. Giggling, he swiped his sleeve through the alcohol. His eyes were shiny black behind his horn-rims.

Peter shook his head. "Are you stoned?"

Ike cackled, confirming Peter's suspicions. He handed
Peter a drink and downed his own. Looking toward the
kitchen, he leaned close to Peter. "What's up with you
and Bram? I saw him the day after my party and he had
this huge scrape across his face. He wouldn't tell me what
happened."

Wren glided into the room and sat next to Peter on the
couch. He cleared his throat. "I don't want to talk about it."

Ike held up the bottle. "You want a drink, Wren?"

"No."

He mixed another one for himself and refilled Peter's
glass. Conscious of Wren's glare, Peter sipped his second
drink like he was taking high tea. Ike noticed the paintings
propped up along the walls of the living room. "Hey, did
you do these, Wren?"

"Yes."

"Pretty. Are they real places?" He shuffled around the
room and examined the pictures.

"Yes."

He waited for Wren to explain, but she just stared
at him. Peter spoke for her. "Most of them are in Wise
County."

"Oh. Down there in Appalachia, huh? I didn't think it
would be so pretty."

Peter finished his drink and eyed the vodka. "Why?"

"Well, with all the strip-mining and stuff, I figured it
was pretty barren."

"Not all of it." Wren answered that time. She jumped
up and guided Ike around the room again, explaining what
part of Wise County each painting represented.

Peter mixed another screwdriver while Wren talked to
Ike. When she finished, Ike turned to him and grinned. "I
guess I see why you want to go back after you graduate. Just
seems like everybody else I've met from down there can't
wait to escape."

Peter leaned forward and slammed his empty glass on

the table. "Escape what? I'm not ashamed of where I come from. I like Southwest Virginia. I like Wise County. Kids from home get up here and decide they're never going back. They hear people here make fun of the way they talk, so they try to change it. And it really ticks me off to hear them degrade home!" He leaned back in the couch cushions and hot liquid sloshed around his stomach. He felt an ellipsis of sweat on his upper lip.

Ike held his palms out to Peter. "Hey, man. Don't preach to me. I was just saying. But, it's true you guys don't have much of a job market down there for professionals. Right?"

"And we never will if we all leave and never come back." Peter smacked his lips and belched. Orange juice. Yuck.

Wren grabbed the Absolut and handed it to Ike. "I think you should go now. He's got homework."

Ike saluted her. "Yes, ma'am." He winked at Peter. "See you later, man."

Peter nodded and followed him to the door. "See ya." When he shut the door and turned, the room was empty. He blinked. "Hunh. Hey, Wren, where'd you go?"

She came out of the bedroom pulling a sweatshirt over her head. "I'm going for a walk."

"Now? It's kinda late to go out by yourself."

"I need some fresh air."

"Well, wait up and I'll go with you." He reached for his shoes.

"I don't want you to go with me," she snapped.

Peter let his shoes fall with a thunk. "Who pissed in your cornflakes?"

Wren shoved her sneakers on her feet as she spoke. "You have a problem. You need help."

A problem? Help?? Anger boiled up into his chest. "That's kinda like the pot calling the kettle black, isn't it? Seems to me you're the one with all the damn problems!"

Wren froze. "What?"

"Yeah. You're the one who needs help, Wren." Just shut

up. Just stop talking. But the vodka had loosened his tongue until he thought it might just flap right out of his mouth. "Good grief, I can't even get near you without you curling up your lip like you smell something bad! I've been trying to help you!" Peter crossed his arms in a tight knot.

She snorted. "Help me? You can't help me. Take a good look at yourself, Peter. You're nothing but a damn drunkard!"

When Peter stepped forward, she drew back. "I'm not a drunk." He ran his hand through his hair and rocked back on his heels. "What do you know about me anyway? You're too caught up in yourself to know anything about me. If anything or anyone intrudes on your little world, you just run away."

"My own little world? What do you know about my world?"

"Enough to know I've done everything I can to help you. But, Wren, no matter what I do, you don't trust me. I think by now I should have earned your trust."

"Trust?" Wren laughed and the sound of it made Peter's skin crawl. "Let me tell you about trust, Peter. You can't trust anybody. People let you down. Even God lets you down. You have to take care of yourself." She jerked open the door and twisted the knob back and forth in her fist. "And I didn't ask you to help me! What do you want from me? Eternal thanks? You want me to fall at your feet and kiss them? Fine!"

She dropped to her knees, crawled to Peter's feet, and wrapped her hands around his ankles. "Oh, thank you, Saint Peter," she chanted, and began to kiss his feet.

Horrified, he pushed her away and she fell on her back. He clutched her waist to pick her up, but let go when she hit him. She flailed at him with furious slaps, scratching his face and arms until he withdrew.

Peter backed against the wall and slid down to the floor. His face felt sticky and he wiped away blood with his shirt. Trying to catch his breath, he stared at Wren. She writhed on the floor with her fingers shoved in her mouth. He heard her gag, but her eyes were dry and distant. Crazy. *She's crazy.*

"What's going on down there?" His upstairs neighbor was standing at the top of the stairs with his head ducked to see inside Peter's apartment. All Peter could see was the man's naked legs and his pale feet encased in ragged slippers. "Do I need to call 911?"

At that question, Wren sat up and stared at Peter with wide eyes. She shook her head side to side, as steady as a metronome. He opened his mouth to say, *Yes, please call the police. There's a crazy woman in my apartment. Tell them to come take her away.*

Instead, he heard himself call up to the man, "No, don't do that! We're just having a little argument. Sorry if we woke you up."

"Some people gotta work weekends, you know! Keep it down or I'll call the police next time!" The naked legs disappeared up the steps and a door slammed a moment later.

Wren stood and walked stiff-legged back to the door. Peter wanted to follow her, but he felt as taut as a new guitar string. "Wait," he said.

She didn't turn around when she spoke. "I'm going for a walk." The door shut behind her with a loud click.

"Shit," he muttered. He stumbled to the couch and waited for her to come home.

~~~

Peter awoke the next morning on the couch, where he had fallen asleep waiting for Wren. He staggered to the bathroom and stared at the stranger in the mirror. Scratches ran down both sides of his face like dark brown tributaries. Similar marks covered his arms. He ran his hand through his hair, pulled it back into a small ponytail, and twisted one of Wren's hair bands around it to secure it.

He washed blood from his face and arms, changed his shirt, and walked outside. Where are you, Wren? He leaned against the banister at the bottom of the stairs. The cold metal soothed the throbbing skin on his arms. Peter laid his head down on the rail and absorbed the morning's sensations.

Gravel popped as a car cruised through the parking lot. A distant door slammed. His neighbor's dryer vent exuded the scent of fabric softener and Peter inhaled its heavy perfume. The banister vibrated as someone ran down the stairs.

Peter sensed a presence and he raised his head to see a tow-headed boy staring at him. He held a ragged Hershey bar in one hand. A brown ring of chocolate lined his lips, making him look like a clown. Peter swallowed a laugh and laid his head back down on the rail.

The boy began to kick the stairway railing with precise, gentle taps. The banister vibrated and Peter clenched his teeth. He raised his head again and glared at the child. "Hey, don't do that."

The boy licked some of the chocolate from around his mouth and pointed at Peter with his candy bar. "You got scratches all over you," he observed as he bit off a square of chocolate.

Peter ran his tongue across his teeth and rolled it into his cheek. "The monster almost got me last night," he said.

The little boy paused in mid-chew. "What monster?"

"The one that lives in the stairwell downstairs."

The child peered down the steps toward the basement, and then back at Peter. He shook his head without conviction. "There's no such thing as monsters. Is there?"

Peter shrugged and rubbed his face. "Well, I didn't dream up these scratches. If I were you, I wouldn't go downstairs. I probably just whet its appetite."

The boy stood on his toes, lifted his head, and stared down his nose in the direction of the basement again. "I don't see nothing."

"That's how it gets you. Just when you least expect it, it sneaks up on you and *gahhh*!" Peter slammed his fists on the banister as he shouted.

The little boy jumped, dropping his Hershey bar, and ran up the stairs. "Mommy!" he wailed. When Peter heard the apartment door slam, he laid his head back down on the rail and laughed.

The sun melted his muscles and he wondered if he could fall asleep leaning against the railing. Just as he started to drift, he sensed he had company again. Without raising his head, he spoke. "I told you if that monster gets loose, it'll eat you alive."

"How did you know about the monster?"

Wren! Peter turned to see her leaning against the wall of his apartment. She had removed the sweatshirt and tied its arms around her waist. She stood with her hands in her pockets and scuffed the welcome mat with the toe of her sneaker.

He stepped toward her, but stopped short, afraid to touch her. He lifted his arms and held out his palms as if he were a mime in an invisible box. Wren lifted her head and gazed at his injured face.

A tiny "oh" escaped her lips and she touched the scratches with her fingertips. She let her hands slide down his neck and shoulders to stroke the scratches on his arms. She swallowed hard and, closing her eyes, slid her hands down to his. Weaving their fingers together, she guided their arms down. Without letting go, Wren stepped close and pressed her cheek against Peter's chest. He held his breath, not sure what to do.

"I'm sorry," she said.

"Me, too," he whispered. He bowed his head and nuzzled her auburn curls. He thought the nimbus of morning sunlight in her hair made her look like an angel.

~~~

Peter finished his final project in May. His classes dwindled, he finished his exams, and he prepared for graduation, which was one week away. Free from school, Peter suggested a hike on Skyline Drive. "The weatherman said there would be meteor showers tonight. We should have a good view up there."

Wren packed dinner and Peter set the box of food on top of a blanket in the back of his truck. They traveled Interstate 64 toward Waynesboro, but left the interstate on top of Afton Mountain.

Peter pulled into a gas station parking lot and showed Wren a map of the drive. "Going south, the Blue Ridge Parkway goes down Virginia, past Roanoke, all the way down to Fancy Gap. If we went that way, eventually we'd end up in North Carolina, somewhat close to our neck of the woods. If we go north, it's called Skyline Drive and it's part of the Shenandoah National Park. It goes all the way to Front Royal, which is just spitting distance from West Virginia and Maryland."

"Which way are we going?" Wren asked.

"We'll go a little ways north," Peter said. "There are all kinds of trails and waterfalls and overlooks."

The road climbed high into the mountains. Wren caught glimpses of trillium in the shadows of oak, hickory, and maple trees. Peter pointed out deer in clearings near the road. At the Loft Mountain overlook, they watched a hawk dance with the clouds. They passed abandoned pastures and old orchards. "People lived up here?" Wren asked Peter.

He ran his hand through his hair before he answered her. "Well, the Indians lived here for thousands of years, I guess. And when people came over from Europe and settled in Virginia, some came up here. They cleared a lot of the trees and made pastures and farmed during the 1700s and 1800s. I remember reading once that the government bought out a lot of people's land so they could turn this into a national park."

"It makes me sad," Wren said. "All those people living up here, living and loving and dying, not knowing there'd be nothing left a hundred years later but the bones of their homes." She propped her elbow on the open window, cupped her chin in her hand, and stared at the mountains.

Peter shivered as he gazed at her. Who are you? They stopped at Bearfence Mountain and climbed the trail to perch on rocks that offered a panoramic view of blue mountains, green valleys, and patchwork farmland. Wren scooted close to him when the wind swirled up the mountain. They traveled higher up the drive and ate their supper while sitting on a stone wall near Big Meadows.

After they ate, they hiked to Dark Hollow Falls. Wren tickled ferns with her fingers and pulled off her shoes so she could sink her toes into the moss. They both shuddered when the waterfall draped icy mist across their shoulders. Dusk began to settle across the mountains as they returned to the truck.

Peter found a meadow and pulled the truck into the scrubby grass. "This looks like a good place to watch the meteor showers," he said. He retrieved the blanket and spread it on the ground. Wren dug around in the box of food and pulled out a bottle of wine and two glasses. "Hey," Peter said, "I didn't see that in there."

"I found it in the back of the cabinet the other day. I didn't know they made wine in Russell County." She rubbed her thumb across the label, although it was too dark now to read it. She handed Peter the bottle of wine.

He wrapped his fingers around its neck. "Are you sure?" She nodded. "One glass each."

He pulled out his pocket knife, found the bottle opener, and removed the cork. He filled the glasses, but neither of them drank right away. They sat side by side, elbows and knees touching, without speaking. Peter thought the moment felt as sacred as those times of reflection right before he took communion at church. They looked at each other and he saw her eyes shining, catlike, in the dark. He held up his glass in a silent toast and she touched it with her own.

Peter rolled the wine around his mouth, savoring it. He could actually taste home in it: woods that smelled like coriander, peppery greens, ripe blackberries, and rich earth. He looked at Wren, but she was leaning back on one elbow with her eyes closed, the wine glass pressed against her lips. *I wonder if she tastes home, too.*

Wren had changed since the night of their fight. Now she let him hold her hand or put his arm around her shoulders. Sometimes she laid her hand on him when they passed in the apartment. She laughed more. And she told him stories about her childhood on Pawpaw Ridge. Peter absorbed it all with an odd urgency, as if he needed to memorize it before it was lost forever.

Still, she hasn't told me everything. I don't know what happened after she got to Richmond. He sighed, mentally shrugging off the cloak of doubt. *I guess she'll tell me when she's ready.*

Peter stretched out next to Wren and closed his eyes. Dew covered his skin with a gentle mantle of cool moisture and he shivered. The measured beat of tree frogs and crickets rose around them and he imagined they matched the very pulse of the earth. *The world is alive all around us.* From deep within the dark woods, an owl confirmed his thought.

He turned his head and saw that silver moonlight had dusted Wren's skin. The cold light imbued her with a terrible beauty; she looked like a creature of myth. He was stricken with a feeling that he had fallen into a fantastic dream where dryads, sylphs, and nixies really did exist. Peter lifted his hand and touched her cheek to reassure himself she was still flesh and blood.

Wren smiled, opened her eyes, and turned on her side to face Peter. "You look so serious. What are you thinking?"

He laughed. "That you're a real dream girl."

She rolled her eyes and flopped back over to stare at the sky. "This is the first time I've felt close to home since Daddy died. It seems like we spent a lot of time outside, looking at the trees and the sky and the animals."

Peter clasped her hand. He stroked her thumb with his, but he didn't say anything.

She sighed. "Sometimes I feel so homesick. It's terrible to miss a home that no longer exists." A bright light streaked above them and she drew in a quick breath. "Did you see it?"

"Yeah," he whispered. He pointed to the heavens. "Look, there's more."

Meteors glided across the sky one at a time, then in groups. Peter and Wren gaped at the luminous light show. Dizzy with the brilliant spectacle, they both clutched the ground and laughed as the stars and meteors continued to reel above the earth.

They turned to face each other and Wren spoke first. "Thank you for bringing me up here. This is wonderful." She laid her hand against his chest.

Peter covered her hand with his and brought it to his lips to kiss it. "I guess we should head back."

"Not yet," Wren said. She wrapped her arm around his waist and scooted close to him. He felt her warm breath against his neck. Her lips moved across his skin with gentle ghost kisses. He ran his hand up her back and rested his fingers on the nape of her neck. She trembled and he waited for her to pull away, but she didn't.

Peter tilted her head to look in her eyes. They were clear. "You want this?"

She nodded. "I want this."

He kissed her. First a light kiss on her brow . . . then two more on the blue skin beneath her eyes . . . then a tender kiss on her lips. She responded.

They twisted into a knot. Tight. Loose. Tight again.

And the stars tumbled above them.

~~~

Dawn. The horizon erupted and spat out the sun. Clouds piled high in the sky like heaps of ash. Thunder rumbled and Peter stirred when it bounced off the mountains. He lifted his head and looked around the meadow. A ragged breeze swept the grass back and forth.

He looked at Wren, asleep next to him. She had pulled the blanket over her bare skin and curled up like a cat. He leaned over and kissed her shoulder. "Hey," he whispered. "Wake up, Sleeping Beauty."

She twitched, but her breathing remained steady. He pulled the blanket down and stared at her. Her fair skin was smooth, her bones delicate. He ran his forefinger down the line of her hip and tickled the angel tattoo. It's like a punctuation mark. One part of your life ended with that tattoo. It's the period on the sentence of your innocence. Peter shook his head and muttered, "You're getting deep now."

He sat up and stretched. Staring into the distance, he saw lightning crack the sky. Without looking away, he reached out and shook Wren. "Wake up, sweetheart."

She sighed and rolled over on her back. "What's wrong?"

"We slept through the night. There's a storm coming." He pointed to the hostile clouds. "We better go."

The wind picked up as they pulled on their clothes. The rain came fast and fat drops pelted them before they reached the truck. They sat in the cab, hair clinging to their skulls, rain dripping from the tips of their noses, and watched the storm drape sheets of grey across the line of mountains. The truck rocked a bit with each gust of wind.

"I guess we'll stay here for a while. Maybe it'll ease off." Peter wiped the back of his arm across his wet face.

"We look like two drowned rats." Wren laughed and pulled her hands through her sodden curls.

"You don't look too ratty to me." Peter slid across the seat and kissed her. "Last night--" he stopped, unsure how to express himself.

"I'll remember it forever," Wren said.

Peter's stomach flip-flopped. Her words rang with such a tone of resignation that he had to pull away to read her face. "Why do you say it that way?"

"When we get back to the apartment, I'm leaving." She stared out the windshield, though nothing was visible but leaden rain.

"What are you talking about? I thought--"

"Thought what?"

"Last night was a beginning for us. You can't leave now."

She turned to him then and he recognized the look on her face: despair had returned. She dropped her eyes and sighed. "Last night wasn't the beginning. It was the end."

"The end? Wren, this isn't a story. You can't just say 'the end' and shut the book on me!" His voice rose in jagged peaks.

A single tear trickled down Wren's cheek and ran into the corner of her mouth. She licked it with a quick flick of her tongue. Peter wanted to grab her then and kiss her hard. Instead, he clenched the steering wheel.

"I'm doing this for you, Peter. Leaving hurts both of us, but staying'll hurt you worse in the long run."

"What're you talking about?" He didn't wait for her answer. He seized her hand and held it over his heart. "This belongs to you. I love you, Wren!"

She freed her hand from his and shook her head. "Don't say that!"

"Why? I feel it. I mean it. I love you."

"I can't love you." She sounded as if she were trying to convince herself. "You can't love me. I'm not worth it."

"Don't say that. Whatever's happened--"

"If you really knew me, you'd hate me, Peter!"

"I could never hate you."

"You'd change your mind if you knew. I've done things."

"What?"

"I can't tell you. Please, just believe me."

Peter grabbed Wren's shoulders. "Whatever it is, it doesn't matter. I love you!"

Wren searched his face until her green eyes found what she wanted to see. She placed her hand back over his heart before she spoke.

"I killed a man."

Eight

Richmond/Charlottesville, 1988-1991

A man stared at Wren as she trudged past the washers and
dryers to the pay phone. He placed one wrinkled black
finger in his book to mark his place and watched her feed
quarters into the silver slot. She tried to ignore him as she
jabbed the buttons on the phone. Waiting for Thomas to
answer, she surveyed the room. The old man eyed her with
suspicion and nudged his empty basket under his seat.

"Hello?"

"It's me, Thomas."

"Don't ever leave me hanging like that! I've been going
out of my mind! Are you okay?"

She ran her fingertips down the metal cord and looked
across the room at the old man. He opened his book and
pretended to read. "Yes, I guess."

"Where are you?"

"Is it safe for us to discuss it?"

"Yeah."

"I'm in Richmond."

"Are you in a motel?"

"Not yet. I'm at a pay phone. What am I going to do,
Thomas?" Her voice rose above the hum of the machines.
The old man looked up from his book; his gaze narrowed.

"Get a room somewhere and sit tight. You didn't tell Gordon or anyone else you were leaving, right?"

Wren rubbed her palm against her chin, then up her face to her eyes. She turned her face to the wall. "No. And I feel really bad about leaving Gordon high and dry. He was good to me."

A dryer seemed to say *tsk-tsk* as it shut off and cooled. The old man pulled clothes from its dark belly and folded them with particular care.

"Well, that can't be helped. Like I said, the best thing now is to find a room, wait a few days, and see what happens."

"I can't go back to Virginia Beach now, Thomas. I'll never feel safe now that he knows I was there. He was a cop. He's going to find me."

He sighed into the phone. "He won't find you. You can start all over in Richmond. We'll help you."

They made arrangements for Wren to call again after she found lodging. She hung up and left the laundry. The sky was steel and the clouds were iron. Rain glazed the parking lot.

Walking on legs as shaky as a foal's, she trained her eyes on the space in front of her feet. Dirty water splashed her ankles and streamed into her shoes. Ugh. She quickened her pace, cringing at the *clop-squelch* of her footsteps.

She stopped at a crosswalk and watched cars roll through the city. A city bus roared by and its black fumes stung her eyes. A sign on the back of the bus encouraged her to "Have a Merry Christmas!" Wren laughed, then she looked back to see if anyone had heard her jittery bird song. The sidewalk was empty.

She looked to the pedestrian signal for guidance, but its message was ambivalent: Walk. Don't Walk. Walk. Don't Walk. Wren plodded through a rainbow in the oily street until she saw a motel with a vacancy sign. She hurried down the block and secured a room for the night.

In the room, Wren kicked off her wet shoes and peeled away her socks. She checked in with Thomas, then abandoned the rest of her clothes and dropped into bed. She pulled a comforter over her head and straightaway fell asleep. She slept through the night without waking.

~~~

That weekend Wren found a job as a server at a gourmet coffee shop in the mall. She also worked extra hours wrapping gifts at the anchor department stores. Desperate store managers asked few background questions with Christmas shopping season in full swing. She added her wages to the money Thomas wired her.

Thomas wanted to come to Richmond, but Wren was afraid Don would follow him. Bailey and Miller had driven by his house several times the week after he broke into Thomas's apartment and they couldn't see any evidence that he was home. "I think he probably did go to Virginia Beach," Thomas told her.

"If he ever finds me--"

"He won't. We'll be more careful this time."

They decided she should change hotels each week until they were sure Don had lost her trail.

~~~

In January, she leased a cheap efficiency apartment. She was happy to have a bed to call her own for more than a week. She felt safe behind the apartment's locked doors and windows, even if it was cramped. It was dreary, though, and she found herself growing depressed staring at her surroundings. After a few weeks inside its shabby walls, she decided to banish the gloom.

One weekend, she painted the walls purple. While the paint dried, she walked to a nearby craft store and bought the items she needed to finish the job. Back in the apartment, she dumped her purchases onto the bed, grabbed a cellophane-wrapped sheet of cardboard, and unwrapped it with her fingers and teeth. She spit cellophane onto the floor and peeled a sticker from the cardboard. She climbed on a chair, grimacing when it wobbled. She pressed the sticker onto the ceiling, and then repeated this action several times. By the time she emptied the cards, night had fallen.

Wren clicked off the lights in the apartment. Her eyes took a few seconds to adjust to the darkness. When they did, luminous spots appeared on the ceiling. She collapsed on the bed and stared up at the counterfeit stars.

~~~

In February, she saw a bus ad for Healing House. It advertised itself as a therapeutic recreation and residential facility for abused women and children. She walked by the house several times during the next few months. One May morning she found herself standing outside Healing House, contemplating a visit.

Healing House was based in a restored antebellum mansion. Crepe myrtles and dogwoods lined its clipped yard and a large bed of tea roses grew in a plot inside the circular driveway. Wren walked several times around the drive, but finally decided to leave. She was headed for the street when a woman called to her from between two marble columns on the porch.

"Hellooo!" She waved to Wren, indicating she should come to the porch.

Great. Too late now. She shuffled to the porch and stood with one foot on the bottom marble step. She greeted the woman with a shy "Hello."

"Hi, I'm Felicia. You looking for someone?" The woman had long blonde hair with dark roots. She wore jeans and a plaid shirt, but her feet were bare. Her toes curled around the rung of the white rocking chair she occupied.

"Uhm, no. I was just admiring the flowers. Sorry if I was trespassing." Wren turned to leave and the woman jumped up.

"Don't go. Do you want to come inside?"

Wren smiled. "No thanks."

"Don't be scared."

Wren crossed her arms and shook her head. Felicia walked down the steps, feet slapping against the marble. "You look thirsty. Come inside and I'll pour you a glass of sweet tea."

It was a simple introduction to Healing House. Inside, Wren found women and children participating in therapy groups, learning skills, playing games, and doing chores. Some of them lived at the house, others visited on day trips. They all greeted Felicia with enthusiasm and respect; later Wren learned that Felicia was the founder and owner of the facility.

~~~

In July, Wren told Felicia about the rape, but she didn't share any other personal information with her. She refused Felicia's suggestion that she should join a therapy group, but she returned to Healing House day after day to watch the activities. The children gravitated to her and she sat in the floor with them and drew pictures.

One day she was surprised to find an infant thrust into her arms by a teenage mother who had a therapy session. Wren took a deep breath and looked down at the baby in her arms. His skin was red, his eyes scrunched tight. He wiggled and plunged his fists into the air. She took his little hand in hers and examined his fingers. His tiny fingernails amazed her.

He bleated and kicked, so Wren gave him a tentative rock. He didn't seem bothered by it, so she continued the gentle motion. She was pleased when he stopped wiggling and opened his eyes to stare at her. "Hi there," she said, and then looked around to see if anyone had heard. Felicia smiled at her from across the room and she blushed. She bowed her head and whispered to him again.

She rocked him until he fell asleep. Felicia sat down next to her and pulled the blanket down to look at the baby.

"You'll make a good little mother one of these days."

Wren burst into tears. She told the woman about her miscarriage. "I wished that baby away," she cried.

"Sweetheart, if babies could be wished away, the world would be a lot less populated than it is now." Felicia put her arms around Wren and rocked her and the baby.

~~~

Wren joined Healing House's therapeutic painting group and surprised the instructor with the maturity of her work. In November, Felicia offered Wren a job teaching art to the children. The wage was more per hour than she earned as a waitress. She accepted the position and dropped her job at the mall.

Facing another lonely Christmas, Wren threw herself into art projects for the children at Healing House. They worked on pictures of Santa, reindeer, angels, and nativity scenes, though Wren hardly felt the holiday spirit. She spent every night getting drunk.

One evening, a few days before Christmas, she rushed along the sidewalk below whirling doves and dirty pigeons. The afternoon traffic had chased its shadow home long ago. The street's neon absorbed the dusk and the unnatural colors of decorations hurt her eyes. Hysterical children voiced their demands for all the shoppers to hear, making her head throb.

In the grocery, her rubber band mouth stretched and snapped back, and she thought the cashier flinched at her effort to smile. Wren cringed at the Christmas music blaring from the store's speakers. She wanted to scream. A person would have to be a hermit to escape this crap, she thought, although she knew that wasn't true. She was practically a hermit now.

Wren arrived home after seven. The apartment was still in disarray from the previous night. She'd been too drunk to wash the dishes or decorate the Christmas tree she'd bought on an impulse.

She stared in disgust at the half-decorated tree. Sighing, she turned on the television and watched a Christmas cartoon. Maybe my heart's three sizes too small, she thought. She clicked the show off in mid-story.

She retrieved a bottle of Jack Daniels and a glass from the kitchen and returned to the living room. Plopping down on the carpet, she leaned against the couch and poured the golden liquid into her glass. She didn't drink it right away. Instead she stared at the tree.

She hadn't celebrated Christmas since she'd run away from Bristol. No reason to start now. Holidays are for families. Wren laid her head down on the coffee table and sobbed. She allowed herself a few minutes of self-pity and then she sat up, blew her nose, and swallowed some whiskey.

She poured another glass. She liked the taste of Jack more than that of beer. She finished half the bottle by midnight. Stumbling to the Christmas tree, she tried to jerk down the tinsel. The tree came with it.

Wren stared at the pitiful tree lying on its side. She kicked it and pine needles dropped into the carpet. The evergreen smell grew thick and Wren felt sick. She ran to the bathroom and vomited.

She fell asleep in the bathroom with her hand hanging in the toilet and awoke late the next day with a hideous hangover. She crept around the apartment for hours and when she felt better, she stripped the tree of its tinsel and dragged it down to the alley dumpster.

She returned to the apartment and packed the lights and shiny globes in a cardboard box. A silver star -- the tree topper -- lay on a bookshelf. Wren grabbed it, prepared to stuff it into the bulging box, but she couldn't bring herself to do it. She placed the star back on the bookshelf and carried the box of decorations to the door.

When she started down the stairs, she saw Thomas. He had dragged her Christmas tree to the bottom of the steps and propped it against the banister. "Need some help decorating your tree?"

Wren dropped the decorations and jumped into his arms. "Thomas! Thank God."

"Bailey and Miller are in Pittsburgh for Christmas, so I figured I'd drop in and see how you're doing. You look a little rough around the edges, Sis."

~~~

Thomas stayed through the holidays. Wandering around Richmond on New Year's Eve, they settled into a leather booth at a bar as midnight closed in on them. They watched the ball drop on television and Thomas clanked his mug of beer against Wren's. "Here's to 1990. It's gotta be better than 1989, right?"

"I sure hope so. I think this is the first time I've rung in the New Year with a live human being. That's a good sign, right?"

Thomas cocked his head and frowned. "Do you ever date, Wren?"

She looked over his head and studied the room. Couples or groups of couples populated the bar. They smiled at each other, laughed, touched. She remembered Michael's hands touching her in the dark. Wren dropped her eyes. "No. It's not for me."

Thomas cleared his throat. "I know what happened was bad. I can't even imagine how you feel. But maybe if you tried going out every once in a while, you wouldn't be so lonely. I mean, look at you. Finding a guy shouldn't be a problem."

"I'm the problem, Thomas. The thought of being touched--" She blushed and her fingers crept to her mouth.

He sighed, captured her hands, and pressed her palms against the table. "I'm sorry. I thought maybe working where you do would have helped."

"Let's not talk about it anymore, okay?"

"Okay."

~~~

The only time Wren felt comfortable being touched by strangers was when she attended church. Sometimes she worshipped at the AME Zion church down the street from her apartment. She loved to be enveloped in the hugs of the older ladies, their skin the color and texture of well-worn paper bags. They made her feel safe.

None of the families she had lived with attended church, so she hadn't been to church since her father died. She had missed it. No matter how tired he was, her father got up on Sunday morning ready for church. He was a deacon.

Sitting in the AME Zion sanctuary on Easter, Wren wondered if her old church was the same as she remembered it. It was a white clapboard building, small, without a steeple. It didn't have air conditioning, so on hot summer days the deacons opened the windows. When the tinkling creek and flittering butterflies threatened to distract his sheep, Reverend Sutton preached loud.

She remembered the Sunday she was baptized. They didn't sit on the front row, and Wren was glad, because the preacher spit when he got excited. It was warm in the church and Wren felt sleepy. She scratched the back of her neck, then her knee, then her ear and arm. She rubbed the polished grain of the pew in front of her. She tried sitting ramrod straight, but slumped as the room got hotter. Her father poked her in the ribs and handed her a cardboard fan. It had an advertisement for a funeral home on one side and a picture of Jesus on the other. Wren flapped the fan back and forth in front of her face, but it didn't bring much relief.

After the service, the congregation gathered on the banks of the creek for the baptisms. Wren watched the preacher dunk believers in the deep part of the creek where the water gathered into a pool before it moved on down the mountain. When her turn came, her father held her hand

and escorted her out to the preacher.

Sunlight shimmered on the surface of the creek, and her eyes watered. Around her she could hear voices rising and a melody floating from the earth to the sky. They were singing "Nothing But the Blood."

Reverend Sutton held her hands asked, "Wren, do you believe that Jesus, the son of God, died for your sins?"

Wren thought of her sins. Sometimes she didn't do her chores. One time she and Katie Phillips made fun of Joe Evans for peeing in his pants at school. She had even lied to her father to get out of a whipping. But she thought those things weren't as bad as killing someone or cursing God.

Then she remembered her dad telling her that Jesus hung on the cross for even the littlest sins. She started to cry and nodded her assent to the preacher. "Do you believe He rose from the dead and ascended into heaven?"

Wren didn't know what ascended was, but she believed Jesus was in heaven looking down at her right now. "Yes."

Reverend Sutton nodded to her father, who placed one hand on her back as he continued to grasp her arm. The preacher did the same. "Katherine Rose Johnson, I baptize you in the name of the Father, the Son, and the Holy Ghost." They tipped her back and the cold water closed over her face.

For a second, she panicked. She remembered the night she fell in the creek. Don't let me drown, Daddy! Suddenly she was up again. She shook her head and water droplets glistened like diamonds against her skin. Light-headed, she started to laugh. She heard other people laughing, and some crying, above the singing voices.

She joined the singing as she waded back to the creek bank with her father. "Oh! Precious is the flow that makes me white as snow; No other fount I know, nothing but the blood of Jesus."

Sitting in the AME Zion church more than a decade later, Wren didn't feel white as snow. She hadn't felt pure or clean since that night. I don't think I'll ever feel clean, Jesus.

~~~

In May, Felicia encouraged Wren to finish her high school education. "You don't have too many classes left to get your GED," she said when Wren balked. She accompanied her to a nearby GED office and helped her sign up for classes.

Wren called Thomas when she received her diploma in October. "Congratulations!" Thomas shouted into the phone. "Now you should think about college."

"Oh, Lord. I don't know, Thomas. That's expensive."

"I bet you could get financial aid."

Wren chewed on her thumb and stared at her GED certificate. "I don't think it would be good for me to get into too much paperwork. I've already made more of a paper trail here than I intended."

"You can't spend the rest of your life looking over your shoulder." She heard a voice in the background and Thomas's muffled response.

"Bailey says Happy 21st Birthday. He wants to know if you got the present he sent you."

"I got it yesterday. Tell him I love it." Inside Bailey's brown-paper package, she had discovered a large rock with fossilized ferns imprinted on its surface. "It's heavy! It must have cost a fortune for him to mail it. I set it on my nightstand."

Thomas relayed her message to Bailey. "He's grinning from ear to ear. Check your mail today and you'll find my birthday gift to you."

"Thomas, you shouldn't. But I'll take it! Thank you."

After they hung up, Wren sat on the edge of the bed and examined the rock again. Ferns feathered themselves across much of the rock. She traced the lines with her fingertips, remembering the fossils Mark used to bring her from the strip mine. She sighed.

I wonder if they ever moved back home or if they're still in Northern Virginia. She chewed on her lip for a few seconds before lifting the phone receiver and dialing information. The directory assistance recording offered her four numbers in Manassas.

She dialed the first one with shaking fingers, but it was disconnected. The second number belonged to Tony and Mark, not Toni and Mark. She hung up. She dialed the third number and stared at the rock again while she waited for someone to answer the phone.

"Hello?" The female's voice was mellow, but unmistakably Toni's.

Still, Wren asked, "Is this Toni Hall?"

"Yes. May I help you?"

"Are you Toni and Mark Hall from Wise County?" Wren held her breath.

"Yes. Who is this?"

"Toni! This is Wren!" Her voice quavered.

"Wren? Katherine, the little girl we used to take care of?" Toni's voice rose.

"Yes!"

"Hold on." Wren heard her shout to Mark. "I'm back. Oh my gosh! Wren! I can't believe it. You sound so grown-up. Wait, today's your birthday, isn't it? No wonder you sound grown-up. How are you?"

Wren hesitated. No need to dump on them. What can they do about it now? "I'm fine. I was just thinking about you and Mark. Didn't know I'd actually reach you. Wow. How are you two?"

"We're great. We have a little boy now. He's four." Mark came on the line.

"Wren. It's good to hear from you. Where are you now?"

"Richmond."

"Oh, that close?" Toni laughed. "You should come visit us."

Wren's heart beat hard behind her breast. "Oh, I don't get out of Richmond very often. I just thought I'd try to contact you and see how you were."

When Mark spoke again his voice was low. "We tried to get you back, Wren. After I found a good job, Toni made some calls about adopting you. When we found out you'd already been adopted, we decided it was best not to contact you and shake up things with your new family. I just wanted you to know we really did want you, honey."

Her throat narrowed into a tight channel, its muscles rigid with grief. "Thank you for telling me that, Mark. That means a great deal to me." She squeezed her eyes shut. "Well, I better get off of here. It was good to hear your voices. Goodbye."

Wren sprawled on the bed. Why did I call? Why? Everything would have been completely different if Toni and Mark had adopted me. Angry, she bit her pillow. It sank into itself and she chewed on the cotton pillowcase. She exhaled, pulled the blanket over her head, and cried herself to sleep.

She dreamed of water. It swirled around her feet until they grew numb in its cold depths. A tree limb floated past her and caught her sleeve. She felt herself being lifted and pulled along the current. The tree rolled and Wren rolled with it. Water burned her nose and eyes. She opened her mouth to scream and water filled her throat.

She woke with a choking sound and threw off the blanket. Sweat soaked her clothes and she peeled them away in disgust. She ran to the shower and stood shaking beneath the hot water. Haven't dreamed that in a long time, she thought as rivulets of water slid down her skin.

She stepped out of the shower and shook like a wet dog. Water splattered the bathroom. Wren wiped water from the mirror and stared at herself. Her red hair was slicked back across her skull. The scar was white and shiny against her eyebrow. Steam crept across the glass and her image disappeared.

She drew a circle with two dots for eyes and a bow for

a mouth. The face frowned at her. She sighed and added two marks to the corners of the mouth. The frowny face morphed into a smiley face. She erased the entire face with her fist and finished drying off in the other room.

~~~

Thomas called her on Valentine's Day. "How's my number one sweetheart?"

"You mean Miss Lonely-hearts? I'm fine. What's up?"

"Wanted to let you know I'm going to be out of town, out of the country, actually, for a while. Bailey, Miller, and I are going to Japan."

"Oh, wow. How come?"

"We're going to study with some Japanese tattoo artists. I'm really psyched about it."

"That's great." She hoped she sounded more excited than she felt. You'll be halfway around the world, Thomas. "How long will you be gone?"

"We're leaving tomorrow morning and won't be back until June. Excuse me." He sneezed. "Got a pen and paper?"

She took down his contact information in Japan and stuck it on the refrigerator. "Four months is a long time. Can you guys afford to take so much time off work?"

"It'll be worth it in the long run. Miller's been talking about moving the business or revamping the shop, anyway. This will give him time to think about what he wants to do."

Wren sighed. "Are you sure this is such a good time to go? I mean, with all the stuff happening over there in Iraq and Kuwait, I'll be worried to death about you."

"We'll be fine. Don't worry."

"I'll miss you, Thomas. Will you call me?"

"Soon as we get settled in to our new digs. In the meantime, be careful and keep my number handy. I love you, Wren."

"I love you, too, brother."

~~~

She tried not to listen to her coworkers discussing Operation Desert Storm. For a week she avoided the news; the images of SCUD missiles and exploding bunkers set her teeth on edge. By the weekend, she was climbing the walls. She decided to wash clothes to calm her nerves, so she gathered her dirty clothes and walked across the street to a coin-operated laundry.

She leaned back in a hard plastic chair, folded her arms, and let her chin drop. She inhaled the air, bleached clean and perfumed with fabric softener. The soft whisk of the dryers relaxed her and she allowed herself to float in a state of half-sleep. Cold fingers prevented her from sinking deeper; they gripped her shoulder. She jerked upright and discovered a young girl shaking her. "I think your clothes are finished."

Wren shook off sleep and folded her clothes into a wicker basket. Returning to the apartment, she noticed the ripe odor of the garbage. She dropped the basket next to the couch, gathered the trash, and carried it down to the alley dumpster. She walked back up to her apartment, locked the door behind her, and reached down to grab the laundry. A furtive movement caught her eye and she froze. Don stood in the bathroom doorway.

His thick grey hair was slicked back in a ponytail. He wore crisp blue jeans, a grey shirt, and steel-toed boots. He clutched a box cutter in his right hand and a revolver in his left. He smiled briars and thorns.

Her palms grew slick with sweat and her legs felt as sturdy as cooked spaghetti. Bile rose in the back of her throat and she shoved her fist against her mouth. She heard a child crying and looked around the apartment before she realized she was hearing her own sobs.

"Hello, little girl. You've given me quite a chase, you know that? I don't appreciate all the trouble you've caused me." He entered the living room favoring his right leg.

He stepped into the lamplight. One of his blue eyes was

now milky. He turned his face so she could see it. "Thomas's got quite a temper when it comes to you."

Her chest contracted as she stumbled backwards to the door. Don slammed her against the door before she could get it open. He held the box cutter to her throat. "You and me, we've got a lot of catching up to do."

Wren shut her eyes tight and tears streamed down her face. He kissed her earlobe and she expelled loud hitching sobs. He ran the gun down her side and used it to pull her waistband away from her skin. "You're more beautiful than ever, Wren. I've been wanting to see that angel again. Yeah."

Don dragged her across the room and threw her on the bed. She kicked out at him but he wouldn't let go. He dropped the gun on the floor, but the box cutter still flashed in his hand. She twisted away from him, but he yanked her down on the mattress and pushed her onto her stomach.

"Thomas should've killed me. After I'm done with you, he's next."

When Don tried to pull his pants down, Wren panicked. Not again! She turned over and pushed him in the chest. He fell back, slashing the air in front of her face with the box cutter. She scooted backwards on the bed to get away from him, but he fell upon her and pressed his hand against her neck.

Her vision began to darken at the edges as he writhed on top of her. For one crazy moment she thought him a fat spider with a pale sack of bitter poison. She would have screamed then, but she couldn't breathe.

Don couldn't hold her and the box cutter and get his pants down, so he let go of her neck to unzip. Her arms flopped across the bed and she banged her knuckles against the nightstand. Her hand rested on the rock Bailey had sent her. Without thinking, she lifted it. When she grunted with its weight, Don looked up. "What do you--"

Wren smashed it into his temple with all her strength. It hit his skull with a thunk that made her sick. Without a sound, he fell over in a heap, one hand in his pants. Blood spurted in ropy jets from the side of his head. He twitched, then lay still.

She grabbed the nightstand and pulled herself to her feet. Black specks floated before her eyes, looking very much like blackbirds or crows. A murder of crows. She expelled a jagged laugh and lurched toward Don, wary of the box cutter still clenched in his fist; he remained still.

Wren stared down at him. She nudged him with the tip of her shoe, but he didn't move. Dead! Oh, God. I didn't mean to kill him. Blood tatted crimson lace across his face. She leaned down and touched his neck; it was sticky. She rubbed the blood from her hands onto her shirt.

She staggered to the bathroom. Sobbing, she peeled off her clothes and climbed into the shower. The hot water washed away the blood. Wren dropped to her knees and jammed her fingers into her mouth to crush the fluttering black wings of a scream. She leaned her head on the faucet and let the hot spray of water beat against her back. Eventually its steady stream soothed her into a stupor. When the hot water turned cold, she turned it off and stepped out of the tub.

She peered into the other room. Don remained where she'd left him. She edged her way around his body and pulled clean clothes from her dresser. White for purity, she thought, as she pulled on a plain white T-shirt and jeans. She giggled and mashed her mouth with her fists. She covered the bruises on her neck and wrists with the leather cords Thomas had given her so long ago. Grabbing all the cash she had on hand, she stuffed it in her purse and ran to the door.

She turned and looked back into her apartment. Don's blood had darkened into a black mask. He looked like a monster. Wren slammed the door and ran down the stairs.

~~~

She hitchhiked her way out of Richmond on a potato chip

delivery truck. She cringed each time news reports came on the radio and ducked her head when they passed state troopers. The driver dropped her off on Interstate 64 near Charlottesville, telling her she made him nervous. "I'm sorry, miss, but you seem like you're in trouble and I don't need any."

She walked along I-64, hugging her bare arms, willing her feet to move even after she lost sensation in them. A driver in an SUV stopped and gave her a lift to Route 250. From there Wren wandered down into Charlottesville, at the fringe of the city. She thought she might be on the verge of freezing to death when she saw the bar.

Inside, she walked to a pay phone in the corner and picked up the receiver. Then she realized she had left Thomas's contact number on the refrigerator. Great! I can't go back now. She pictured Don's body stiffening in the dark apartment. Wren shivered and let the phone fall back into its cradle. I'm all alone. And now I'm a murderer. I can't do this to Thomas anymore. I've caused him enough grief. I've got to take care of this myself.

She shuffled across the room and perched on a barstool. The room vibrated with music and voices. Bodies crowded around her and she felt her muscles go slack in the heat. She stared at the silent television, wondering if Don's murder would make the news beyond Richmond.

She ordered a shot of whiskey and drank it in one big gulp. It threatened to come back up and she swallowed hard to keep it down. She tipped the glass toward the bartender and he filled it again. Wren drank it without looking away from the television, where images of war filled the screen. But all she saw was the dead man.

What am I going to do?

Two voices began to pierce the shroud of her dark reverie. The young men on either side of her were speaking across her and to her. She didn't know how long they had been talking, but they battered her with suggestions of what she could do for them in bed. She watched the television, trying to ignore them, but her vacant stare had no effect on their efforts.

She heard another man speak. "I'm getting a little tired of that name." His voice jerked her across the years, across the state, into the coalfields. Hearing her mountains in his words, she turned to stare at the source of the voice.

He was tall, lean, and hard. His hair, black and shiny as crow feathers, fell well below the collar of his leather jacket. His eyes reminded her of dark chocolate, melting, bittersweet. He spoke again and his voice made her homesick. "Now come on, give her a break."

Waves of desire, for him and for home, swept across her, and it made her feel tired and dirty. Home. I don't have a home. All I have is blood. Blood and death and filth. Dirty. Dirty. Dirty. Fear and despair enveloped her then and she turned back to the television.

The young man next to her touched her knee and she cringed. All three men stood and she realized they would fight. When they crashed onto the floor, Wren jumped up, threw some money on the bar, and fled into the cold night.

She ran down the road and stepped onto a bridge that spanned a black river. She walked to the halfway point of the bridge and leaned over the side to stare at the turbid water. It was hypnotic.

Wren remembered the way the water had felt the night she fell in the flooding creek. It had carried her away and covered her until the world grew dim and distant. That seemed a good thing to her now, to be far away from the world. She climbed up on the bridge and pivoted so that her legs hung over the side.

She let her purse dangle between her legs a moment, then dropped it and watched it disappear beneath the current. That was easy, she thought. She looked up at the sky, at the stars. They're not really angels.

A truck crossed the bridge and ran into the side of it.

Someone climbed out of it and, falling, cursed. Wren turned and saw the young man from the bar. He froze, staring at her with eyes as black as the river below. "You okay?"

She looked back to the heavens, confused now. He spoke again, naming the stars, and her heart did a jig. She lifted her arm to the sky and spoke without knowing what she said.

The boy was closer now, within arm's reach. His face was ghoulish in the streetlight. It was swollen along his jaw line and she saw handprints on his neck. She touched her own throat.

Did Daddy send you? She laughed and tried to grab a star, but it disappeared. Wren cried and fell forward into the welcome depths of dark water.

Nine

Charlottesville/Southwest Virginia, May 1991

Dark water trickled down the windshield like teardrops. The rain had stopped but a grey mist covered the meadow. Peter couldn't even see the spot where they had made love hours ago. "Why didn't you call the police?"

Wren laughed. "And tell them what? I bashed in the skull of a retired police officer? A decorated policeman! Anyway, I wasn't thinking straight. I just did what I've always done when I get scared. I ran."

A dull ache set up behind Peter's eyes. He propped his elbows on the steering wheel and rubbed his thumbs along his eyebrows. Now what? What are we going to do? Something. Something. Have to do something. I need to talk to Dad. He'll know what to do.

"Peter."

"What?"

"What are you thinking?"

"I'm trying to figure out what to do."

Wren touched his ear, caressing the lobe between her thumb and forefinger. "Well, stop. It's not your problem. I shouldn't have told you, but I wanted you to understand. I should have left a long time ago, but I started feeling--"

"What?"

"Nothing." She rolled down the window and mist drifted into the cab. "Wow. We'll never get out of this."

"Yes, we will. I'll call my dad. He'll help us figure something out."

"I meant the fog, Peter." She chewed on the edge of her thumb before she continued. "You can't tell your parents. I mean, they don't even know I've been living with you for the past three months. What are you gonna tell them? I'd like you to meet my girl. Oh, by the way, she's a murderer!"

Peter grabbed her by the shoulders and shook her. "Don't say that! What happened wasn't your fault. You're not a murderer! It was self-defense. The police will understand." He ran his hands down her arms and gripped her fingers. "But you have to tell them."

Wren pulled her hands from his and covered her mouth with two fists. She bowed her head. Peter leaned back against the seat and closed his eyes. The dull ache turned into a painful throb.

They sat in silence as tendrils of mist curled around them. With his eyes still closed, Peter reached out and turned the key in the ignition. The sound of the engine fell flat against the insulating fog. He sat up and wiped film from the inside of the windshield. Without looking at her, he pulled onto the road and directed the truck toward Charlottesville.

~~~

Peter sat at the kitchen table rolling a saltshaker between his palms. He looked toward the bedroom and shook his head. How long is she going to sleep? She had crashed on the couch as soon as they returned from Skyline Drive. Once she was asleep, Peter carried her to the bedroom and deposited her in his bed. That had been nine hours ago.

He dropped the saltshaker on the table and padded to the bedroom door. He stared at the door panels as if he might find a solution inlaid in the wood. Nothing but splinters.

Sighing, he returned to the kitchen and drew a glass of water. He looked up at the cabinet. Within its dark confines, an unopened bottle of Maker's Mark rested behind cans of chicken soup and boxes of macaroni. Peter pushed his tongue against the roof of his mouth and the desire for a drink out of his mind. He swallowed a sip of water and set the glass down on the sink. He studied the floor, rubbing his bare foot against the dimpled linoleum. Muttering a string of curses, he went to the bedroom and flung open the door.

"Wren." Peter pulled the blanket away from her face and rested his forefinger beneath her chin. When she didn't respond, he tipped her face up to his. "Wake up."

She pushed his hand away and tugged at the blanket. "Go away," she mumbled.

"Come on. Get up." He yanked the covers down, releasing warm air tinged with the scent of vanilla. Wren covered her face with her hands and curled up in a fetal position. Peter pulled at her shoulder till she was lying on her back. "Hey!"

"Leave me alone."

"Wren, damn it, if you don't get up, I'll drag you out of this bed!"

She didn't answer him. Anger clenched his chest, so he slid off the bed and grabbed her ankles. She kicked the air, but he didn't let go. Instead, he jerked her off the bed and she landed on the carpet on her butt. *Thump*!

Peter dropped down on top of her before she could crawl away and pinned her arms to the floor. Strangled sobs escaped her chest. He hated himself then, but he didn't know what else to do.

"Sleeping is just another form of running away," he hissed. "I want you to get up so we can figure this thing out."

He felt her body go limp. She stared at a spot on the ceiling. He blocked her view with his face, forcing her to look at him. "I'm sorry. I don't want to hurt you. Believe me, that's the last thing I want to do. I love you."

Tears streamed down her face. "If you loved me, you'd leave me alone."

Peter closed his eyes and rolled off Wren. "Go wash your face and pull yourself together."

He stayed on the floor while she was in the bathroom. His headache returned and he pressed his knuckles against his temple. *Running away is looking better and better. I could do it myself right now.* He sat up, leaned against the bed, and listened to the running water.

You're in your own little world and I'm just orbiting it. Somehow I got sucked in by its gravitational pull. Why am I bothering with you anyway? I'm not getting anything in return. You've never said you loved me. Maybe I'm wasting my time trying to help you. When she emerged from the bathroom, he started. He couldn't look at her, afraid she might be able to read his thoughts in his face.

He stood, took her hand in his, and led her out of the bedroom. Peter sat in the armchair and pulled Wren down onto his lap. He wrapped his arms around her, half afraid she would scream. Instead, she leaned her head against his chest. His throat constricted and he wondered how he could have ever thought of abandoning her.

He placed his mouth against her hair and spoke. "I've been thinking," Peter said. "We should go to the police. You can explain you didn't mean to – to kill him. He would have killed you after he was done with you. You were just defending yourself."

She trembled and he pulled her tighter against his body. She looked up at him, her green eyes wide with fright. "I can't."

Peter rocked Wren as if she were a baby. "I'll help you. It'll be okay." *But will it really?*

~~~

A Charlottesville police investigator sat at a table in a large grey room with Peter and Wren. He pushed his bifocals to the tip of his nose and reread his scribbled notes. "I'm going to contact the Richmond authorities to confirm your statement, Miss Johnson. This may take a while. I'll have someone bring you something to drink. Excuse me."

Detective Webster pulled on his jacket and left the room. Wren laid her head on her arms. Her eyelids were puffy and her nose was red. Peter scooted close to her and handed her a tissue. She blew her nose, wadded the tissue into a ball, and tossed it into the trash can next to the door. Resting her head again, she rubbed her forehead against her arm.

Peter ran his hand through her hair with gentle strokes. "Look at those curls. My sisters never had a curl on their heads. Always hollering for perms." He wound an auburn strand around his finger and rubbed it with his thumb. "There was a little girl who had a little curl. When she was good, she was very good. And when she was bad--"

"She was horrid," Wren finished. She lifted her head and half-smiled at Peter. "My daddy used to tell me that when he brushed my hair." She burst into tears again.

A uniformed police officer stepped into the room with two sodas. "Detective Webster is still talking to Richmond. He'll be with you as soon as he can."

More than two hours passed before he returned. The officer sat down and crossed his arms. Rubbing his chin with his thumb and forefinger, he studied Wren. Unable to read Detective Webster's expression, Peter's heart sank. "What's going on?"

"Miss Johnson. Or Miss Palmer. That's your adopted name, I guess." He rested his chin in the palm of his hand. "Have you ever received treatment in a mental health facility?"

Frowning, Wren looked from Webster to Peter and shook her head. "I don't understand."

"Don Palmer is not deceased."

"What?"

"According to the Richmond authorities, Mr. Palmer reported you missing back in February."

Peter leaned on the table. "What are you talking about?"

The detective cocked his head at Wren. "A neighbor discovered your father crawling down the steps from your apartment back in February. He was covered in blood, so she dialed 911. At the hospital, he told the police that you were a runaway and that he had been tracking you. He said when he finally found you, that you assaulted him with a rock."

"Assaulted him?" Peter's voice rose. "Didn't you listen to what she told you? The man raped her once before and tried to do it again in February! She's the one who was assaulted!"

Detective Webster's mouth turned down at the corners. "Son, are you sure you can be objective about this? You weren't there, were you? What do you really know about this girl?"

"I know enough to know she's telling you the truth! You're going to take his word over hers?"

"The Richmond police checked Mr. Palmer's background. His record is completely clean. He's a decorated police officer who retired from the Detroit police force." Webster shrugged and cut his eyes to Wren. "According to Mr. Palmer, his daughter has some mental health problems."

Peter's skin itched, but he didn't look down at the faint scratches on his arms. He focused on the wall behind Detective Webster and remembered the night Wren had scratched him. There's a crazy woman in my apartment, he had thought.

Wren mashed the pop can between her hands, twisting her wrists back and forth. Aluminum gleamed beneath the fluorescent lights and Peter's eyes watered at the sight. He rested his knuckles against hers to still her hands.

"Mr. Palmer didn't want to press charges against her. He just wanted to make sure she was found. Katherine, if your father really assaulted you, why didn't you report it?"

She didn't look at him as she answered. "He said he would kill my brother. And he was a cop. I didn't think the police would believe me. And I was right!" Her tears splattered on the table.

"Why don't you ask her brother?" Peter suggested.

"I believe the Richmond police did try to contact him in Japan, but he wouldn't speak to them about Mr. Palmer. At any rate, I'm not sure that Thomas Palmer is credible. After all, he served time for assaulting his father. There seems to be a family pattern here."

Wren jumped to her feet. "He was defending me! I need to talk to Thomas! Is he back in the country?"

"Calm down, Miss Palmer." Webster held his palms up to Wren. "We're going to contact your father and your brother and try to get this straightened out."

"No!" Wren grabbed the policeman's arm. "You can't tell Don I'm here. Please! You don't know what you're doing. He'll kill me!"

Detective Webster removed Wren's fingers from his sleeve. "Excuse me, I'm going to call Richmond again and see what they want us to do with you. I think they'll want to call Mr. Palmer in and question him about the alleged rape. You two just sit tight." He left the room.

Wren knelt before Peter. "We have to leave. Now!"

Peter rubbed his forehead. "Wait. I need to think."

"Peter, we don't have time for you to think. You heard what that man said. When Don finds out where I am, he'll be here."

Peter squeezed his eyes shut and shook his head. "Wren--"

She pulled his face to hers and kissed him. Her eyes brimmed with salt and misery. "You promised me, Peter. You promised you'd help me. You said you loved me."

And God help me. He nodded. "Okay."

~~~

They sneaked out of the police station without any trouble. Curled up in the corner of the truck, Wren leaned her head against the window and stared at traffic. Peter rested his hand on her leg, but she didn't speak. She didn't move to get out of the truck when he pulled into the parking lot. He opened the door and lifted her from the cab. "Come on."

They sat at the kitchen table in silence. Staring at nothing, Wren folded and unfolded a dish towel on the table. Peter had to restrain himself from snatching it out of her hands. Finally, she laid it aside and looked up at him. "I need a drink."

He jumped up, pulled the bourbon from the cabinet, and poured drinks for both of them. Wren sipped hers while he gulped his. She refilled his glass and leveled her own. "That police investigator will probably be knocking on the door before the night's over."

"He doesn't have my address."

"No, but he knows your name and that you're a student. It won't take long for him to find us." Wren filled his glass a third time. She swished some Maker's Mark around in her mouth and swallowed it with a cough. Her lips stretched into a grotesque smile.

Your face is going to freeze that way. When he was a child that was the warning Peter's mother had given him every time he made a face at someone. He looked away from Wren when he spoke. "I love you." Tell me you love me.

"Well, you're dumber than a coal bucket, then." Wren pulled her fists up and pounded her chest. "There's nothing here worth loving. Don't waste it on me."

He pulled at one of her ginger curls. "You remember what I told you? There are fires banked down in you. They're in me, too. We burn together."

Wren shook her head and stared at a point behind him.

171

He tried to nurse the third drink, but found himself staring into the bottom of the glass sooner than he intended. He rolled the glass in the palm of his hand, but didn't reach for the bottle. Wren sighed and poured him another drink. He was embarrassed to feel grateful. Slow it down, Pete. This isn't going to help.

She grabbed the bottle and her glass and tottered into the bedroom. Peter followed and found her stretched out across the mattress. He reclined next to her, spilling some of his drink on the bedspread. "Oops."

She rolled onto her back and rested the glass on her stomach. Peter stroked her cheek. Her teardrops ran between his fingers and he licked the salt from his knuckles. He chased it with the rest of his drink. Wren handed him her bourbon. He finished it and let the glass drop onto the carpet. The clunk sounded funny to him and he tittered.

She scooted close to him and wrapped her arms around his waist. She ran her hands up his shirt and rubbed his back. The steady rhythm of the massage and the soporific liquor mesmerized him and he sighed. I've got to close my eyes for a second, he mouthed, unable to speak aloud. He felt himself sink into downy sleep.

~~~

When Peter woke up, his tongue felt like a woolly worm. He smacked his mouth and sat up clutching his head. His blood pulsed with each ring of the phone. Shit.

Ignoring the phone, he climbed off the bed and crept into the living room. The answering machine picked up the call and he heard Detective Webster's voice, although what he said didn't pierce the fog of his hangover. He squinted at the window and saw morning lighten the parking lot by slow degrees.

Wren wasn't in the kitchen. Peter went to the bathroom door and called to her. When she didn't reply, he stuck his head in the bathroom, but it was empty. He splashed cold water on his face and returned to the living room. The answering machine's light blinked angry red at him and he turned from it. A piece of paper pinned to the apartment door caught his eye. He snatched it down and unfolded it.

Dear Peter,

Please don't be mad at me. I had to get out of town and I couldn't take you with me. I know you're tenderhearted, but please try not to let this hurt you. Don't dwell on it. By the time you wake up, I'll be far away. Don't try to find me.

There's nothing you can do to help me. But I can help you by getting out of your life. As long as Don is hunting me, the people I care about (Thomas and you) are in danger. I can't bear the thought of Don hurting either of you.

Thank you for everything. You can't possibly know what it means to me. Have a good life and find someone worthy of your love.

Wren

"By the time you wake up, I'll be far away." Cursing, Peter wadded the note and threw it across the room. He stood in the middle of the room and pulled his fingers through his hair. He lifted his face to the ceiling and howled. Blood rushed to his head until he felt it might split. Good. I hope it does. Maybe what brains I have will just spill out on the carpet and I'll die.

He kicked the coffee table and it landed on its side with a satisfying crash. He yanked cushions from the couch and tossed them across the room, but the swish was disappointing. He stomped into the kitchen and pulled pots and pans from the cabinets. A volley of tinny bangs made him feel better. He was throwing dishes against the refrigerator when Detective Webster rushed into the apartment.

He jerked a plate from Peter's hands. "What the hell are

you doing?"

Peter sagged against the counter and shook his head. "I don't know." He looked at the policeman. "I don't know what I'm doing."

~~~

"Peter! Are you dead in there? Get up!" His mother's voice called to him through his bedroom door, then she banged on it.

"I'm awake. Give me a minute!" He threw back the quilt and sat on the edge of the bed ruffling his hair. Crossing the room, he threw open the curtains and turned his head.

Late morning sun gilded the landscape outside his window and he squinted against its unwavering cheer. Sunshine gobbled limpid dew from the ground. Above green and golden hills, crows called to each other with hoarse delight. Cows moped along well-worn paths, flicking flies with their bottlebrush tails. Metal twinkled in the shimmering distance as impatient cars passed a coal truck struggling up the mountain.

Peter leaned out the window and filled his lungs with fresh air. He had graduated the previous week, and it already seemed a distant memory to him. He had walked down the University's famed lawn in a daze, mortarboard tipped to one side, robe fluttering behind him. While his parents snapped his picture, his mind was on Wren.

Detective Webster had called his home in Wise County. Neither he nor the police had been able to locate Don. He spoke with Peter's parents, but Peter refused to answer their questions about Wren.

He was home a week before he spoke of her. They tried to convey understanding, but Peter knew they were relieved she was gone. He was devastated. He had spent most of the week in bed. Fed up with Peter's dark mood, Ginny had taken to pounding on his bedroom door the past few mornings.

Pull yourself together, he thought as he dressed.

You can't show up for your internship tomorrow in this state. He sighed and trudged downstairs, the old steps squeaking beneath his heavy tread. Bleach hung in the air and he followed its scent to the laundry room. His mother hummed as she folded clothes with efficient industry.

"I was beginning to think you was going to sleep all day. You never used to be this sorry. What's wrong with you?" She didn't look up from her work as she spoke.

Peter crossed his arms and rubbed his chin against his shoulder. "You know what's wrong, Mom."

"Well, enough is enough."

"I love her."

Ginny snorted and plopped a stack of clothes into a plastic basket. "Love? You got a lot of growing up to do yet, Big'un. It's too soon for you to be hitching your wagon to a horse. Especially the wrong horse."

"Wagon? Horse? What--" Peter stuttered. "Look, you always told me to do good for others when I could. I can't think of anybody who needed more good than Wren."

Ginny moved to Peter and seized his shoulders. "I'm proud of you for wanting to help that poor girl, but you just graduated from college. You've got a whole new life waiting for you." She dropped her arms. "Besides, there's nothing else you can do for her. She's gone now."

"But--"

"There you are. I been waiting for you to get up. What time are you leaving to go back?" Peter's father stood in the doorway.

"I'm fixing him a bite to eat," Ginny said. "Meade, will you carry these clothes upstairs for me?" She thrust the basket into his hands before he could respond. He chuckled as he carried them upstairs.

Peter walked out to the porch and leaned back in a rocking chair. I wish I could talk to Matt. He'd understand. He propped his bare foot on the porch post. The wood was rough against his foot and he scrunched his toes against it. He tipped the rocking chair and watched his knee rise and fall as he rocked. The chair sang to him: *Wren – Wren – Wren – Wren.*

Meade joined Peter on the porch. He shifted his cap to scratch his head as he looked across the yard. His hair was the same shiny black mop as Peter's, though shot through with grey. "I know you got a lot on your mind, Peter. There's nothing worse than not being able to help someone you love."

Peter stopped rocking and stared at his father. "Mom thinks I'm stupid."

"She don't think that. She just wants the best for you." Pulling off his cap and twisting it in his hands, Meade propped himself on the porch railing. "I don't know what to tell you, except cherish the time you knew her and move on."

"She's out there alone. Probably hungry. Maybe ready to kill herself again. And if she doesn't, that SOB is looking for her. She'll never be safe as long as he's around."

"Forget it, Peter! Besides, now that y'all told her story to the police, her daddy'll probably leave her alone. You know they'll ask him about what she told them. That'll scare him."

Peter flattened his feet against the warm porch floor. "He needs to be scared. It's too bad she didn't really kill him!"

"Don't talk like that. Come on, now. Let's go see what Ginny's fixed us for lunch."

~~~

Peter packed his clean clothes into the passenger side of his truck and slammed the door. "Well, I guess I'm ready." He hugged his mother and shook Meade's hand.

"Your sisters will be mad that you didn't wait for them to get back from Norton."

Peter laughed. "If I waited for them to finish shopping, I'd still be here tomorrow. Kiss them for me."

"Call us when you get back in Charlottesville," Ginny shouted to him as he pulled away from the house.

~~~

He was in Abingdon in a half hour. He grabbed a pop at a convenience store and sat in the parking lot drinking it. Peter burped as he pulled a scrap of paper from his pocket. He reread Don's address. After wadding the note, he stuck his hand in the middle of the clothes stacked in the laundry basket. He felt oily steel nestled between his shirts.

His father had given him a pistol when he was in high school. Peter had never been a hunter, but he and Matt liked target shooting. Used to be pretty good. He didn't allow the thought to grow beyond that. He shoved the gun deeper into the clothes and pulled out of the parking lot.

Instead of heading north on Interstate 81, Peter took Exit 14 going south toward Bristol. His hands grew clammy against the steering wheel and he rubbed them against his jeans. His heart beat the devil's tattoo until he grew short of breath. He turned on the radio, but the music jarred his nerves so he snapped it off after a couple of minutes.

He drove around Bristol for twenty minutes before he found the right street. Then he cruised past the house three times before he got the nerve to park. Parking several houses away, he slid down in the seat and scrutinized the neighborhood. Not a lot of traffic on a Sunday afternoon. He removed the gun from the laundry and stuck it in the back of his pants. He pulled his shirt down to cover it and got out of the truck.

Peter stood on the sidewalk and stared at the patchwork of concrete, brick, and peeling paint Wren had once called home. It was a two-story house slapped together with spit and a prayer, probably uninviting even when it was new. Garbage lay scattered across the yard like dead swans. A greasy hamburger wrapper blew across the sidewalk and stuck to Peter's shoe. He kicked it away and walked to the front door.

His dry mouth clicked when he swallowed. The gun pressed into the small of his back like a cold tumor. *What are you doing? This is crazy. Just get back in the truck and go on to Charlottesville.* Instead, he punched a worn button next to the door and heard a distant buzz. Next door a dog began to bark. Peter glanced back over his shoulder and saw a dark-skinned boy riding a tricycle down the sidewalk. He turned his face back to the door and hunched his shoulders together.

He thought he heard movement inside and cocked his head to listen. When no one came to the door, he hit the doorbell again. Finally, Peter twisted the doorknob but stepped back in shock when the door opened. He had expected it to be locked.

Cold sweat covered his back, making his shirt stick to his skin. Peter patted the gun before he stepped inside the house. He held his breath when the floor creaked, and then shut the door behind him with a quiet click. He stood in the middle of a dusty, dim living room. The stale air smothered him.

Pop! Peter jumped then froze. The ceiling popped again as someone walked across the floor upstairs. Reaching back to pull out the gun, he crept to the steps. He lifted iron feet and dragged them up the stairs.

A carpeted hallway stretched before him. All the doors along the hall were closed. Except one. It stood halfway open. Peter stopped short when he heard a bedspring creak in that room. Rivulets of sweat ran from his scalp into his eyes. He swiped the back of his arm across his face. The gun jerked in his hand as he padded to the door.

Step through that door and there's no turning back. It's not too late to leave. He thought of Wren curled up on the floor, her fingers jammed in her mouth. *No. I promised I'd take care of you, Wren, and I will.* He pushed opened the door and stepped inside the room.

A dark young man with a blond ponytail, light blue eyes, and myriad tattoos sat on the bed. He aimed a gun at Peter. "Who the hell are you?"

Peter exhaled and dropped his hand so his gun rested against his thigh. His legs melted beneath him and he let himself slither down to the floor. He dropped his gun onto the musty carpet. The young man cocked his gun. "I said who are you?"

"Peter Sullivan."

"Peter Sullivan." The boy rolled the name around his mouth and pondered it. His eyes widened and he lowered his gun. "You're the guy Wren was living with?"

Peter nodded. "You have to be Thomas."

"She told you about me?" He jumped from the bed and crouched in front of Peter. "If you know where she is, you have to tell me."

"I wish I knew, man. I'd give anything to know where she is." He pulled his knees to his chest and wrapped his arms around his legs. "Has she tried to contact you?"

Thomas shook his head. "No."

"When did you get back from Japan?"

"I found out Wren was missing in late February. The police contacted me and told me Don had filed a police report. I've been looking for her ever since." Thomas rose and returned to the bed. "I read the police report you two filed. She said you saved her life and took her in. Why?"

Peter's mouth turned down at the corners. "I don't know. At first it was her voice. Then her eyes. And that vanilla skin." He blushed. "I can't explain it. She made me feel like I was home."

Thomas grinned. "You sound worse than my friend Bailey." He grew somber again. Pointing at Peter's gun, he frowned. "What were you going to do with that?"

Peter looked down at the gun. Against the brown carpet, its wicked sheen disconcerted him. *What was I thinking?* "I don't know. I don't know what I was going to do."

Thomas clicked his tongue. "For a college boy, you don't seem very bright. If you were thinking of doing something stupid, forget it. I'll take it from here. Anyway, I don't think he'll come back here now. He knows I'm waiting for him."

He rose from the bed, offered his hand to Peter, and pulled him to his feet. Peter picked up the gun and stuck it back in his pants. "I wanted to hurt him. Or maybe worse."

The other man nodded. "I understand." He rubbed his watery eyes. They reminded Peter of a Husky's. Thomas peered into Peter's face. "Did you sleep with my sister?"

Peter opened his mouth then let it snap shut for a moment. "I love Wren," he said, finally. "I'm going back to my apartment in Charlottesville today. I'm in the phone book. If Wren contacts you — if you find her, call me. Please." Peter walked into the hall but turned at the top of the stairs. "Tell her I miss her fire. She'll know what I mean."

Thomas leaned against the banister and called to Peter as he walked down the steps. "Thank you for taking care of my sister. For her to have stayed with you for so long, she must have really trusted you. Does she love you?"

Peter paused at the bottom of the stairs without turning around. "She never said she did."

Ten

News Clippings, 1992-2001

February 1992:

Local Architecture Firm Names New Associate

CHARLOTTESVILLE – Peter Sullivan has joined Bryan and Greene Associates as a junior associate.

Sullivan graduated from The University of Virginia with a bachelor's in architecture. A native of St. Paul, Va., Sullivan will specialize in needs-based community design.

Headquartered in Charlottesville, Bryan and Greene Associates is ranked 25th among all U.S. architecture firms and 4th among Virginia firms.

May 1996:

Central Virginia Architects Expand Services to D.C.

WASHINGTON – Charlottesville-based architecture firm Bryan and Greene Associates has opened an office in Washington, D.C.

The company offers services in commercial, residential and community design. Burns Interior Concepts will collaborate with the firm to provide interior design solutions.

June 1997:

Reed, Sullivan Announce Engagement

Christopher and Pauline Reed of Arlington, Va., are pleased to announce the engagement of their daughter, Anastasia Paulina Reed, to Peter Quinlan Sullivan, the son of Meade and Virginia Sullivan of St. Paul.

The bride-elect is a 1992 graduate of Marymount University, where she received her bachelor's in interior design. She works for Burns Interior Concepts in Washington, D.C.

The prospective bridegroom received his master's in architecture from The University of Virginia, Charlottesville, in 1996. He is employed by Bryan and Greene Associates in Washington, D.C. The couple will be married at the University of Virginia's Chapel in Charlottesville on December 31, 1997.

July 1998:

Ness Center Hires New Art Therapist

PITTSBURGH – The Ness Center has hired Katherine Johnson as an art therapy specialist. Johnson will work with special-needs and at-risk children served by the Ness Center.

Johnson received her bachelor's in fine arts with a minor in social work from West Virginia University in Morgantown.

Founded in 1975, the Ness Center is a leading mental health services provider for Pittsburgh and the surrounding region.

March 1999:

Sullivan Family Announces Birth of Daughter

Peter and Ana Sullivan, St. Paul, are pleased to announce the birth of their first child, Caroline Petra Sullivan. Caroline was born at Memorial Hospital on March 16, 1999. She weighed 8 pounds, 11 ounces, and was 20 inches long. Grandparents are Christopher and Pauline Reed of Arlington, Va., and Meade and Virginia Sullivan of St. Paul.

October 2001:

No Charges in Death of Former Bristol Resident

PITTSBURGH – Prosecutors have declined to press charges against Bailey Kiser for the death of Donald Palmer, a former resident of Bristol, Va.

Kiser shot and killed the Michigan native and retired police officer during an altercation after Palmer allegedly broke into Kiser's home on September 11. Kiser claimed he was acting in self-defense when he fired his Ruger pistol at Palmer.

Citing a lack of evidence to the contrary, the district attorney did not pursue charges.

Kiser, also a former resident of Bristol, is a tattoo artist serving high-end clients at an elite tattoo design shop in an affluent suburb of Pittsburgh. Kiser could not be reached for comment. Three other people who were in the house at the time of the shooting also declined to make statements to the media.

Eleven

St. Paul/Wise County, 2001-2002

Morning dawned bright and clear, the kind of crisp October day that lingers in memory. Peter decided to walk to the office. A clean breeze ruffled his hair as he ambled along the sidewalk several blocks through St. Paul. He waved at seniors rocking on the porch of their building. Once a hotel built during the railroad boom of the early 20th century, the building now housed apartments for older people.

Better enjoy this weather while it lasts, he thought as they waved back at him. Snow'll be flying pretty soon.

Peter turned onto a side street and pulled his keys from his pocket to unlock his office. He tossed his jacket on a chair and walked across the street to collect his mail from the post office. He shuffled through the envelopes and newspapers. Below stories about the search for Osama Bin Laden in Afghanistan, a stark headline in the daily newspaper caught his eye.

No charges in death of former Bristol resident. Closing the door behind him, Peter unfolded the paper and read the story. He laid the newspaper aside, then picked it up and read the report again. Three other people. Thomas. Miller? Wren?

He hadn't seen her in more than a decade. Peter leaned back in his chair and savored the memory of her sloe-eyed gaze. Sun-kindled hair. Creamy complexion. Cinnamon freckles and vanilla skin. And always the fear. Fear of being loved. Fear of being found. Fear of being touched.

He thought of Don, shot dead, and disliked himself for being glad. He remembered his visit to Don's house that Sunday afternoon, his pistol hard against his back. Could I have really done it?

Wren's presence had brought him self-revelation months before that day: a man might kill or die for a woman. Maybe Bailey had that revelation, too. If it was Bailey. I wonder. Peter had met Thomas that day in Don's house, and his feral blue eyes had flashed when he spoke. I'll take it from here.

Peter pulled scissors from his desk and clipped the news story. He read it again. Pittsburgh. Have you been there all this time, Wren? Why didn't Thomas let me know? Why didn't you call me?

Turning on his computer, Peter pulled up directory assistance on the Internet. He typed in variations of Wren's first and last name. He found five Katherine Johnsons, two Kathy Johnsons, one K. Palmer, and one Kate Palmer. He printed the list and then did a search of tattoo shops in Pittsburgh. Grabbing the printout, he studied it.

Peter dropped the paper and rubbed his finger along the frame of a picture that sat on his desk. Ana, propped against pillows in her hospital bed, cradled their newborn daughter, Caroline. Peter perched on the side of the bed with his arm around them. Caroline's face squished together as she cried; it reminded Peter of one of those dried-apple doll faces. He thought she was the most beautiful creature he had ever seen.

He looked down at the printouts and sighed. Are you crazy? You would risk your whole world for unrequited love? Peter shook his head, folded the papers, and stuck them in a paperback novel.

~~~

"You're growing faster than a weed, kiddo." Peter watched Ana tug a skunk costume over Caroline's diaper.

Ana grunted and exhaled. "It's just too tight." She handed Caroline to Peter and flopped down on the love seat in his home office. "I think your mother made it too small."

Peter rolled his eyes. "She didn't make it too small. The baby's just growing faster than we can keep up." Caroline giggled as he tried to pull the costume up around her. "There!"

Ana stared at Caroline with doubt. The costume bulged at the seams. Sweat rolled down the baby's face and Peter dabbed it away with his shirt. He spun her around and examined the outfit. "I think if we loosen the seams here and there, it'll be okay. What do you think?"

"Maybe."

"Grab an X-Acto knife from my desk. Let's see what we can do."

Ana poked around Peter's desk until she found the tool he wanted. "Got it," she cried. She knocked a book to the floor and papers fluttered out of it.

Wiping Caroline's face with a damp cloth, Peter took no notice. "I don't know if we should take you trick-or-treating. Looks to me like you've already been in some chocolate. She didn't eat all the candy we were gonna give out, did she?"

When Ana didn't respond, Peter turned and saw her crouched in front of his desk. Her face was chalky, her expression unreadable. She held a creased printout in her trembling hands. His tongue cleaved to the roof of his mouth. He set Caroline on the love seat. "Ana."

"What is this?" She clenched the papers in her fists and carried them to Peter.

"It's nothing. I meant to throw those away." He

stretched his hands out to grab the printouts and she jerked them out of his reach.

"Nothing? You've been trying to find that girl? I wouldn't call that nothing, Peter!"

Peter held his palm up to Ana. "Lower your voice." He looked back at Caroline. "It's not what you think."

Ana waved the papers in his face. "I think you're still in love with her."

Peter felt his face flush. "Ana. You're overreacting. I saw something in the newspaper a few weeks ago that--"

Ana snorted. "I know you think about her. How can you still mourn over some girl you hardly knew a decade ago? And a crazy one!" She flung the papers in Peter's face.

Flinching, he spoke in a hoarse whisper. "You have no idea what you're talking about, Ana."

She started to cry. "How do you think I feel knowing you'll never give me all of yourself the way you did her?"

Seeing her mother's tears, Caroline cried, too. Peter dropped his head and sighed. Picking up his daughter, he thrust her in Ana's arms. "Don't cry, baby. Look, Mommy's okay."

Stooping, he gathered the papers and shuffled them together. He rose before Ana and laid his hand against her cheek. "I'm sorry. I love you. I do. Look."

Peter ripped the papers in half, then quarters, then eighths. Shredding them, he rolled them between his palms and tossed them into the trash can. "Come on. Let's take Caroline trick-or-treating."

~~~

"Trick-or-Treat!" Peter and Ana called in unison through the door of his parents' house. He held Caroline in his arms and she offered a broad smile to Ginny and Meade.

Ginny clapped her hands and pulled Caroline to her chest. "Lord have mercy! She's as cute as a speckled pup. That costume turned out good, didn't it?"

Ana pulled the hood back. "We had to make a few

adjustments. I think she's hot now." She smoothed down Caroline's black hair and patted the roses in her cheeks. "I'll get her some cold water in her sippy cup."

"Sippy!" Caroline bounced in Ginny's arms.

"Got your favorite, Knothead! Peppermint Patties." Meade waved candy in front of her face. Her chocolate eyes darkened and she reached for it. "She looks more like you every day, Big'un."

Peter laughed and kissed her on top of the head. "Where's Abigail?"

Abigail was the six-year-old daughter of Matt and Rachel. Meade set the bowl of candy on the hallway table and said, "They've come and gone. One of her friends was having a Halloween party and she wanted to go."

Ginny carried Caroline to the living room. "They waited as long as they could. Figured you'd be here a lot sooner."

Peter cleared his throat. "We had a hard time getting the brat into her costume. She's a wiggly little devil."

Ginny narrowed her eyes at Peter, so he turned his head to study the decorations. Ana returned with Caroline's water and handed it to Ginny.

"Here, baby," Ginny said. "Drink you some water." She held the cup for Caroline as she slurped it.

Ana sat on the far end of the couch from Peter. An awkward silence filled the room, punctuated by Caroline's laughter. Meade shifted in his seat and cocked his head at his son. "How's work?"

Peter jumped up and paced the room. "Great, Dad. As a matter of fact, I won the bid to design that center over in Lebanon."

"That kids' center?"

"Yeah. This is the biggest project I've landed since I struck out on my own. I intend it to be the first jewel in my crown, so to speak."

"That's wonderful, Peter." Ginny bounced Caroline on her knee. "I bet you're real proud of him, Anastasia."

Ana chewed on her lower lip for a moment. "He's something else, isn't he?"

Peter grabbed a piece of candy from the bowl, unwrapped it, and stuffed it in his mouth. The dark chocolate was rich, but the center was minty sweet. It reminded him of peppermint schnapps. He shivered as he swallowed it.

~~~

"You look as beautiful today as you did the first time I saw you," Peter said. He held up his wine glass to his wife.

Anastasia smoothed her hair with her hand; her honey-colored locks were pulled back into a neat French braid. She wore a pink cardigan and crisp blue jeans. She gave the impression of cool poise until her other hand began to agitate the signature strand of pearls at her throat. "You talk too much, Peter."

Peter smiled across the table at Caroline. "And there's the most beautiful girl of all." Around the table, his family laughed.

Ana gazed at the child seated beside her. "It is a sweet face, isn't it?"

Caroline smacked her hand in her mashed potatoes. Peter started to laugh but Ana shook her head at him. She swiped at their daughter's fingers with a napkin. "If you're not going to eat your food, you're certainly not going to play with it."

"Hey, don't fuss at her," Peter said. "She's a sensory kid. She's just trying to figure out the texture."

"You always make excuses for her, Peter!" she snapped. "She's making a mess and dragging her sleeve through her food." She glared at him as she picked up the little girl. "Come on, Caroline. Let's see if we can get the gravy off your face."

Peter pushed his plate away and stared at the tablecloth. Silverware clanked against porcelain, setting his teeth on edge. Ginny motioned to Rachel and Theresa. "Will you girls help me clear the table?" She clicked her tongue. "It's terrible to celebrate Easter by stuffing ourselves with all this food. I'll never find a place to put all these leftovers!"

When Peter rose from the table, Abigail ran up behind him and wrapped her arms around his waist. "Play Monopoly with me, Uncle Peter!" Her dishwater blonde hair hung down her back as she stared up him. He gave her nose a light pinch and extracted himself from her grip.

"Not right now, Sugarbooger."

Theresa's husband, Murphy, and Matt pushed themselves away from the table. "Abby, stop pestering him," Matt said.

"Aww, Daddy, I'm not bothering him. Am I, Uncle Peter?"

"No, sweetie. But why don't you go see if your mom needs help?"

"Okay." Abigail skipped to the kitchen.

"I think I'll go for a walk," Peter said.

"Want some company?" Meade asked.

His son shrugged. "Sure." They grabbed their jackets from the hallway tree and walked out to the porch. Meade pulled a cap onto his head and followed his son out into the yard.

Peter's parents lived on a ridge in the eastern part of Wise County. Little traffic passed by their house, so they felt free to walk down the middle of the hardtop. The sun clung to the shoulders of the hills, and Peter shivered as they passed into the shadows that stretched across the road. He detected the faint scent of coal smoke in the crisp air. Scanning the horizon, he saw a black ribbon curling into the sky.

"I thought Mrs. McReynolds got a heat pump?"

"She did. Her boy installed it for her, but she won't use it. I hauled a load of coal up there to her a couple of days ago. Told me that heat pump just didn't keep the house warm enough to suit her. Today's the last day of March, but

I guarantee she'll be heating her house up into June."

Peter laughed and shook his head. "Old bones are hard to keep warm, I guess." He picked up a stone and tossed it into the brush alongside the road. A deer crashed through the bushes and retreated into the woods. "Sorry about that," Peter called to it.

"Why don't y'all spend the night tonight?"

"I guess we'll head back to St. Paul after while. Ana says she'd rather sleep in her own bed in her own house. You know how she is." Peter stuck his hands in his pockets to warm them.

"No, son," Meade said, "I guess I really don't. Most women are hard to figure, but she takes the cake. Seems to me she's unhappy no matter what."

Peter sighed. "She still hasn't adjusted to living down here."

"Shoot, you've been down here more than three years. Surely to God she's had time to adjust."

"Dad, if you'd lived your whole life in Northern Virginia and Washington, D.C., you'd have a hard time fitting in down here. It'd be the same the other way around, wouldn't it? Moving from the mountains to the city?"

"Adjusting to the city? I couldn't do it. But I don't understand anybody not loving this place. Maybe if she'd try harder to be friendly-like to everybody, she might not have such a hard time. Theresa said she walks around town with her nose up in the air. Gives people the impression she thinks she's better than they are."

"She doesn't think that! Anyway, Theresa needs to mind her own business. Look, Ana gave up her career to move because I wanted to start my own business here."

Meade tipped the bill of his cap back and stared at his son. "And she don't ever let you forget it, does she?"

Never.

~~~

Ana shifted beneath the sheets when Peter sat up on the

edge of the bed. He rubbed his eyes and stared at the clock on the nightstand. 4:15. *Shouldn't have taken that nap on the couch last night. I ate too much Easter supper.*

He pulled on his jeans and walked down the hall to Caroline's bedroom. He padded across the carpet and stood beside the bed to stare down at his daughter.

Nothing as pure as a sleeping child. She lay with her cheek mashed against the mattress, her arm dangling over the side of the bed. Her pillow had fallen to the floor. Peter picked it up and placed it back under her head, careful not to wake her. He lifted her arm and placed it beneath the blanket. Her arms still had faint rings around them, remnants of her baby fat.

Peter pushed her dark hair back to kiss her forehead and inhaled her sweet, sweaty scent. It astonished him that he had helped create this amazing little human being. *Years ago, I thought I knew what it meant to be consumed by love.* Wren's face flashed before his eyes and he sighed, blowing away the memory. He looked at Caroline and smiled. *I had no idea.*

He trudged downstairs and poured himself a glass of wine, thinking it might help him sleep. He carried it to his computer and sipped it while he checked his E-mail. His office was downtown, but he sometimes worked on his projects at home. After two years on his own, Peter had built a solid client base. He had worked on projects throughout the nation, but most of his clients were in Virginia, Tennessee, Kentucky, and North Carolina. Occasionally his old firm referred projects to him.

Peter responded to some inquiries about his services, then read an e-mail from Ike. He still couldn't believe his old college friend was running for office in New Jersey. Shutting down the computer, he wandered over to his drafting table and stared at the plans for their new house. He couldn't seem to finish them. He had bought a piece of land when they first moved home, to Ana's great dismay, but he hadn't done anything with it yet. He wanted to design their home before he touched the land. Often, though, he found himself daydreaming or doodling instead of drawing. Now he stared at the two-year old plans with disgust.

This is ridiculous, he thought. I need to just do this! He picked up his pencil and began to work. The scratch of pencil against paper comforted him and he relaxed. After a few minutes, he yawned and shook his head. Of course, now I'm sleepy.

"What are you doing down here?" Ana spoke into his ear.

Peter jumped. "Give me a heart attack! I didn't hear you come downstairs." He dropped his pencil and turned to face his wife. "I couldn't sleep, so I thought I'd work on our house for a while. I'm sorry if I woke you up."

Ana looked over his shoulder at the drawings and frowned. "Our house? When did you ever consult me about 'our' house? You bought that land without even asking me about it. You've been designing that stupid house without ever once stopping to see what I thought about it. There's no 'our' to it, Peter."

She turned away, but Peter grabbed her shoulder and twisted her around to face him again. "Did you come down here just to start a fight with me? Let's not do this now."

"When, then? You mean let's not talk about this ever. I'm not fighting with you, Peter. I'm just stating the facts. You're in your own little world and you don't give a fig what I think."

"That's not true, Ana. Be fair. You don't want to be part of my world!" Sighing, he ran his hand through his hair. "When we first met, you wanted to be near me all the time. We couldn't get enough of each other. Remember?"

Peter slid his arms around her waist and pulled her close. She was unyielding in his embrace, and he felt like he was hugging a thorn bush. He pulled back and stared into her face. Her eyes looked as hard as blue marbles. He released her and stared at a point on the wall behind her.

Ana retreated upstairs. Peter drained his glass, waiting until he thought she might be asleep before he returned to bed.

~~~

The sun was high on the bedroom walls when Caroline crawled into bed with them. She pulled Peter's right eye open and peered into the black orb. "You in there, Daddy?"

"Nope. Daddy's gone fishing. Come back later."

Caroline giggled and stretched his eye open wider with her fingers. "Daddy!"

Ana rolled over and pulled the sheet across her shoulders. "Go back to bed, Caroline."

"I want Daddy to play!" She bounced up and down on Peter's chest until he grunted. He grabbed her and tickled her. She laughed and kicked her feet up and down on the bed.

Ana threw off the blanket and stomped to the bathroom. Peter picked up his daughter and she curled her arms around his neck. "Come on, kiddo. Let's go get leftovers at Granny and Granddad's, okay? I think Mommy needs some quiet time today."

~~~

"Lord, she's as mean as a striped snake." Ginny shook her head as she said it. Caroline had stuck her doll in the microwave, and mashing the buttons as she had seen the grown-ups do, she managed to cook the toy.

Peter grunted as he scraped melted plastic from inside the oven door. "She's no meaner than any other kid in the family. Remember when Abigail tried to baptize the cat a few years ago?"

Meade smacked his knee and laughed. "How can we forget? She's got two long scars up her arms from poor old Chester. It's a wonder he didn't put her eyes out."

"I'm just glad the microwave didn't explode. Somebody

might have gotten hurt." Peter looked across the room at Caroline. She and Abigail sat at the kitchen table drawing pictures on notebook paper with magic markers.

Ginny washed the oven with soap and water after he removed all the plastic. He carried the remains of the doll to the table and sat down next to Caroline. "Look here at Molly. She's ruined now. Why'd you put her in the microwave?"

Caroline poked her marker at a clump of blonde hair in the middle of the plastic and shrugged. "Tanning bed."

Peter rolled his eyes and leaned back in the chair. "Okay, no more trips to the beauty shop with Rachel. Caroline's seen all those girls frying themselves in the tanning bed."

Theresa walked into the kitchen and wrinkled her nose. "Pshew! You sure that thing didn't emit some kind of toxic fume when it was cooking'? It stinks in here."

"Hey, I'm not a chemist," Peter said. He took a breath and frowned. "Then again, it might not be a good idea for all of us to be sitting in here right now." He picked Caroline up and propped her on his hip. "Let's go see the calf, you want to?"

Since his retirement, Meade had decided to keep a few animals, although they hadn't raised cows or pigs since Peter was a child. Meade bought a large freezer for the basement. "We'll have us some good pork chops and steaks." Peter had avoided visiting them the week they killed the pigs, but he wasn't averse to eating the sausage and tenderloin his mother set on the table in the following months.

A neighbor's bull had gotten loose and now Meade had a calf. The first time Caroline saw the calf she became attached to it. She named it Spot for the black smudge around its eyes. He wondered if his father would be able to kill it now that Caroline had adopted it.

They walked into the backyard and through the gate. Behind the house, trails crisscrossed the hill like dirty ribbons. Glistening spider webs seemed to hold the pasture's leaning fence posts together. Caroline reached for the barbed wire and Peter gave her hand a light smack.

He paused beneath an old maple tree and laid Caroline's palm against its trunk. She smiled and traced tracks of moisture running down the wrinkled bark. She and Abigail ran around the tree kicking up a pungent mass of leaves, delighting in the angry crunch.

He squatted on the ground and stared at his family. Ginny fussed with Meade's coat buttons. Murphy tickled Theresa's ear with a piece of long grass. Rachel leaned against Matt and he rubbed her belly, swollen with Abigail's baby brother. If Ana was here, it would be perfect. Then again, probably not. She'd be fussing about something.

He blinked and looked up at the sky. Peter thought it was as blue as he had ever seen it. Crows peppered the white clouds, and it seemed to him they called to each other with raucous joy. Caroline echoed their chatter, her cheeks pink with cold. She scampered to Peter and threw her arms around his neck. "I love you, Daddy."

He felt as if he might float off the face of the earth. "I love you, too, baby."

He picked her up, hoisted her onto his shoulders, and they continued up the hill to the lot where Meade had penned up the calf with its mother. The cow turned a wary eye to them as they approached, but the calf wobbled to the fence and stared at them with dumb, round eyes. "Spot!" Caroline smacked the top of Peter's head.

"Ouch! Are you trying to kill Daddy?" He set her on the ground and they sidled up to the fence. "Easy now." He cupped Caroline's hand in his and stuck it through the fence. The calf nuzzled their hands with its rough, wet nose. *Snuffle.* The mother cow bawled, but she didn't move.

Meade kneeled next to them and rubbed the top of the calf's head. "She's getting horns."

Peter moved Caroline's hand up the side of the calf's

face to the top of its head. She emitted a soft "ooh" when she felt the two nubbins. Abigail crouched next to them and rubbed the tiny buttons, pronouncing them "neat!"

"I'd say the house is safe now," Ginny said. "I left the kitchen windows open. Abigail! Caroline! Let's go."

"Ahh, Granny, can't we stay a while longer?" Abigail kicked the ground in front of her.

Rachel shook her finger at her daughter. "Don't argue with your grandmother."

Peter stepped behind his niece and placed his hands on her shoulders. "You know what happens to little girls who don't behave?"

She tilted her head back to look at him and grinned. "What?"

"They get their toes dipped in a cow pie!" He wrapped his arms around her, picked her up, and dangled her over a fresh pile of cow manure.

Abigail squealed and lifted her legs when Peter threatened to set her down in the cow patty. "Are you gonna be good?"

"Yes!" She screamed when he dipped her down.

"Promise?"

"I promise. I promise, Uncle Peter. Don't!" She giggled when he swooped her through the air and set her down on the other side of the cow pie. She wrinkled her nose and backed away from it. "You wouldn't really dip my toes in that, would you?"

Theresa snorted. "Don't be so sure. One time he pushed me over right into the middle of one."

Peter laughed. Well, sometimes life can be a big pile of crap. You just have to get up, clean yourself off, and get on with it.

~~~

As April bled into May, Peter worked longer-than-normal hours at his office downtown. Designing the center in Lebanon for troubled children turned out to be an even bigger project than he imagined, although he enjoyed working on it. Sitting at the computer, he let himself get lost in dreams of a safe place for kids.One rainy night, when he returned home after ten o'clock, Ana flew into him before water had time to evaporate from his hair. "Do you know what time it is?? Your dinner is ruined!"

Peter shrugged off his raincoat and hung it in the hallway closet. He clutched a six-pack of beer to his chest. "I'm sorry, Ana. I got caught up in the design for this new center and lost track of the time. I'm not really hungry anyway."

"Caroline waited and waited for you to come tuck her in. She finally fell asleep on the couch and I put her to bed."

He set the beer on the hallway table. "I'll go look in on her." He started up the stairs, but Ana grabbed him by the elbow.

"No! Don't wake her up now. She'll want to get up and I'll never get her back to sleep."

Peter grabbed the beer, shoved past Ana, and walked into the living room. He slumped on the sofa and clicked the remote. The television filled the room with blue light. He twisted the top from a bottle and chugged the frothy liquid

Ana followed him and stood in front of Peter with her hands on her hips. He leaned to the right to see around her and she slapped the remote control from his hand. It hit the hardwood floor with a cracking sound.

Peter shoved his palms against his eyes and rubbed them hard. He balled his hands into fists, laid them against his knees, and glared at Ana. "What do you want from me?"

"First of all, I'd like you to slow down on that stuff." She pointed to the beer. "Second of all, I want us to move back to Washington."

"Forget it. We're not moving."

Ana crossed her arms. "Oh, just like that, Peter the Great speaks and that settles it? Don't I have a say?"

"Yeah and you've been saying it for the last three years! You agreed to live with me here." He looked up at his wife. Blue light poured around her, hollowing out her face with black shadows, so he couldn't read her expression.

"I thought you'd be willing to move after a few years if I didn't like it down here. I thought you'd love me enough to move if I asked you to." Her voice wavered. "I guess you don't."

"Ana, you know I love you. It's not that simple." How do I make you understand? Home runs through my veins as surely as coal runs through the hills. Make me leave and I'll die!

"It *is* that simple," she argued. "If you really loved me, you'd do this for me."

A sharp memory pricked his heart. Wren lay on the floor of his bedroom and he rested on top of her. If you really loved me, you'd leave me alone. He sighed and tried to shake off the image, but it gripped his heart. Why'd you leave me, Wren?

"Are you listening to me?" Ana snapped her fingers in Peter's face. "I hate it when you do that!"

He shoved her hand. "Do what?"

"Daydream when I'm talking to you about something important. And I know that look. You're thinking about her!"

Peter felt his ears grow warm. "You don't know what I'm thinking, so stop riding me! How many times do I have to apologize? Every time you get pissed off, you bring up Wren. It's getting old!"

"Daddy? Mommy?" Caroline stood at the bottom of the steps, eyes wide and brimming with tears.

Peter sprinted to the stairs and picked up his daughter. He felt her tremble and gave himself a mental kick. Idiot! "Here now, it's all right, Caroline." He dropped down to rest on the bottom step.

The little girl looked from her father to her mother with

raw fear. "What's wrong?"

Ana wiped her eyes and laughed. She sat down next to Peter and patted Caroline's arm. "It's okay, baby. We were just talking to each other and got a little excited, that's all. Don't be scared."

Caroline looked up at Peter and he saw himself in her black eyes. "Do you still love me, Daddy?"

He felt as if his heart were being squeezed in two. *How am I going to fix this?* "Of course I love you, baby. You don't have to ever worry about me not loving you. You are the most important person in the world to me."

Caroline kissed him on the neck, then her lips fluttered against his throat. "Daddy loves Mommy?"

Tears blurred Peter's vision. He looked up at the ceiling, willing them to disappear back into his head. "Yes, I love your Mommy."

Ana hugged herself as she tried to smother a sob. She ran her hand through Caroline's hair, whispering to her, "Go to sleep, sweetheart."

Peter rocked Caroline until her breathing grew steady. They sat on the steps and watched the darkness settle around them.

~~~

Ana and Peter argued all through spring. She wanted to take Caroline to Washington for the entire week leading up to Memorial Day. "Caroline needs to spend more time with my family," she told Peter. "It would be nice if you'd spend more time with them, too."

"Why?" Peter asked. "So your father can tell me jokes about the Beverly Hillbillies? Or so your mother can smirk at the way I talk?"

"You're so unfair, Peter! You expect me to be with your family all the time, but you won't do the same for me."

"Your family makes me feel unwelcome."

"They don't try to make you feel unwelcome."

"You're right. They don't have to try. It comes naturally

to them."

In the end, they spent the week together with her family. When Peter packed Caroline into the Lexus to return to St. Paul by Memorial Day, Ana stood in the driveway with her arms crossed.

"I wish you'd come back with us today," he said.

"I'll be back after Memorial Day." She leaned into the vehicle and checked the straps restraining Caroline in the seat, then kissed the little girl on the forehead. "Be good for Daddy, okay?"

Peter shut the door and leaned against the car. Ana picked an invisible piece of lint from his coat and flicked it away. "Be careful driving back, okay?"

"I will. Precious cargo, right?" They stared through the window at Caroline. She was already asleep.

Peter wrapped his arms around Ana and she rested her head against his chest. He looked back at the house and saw her mother staring out the window at them. Peter sighed and kissed his wife's forehead. "Well, I guess I'll see you in a few days, then."

She nodded and followed him around to the driver's side of the car. He climbed in behind the wheel and buckled the seatbelt. Ana reached in and rested her hand against his cheek. He pulled it to his mouth and kissed her fingers. "I love you."

"Goodbye, Peter."

When Ana returned home, they tiptoed around each other, afraid to stir the false peace they had concocted. It lasted through summer and autumn.

~~~

Ginny decorated for Christmas with great fervor. Meade had stopped by Peter's office the day before to tell him she was driving him crazy. "I don't know what it is about that woman and holidays. She acts plumb wild."

Peter leaned back in his chair and laughed. "I guess it's because she never had much until she was an adult."

Meade nodded. "That must be it. When you grow up as poor as Ginny did, you want your kids to have better. But, Lord God Almighty, she does go overboard. And I think she gets worse the older you children get."

"Yeah. And after Christmas, we've got New Year's and Valentine's Day and my birthday and Caroline's. Then we'll be safe until April, when Rachel's birthday hits. It'll be warm then and you can get out of the house."

"That don't make me feel any better, son." Meade pulled his cap off, scratched his head, and jammed the hat back in place. He looked around the office. Completed renderings, plaques, and architecture awards hung on the walls. Drawings still in progress covered Peter's desk and all the tables in the room. "How's that Lebanon job going?" Meade asked.

"The Board asked me to make a few minor changes. That's what I'm working on now, as a matter of fact." He pointed to his computer.

Meade nodded. "Well, let's get up on the mountain."

"Ah, I better not. I'll see y'all tomorrow. Don't let Mom worry you to death."

"Too late."

Peter shook his head and smiled at his father's back as Meade walked out the door. Outside Meade looked up at the sky and pulled his collar up around his neck. Peter walked to the door and saw snowflakes tatting a lace pattern in the street. He shivered as he returned to his work.

~~~

Caroline shook him awake the next morning. "Wake up, Daddy! It snowed and snowed and snowed all night! Let's go make a snowman."

Peter sat up and stretched as Ana entered the bedroom. "Caroline, I told you not to wake him up. At least let him sleep late for Christmas Eve and Christmas Day."

The little girl put her hands over her mouth. "Oh, I forgot!" She climbed up into the bed and sang *O Christmas*

Tree to him, then she whispered into his ear, "Now can we go build a snowman?"

Ana sat on the edge of the bed and shook her head. "Go get dressed. I laid your clothes out in your room."

Caroline jumped off the bed and landed on the carpet with a thump. She ran out of the room and they heard her bare feet slapping the floor all the way down the hall. Ana walked to the window and stared at the snow. "It looks pretty bad out there. Maybe we should stay home today."

Peter joined her at the window. Spun sugar treetops cast shadows across their yard, which looked like it had been encased in marshmallow crème. Mysterious mounds destroyed the familiar landscape, and Peter tried to think what might be beneath each one. *That's that old tree stump. There's the lawn chair I forgot to store with the others. That must be Caroline's tricycle. And I have no idea what that might be.*

"Well, what do you think?" Ana clutched the curtain with one hand and tugged at the pearls around her neck with the other.

"Stay home on Christmas Eve? Mom would kill me if we didn't come. Anyway, we've got four-wheel drive. It'll be fine."

Even with the F-150, the drive was treacherous. Cars were strewn along the side of Route 58 and in the median. Large yellow trucks pushed snow off the road or dropped salt on it.

"They probably won't even touch Mom and Dad's road till tomorrow, if then," Peter remarked.

When they reached the base of the mountain where Meade and Ginny lived, Ana clutched Peter's arm. "I think we should go back home."

"We're practically there now, Ana." He looked down at Caroline sitting between them. She was staring out the window in wide-eyed wonder.

They turned off Route 58. The road wound around the

mountain, shaded by trees and outcrops of sandstone. The pickup wiggled on the sheath of ice and Peter gripped the steering wheel. "Road's slicker than snot on a porcelain doorknob."

Ana laughed, but it sounded to Peter like a violin being plucked by a madman. They rounded a curve and saw a van spinning its tires. It moved forward a few inches before its rear moved sideways. The driver eased off the accelerator and the vehicle slid backward and wedged against the guardrail.

Peter eased the truck around the distressed vehicle and stopped. When he opened his door, Ana restrained him. "What are you doing?" she asked.

"The road flattens out just a little ways up. I'm going to pull him up to there, so he'll at least be out of the way."

"Let's just go! Let somebody else help him."

Peter stepped out of the truck. "It'll just take a couple of minutes. Stay inside." Slamming the door, he retrieved a chain from the back and hooked it to the truck. Dragging it through the snow, he hailed the man in the van. They connected the chain to the stranded vehicle and Peter returned to his truck.

"Hang on to your drawers, girls." He shifted gears and they crawled up the hill with the van in tow. Caroline clapped and laughed when they reached the top of the hill and pulled to the side of the road.

Peter jumped out and removed the chains. He returned to the truck and they continued up the road to his parents' house. They rolled into the yard, where Abigail and Matt were building a snowman. Caroline rocked back and forth in her seat. "I want to help!" she yelled through the car window. She pulled at the straps and buckles that held her against the seat.

"Daddy, get me out! I want to build a snowman, too!"

"Hold your horses." He extricated her from the car and set her on the ground.

Caroline plunged through the snow. "Wait for me!"

Laughing, Peter looked across the interior at Ana. She stared out the windshield without moving. "What's wrong now?"

She shook her head without responding. Peter sighed and reached across the seat to touch her shoulder, but she jerked away from him. Anger rose up and thumped against his chest with each heart beat. "Who licked the red off your candy today, Ana?"

She jumped out of the car, slammed the door, and trudged to the house. Cursing, Peter followed. He stomped the snow off his shoes and walked into the kitchen. Ginny enfolded him in her arms a brief moment. "Lord God, I was beginning to get worried about y'all. Have any trouble?"

Peter looked at Ana. She leaned against the sink and stared out the window, her face blank.

He smiled at his mother. "Nope."

~~~

Peter leaned back in his chair and patted his stomach. "I feel fatter than a tick. That was good, Mom. Thank you."

Murmurs of agreement rose around the table and Ginny smiled. "That's just dinner. You haven't had dessert, yet!" She jerked her thumb over her shoulder at the sideboard. A host of sweets were stacked across its surface: pecan pie, rum cake, oatmeal cake, chocolate fudge, banana pudding, molasses cookies, and peanut butter roll.

Peter groaned. "Why'd you fix all that?"

"Well, I wanted to make sure I had something for everybody. And there's plenty for everybody to take home, too." Ginny passed dessert plates around the table as she spoke. "Now, who wants what?"

"I want cake!" Caroline shouted.

"Caroline Petra Sullivan! Lower your voice." Ana glared at her daughter. "Anyway, you don't need any cake." She looked at Ginny. "Do you have any fruit?"

"I don't want fruit. I want cake!" Caroline smacked the

table with her hands.

"Hey." Peter shot his daughter a warning look. Looking across the table at Ana, he said, "A piece of cake won't hurt her."

Ana clenched her jaw as she spoke. "I said no."

Peter flushed. He walked to the sideboard, cut a piece of oatmeal cake, slapped it onto a plate, and shoved it in front of Caroline. The clattering of the plate against the table was the only sound in the room. "Go ahead, baby. Eat your cake."

Rubbing the edge of the plate with her forefinger, Caroline tilted her head, and looked at her mother. "Mommy?"

Ana's nostrils flared as she worried her pearls with both hands. She spoke in an even voice. "If your Daddy said you can have it, then you can have it. After all, he's the ruler of the roost, isn't he?"

Caroline picked at the cake with her fingers. Never taking his eyes off Ana, Peter leaned down and kissed the top of his daughter's head. Meade stirred in his chair. "Well, Ginny went to a lot of trouble. Let's everybody eat. Let's not have a big fuss on Christmas, okay?"

"We're not fussing, Dad," Peter said.

"Well," Meade said.

The family ate dessert in silence. The sugar turned sour in Peter's stomach and his head started to ache. He scowled at Ana across the table, but she just gazed at a point right above his head.

Finally, Rachel dropped her fork into her plate and lifted Martin, her son, into her lap. "Well, who's ready to open presents?"

Abigail and Caroline shouted their delight in unison.

~~~

The drive home was quiet and grim, outside the truck and in. Caroline slept, although she cried out once or twice. At home, Peter carried her upstairs and put her to bed. He kicked off his boots in the hallway and walked downstairs in his socks. He grabbed a bottle of bourbon and a glass from an upper cabinet and a carton of beer from the refrigerator and carried them to the living room.

Ana was curled up on the end of the couch, flipping through an old Vogue. Peter plugged in the Christmas tree, set his drinks in the floor, and collapsed in his favorite chair. He crossed his legs, propped his feet on the coffee table, and opened a bottle of beer. He chugged it, belched, and opened another. He finished that one as he gazed at the lights on the tree.

Ana had decorated the tree with a candy cane theme. Candy canes, red bows, and red-and-white decorations gleamed in the glow of blinking lights. A red foil star topped the tree. Peter stared at it until his eyes watered. "Are you going to ignore me the rest of the night?"

Ana turned over onto her back, propped the magazine on her knees, and thumbed through the pages. Peter shrugged and opened the bourbon. He poured three fingers of liquor into the glass, turned it up, and let it tumble down his throat. Warmth spread across his stomach, through his veins, until he felt lit from within. He smiled to himself.

He pulled another beer from the carton and rolled the bottle between his palms. Foam spilled over the lip and down his wrist. He licked the amber froth from his skin and finished the beer in five easy gulps. He smacked his mouth and banged the bottle down on the coffee table.

Ana jumped. When he poured another glass of bourbon, she glowered at him. "Are you going to sit there and get drunk?"

"Yep. I intend to get as high as a Georgia pine."

"Yeah, that'll really help! You think the answer to all your problems sits in the bottom of a bottle."

"Whatever." His heart began to bang against his chest as if it were trying to break through his rib cage. He bounced the glass against his thigh. He felt an urge to fling it over her head. Not good. Not good at all.

"I have to tell you something, Peter." Ana tossed the magazine onto the coffee table. She leaned her elbows on her knees and stared at the carpet between her feet.

"So tell me." Peter drained his glass.

"Jeremy called me yesterday."

Peter squeezed his eyes shut. "Jeremy? Who's Jeremy?"

Ana rolled her eyes. "He was the senior designer at my old firm. Well, he owns it now."

"Great. Good for him. Why are you telling me?" Sharp suspicion began to pierce Peter's thick shield of alcohol. He fumbled around the beer carton and retrieved another bottle.

"He offered me a job. I would be making more money than I was when I left and it would be a promotion." Ana spoke without raising her head. "I'm going to take it."

"Gonna be one helluva commute," Peter growled. "St. Paul to Arlington."

She rose and walked over to Peter. Kneeling on the carpet, she laid her hands on the arm of the chair. "I'm taking the job, Peter. I'm leaving you. I've already contacted my father's lawyer about proceeding with a legal separation and a divorce."

The fire inside him began to die. His stomach felt cold and heavy with poison. He threw the bottle and it flew across the room and shattered against the wall. Golden foam bled down the wallpaper, but Ana didn't flinch.

"Don't do this, Anastasia."

"I have to, Peter. I'm going crazy here."

"You don't love me, fine. I can live with that. But don't do this to Caroline." He rubbed his fingers across Ana's hands.

She began to cry. "You just said it, Peter. You can live without my love." She rose and ran her sleeve across her face. "I'm packing tomorrow and I'm taking Caroline with me."

"No!" Peter stood up and staggered. "If you want to leave me, go! But you're not taking my little girl!"

Ana backed away from Peter. "We'll figure something out after I talk to the lawyer. Half the year down here and half the year with me or something like that. But for now, I want her with me."

Peter stumbled over the beer carton and grabbed Ana's wrist. She tried to pull free, but he wrapped his arms around her. "I'll go with you, then. If that's what it takes to make it right for Caroline, I'll move up there." He mashed his mouth against Ana's, but she twisted her head.

She spoke against his shoulder. "No. Either way -- me down here or you up there -- somebody's going to be miserable. We don't fit right anymore, if we ever did. If we stay together, we'll end up hating each other."

Ana stepped out of Peter's arms and retreated to the hallway. Standing at the side of the staircase, he curled his fingers around the maple spindles and watched Ana's feet fit square against each step as she walked upstairs. He heard the *snick* of the bedroom door being shut.

Leaning back, he let the balustrade support his weight. He focused on the ceiling, but the angles looked crazy. He blinked and the walls pitched inward. His hands slipped and he landed on the floor flat on his back. The room began to spin.

Peter lurched to his feet and fumbled for the front door. Staggering out into the yard, he fell into the snow. It frosted his hands, his face, and his feet. His stomach muscles seized up and he vomited. The puddle steamed in front of him and the sight of it made him retch again.

He shoved himself backward and lay on the stoop, shivering and staring at the sky. It was black, a great bed of coal stretched above the earth instead of within it. Suddenly a spot of white grew in his sight. He reached for it, thinking it a star, but it was nothing more than a solitary crystal of snow. Peter closed his hand around it and felt it melt.

Twelve

Russell County/St. Paul, Spring 2004

Wren took a deep breath and inhaled the sweet smell of
clover and close-shaven grass. She laughed and spun in
a circle. All around her she saw fields swell and shrink in
shades of green. Neat bands of houses lay beyond the horse-
freckled, cow-speckled pastures of Castlewood. She closed
her eyes and lifted her chin for the May sun to warm her
skin.

"I take it you like the view?" The realtor leaned against
his car with a sheaf of papers tucked under his arm.

"You take it right, Mr. Asbury." Wren dropped her head
and squinted at him. "The house needs a little work. If you'll
have that taken care of like we discussed, I'll definitely rent
it."

"Are you sure you don't want to look at that other place
I told you about? It would be closer to your new job."

She studied the house one more time. It was compact:
one floor, four rooms, and a stubby porch. Pink peonies
blushed against the foundation of the house. A motley
assortment of tulips, primrose, and phlox decorated uneven
flower beds. Irises and day lilies marched beside the
shattered sidewalk. Just beyond the house, clouds floated in
the still surface of a small pond.

Wren shook her head. "No. This is perfect."

Mr. Asbury jangled his key ring. "Well, let's go the office and take care of the paperwork."

~~~

Thomas and Bailey helped her move in a week later. The realtor had had the utilities connected for her and the phone rang as they carried in the final boxes of her belongings. "Hello?"

"Well, are you all settled in?"

"Hey, Felicia. Just about. I'm going to have to do some serious cleaning. It's pretty dusty right now."

"Well, that'll give you something to do until you officially start. Are you excited?"

"Yeah. And a little nervous, of course." Bailey held up a box marked JUNK with a questioning look. Wren shrugged and gestured for him to take it to the bedroom.

"You'll be fine. The kids will love you, just like they have in your other jobs."

"I really appreciate you recommending me for this job."

"I've always believed in you, Wren. You just needed to believe in yourself."

Wren laughed. "I never thought I would have even the semblance of a normal life. Things have really turned around since--"

"Hey, Sis, where do you want these books?" Thomas pushed a bulging box through the front door with his foot.

"Just leave them in the middle of the floor. I'll figure out where they go later. Listen, I've gotta go. I'll call you in a couple of days."

"Take care." Felicia's voice grew deep. "Wait, how does it feel to be back down there?"

"Well, I'm not freaking out yet, if that's what you're trying to ask me. We took one quick trip into St. Paul to get some cleaning supplies, but that's as far as I've gone. I need to get settled in a routine before I tackle Pawpaw Ridge."

"Give me a call if you need to talk."

"Thanks, Felicia. Well, I better go. I think we'll run out and grab a pizza before I unpack all this junk. Talk to you later."

~~~

Thomas tossed a gnawed pizza crust into the empty box. "Are you sure you don't want us to stay with you for a couple of days?"

Wren pulled a string of cheese from her slice, wrapped it around her finger, and stuffed it in her mouth. After she swallowed it, she responded. "I'll be fine."

Bailey stole a pepperoni slice from her pizza and popped it in his mouth. "I don't know. This will be the first time you've been alone this far away from us in a dozen years. I think we should hang around a while."

Wren smiled and ran her thumb along the scar on his face. She leaned over and kissed him on the cheek. "What would I do without my two sweethearts? But you guys need to get back to Pittsburgh. I bet Miller's pulling his hair out right now."

Thomas laughed. "Impossible. He doesn't have any hair left to pull out."

Wren dug her bare toe into her brother's thigh. "Neither do you. I wish you'd stop buzzing your hair, Thomas."

He chuckled and ran his hand across the golden fuzz on his head. "I think I'll grow it out and get dreads."

Wren rolled her eyes and shook her head at Bailey. He ran both hands through his own blond hair and twisted it behind his head, exposing the tattoo on the nape of his neck. WREN was stylized in purple script and minute scarlet hearts trailed off the tips of the letters.

Wren clicked her tongue at her brother. "You're not gonna leave Becky alone, are you?"

Thomas sighed and stretched. "Probably not a good idea. She told me she'd knock me down a rat hole if I don't come back when I'm supposed to. And I believe her."

She laughed at Thomas's assessment of his wife's threat.

"Well, with a baby on the way, you should be home with her. I can't wait for him to get here."

"Between you and Becky, this kid will be totally spoiled. Which reminds me, I need to pick up paint before I get home. She wants to start on the nursery." He looked at Bailey. "You about ready?"

"Not really. But I guess I have to go, huh?" He offered Wren a hopeful expression, his hazel eyes wide.

She pursed her lips. "You have to go."

Escorting them to Thomas's Jeep, Wren hugged her brother. "Don't drive fast."

He pretended to be insulted. "Me? Speed? What do you take me for, some kind of lawbreaker?"

Wren giggled and punched his arm. She turned to Bailey and wrapped her arms around his waist. Leaning back, she smiled up at him. "Thank you."

He planted a chaste kiss on her lips, but his hands ran up her sides and lingered beneath her breasts. She allowed it for a few seconds, then laced her fingers between his and turned their hands into a partition. He dropped his head but lifted his eyes to gaze at her beneath hooded lids. "I love you."

Oh, Bailey. "I love you, too."

~~~

After they left, Wren sat on the back porch and stared across the yard. The apricot sunset wiped the hills dry and burnished the pond. From the water's depths, frogs sang gleeful peeps.

She rested her elbows on her knees and twisted the ring on her left finger. Bailey had given her a diamond engagement ring a year and a half ago, for her thirty-third birthday. They still hadn't set a date, but he seemed content that she wore the ring.

She sighed and walked back into the house. Removing the ring, she placed it in her jewelry box. She spent the evening scrubbing the kitchen and the bathroom. When she was done, she flopped down on the couch and stared at the boxes piled throughout the living room. Well, they're not going to unpack themselves.

Wren stood and stretched and cracked her knuckles. "Now is as good a time as any, I guess." She ripped packing tape from the lips of the closest box and opened its cardboard maw. Dishes go in the kitchen. She set the box on the kitchen counter and opened another one.

A framed diploma rested on a stack of papers. Wren wiped it with the tail of her shirt. The general faculty of West Virginia University has conferred the degree of Bachelor of Arts upon Katherine Rose Johnson . . . . She shook her head in disbelief.

After she had fled Charlottesville, Wren spent three months running from motel to motel in North Carolina. When she finally contacted Thomas, she discovered that Miller planned to move his shop to Pittsburgh. When he did, she joined Thomas and Bailey at their new apartment. Feeling secure, she contacted Felicia to explain her flight and apologize. She swore her to secrecy.

Felicia and Wren stayed in contact. In 1994, Felicia helped her find funds to go to college. Wren chose the school as much for its location as its academic program. In many ways Morgantown reminded her of home. After graduating in 1998, she got her first job as an art therapist in Pittsburgh.

She worked at the Ness Center for three years, leaving right after September 11. Wren landed another art therapy job back in Morgantown. In January 2004, Felicia told her about the job in Lebanon, Virginia. Wren applied for it immediately. And here I am, she thought. So close to home I can almost smell the honeysuckle.

She laid aside the diploma and dug to the bottom of the box. She retrieved a picture album that Thomas had discovered in Don's attic. It was in a box she had brought with her when Don and Cindy had adopted her. Wren flipped through its pages. The snapshots were faded and ragged around the edges, much like her memories of the moments the pictures were taken. She ran her fingers across the plastic that protected the photos and smiled.

In one shot, she sat on a porch swing inside the crook of her father's arm and grinned at the camera. Her father seemed to be speaking to the photographer. His mouth was open and one eye was closed halfway. He was dressed in work clothes and his lunch bucket sat on the floor beneath the swing.

In another picture, she and Maryann leaned on the rough railing of the bridge that crossed the creek near the house. Sunlight transformed their faces into two moons. Their mouths and eyes were thin slashes.

She flipped to the back of the album and found her favorite photograph. The picture had been taken in their living room. She sat on her father's lap and a doll rested in hers. It was a miniature version of her, with wide green eyes and bright orange hair. Her father's arms encircled her waist and his cheek mashed against hers. Both their faces were distorted by wide smiles. She and her father were caught in a slice of time, unaware of the dark future.

She carried the album to the bedroom and stored it on a bookshelf. Returning to the living room, she walked outside and sat in the porch swing. Although it was past nine o'clock, the thermometer showed eighty degrees. If spring is this hot, I wonder what summer will be like, she thought. Wren rocked the swing to stir the air. She closed her eyes and thought of Peter. She replayed the night she had spent with him on Skyline Drive.

His long hair tickled her shoulders when he bent to kiss her. She ran her fingers up into it and pulled his face closer to hers. His pupils dilated in the dark and his hot cocoa eyes turned the color of black coffee. She slid her hand down to the small of his back and kneaded the muscles that rolled beneath his skin there.

He was a gentle lover, and she'd never found another to fill the empty spaces like he had. Wren rubbed the back of her neck, twisting her head to stretch the muscles. She jumped up from the swing and it banged against the wall. Returning to the living room, she grabbed the phone book and ran her finger down the S section.

Sullivan, Meade & Virginia. Sullivan, Peter & Anastasia. Anastasia? Her heart contracted. Come on, Wren. You didn't really expect him to put his life on hold until you got yours together, did you?

She picked up the phone and then slammed it back down on the counter. Don't screw up his life again! Catching herself bringing her fingers up to her mouth, she splayed her hand flat against the marbled countertop. She took a deep breath, picked up the phone again, and dialed the number with trembling fingers. She expected to hear a woman's voice and she did, but it was a phone company recording. "The number you have reached has been disconnected. Please call directory assistance for a new listing. Thank you."

Relieved, she set the phone on its cradle and resumed unpacking.

~~~

Wren ventured out of Castlewood the next day to buy some groceries. She drove past the high school, turned onto Route 58, and headed to St. Paul. Crossing the Clinch River, Wren remembered the big flood in 1977. Wonder what ever happened to that Volkswagen, she mused.

The area had changed a lot since then. The river had been rerouted in 1983 to prevent other devastating floods. Since then the Clinch River had experienced a renaissance. A legion of fans, touting the river as a source of natural beauty and a home to rare species of fish and mussels, had even organized an annual festival. She vowed to check it out as she turned into a shopping center in St. Paul.

After she packed her groceries into the car, she decided

to take a quick cruise through town. It had been more than two decades since Wren had been in St. Paul. A little more than a thousand people lived there. Trees shaded tidy streets, flowers brightened yards, and residents stood on sidewalks or in parking lots discussing friends and neighbors, weather and politics. Wren noted with dismay that the soda fountain shop was closed. The old hotel had been renovated; now it housed seniors. When she turned at the post office, a business caught her eye.

She whipped into a parking space and stared at the name painted across the glass. Unadorned, unpretentious letters lined up to form a simple message: Sullivan Architectural Services. Wren gripped the steering wheel with both hands and tried to stare through the glass. The morning sun frustrated her efforts; all she saw was her own reflection, a pale woman clutching a steering wheel like it was a life preserver.

She climbed out of the car and walked across the sidewalk. Her feet resisted and she dragged them along like anchors. She framed her face with her slender hands and looked through the window. The room was dim but she could make out architectural renderings and photographs of buildings hanging on the walls. She saw two computers, wide filing cabinets, and a drafting table. Papers, curling at the edges, covered tables and chairs.

Wren reached down and twisted the door knob. Locked. She laughed. Of course it's locked, stupid. It's Sunday. She retreated to the car and drove home.

~~~

She spent the next week corresponding with the mental health professionals and child development specialists who would be working with her at the Childhood Wellness Center in Lebanon. The facility's grand opening would be June 1, only two weeks away. In between bouts of cleaning, Wren worked on her art healing program, which was based on her work in Pittsburgh and Morgantown.

She called Felicia often. Since she sat on the board of directors for the center, Felicia had championed Wren as her choice to be art therapist. When you're powerless, it pays to know the powerful, Wren thought.

~~~

She saw Peter once and the seeing was as sweet and as bitter as blackberries that hang too long on the vine. She had gotten into the habit of driving around St. Paul every evening just to reabsorb her memories of it. Sitting at an intersection, she glanced out the car window and saw him coming out of a convenience store.

He wore ragged jeans, a dark blue T-shirt, and sandals. His shaggy hair was black as coal and he pushed it back from his face in a gesture so familiar to her that she ached. A little girl held his hand and she looked so much like him that Wren had no doubt she was his daughter.

The child was eating an ice cream and it dribbled down her chin and arm. Peter crouched next to her and wiped the chocolate from her face with a paper napkin. When he smiled at the girl, Wren started to cry. She recognized the look on his face; her own father had smiled at her like that when she was a child.

A car horn sounded behind her and she pulled through the light. She wiped her eyes with the back of her hand and tapped the accelerator. She had work waiting at home.

~~~

One night she tried to contact Maryann. A man answered the phone. "Hello?"

"Uh, hello. May I speak with Maryann Trent please?"

"Who's calling?"

"Oh, Katherine Johnson. She, uhm, used to babysit me when I was a kid."

The man cleared his throat. "Katherine. Are you the little girl whose father was killed in a mining accident?"

"Yes."

"Maryann told me about you. She often wondered

218

where you were her last few years. I'm sorry, Katherine, but she passed away two years ago from a stroke. I'm her nephew."

"Oh. Well, I'm sorry to hear that. I hadn't seen her in more than twenty years. I just wondered – well, anyway, I guess it doesn't matter now."

"Is there anything I can help you with?" She heard kindness in the man's voice.

"Would you happen to know if anyone is living in my old house? It's the one right down the road from Maryann's house, down in the little valley." Wren held her breath.

"Nooo." He drew out the word. "Actually, that house burned down about ten years ago. I'm not even sure who owns that property now, but it's pretty grown up with brush and weeds."

Disappointment settled in Wren's chest and she coughed. "Well, I wasn't expecting that. Oh, goodness."

"I'm sorry. I guess I'm full of bad news for you."

"Oh, don't apologize. Thank you for letting me know. And, again, I'm sorry to hear about Miss Trent." As she hung up, she was surprised to find she really was sorry.

~~~

Wren woke up in a sheath of sweat. She pushed away nightmares of black water to answer the phone. "Hello."

"You sound out of it. Did I wake you up?"

"Hi, Bailey. Yeah, but I'm glad you did. I was having a bad dream. What time is it anyway?" She squinted at the clock on the nightstand.

"A little after midnight. I thought you'd still be awake. Sorry." Music rose in the background: Lou Reed sang about "Sweet Jane."

"I've been going to bed earlier than normal. I want to be well-rested for my new job. What's up?"

He sighed into the phone. "I was just thinking about you. Missing you, really."

Smiling, Wren sat up and propped her pillow behind

her back. "I miss you guys, too."

"Do you ever think of me just by myself, without Thomas in the equation?"

Wren frowned. "You know what I mean, Bailey." When he didn't respond, she continued. "What's wrong?"

"I think we should set a date to get married."

She rolled onto her stomach and pressed the phone against her ear. "What's the hurry?"

"Hurry? We've been engaged for more than a year." The music behind his voice changed and Nine Inch Nails jarred the air.

Come on, Wren. It's time to tie the knot or cut him loose. Be fair. But I can learn to love him like he needs me to. What he did for me—

"Are you there?"

"Yeah. I was just thinking. I may be down here for a long time with this job. I can't ask you to leave your job when you guys are doing so well up there."

"I don't care." He cleared his throat. "Look, I know you don't love me the way I love you. I accept that. I just want to be with you."

An image popped into her mind of Miller's pet terrier. Dubya was the world's worst beggar of table scraps. He circled the table at every meal, imploring with his sad eyes until one of them took pity on him and tossed him a crumb. Wren pushed away the thought, rebuking herself for such a cruel comparison.

Bailey was a decent, beautiful human being. She gnawed on her thumb a moment before speaking. "Okay. How about October 16? An autumn wedding would be pretty."

"October 16? Okay. Yeah, October 16."

"Go to bed, Bailey." She hung up before he could respond.

~~~

Wren rose early on June 1. The weatherman warned

television viewers that he expected it to be the hottest day of spring. "Great," she said to herself as she dug through the closet. "Just what I need when I'm already nervous – something else to make me sweat."

She pulled on lavender pants that flared slightly at the bottom and a matching fitted jacket. A floral print scarf completed the outfit. She ran some gel through her auburn hair. Cropped short now, it curled around her ears and at her neck. She dusted blush across her eyelids and cheeks, slicked some cocoa butter on her lips, grabbed her materials, and headed for the door.

She set aside her nervousness to enjoy the drive between Castlewood and Lebanon. She took the old road, a two-lane stretch that coiled around hillocks and meadows. In one pasture, a flock of sheep gathered in the shade. Horses occupied another field. They lifted their heads and shook their manes as she passed. The drive soothed her nerves. By the time she reached the meeting facility, she felt a professional composure settling around her like a supple glove.

Felicia greeted her with a hug in the parking lot. "You look great!"

"Is everyone else here?"

"All staff members and board members are here. We're missing a few politicians. The reporters are supposed to be here in about twenty minutes. I'll be glad to get this over with."

"You didn't get a hotel, did you? Cause you're still welcome to stay with me."

"Actually, I got a room at the Martha Washington Inn in Abingdon. Johnny wanted to come with me, so I figured we'd do the whole romantic getaway thing." Felicia laughed and rolled her eyes.

"Shoot. I thought we'd get to spend some time together." Wren jammed her folio under her arm and hiked her purse up on her shoulder.

"Next time I'll leave Johnny at home and we'll have a girls' night out!" Felicia eyed the Center as she spoke.

The building sat on a hill high. The two-level facility had a distinct Mediterranean look. The mauve stucco walls were topped with a magenta tile roof. A flagstone terrace ran into the shadows beneath arched entries. A landscaping crew piled pink pebbles around shrubs and small trees in a last-minute tweaking effort.

"Is this the first time you've seen it, Wren?"

"No, I came out when I first got down here and took a look at it. I drove up one Sunday and walked around the building and peeked in the windows. They've done a lot to it since then. The kids are gonna love all the open space and light."

A BMW pulled in next to them and parked. A local delegate exited the car and greeted them with a wide smile. Wren thought his head looked like it might split in two if his smile got any bigger. His appearance seemed to draw others and local officials descended on the property like locusts. Entering the building en masse, the VIPs scattered to examine the interior.

Wren sighed when the cool air enveloped them. She and Felicia walked through the foyer, admiring the mosaic marble floor. She rubbed her fingertips along a coral stone fireplace. Exploring the first floor, she was delighted with the art area. "It's perfect! I couldn't have designed it better myself!"

"Come on." Felicia gestured to the stairs. "Let's see what the administrative offices look like now." They tiptoed up the stairs and admired the second floor.

Wren glanced at her watch. "About time for the news conference. We better head back down."

Lingering on the steps, Wren rubbed the wrought iron railing as she stared at the indoor waterfall in the main entryway. I can't imagine a more peaceful setting for the kids we're going to help here, she thought.

She shook her head and looked across the open space.
Felicia glided across the marble floor toward a large group
of board members, politicians, and reporters. People began
to take seats as Mr. Sexton, the Board's chair, readied
himself at the podium. Felicia motioned Wren to hurry.

As she continued down the stairs, she caught sight
of a latecomer passing through the doors. Traversing the
foyer, the man happened to glance up in her direction. His
face blanched when he saw her and she froze in mid-step.
Peter!!

Dressed for business, he wore khakis, a white shirt, a
light jacket, and a purple tie. His hair was pulled back into a
short ponytail that curled at his collar. He frowned, looked
down at the ground, and rubbed his eyes with his thumb
and forefinger. He looked back up at her, but she couldn't
read his expression.

The Center director approached Peter and led him to
a seat in the front row of folding chairs. Keeping her head
down, Wren swept down the steps and found a seat in the
back row. Felicia, seated near the front, turned and gestured
for her to sit next to her, but Wren shook her head and
crossed her arms.

I should have known. Surely somebody has mentioned
his name to me in discussions about the Center. No. If they
did, I missed it. Wren stretched her neck to see Peter.

A short, stocky gentleman with grey hair leaned toward
him and whispered in his ear. Their hushed conversation
was animated, punctuated with grins and nods, but Peter
looked distracted. He turned his head this way and that to
inspect the audience. He's looking for me, she thought, and
a jolt of excitement tightened her spine.

Mr. Sexton cleared his throat, tapped the microphone,
and opened the news conference. Wren tried to concentrate
on the speakers, but found herself staring at Peter's back.
He fidgeted in his seat. When he tugged at his ponytail and
rubbed the back of his neck, she wondered if he sensed her

eyes on him.

Mr. Sexton called Peter to speak. He ambled to the podium, but Wren thought he might not be as relaxed as he looked. Scanning the audience, he finally spied her in the back row. She slid down in her seat and covered her mouth with her fingers. She held her breath when he cleared his throat and placed his palms on the podium top.

"Thank you, Mr. Sexton. I'm not fond of public speaking, so this will be short and sweet. I'd like to thank everyone, including the community agencies, for their support and suggestions during this project. It was a productive collaboration and I enjoyed the opportunity to create a safe space for children. I wish the Childhood Wellness Center great success!"

The audience applauded as he returned to his seat. The news conference continued with speeches from several local governing officials. Wren didn't hear another word. As soon as the event ended, reporters descended on the speakers, including Peter. Wren slipped from the assembly and hovered around the front door, waiting for Felicia to join her.

"I didn't know, Wren," Felicia insisted. "I swear. I mean, I knew the name of the architect, but it never occurred to me it was him." She patted Wren's arm. "To be honest, it's been such a long time, I forgot about him. But as soon as I saw your face, I realized—well, anyway, are you okay?"

Wren laughed, leaning her back against the wall and crossing her arms. "I really don't know. I saw him once before, a couple of weeks ago, in town, but he didn't see me. But having him look me straight in the eye is a completely different experience." She rolled off the wall until only her left shoulder rested against it and she faced Felicia. "He's married, you know."

"And you're engaged."

Wren dropped her eyes and examined her feet. "Yeah."

Felicia sighed. "Honey, can I tell you something? I

think--"

An exodus of VIPs interrupted her and she scooted away from the entrance. Mr. Sexton caught sight of them as he escorted Peter and his grey-haired friend outside. "There you are, Felicia! I'd like to introduce you to the men who made this beautiful building."

He placed his hand on Felicia's arm. "Gentleman, I'd like to introduce you to Felicia Rockett. She's our Richmond board member. Felicia, this is Shannon Gilbert. He's the president of the construction company. And this is Peter Sullivan, the facility's architect."

"I'm pleased to meet you," Felicia said. She shook their hands. Placing her arm across Wren's back, she held out her hand to Mr. Sexton. "Bill, this is Katherine Johnson. She's a member of the Center's staff – our art therapist."

Hyperaware of Peter, Wren offered Mr. Sexton an intense smile as she extended her hand. "How do you do, Mr. Sexton?"

The man smiled as he pumped her hand. "Pleased to meet you, Miss Johnson. We're looking for great things from the Center's staff."

"Well, I hope we don't disappoint you." Turning to Mr. Gilbert, Wren nodded her head at him as she shook his hand. Then she turned her attention to Peter. "Hello."

He blinked. His lashes were sable against his pale skin, his eyes blacker than she remembered. Darker than bitter chocolate, she thought. She had to search for it, but after a few seconds, she found the tiny white scar on his cheek. She wondered if he thought of her when he looked in the mirror.

Wren held out her trembling hand. "How have you been, Peter?"

Thirteen

St. Paul/Castlewood, Spring & Summer, 2004

Peter grasped her hand but he didn't shake it. His wedding band felt cold against her hot palm and it clinked against her own ring. He gazed into her face, trying to reconcile his memories with the flesh-and-blood entity standing before him.

Different but the same. Superimposed over the now Wren was the then Wren in his memory. It was like looking at an old black-and-white picture someone had filled in with vivid colors.

She had cut her hair and its pixie curls emphasized the curves of her face. That quizzical scar through her eyebrow hadn't faded. Spring – with all of its possibilities – was vibrant and green in her almond-shaped eyes. She had knotted a purple scarf around her slender neck; Peter wanted to pull it loose and kiss the soft skin in the hollow of her throat.

"You two know each other?" Mr. Sexton asked Peter.

When he didn't respond, Wren answered for him. "Oh, a lifetime ago. Isn't that right, Peter?" she said with a smile.

He gave himself a mental shake, released her hand, and turned to Mr. Sexton. "Oh, yeah. We knew each other years ago." He looked at Wren again. "It's good to see you.

Katherine."

He didn't hear the rest of the conversation. Everything disappeared around him as he watched Wren talk to Felicia, Shannon, and Mr. Sexton. She radiated self-confidence and contentment, but he saw she still wrestled with one old mannerism. Her fingers crept to her mouth before she realized it. Each time they did, she pulled her hand down and gripped the purse hanging at her side.

Once she ducked her head and shot him a sidewise peek. She cocked an eyebrow at him and he wondered what she was thinking. Are you happy to see me? Embarrassed? Or don't care one way or the other? A hundred questions turned over in his mind. "Will you shut up?"

When they all turned and stared at him, he realized he had said it aloud. His face grew warm. "I mean will you shut up the building until you're officially open?"

Felicia smiled at him. "No. Actually, the staff members are going to meet here this afternoon for a few minutes."

"That's nice," Peter mumbled. "I have to go now." He nodded goodbye in no particular direction, turned on his heel, and marched to his car. He threw his briefcase into the passenger seat of the Mustang, then ripped off his jacket and tossed it in on top of the attaché. He jerked his tie loose and unbuttoned his collar. Leaning forward against the car door, he willed his heart to stop racing. He was angry but he didn't know what to do with the black emotion.

"You don't look like you're in any condition to drive." Wren's soft voice startled him and he jumped.

A guttural laugh tore his throat and he turned to face her. "How could you stand there looking so calm, like it was the most natural thing in the world for us to see each other?"

She stretched her arm back and pointed at the building. "My employers are in there. It wouldn't be very wise for me to fall apart in front of them, would it?"

Peter inhaled the hot, humid air. It burned his lungs and he coughed.

"Are you okay?" Wren asked. Stepping forward, she reached out to him, but he shrank away from her touch. "I'm sorry. I don't know what to do or say." She crossed her arms and looked down at the ground. Sun baked the fresh asphalt and its bitter smell rose around them.

Peter pressed his palm against his forehead as he gazed at the hills shimmering in the heat. He sighed before he spoke. "It's really hot out here. I think I'm going to grab a cold drink somewhere. Would you like to join me?"

~~~

Wren looked out the window of the ice cream shop and admired Peter's car. "Nice Mustang."

"Matt and I did the work on it. Took us three years to restore it. It's a '65 Shelby GT350. I don't drive it very often." He pumped the straw in his lemonade up and down, rattling the ice, wishing it contained vodka.

"I saw you in town a couple of weeks ago. You had a little girl with you. Your daughter?"

Peter smiled. "Caroline. She's five. Sharp as a tack."

"She's beautiful. She looks just like you." Wren moved her cup and it left a circle of water on the table. She rubbed away the ring without looking up at him. "You and your wife must be very proud of her."

"My wife?" He twisted the ring on his finger. "Actually, I'm divorced now."

Wren lifted her eyes. "Oh."

"We split up last year. It became official this past February." He sipped his lemonade; its tart taste made his mouth draw together in a knot.

"I'm sorry. You're still wearing the ring so I assumed--"

He tapped his finger against the table: *clink-clink-clink.* "Strange. You get used to something, like a ring on your finger, and it feels funny without it."

"You still love her?"

He propped his elbows on the table, crossed his arms, and shrugged. "I didn't want to get divorced."

She peered into his eyes. "You didn't answer my question."

He stared back at her without blinking. "Well, she is my baby's mother." He jerked his chin at her ring. "That's some rock you got there on your finger. An engagement ring?"

"Yeah." Wren removed the plastic lid from her cup and examined its contents. Looks like she's reading tea leaves, Peter thought.

"Who's the lucky guy?"

Wren cleared her throat. "Bailey."

"The guy from the tattoo shop? Wait, isn't he the one who shot your father?"

Her hand jerked and tipped over her cup. Lemonade crept across the table and they sopped it up with napkins. Stuffing the sodden paper in her cup, she licked her lips and looked at Peter. "How did you know about that?"

"It was in the papers down here." Silence fell on them, thick as syrup, but not sweet. Wren tugged at the scarf around her neck.

Peter rocked his cup back and forth on the table. "How long have you been engaged?"

"A little more than a year and a half." She continued when Peter looked skeptical. "We've set a date. October 16."

"Congratulations."

"Thank you." She smacked the table. "I guess we should get back. I have a meeting at the facility."

"Sure thing."

The afternoon sun glared in the windows of the vehicles when Peter pulled into the parking lot. He jumped out of the car and hurried to the passenger side to open the door for her. She spun her key ring around her index finger. "Well, it was nice to see you again."

Peter panicked when she stepped forward, so he pushed the door open wider with his knee to block her path.

"Wait!"

She backed up a step. "What is it?"

"This is stupid. You're not going to just prance off without giving me an explanation!"

"An explanation?"

He squeezed his hands together into two fists. "Stop playing dumb, Wren. I think I deserve some answers. You deserted me! You didn't even have the guts to give me the kiss-off in person."

She crossed her arms and jangled the keys against her elbow. "I had to do it, Peter. Don would have gone through you to get to me. I did it for you."

Peter laughed. "Oh, please! You don't really believe that. I sure don't. You wanna know what I think?"

Blood rushed to her face and her nostrils flared. "What?"

"You were a coward. You were afraid to stay with me because we were getting so close. You were afraid of your own feelings. You were scared to tell me that you loved me."

Wren laughed and shook her head. "This coming from a man who can't say whether or not he loves his wife?"

"Ex-wife! And we're not talking about me loving Anastasia; we're talking about you loving me."

"God, were you always this arrogant? What makes you think you were the center of my world?"

A lock of hair had pulled loose from Peter's ponytail and it hung in his face. Flipping it out of his eyes, he backed Wren against the car and gripped her elbows. She dropped her keys onto the pavement between them. Bending his head so that his left cheek touched her left cheek, he breathed into her ear, "You were the center of mine."

They stood motionless for a long time before he stepped away from her. He stooped to retrieve her keys and was surprised at how cold they felt. He held them out to Wren and she scooped them out of his palm.

"I couldn't depend on you, Peter." Her mouth turned down at the corners. "You were a lush."

Peter felt a mantle of blood settle across his face. "That's not fair! And it's not true."

"God, it's been what? Thirteen years? And you still can't admit you had a drinking problem."

"Look, I haven't touched a drop in a year. Not since I separated from my wife."

Wren's face softened. "I'm glad. Especially for your little girl." She shouldered her purse and stepped around him. "It doesn't matter now, anyway. The world didn't stop on its axis when I left. I'm okay. You're okay. La-de-dah. La-de-dah."

Peter's fingers twitched, but he refrained from grabbing Wren and shaking her. "You can pretend everything is fine and dandy, but I'm not stupid! You were afraid of loving me then. What are you afraid of now? And what about Bailey?"

"What about him?" A white ring lined her mouth and her cheeks sported cherry blotches.

"Do you tell Bailey you love him? *Do* you love him? Or is this a marriage of convenience?"

The force of her slap rocked his head to the side and he bit his tongue. He covered his stinging cheek with his palm. Leaning against the car, he spit blood onto the pavement. Wren lifted her fingers to his face, but he ducked his head. "Don't touch me."

"I'm sorry. But you had no right to say those things. You don't know Bailey. And you don't know me. Not anymore." She scanned the horizon, squinting her eyes against the sun. "You're right. I was afraid of a lot of things back then. But I'm not afraid now." She turned, stalked across the parking lot, and flung open the Center's door. It slammed shut behind her.

Peter echoed it by slamming the Mustang's passenger door. He marched around the car and flung open the other door. Cursing, he laid his forehead against the roof of the car. His head thumped with each beat of his heart. He spit again, then climbed into the driver's seat. Peeling out of the parking lot, he left a black rubber track of tears down the pavement.

~~~

"Daddy, I don't like green beans. Do I have to eat them?" Caroline stirred her food around on her plate.

I know another little girl who didn't like green beans. "You like carrots, don't you? Eat two helpings of carrots and you don't have to eat your green beans." Peter scraped her beans on to his plate and gave her another serving of carrots.

"Beans'n'carrots, beans'n'carrots, beans'n'carrots," she chanted as she ate.

"Don't sing at the table, young'n." Ginny shook her head at Caroline before turning her attention to Peter. "You're awful quiet tonight. Anything wrong?"

Peter sighed. "When I went up to the news conference for the Childhood Wellness Center, I ran into someone I thought I'd never see again." He jabbed a green bean with his fork. "Wren was there."

Ginny rested her elbows on the table. "Wren? That girl that--"

"Go out in the backyard and play if you're done eating," Meade told Caroline. She was making grid marks in her mashed potatoes with her fork. She jumped up from her chair and ran from the room. "And stay away from that water barrel!" Meade shouted. They heard the kitchen door slam a few seconds later.

Ginny stacked Caroline's plate on top of hers. "What was she doing there?"

"She's a staff member. An art therapist. I talked to her after the meeting. She's been in Pennsylvania and West Virginia all this time."

Meade handed Ginny his empty plate. "Well, ain't that something? Really turned her life around, did she?"

Ginny's mouth was a thin seam. "And now she's fixing

to flip yours around. Whyn't she stay up there?"

Peter rested his chin in his hands. "She's got a right to live wherever she wants to, Mom. She's renting a house over in Castlewood."

Ginny shook her head as she continued to gather the dirty dishes. "You don't need this right now, Big'un. You've spent the past year trying to keep it together, and Ana jerking you along the whole way. Caroline's just now getting used to being shuffled back and forth between the two of you. How are you gonna explain Wren to her?"

Peter threw his fork onto his plate. "I've got nothing to explain. Wren's engaged. Anyway, if she'd cared about me, she would have contacted me at least once in all these years."

Meade lifted his head and looked at Peter through the bottom of his bifocals. "Well, no use in acting like a sore-tailed cat, son. Your mother's just concerned about you and Caroline, that's all."

Peter sighed. "Sorry." He stood and threw his napkin on the table. "Watch Caroline for me? I'm going for a drive. I'll be back in a little while."

~~~

He drove around the back roads, taking the curves a little too fast. His headlights grew bright as night dimmed the sky. Holding his hand out the window, he pressed against the resistant air, which was, by turns, hot and cold. Peter drove up Pawpaw Ridge and into Dickenson County.

The road writhed past houses that seemed to huddle together for protection from the mountains. He drove through Trammel, Dante, and into St. Paul. He stopped at a convenience store and bought some watermelon bubblegum for Caroline. He hated to smell the stuff, but she loved it.

Heading to the check-out counter, he took a detour to the back of the store. Cartons of cold beer stood in neat rows behind thick glass. Peter stared at the bottles, squat ponies and tall long-necks. Pale ales, smooth lagers, and rich stouts gleamed in the fluorescent light.

The quick pop of a beer cap echoed in his head. He closed his eyes and pictured a frosty bottle in his hand. Vapor rose from it like a genie released from a lamp. He lifted it to his nose and inhaled the intoxicating perfume of floral hops and sweet grains. The bottle was at his mouth when a nervous voice jerked him from his daydream. "Excuse me." A young woman in a halter top and tight shorts stood next to him. "I need to get in there." She pointed at the beer.

"Sorry." Peter retreated to the counter and paid for Caroline's gum. Returning to his vehicle, he sat beneath the flickering lights in the parking lot and watched cars and trucks cruise through town. His eyes felt like they had grit in them; he rubbed them with the palms of his hands. Revving the Mustang's engine, he pulled out of the parking lot, crossed the Clinch River, and headed into Castlewood.

He turned off Route 58. Wren had given him a general idea of where she lived. Just want to see what her house looks like, he told himself. Lights twinkled throughout the low hills. He topped a rise in the road and slowed to examine cars parked in the gravel driveways of houses built in the middle of old pastures. Peter thought he recognized her car, a metallic pink Geo.

He turned into the long driveway, but didn't drive to the end. He parked at the bottom, cut the engine, and listened to frogs and crickets serenade each other. A yellow square of light advertised her waking presence inside the little house.

Now what? If she sees me out here, she'll think I'm stalking her. This is stupid. Just go up and knock on the door. He reached for the door handle, but changed his mind. He ran his hand through his hair and stared at the house.

You could have called me just once, he thought. At least let me know you were okay. But you don't think about other

234

people, do you? You've always been selfish. A silhouette appeared at the window and drew the curtains. Peter started the car, backed out of the driveway, and headed home.

~~~

Caroline jumped into his arms when he walked into the living room. "Where've you been, Daddy? Why didn't you take me with you?"

"You think every time somebody grabs their car keys that you should go with them." He swung her around in a circle and she squealed.

Meade looked up from the book he was reading. "Was starting to get a little worried. You said you'd be back in a little while. It's been more than two hours."

Peter shrugged as he set Caroline on her feet. "Sorry. I was just riding around. I didn't realize I was gone that long. Where's Mom?"

"Talking on the phone in the kitchen. She's trying to tell Theresa how to keep the deer from eating her flowers."

Caroline rested her bare feet on Peter's shoes, wrapped her arms around his waist, and leaned back to smile at him. "I think it's time for bed," he told her. He lumbered across the room with her still standing on his feet. "Go brush your teeth and wash your face. I'll be up in a minute." He shook his head as she thundered up the stairs.

Meade closed his book and laid it on the end table. Removing his glasses, he stuck them in his shirt pocket. "Everything all right?"

"Yeah, I guess. Did a lot of thinking while I was out riding around."

"Thinking about drinking?"

Peter flushed. "That and some other things."

"You've done good this past year, Peter. Don't turn back now." Meade stood and placed his gnarled hand on his son's shoulder. "I know your mother gave you a hard time at dinner, but she was worried. Don't be mad at her." He patted his shoulder and started up the stairs. "You never did stop loving that girl, did you? I know you can't help it, but it might be to your ruination."

Peter followed his father up the steps and went to Caroline's room. She was sitting in the middle of the bed playing with a doll. He pulled the bubblegum from his pocket and laid it on her nightstand. "There, I brought you something. Don't mess with it until tomorrow, okay?"

"Thanks, Daddy." She tucked the doll between the sheets and cocked her head at him.

"Did you brush your teeth and wash your face like I told you?"

"Yes." She stretched her legs out and draped them across his lap. He lifted her feet and frowned at the layer of dirt on her soles.

"You must be a member of the Blackfoot tribe. Look at those nasty feet!" He retrieved a soapy washcloth from the bathroom and wiped the dirt from her soles.

Caroline giggled while he dried them. "That tickles!" She climbed beneath the bed coverings and let her head sink into the pillow. Peter kissed her on the cheek and then she kissed him.

He pushed her hair back behind her ear and watched her yawn. God, I dread seeing her go back to D.C., he thought. She's my life. I really screwed things up. I can't do anything else that might make it worse.

"You look sad, Daddy."

"I don't mean to, Caroline. I was just thinking about how much I love you. Do you know how much?"

She spread her arms wide. "This much?"

"More than that. More than anything else in the whole entire world!"

"I love you that much, too," she said. She yawned again and closed her eyes. "Night, Daddy."

"Sleep tight, Knothead."

~~~

Peter parked next to Wren's car and looked at his watch.

Five o'clock. She should be out in a minute. He stepped out of the car and rested his butt against the door. Employees streamed out of the Center in clusters of two and three. Accompanying a dark-skinned older woman across the parking lot, Wren threw her head back and laughed at something her companion said. A silver thrill chilled Peter when he heard it.

Wren was in the midst of a lively conversation when she saw him. Her mouth snapped shut and her smile disappeared. Peter couldn't hear what she said to the other lady, but the woman hugged her and veered off to her car. Wren shook her head as she approached him. "What are you doing here?"

"I don't feel good about the way we parted the other day. I wanted to apologize for the things I said."

She tossed books and her purse into the car and spoke without looking at Peter. "Apology accepted. I'm sorry, too. So, I guess we're good now." She climbed into the car, but Peter leaned in behind her.

"Don't run away from me."

She ran her palms back and forth along the steering wheel and stared out the windshield. "What do you want from me?"

"I just want to know you. That's all. I want to know about your life." Crouching down next to the car, he rested his elbows on his knees. He weaved his fingers together and rubbed his left palm with his right thumb as he talked. "How about a movie Saturday night?"

"You know I'm engaged." She sounded impatient.

He held up his hands. "Not a date! Just two people – two friends – catching up with each other. I won't even buy you dinner. How's that?"

He was pleased when she smiled. She sighed. "Okay."

"Great. I'll pick you up at seven."

"No, wait. Uhm, let's do a matinee."

"Afraid to be with me after dark?" He meant it as a joke,

but she blushed. "Okay. I'll pick you up at – uhm -- one?"

"Let me give you directions to my house."

"No need. I know where it is."

Wren stared at him a moment, then shut the door and pulled away. Waving goodbye, Peter watched her disappear into the distance.

~~~

During the ride to Abingdon, Wren told him about her college and work experiences. She didn't mention Don, Thomas, or Bailey, and he didn't ask about them. She listened while he talked about his job, his drinking, and his divorce. The conversation faltered as they neared the movie theater, so Wren asked him, "What's been your greatest accomplishment so far?"

He didn't hesitate. "Caroline."

She smiled. "Is it difficult for you when she goes back to her mother?"

"I can't express how hard it is! As soon as she got down here this spring, I started dreading her going back this fall. I wish — well, it doesn't matter. Things are the way they are and that's it. I just try to make the best of it."

They hurried into the theater lobby, grabbed popcorn and drinks, and seated themselves in the auditorium. Peter studied Wren out of the corner of his eye. She wore jeans and a sheer blouse with ruffled sleeves. Its port wine hue made her skin glow.

"Stop staring at me."

"Sorry." He cleared his throat and stared at the blank screen.

"You lied to me."

Peter jerked his head around. "What?"

Laughing, Wren held up her popcorn. "You said you wouldn't buy me dinner." The lights dimmed then, and her feline eyes gleamed in the dark. Peter shivered beneath her gaze.

Packed with explosions and the latest CG effects,

the movie threatened to burst the speakers that lined the auditorium walls. Once Peter glanced over at Wren and discovered her watching him. The light from the screen whitewashed her face, giving her features an odd one-dimensional appearance. She looked like a cardboard cutout.

They remained in the theater after the screen died its grey death. Wren stuffed her buttery napkin into the greasy tub and covered the remains of the popcorn. When she turned to him and smiled, he saw a grain of salt clinging to the corner of her mouth. He felt the urge to lick it with a quick flick of his tongue. He gripped his soda cup so hard the plastic cracked and pop leaked from it. "We better go," he said.

~~~

They talked by phone every evening after Caroline went to bed. Thursday night Peter finally broached the subject of her engagement during a lull in their conversation. "I'm curious. Most women who are engaged never stop talking about their wedding plans and their husbands-to-be. You haven't said a word about yours."

For a moment, she breathed into the phone in silence. "I'm not most women."

"Well, that's true. I just wondered. Where are you holding the ceremony?"

She cleared her throat. "We haven't decided."

"Oh. What's your dress look like?"

"I haven't bought a dress yet."

Peter leaned back in the rocking chair on the porch and pressed the cell phone against his ear. Stars pierced the sky. "Shouldn't you be getting all this stuff together? You've only got a few months."

"What are you? A wedding planner? I don't want to talk about it!"

"Do you feel obligated to him or something?"

"What? Hold on." Peter heard a muffled thump and

Wren's footsteps. She muttered a string of curses as she came back on the line. "Just drop it, Peter."

"The thing is . . . I can't. It's obvious you aren't real excited about this wedding. If you don't love Bailey, why did you agree to marry him? Because he murdered your father?"

"Don wasn't my father! And Bailey's not a murderer!" Her voice screeched and the phone crackled. "I don't want to talk about this. I've got to go."

"Wait! Hello? Hellooo?" Peter clutched the phone to his chest and shut his eyes. The problem with cell phones is they don't convey the finality of a phone being slammed in anger.

~~~

Wren didn't answer the phone or return his calls Friday. That Saturday Peter took Caroline with him to the grocery store. She entertained him with her constant chatter as they walked up and down the aisles. They got bogged down in the cereal aisle, as they always did when she was with him. "I want this one," she insisted, hugging a bright box to her chest.

"You won't eat it," Peter argued. "The last time we got some, you pulled the toy out of the box and wasted the cereal!"

"I'll eat it this time. I promise."

Peter shook his head. "No, ma'am. Put it back on the shelf, like I told you."

"You're mean, Daddy!"

He grabbed a jar of peanut butter and dropped it in the buggy. "Yeah, I'm a real tyrant."

"What's a trant? Turant?"

"Get your Granny to look it up in the dictionary for you when we get home."

Caroline pushed the buggy down the aisle and around the corner. Peter heard it crash against another and stepped into the next aisle, prepared to apologize. Wren was disentangling their carts and smiling at his daughter. She wore a short denim skirt, pink T-shirt, and sandals. She flushed red when she saw him.

"Sorry about that," he said. He scooted the grocery cart to the side and frowned at Caroline. "What have I told you about getting ahead of me?"

"I'm sorry." She shrugged and grinned.

Wren laughed. "It's okay. No harm done."

He rested his hand on the cart handle and rolled the buggy back and forth in nervous jerks. "I guess not."

Caroline backed up against Peter's legs and stared up at her father, and then back at Wren. Peter curled his arm below his daughter's chin. "You ready to finish shopping?"

"Aren't you going to introduce us?" Wren kneeled in front of the little girl.

"Oh, uhm, yeah. This is my daughter, Caroline. Caroline, this is my – this is Wren."

Wren extended her hand to Caroline. "I'm pleased to meet you. You're very pretty."

Caroline clasped her hand and smiled. "So are you. I wish I had green eyes like yours."

Wren chuckled, stood, and brushed dust from her knees. "Well."

Peter nodded agreement, to what he didn't know. "Well."

She held up her shopping list. "Better get it over with."

"Yeah, me too."

"Goodbye."

"Bye."

Wren rolled her cart a few feet down the aisle. Caroline pulled away from Peter and ran after her. Wren turned when the little girl tugged on her skirt. "Yes, Caroline?"

"My Sunday School teacher said we should invite someone to church. Will you go to church with us tomorrow?"

Peter reached her as she extended the invitation. "Caroline! Don't put people on the spot like that." He grabbed her shoulder. "I'm sorry about that."

Wren covered a smile with her hand. "Oh, that's okay."

He tried to pull his daughter away but she stood her ground. "Well, will you? You'll like it. Reverend McGraw tells funny stories!"

"Oh, well, I don't know." Wren looked to Peter for direction.

He shrugged. "Up to you. You'd be welcome." What? Have you lost your mind?

Wren seemed to mull it over and the nodded. "Okay." She smiled at Caroline. "I'd like that. Thank you for inviting me."

Fighting a sinking sensation in his stomach, Peter gave her directions. Caroline waved at her as they continued down the aisle. Well, this'll go over like a lead balloon, he thought as he grabbed a pack of pudding from a shelf.

~~~

Their church, a brick building with a tall white spire, was set back hundreds of yards from the road. Weeping willows tickled the ground around it while sweet william and dianthus graced flower beds at the entrance. Peter paced in front of the double doors, wondering if Wren had changed her mind. He glanced at his watch. 10:59.

Caroline will be disappointed, he thought. Just as he turned to go inside, Wren's car rolled into the parking lot. Gravel crunched beneath its tires. She stepped out of the car, grabbed her purse, and tottered across the lot in high heels. She wore a peacock-blue sundress with a matching sweater. Sunlight gleamed in her auburn hair.

Peter adjusted his tie before throwing up his hand to her. "Have any problems finding us?"

"No. I think I've been to this church before. Maybe Daddy brought me to a revival here once when I was little." She looked around the churchyard. "Where's Caroline?"

"She just got out of Sunday school class. I'd say she's running up and down the aisle right now worrying everybody to death. I guess we better go in."

She cocked her eyebrow at Peter. "Is this okay with you? I don't want to make you uncomfortable."

"No, it's fine. Uhm, my family goes here, so you'll get to meet the whole lot of them."

"Oh, wow." She tugged at her curls and inhaled a deep breath. "Okay, I'm ready."

Peter opened the door for her and they passed through the vestibule into the sanctuary. A low murmur swept up the aisle and across the pews when they walked in and sat down with his family. Peter felt his face growing hot and he ducked his head.

Caroline crawled across Meade's knees to greet them. "You came!" She wedged herself between Peter and Wren.

Meade and Ginny leaned forward to say hello to Wren. The rest of the family craned their necks to stare at her. "We'll make proper introductions after church," Peter whispered.

Piano notes floated in the air and they turned their attention to the choir. The choir sang three songs, and then two men passed the collection plate. The pastor stood in front of the pulpit to make his announcements.

"Let's excuse the kids for children's church," Reverend McGraw said. The crowd thinned as children left the pews and headed to the fellowship hall in the back of the church.

Peter tugged on Caroline's blouse when she stood. "Behave yourself."

When the children finished filing out, the pastor ascended the pulpit, opened his Bible, and stared at the congregation. Someone coughed, a baby wailed, and gilt-edged Bibles fluttered in the air conditioning.

Today," the preacher intoned, "we'll be preaching from a book of the Bible that's often ignored: the Song of Solomon, also called the Song of Songs. If you have your Bibles with you, please turn to chapter two, verses ten through thirteen. Please stand as we read the word of God."

Members of the congregation rose, Bible pages flapping as they tried to locate Song of Solomon. The preacher didn't wait for them. "My beloved spoke, and said to me: 'Rise up, my love, my fair one, and come away. For lo, the winter is past, the rain is over and gone. The flowers appear on the earth; the time of singing has come, and the voice of the turtledove is heard in our land. The fig tree puts forth her green figs, and the vines with the tender grapes give a good smell. Rise up, my love, my fair one, and come away!'"

"You may be seated." Reverend McGraw began to pray. When he finished, he leaned his elbows on the pulpit and stared at the assembly. "When God made Adam, he said it is not good that man should be alone. The Lord meant for us to love and to be loved. And that's what we're going to consider today."

Perspiring, Peter tried not to think about Wren, but her ankle rested against his. He shifted in his seat and sneaked a peek at his watch. It's going to be a long service, he thought.

After the church service ended, the family walked out to the parking lot, greeting friends and neighbors. Peter introduced Wren to his family. She held Rachel's son, Martin, while Abigail and Caroline walked circles around her, babbling and tugging at her skirt. "Looks like they've taken a shine to you," Meade said.

Wren threw her head back and laughed. It reminded Peter of the first time he heard her laugh long ago in his tiny apartment in Charlottesville. It was so cold then.

But it's not cold now. Sunshine covered his back with a blanket of heat. Leaning against her car, he felt drowsy. He wanted to pull her down into the grass under the weeping willows and sleep in her arms beneath the dappled shade. His head nodded just before Ginny poked him in the arm.

"Looks like you're in need of a nap, Big'un. Getting worse than Meade."

"Are we going home now?" Caroline asked. She leaned

her head against Peter's stomach and yawned.

"Yeah, here in a minute," he said.

"Can I ride with Theresa and Murphy?"

"If they say it's okay."

Theresa walked Caroline to her Tracker. Peter watched his sister buckle her in before he turned back to the others. Wren smiled at him. "I enjoyed this. Thank you."

He nodded and nudged Ginny's side. "Why don't you come up to the house?" his mother asked. "We're fixing to have Sunday dinner. We'd be proud to have you join us."

Wren looked at Peter. "It's not far from here," he said. "Come on up."

<center>~~~</center>

"You sure you don't want some more of this strawberry pie?" Ginny held the dish over Wren's plate.

"Oh Lord, no. I'm stuffed. I haven't had food this good since I was a kid." Gazing at the table, she sighed with pleasure. "Fried green tomatoes, pickled corn, fried potatoes, greens, and pork roast. Pshew, I'm about to bust!"

Ginny beamed at her. "Well, I'll fix you up a plate to take home with you."

"Can I wash the dishes for you?" Wren asked.

"We've got them," Theresa said. She and Murphy jumped up and began scraping the plates.

Caroline clutched her elbow. "Wren. Come upstairs and see my bedroom."

Peter narrowed his eyes. "Let her be, Knothead. She doesn't want to see your room."

"Oh, sure I do. I need the exercise, anyway," Wren said and thumped her belly with her forefinger. Caroline motioned for them to follow her upstairs. Her room was decorated in shades of purple. "Wow," Wren said. "This is a great room. You know, purple is my favorite color."

"Daddy painted it for me," Caroline said. "Granny doesn't like it." She ran to the window and pointed to the hill behind the house. "That's where Granddad keeps his cows."

Wren followed her around the room, admiring each trinket and toy she showed her. Caroline retrieved a framed picture from her nightstand. "This is my mommy."

The young woman sat on the front steps of a house with Caroline between her legs. Her honeyed braid hung down over her right shoulder. She smiled but her blue eyes were solemn. "She's pretty," Wren said.

Caroline nodded. "I know. She lives in Washington, where the president lives. She's an inter, an inter--"

"An interior designer," Peter said. He leaned against the doorframe with his arms folded across his chest.

"Yeah, that's it! Anyway, I live with Daddy during the summer and at Christmas and Easter, and with Mommy the rest of the year." She placed the photograph back on the nightstand with care. "Where do you live?"

"Castlewood."

"We used to live in St. Paul, but Daddy sold the house. He's going to build us a house on Pawpaw Ridge one day."

Wren gaped at Peter. "Where?"

Avoiding her eyes, Peter rubbed the edge of the door with his thumb. "Where you used to live."

"You own my house?"

"The house has been gone a long time. Electrical fire. I bought the land a few years ago, intending to build our home there, but things didn't exactly work out like I planned."

"You were going to build a house for your family on *my* land?" She stalked across the room and glared up at him.

It bothered Peter the way she said "my land." *I don't have to explain myself to you. How did I know you'd be back?* "Technically, Wren, it hasn't been your land for more than two decades."

Her face became an avalanche of sorrow and he regretted his words. "I'm sorry. I didn't mean for it to come out that way."

"No, you're right. I've got no claim to a home there anymore." She touched her mouth with her fingers and chewed on her thumb for a second. "Caroline, thank you for showing me your room. I really like it. I better be going, though."

"Oh, don't go! Can't you stay longer?" Caroline jumped from the bed and followed Wren into the hallway.

"I'm sorry, sweetheart. I've got to get ready for work tomorrow."

"Will you come back? Or can we come visit you?"

"Caroline! Leave her alone." Peter smoothed Caroline's hair. "Why don't you go play with Martin and Abigail for a while? I'm gonna walk Wren out to her car."

"Phooey!" Caroline stomped down the stairs. Peter shook his head and followed Wren down the steps and out of the house.

"You're not leaving now?" Meade called to them from the porch swing. "Ginny's fixed a plate of food for you. Don't go yet!" He walked into the house and the screen door slammed behind him.

Wren rested on the bumper of her car and watched Peter tap his foot against the back tire. Neither spoke until Peter's parents came outside. "Take this with you, Wren." Ginny handed her a plastic plate wrapped with aluminum foil. "You're welcome to stay for supper, though."

"Thank you, Mrs. Sullivan, but I have to be going."

Meade patted her arm. "Come back and see us sometime. Anytime."

Wren smiled at him. "Thanks. Goodbye." She watched them walk back to the house, then, turning to Peter, she said, "Well, goodbye."

"You're mad at me," he said.

"I'm not mad."

"Then what?"

When she shrugged, he pulled the plate from her hands, set it on the hood of the car, and weaved his fingers

247

between hers until their palms pressed together. "My buying the land . . . that hurt you."

She lifted her shoulders. "A little." She pulled his hand down and examined his bare finger. "You took off your ring."

"I've got no use for it now."

She pulled his hands down to her waist. He leaned into her and felt that she was softer and fuller than she had been years ago. He liked the way her curves fit against him. She let go of his hands. Wrapping his arms around her waist, he bent his head and let his lips rest against her slender neck. He inhaled her skin and smiled at its vanilla fragrance.

"Peter."

"Hmm?" He'd never had a high that felt this good.

"Peter."

"What?" He pulled back to stare into her face.

"We can't do this."

He groaned and stepped away from her. Grabbing her hand, he examined the engagement ring. The diamond sparkled in the sunshine. "Give it back."

She slid her hand from his grasp. "What??"

"Give it back to him."

"You can't be serious."

"I'm dead serious." He plucked at a thread on her sweater. "I thought I could do it, Wren. I thought I could be your friend, but I was wrong. I still love you. More than I did before."

Eyes watering, she looked around the yard and blinked hard. "Well, I guess you have a real dilemma, then, because I'm marrying Bailey in October."

Peter pulled her face close to his. "What happened on September 11th? The whole world had its eyes on New York City. It was easy for you all to fall through the cracks, huh? You and Thomas and Bailey. What did you all do, Wren?"

Moaning, she let her head fall back and squeezed her

eyes shut. Tears beaded her lashes like fat dewdrops on grass. Peter gripped her face between his hands and touched his lips to her eyelids. Saltwater ran into the corners of his mouth and stung his skin. He kissed the top of her head before he spoke.

"Look me in the eye and tell me you love him. You do that and I'll leave you alone." He held his breath.

Wren wiped her eyes and stared at Peter. She spoke with deliberate precision. "I love Bailey."

Fourteen

Castlewood/St. Paul, Summer 2004

Watching Peter turn to stone crushed her. She saw his
jaw muscles work as his mouth stiffened around his teeth.
His brown eyes darkened into two pieces of charcoal that
smudged his pale face. She noticed again the pearly scar on
his cheek, a miniscule reminder of their time together more
than a decade ago.

You don't understand. If you knew--

"If you're truly happy," he began, but faltered.
Tempering his voice to match his countenance, he chiseled
his words with care. "If you're truly happy, then I'll try to be
happy for you."

He spun around and stalked across the yard to the
house. She started when the door slammed behind him.
Shaking, Wren grabbed the plate, climbed in the car, and
headed home.

~~~

Peter didn't contact her anymore, and he wouldn't come to
the phone when she called his house. Wren drove by his
office a couple of times, but she couldn't get up the nerve to
stop. She considered visiting his church again, and even got
dressed one Sunday morning, but then thought better of it.
No use putting his family in an awkward situation. Peeling

off her pantyhose and shimmying out of her skirt, she threw herself on the bed and burst into tears. What do you want, Wren? She found she couldn't answer that question.

She immersed herself in her work. She discovered how necessary the Center was as they began to serve an increasing number of children. The number of neglected and abused kids broke her heart. She and the other staff members knew they could make a difference in the community, but sometimes it was difficult to remain optimistic. A grey fugue enveloped her as summer wound up, then wound down. Many days she couldn't even recall the drive home.

Friday evening one August weekend, she arrived home to find two motorcycles parked in her driveway. Bailey and Thomas sat on her porch swing drinking pop and reading the newspaper. She ran up the steps and hugged them. "What are you two doing down here?"

"Checking up on you," Thomas said.

Bailey pulled her into the swing with them. "You sounded kinda down the last couple of times I talked to you."

She squeezed his arm. "I'm fine." Leaning back, she cocked her head and frowned at him. "You cut your hair!"

He lifted his shoulders and tousled his hair. "What do you think?"

Brushing his blond locks with her fingers, she grinned. "I like it. Now I can see those big hazel eyes."

She turned to Thomas and punched his shoulder. "Here you are again and Becky ready to pop any minute."

"I thought we'd spend the weekend together. Becky doesn't want to get out in the heat, anyway. I think Bailey's going to stay a little longer."

"If that's okay with you?" Bailey rested his hand on her knee.

She hesitated. "Uhm, yeah, that's fine." She felt like a jerk when he offered her a dimpled smile. "You guys come on in and rest your tailbones while I fix us some dinner!"

~~~

That night she and Thomas sat on the back steps and counted fireflies while Bailey took a shower. "I always wanted to be a lightning bug," she told her brother.

Thomas laughed. "I don't know. You'd probably blink so much you'd flame out." She laid her head against his shoulder and he wrapped his arm around her. "Anything you want to talk about, Sis? Anything wrong?"

Everything! "Nothing."

"Hmmm. That nothing sure is hanging heavy in the air around you."

Tears streamed down her face before she could catch them in her fists. Thomas jumped up, walked in the house, and returned a few seconds later with a paper towel. "Every time you make a snotty mess, you never seem to have a tissue."

Wren cracked up. Smiling, she blew her nose and stuffed the tissue in the pocket of her shorts. "No matter how blue I am, you can always make me laugh."

"Blue, huh?" He leaned back and considered her face. "I don't know. You look more aquamarine to me."

She smiled and shook her head. "I don't know. I love what I'm accomplishing with the kids. But moving back down here hasn't been what I thought it would be. It's different. Something's missing."

Thomas stretched before he spoke. "What's missing is family. You thought what you missed was a place, Wren, but it's not the place that makes home. This--" He swooped his right arm out across the darkness. "It's just a spot on a map. Home is not a place, it's people . . . people that love you."

"Was I wrong to want to come back?"

"I can't tell you what's right and what's wrong. I just want you to be where you're happy."

If you're truly happy, then I'll try to be happy for you. She pushed away thoughts of Peter's hard face. "I'm gonna go pull the couch out for you, Thomas."

~~~

She found Bailey crouched on her bedroom floor, digging through his duffel bag. She perched on the edge of the bed and watched him. "What are you looking for?"

"I brought you a present, if I can find it." Out of habit, he tossed his head as if hair still hung in his eyes. He wore jeans, but he was barefoot and shirtless. He had a sunburn and Wren contemplated the eerie beauty in the mother-of-pearl scars that decorated his pink skin.

"Here it is!" Retrieving an envelope, he sat down on the bed next to her and watched her open it.

She unfolded a certificate that indicated a star had been named in her honor. Papers accompanying it gave the coordinates of her star, as well as general information about astronomy. "My very own star? Bailey, this is the silliest, sweetest gift!" She embraced him, inhaling the clean scent of his still damp skin.

They lay back on the bed, their knees, toes, and noses touching. Resting her hand on his hip, Wren hooked her thumb through a belt loop on his jeans. He draped his arm across her waist and stroked her back.

Although he was a generous lover, it had been more than a year since they had been intimate. He never pushed her for it, nor did he seem angry when she withdrew from him. Unwilling to hurt him, Wren hid from Bailey the things she saw in the dark. Sometimes when they made love, Peter and Don floated before her eyes, the comedy/tragedy mask that directed her life.

"What are you thinking?" he asked.

"Not much. Getting a little sleepy."

He got up, padded across the room, and clicked off the light. She crawled between the sheets and listened to him undress in the dark. Climbing in bed, he stretched out and folded his arms around her. He kissed her shoulder, then let his forehead rest against the back of her neck. When he fell asleep, his steady breath swept her spine. She lay awake a long time, staring into night's bleak void.

~~~

"You better hurry!" Wren poked Thomas in the back of the head.

He rolled his eyes as he pulled on his boots. "You might want to reconsider, Bailey. She's turned into a real nag!"

Bailey laughed and walked outside with her. He started his motorcycle and she climbed behind him. Thomas ran down the steps, hopped on his bike, and followed them out of Castlewood. They stopped at a hamburger stand.

Wren folded and refolded her ticket and read a Support Our Troops poster while she waited for their order. Funny how Peter and I connected within the parentheses of two Iraq wars, she thought. She caught sight of Caroline and Abigail running across the parking lot.

"Wren! Are you getting ice cream, too?" The girls threw their arms around her waist.

"Whoa! You're gonna knock me down!" Laughing, she looked up and saw Peter walking from a Ford F-150. He wore khaki shorts, a peach polo shirt, and a cap that read Sullivan Architectural Services. He lifted his hand as he approached.

"Hello."

She glanced across the parking lot, but Bailey and Thomas were engaged in a conversation with two other motorcyclists. "Peter. How have you been?"

"Fine as frog's hair." His voice had a false bounce in it.

"Really?"

"What do you expect me to say?" Caroline tugged on his shirt. "What, honey?"

"I want a vanilla ice cream cone with a curl on top."

"Me, too!" Abigail grabbed his hand and danced a jig.

"In a minute." He lifted his chin to Wren. "I didn't see your car."

The loudspeaker sputtered into life and called her

number. "That's me. Uhm, I'm here with Bailey and Thomas." She pointed at them. They hadn't seen Peter yet, but he stared hard at them.

She paid for their food and gathered the greasy bags in her arms. "Well, it was good to see you." She stepped around him, but he restrained her with a light touch.

"Listen. I want to take you up on the mountain. To your old homeplace."

"Why?"

"You want to see it, don't you?"

"It's funny. All these years I wanted to get back home, but now that it comes down to it, I'm scared to go back. I'm afraid what I see will destroy what I know."

Peter shook his head. "It won't."

"Well." She shifted the food in her arms. "When?"

"Tomorrow?"

She looked over at Thomas and Bailey. Now they were watching her and Peter. Her heart raced when Bailey ambled across the parking lot, so she tipped her head in their direction. "Can I bring them with us?"

Peter hesitated. "The road is washed out pretty bad. I'll have to pick y'all up tomorrow."

"Come on, Daddy!" Caroline grunted as she pulled his arm. Peter looked back at Wren as his daughter and niece led him to the order window.

Bailey took the food from her. "Is that him?"

"Yeah. That's him." Finding her fingers creeping to her mouth, Wren curled them into a knot as she followed Bailey.

~~~

She tried to hide the apprehension in her voice. "I'm glad to see this road hasn't changed," she said. "The new road around St. Paul and the bypass at Coeburn freaked me out when I first came back."

"Better roads mean jobs. Or so they say." Peter shifted gears as they rounded the mountain's curves. Wren sat between him and Bailey, Bailey's hand on her knee. Thomas had bowed out, saying he wanted to sleep late.

Bailey stared out the window as they navigated the mountain's switchbacks. He hadn't said a word since they'd climbed in the truck a few minutes earlier. Caught up in her own thoughts, Wren didn't notice his silence.

She stared out the window. The trees – poplars, oaks, maples, locusts – looked as if they might slide off the mountainside into the road. Kudzu tugged the trees earthward with persistent vines. Honeysuckle and blackberry brambles filled the ditch. Peter pointed to a blacksnake, curled like an ampersand between the road and the weeds.

They reached the entrance that fell off the road into the little valley. Peter stopped the truck and turned to her. "You're still up for this?"

She leaned forward and stared across the hood of the truck. "Yeah."

"Okay. Hang on. The road's in pretty bad shape." He maneuvered the truck down the driveway with care, but they still bounced up and down as they drove across ruts and cracks. The gravel had disappeared and a spiral of dust followed them down into the valley. They came to a sudden stop beneath an apple tree.

Green apples, spotted and misshapen, hung heavy on the limbs. When they got out of the truck, their feet sank into piles of half-rotten fruit. The apples burst with tart explosions that smelled like vinegar. Yellow jackets buzzed around the tree.

Peter took Wren's hand and guided her around the front of the truck and into the sun. Squinting in the bright light, she appraised the landscape. Catching a glimpse of a bony foundation, she waded through the tall grass toward the skeleton of the house. Bailey followed close behind.

"Better watch for snakes," Peter warned.

They disturbed butterflies, which launched themselves

from milkweed pods and wild roses. Grasshoppers pelted their jeans: *flick-flick-flick*. Wren reached the crumbling foundation and saw a ragged cedar tree growing in the midst of tumbled blocks and blackened timbers. She walked across the concrete, through dead rooms and living memories.

Peter rested on a fallen oak and watched them pace the remains of the house. Wren spoke in a low voice. "This was the kitchen," she told Bailey. "Seems like we lived in the kitchen. And the living room was here, I think. Daddy used to sit on the couch and read the newspaper while I laid on the floor and drew pictures on the backs of old calendars."

Looking up at the blue sky, she saw the ceiling. "My bedroom had a perfect view of the creek. From up there, I could see or hear every animal that passed through this valley." When Bailey stood behind her and massaged her shoulders, Peter looked off to the side.

Finally, Wren noticed the lack of conversation. She shook away the memories and looked at the men as if she were seeing them for the first time. "I'm sorry. I guess this is boring for everyone but me."

The men spoke at once, trying to reassure her they weren't bored. Wren laughed and walked to where Peter sat. Examining the tree, she said "This is — yeah, I think this is the tree where I had my tree house. The one I fell out of." She plucked at the scar on her eyebrow.

Peter patted the trunk and she sat down next to him. Bailey rested next to her, his forefinger running the length of her pinky over and over. They listened to the place speak to them. Far away a dove called to its mate with a mournful cry. The tinkling creek tickled stones smooth. A cicada performed a buzzing aria. Honeybees droned as they mined for treasure in the lush overgrowth of flowers. Wren sighed.

"Have you been up to the graveyard?" she asked Peter.

"I never have," he answered. "We can try to get up there, if you'll point me in the right direction."

"There are two ways. Cross the creek, go up through the woods, and across the ridge. That's probably the hardest route, since it's so overgrown now. There used to be a road that went in the back. That's how they got the hearse and the gravedigging equipment up there. Let's try that."

They returned to the truck and left the valley. Wren turned around in her seat and watched her home disappear as they climbed the hill. On the main road, Peter kept the vehicle at a crawl while they looked for the old road. "Is that it?" he asked when he spotted what looked like an old trail in the weeds.

"I think so. This has to be it. Anything on up the road would be too far."

He pulled to the roadside. "I guess we better walk."

Bailey draped his arm across her shoulder and smiled at her as they followed the old path. Old pine trees formed a tunnel around them. Mossy rocks jutted up in the middle of the road and fiddlehead ferns grew in the old tire tracks. They panted as the earth grew steep. Wren wiped away sweat that dripped into her eyes.

"If this is the easy way, I'd hate to think about the other route," Peter said.

A circle of light appeared before them and they walked from the shade into the white sun. They stood on top of a hill. Golden sage grass crackled as they waded through it. They spotted a rusty barbed wire fence. Honeysuckle choked it until it almost touched the ground.

The vine smothered the entire hilltop, including the little graveyard. Lush white and yellow flowers emitted a heady fragrance. I'm drowning, Wren thought as she breathed deep the sweet scent.

Peter plucked a tiny yellow trumpet from the vine and slid the stamen out the back of the tube until a clear drop of liquid emerged at the end. He held it out to her. Ignoring Bailey's eyes on them, Wren touched her tongue to it. The nectar was sweeter than sugar, richer than honey. She imagined she might get drunk from it.

She found a clear spot in the fence row and climbed across it. The men followed her, shaking off honeysuckle vine that coiled around their ankles. The tops of two granite headstones gleamed in the sun. She kneeled and tugged at the vine to clear the graves. Peter and Bailey joined her. Sweat dripped down their backs as they worked.

It took them more than an hour to clean off the graves. When they were done, they rested on the ground between the two mounds. Peter twirled a piece of grass between his thumb and forefinger. He studied the mountains while Wren traced names and dates with her fingertips. Tears and sweat rolled down her face and dripped off her chin.

Bailey rubbed her knee. "Are you okay?"

Nodding, she pulled her shirt up and mopped her face. "There's nobody I would rather share this experience with than you two. I just wish Thomas had come." Bailey and Peter stared at each other without blinking.

"It's getting pretty hot." Bailey stood and pulled her to her feet, nodding to Peter. "We better go."

~~~

Heat turned Castlewood's countryside into a fun house image that stretched and shrank before their eyes. When they passed the bank, the sign's thermometer read 98 degrees. When they reached Wren's house, Thomas's motorcycle was gone. She invited Peter inside. "I made a big jug of sweet tea this morning. It'll be good and cold by now."

While she poured tall glasses of tea for them, Peter wandered around her living room and examined her pictures. He lifted a framed photograph of a young boy who looked like he was about nine or ten years old. "Who's this?"

"That's Richard. He's Toni and Mark's little boy."

Peter spied a little angel on a table near the door and held it up to Bailey. "Wren's twin."

An unpleasant silence fell on the room and Peter shifted in his chair. "I should be going."

She jumped up. "Not yet." Turning to Bailey, Wren put her hands on her hips. "Look, you've barely spoken a word to him. What's wrong with you?"

Peter rubbed his face and sighed. "It's okay, Wren. You don't have to do this. Obviously he doesn't want me here, so I'd better just go."

"It's my house. I can have anybody here I want."

Bailey gulped his tea and smacked his lips. "I think we're all playing with fire." He jumped up, looked at Peter, and nodded. "You're right. I don't want you here. You should go now."

Wren stared at him. "Don't do that, Bailey! You have no right to tell Peter to leave."

"You're wearing my ring on your finger! Inviting him in here makes me feel about this big, Wren." Bailey held his thumb and forefinger close together in front of her face.

"Hey, man, don't raise your voice to her." Peter closed in on Bailey.

They were the same height, and although Bailey was a good deal thinner than Peter, he was quick and sinewy. Either man was capable of damaging the other. Standing chest to chest, they reminded Wren of two rutting bucks.

"Would you both stop it?" She tried to part them with her hands, but couldn't budge them.

"What's going on in here?" The door snapped shut behind Thomas as he walked into the living room. "I could hear you all the way down the driveway."

Peter and Bailey backed away from each other and Wren sighed with relief. "Did anybody ever tell you that you have perfect timing?"

"Well, Becky does occasionally, but that's another story." Laughing and scratching his chest, Thomas looked from Bailey to Peter. "What's up?"

"Everybody's temper, apparently." Wren hugged Thomas

and walked him across the room. "Thomas, let me introduce you to Peter."

Peter crossed his arms. "Wren, did you forget we already met?"

"What are you talking about? When?" Turning to her brother, she saw his bronze skin lighten. "Thomas?"

Peter squeezed his eyes shut a moment and polished his forehead with his knuckles. When he finally looked at Thomas, he was pale, too. "You never told her?"

"Told me what?" She looked from Peter to her brother. Thomas walked to the kitchen and drew a glass of water while Wren stared at his stiff back. "Somebody tell me what you're talking about."

"This explains a lot. A whole helluva lot." Peter's laugh sounded like ball bearings in an iron pot. "I came looking for Don after you left Charlottesville. After graduation, I came home and got my gun and went to Bristol to find him. When I got to his house, Thomas was there."

Wren dropped down on the coffee table. "You took a gun to Don's house? You were going to--"

"I don't know what I was going to do." He kneeled in front of Wren and straightened her T-shirt. "I wanted to hurt him. I just wanted to help you. Whatever it took."

She lifted her trembling fingers to her ghastly-white face and pulled at her lips. The monster, that old black beast she thought was dead, clawed his way out of her throat. Her wail drew Thomas and Bailey, and all three men crowded around her.

"Sissy, don't." When Thomas tried to pull her hand away from her mouth, she struck out at him. It felt good and she flailed both arms until they all fell back away from her.

Tears filled her eyes and she slung them away in anger. "Why, Thomas? Why didn't you tell me?"

Her brother blew out a deep breath and shook his head. "I don't know. It was three months later. I didn't see any reason to tell you."

"I can think of one good reason. You knew how I felt about Peter. All those nights I talked to you about him and you didn't say a word!" Spittle flew from her mouth and she wiped her lips with the back of her hand.

Bailey tried to cup her elbow in his palm, but she twisted away from him. "And you! Did you know about this, Bailey? Did you?"

"No." He splayed the fingers of his right hand flat against his chest. "I swear, Wren."

"He didn't know, Sis. I never told anybody." Thomas looked at Peter and shrugged. "I'm sorry, man. If I had told her you'd been to Don's house, she would have come back down here looking for you. I was afraid Don would find her. I did it for your own good, Wren."

"My own good?" She paced the room, tugging at her curls. "My own good? Do you even realize what you've done?"

"Calm down! What's done is done. What difference does it make now?" Thomas sank down in an armchair.

"What difference does it make? It changes everything, Thomas!"

"Everything?" Bailey's face had the pinched look of someone recovering from a long illness.

Wren ground the heels of her hands against her temples. "Yes, Bailey! Everything." Turning to Peter, she curled her hands into fists and dropped them to her sides. "That night in the police station, when you said you needed time to think, I got so angry. I thought you were weak. I've thought it all these years. Turns out I was wrong. I'm sorry."

Peter shook his head. "I *was* weak. I didn't try very hard to find you, Wren. It was easier to get drunk and put you out of my mind. By the time I found out you were in Pittsburgh, I was married and had a baby." He crossed the room and gathered her into his arms. "I'm sorry," he whispered.

"Wren?" Bailey's wretched voice drew her up short and

she withdrew from Peter.

"Go home, Peter." Her voice was steady. "I have some things to discuss with Bailey and my brother."

"I don't want to leave you."

"Go on. I'll talk to you later." She held the door open for him.

Peter glanced at the two men, but both were staring at the floor. He kissed Wren's cheek and stumped down the steps to his truck. She shut the door when he looked back at the house.

~~~

She gestured for Bailey to accompany her to the back porch, and frowned at Thomas when he rose to follow. "Give us a few minutes, Thomas."

She rested on the top step and linked her arm with Bailey's. Avoiding each other's eyes, they watched dragonflies and damselflies circle the dark pond. Wren leaned her head against his shoulder and spoke in a low voice. "This is really hard for me to say."

"Then don't say it." He rubbed his cheek against the top of her head.

Her throat constricted. Swallowing hard, she raised up and nuzzled the scar that ran down his face. "I don't want to hurt you, Bailey. I can't begin to tell you what you mean to me."

"But . . . ."

"But it wouldn't be right for me to marry you when I don't have the right feelings for you."

He allowed himself a tight little laugh. "I thought maybe you'd learn to love me the way I love you."

"I thought so, too. You are one of the kindest, gentlest souls I've ever known. And a beautiful--"

"Don't." He jumped up and leaped down the steps. When he turned, she saw tears in his eyes. "I've been in love with you for almost twenty years, Wren. No matter what you say or how you say it, this hurts!"

He wavered in her sight as her own eyes filled with teardrops. Sobs tugged her chest and she covered her face with her hands. "I'm sorry, Bailey. What you did for me--"

"You don't owe me anything. I just wanted you to love me for me, not anything I did."

"I do love you for you, Bailey." Wren ran her hands up her face into her hair. "But I can't marry you. Please don't hate me."

He turned, expelling a barking sound. She couldn't tell if he was laughing or crying, but when he looked back at her, his eyes were clear. "I guess I'll go on back with Thomas tonight."

Wren's fingers crept to her mouth. Bailey crossed the grass and drew her hand down to her lap. She pulled the engagement ring from her finger, placed it in his palm, and closed his hand around it. Kissing his trembling fist, she stood and walked into the house. He didn't follow her.

Thomas stood at the front door staring at the distant hills. She walked up behind him and placed her hand flat against the small of his back.

"I have to tell Peter the truth about Don. I have to tell him what we did."

Fifteen

St. Paul/Castlewood, Summer 2004

"You got company coming, Peter." Ginny let the curtain drop and turned to look at him. "I think me and your daddy'll turn in early tonight."

Peter opened the door and saw Wren's car parked in front of the house. She rolled down her window when she saw him walk across the yard. "Sorry for dropping by so late."

He rested his hands on the open window. "That's okay. Everything alright?"

"Not so much, no."

He looked over his shoulder at the house and saw the last upstairs light evaporate. Turning back to Wren, he chewed on his bottom lip a moment. "Let's go for a ride."

Neither of them spoke while she drove. The day's heat had dissipated with the setting of the sun; the night air was crisp. Moonlight passed back and forth through the car, sweeping their skin with its ghastly glow. Wren's face was a scrimshaw of shadows and light. Goose bumps erupted along Peter's arms when he looked at her.

She drove around Dry Fork, down into Crab Orchard, and through Coeburn. She turned up Wise Mountain and they climbed high into the night. Finding a wide spot on the side of the road, Wren parked, cut the engine, and looked at the lights twinkling below them. Peter waited.

Still staring straight ahead, she spoke. "I gave Bailey his ring back."

"I'm sorry." But not that sorry.

"I hurt him." She laid her head against the steering wheel and wept.

"I don't know what to say to make it better, sweetheart." Peter ran his fingers through her curls and pulled her head to his chest. He let her cry. When her tears dried, she sat up and brushed the skin beneath her eyes with her forefingers.

Sniffling, she lifted her head and took a deep breath. "I want to tell you about September 11th."

"Wren, you don't have to--"

"Yes, Peter. I do." She smiled at him but he thought her face looked haggard beneath the full moon. "Don knew where I was, but he never followed. He laid low after we got the attention of the police in Charlottesville. But he enjoyed playing mind games with me. He called me, so I had the number changed. Somehow he always got my new number. I moved and he got my new address. That's why I stopped running. I knew he would always find me."

She sighed and pinched the bridge of her nose. "Anyway, Thomas and his wife Becky bought this huge old house in Pittsburgh in 1998. They rented out the entire back part of the house to Bailey. I moved in with them in 1999."

Peter shifted in his seat. "Were you and Bailey – uhm, dating then?"

"We had dated off and on for a couple of years, but nothing serious. At least for me, it wasn't serious. Bailey was . . . safe." Her eyes were wide when she looked at Peter. "I know that sounds terrible, like I was using him. I guess I was."

Peter cleared his throat, but he didn't speak. Rolling down his window, he hung his arm outside and rubbed the cold exterior of the car.

Wren continued. "I'm not proud of it. Anyway, Don found out I was living with Thomas and he started calling me there. Then Thomas and Bailey came home one day with a bunch of guns and stashed them around the house. 'Just in case,' Thomas told me."

Peter remembered Thomas's cold eyes the day he met him in Bristol. I'll take it from here. Thomas had served a year in jail for assaulting Don. Almost killed him, Wren had said. Wished he'd finished the job the first time.

He jumped when she repositioned her seat to stretch her legs. "When the planes crashed into the towers . . . well, I don't have to tell you what it was like. Miller called and said he wasn't going to open the shop for a couple of days, so we spent all day parked in front of the television. It was just unreal."

Peter nodded. "Ana's dad works near the Pentagon. She freaked out when she couldn't get him on the phone."

"I think the whole country wigged out that day. So, anyway, I decided we needed some fresh air. Thomas and I went out for some Chinese takeout. When we came back--" Her voice caught in her throat.

"Don was there?" Peter cocked his head at Wren, his mouth grim.

Rubbing her eyes, she sighed. "Bailey and Becky were still upstairs watching the news. When we walked in the back door, it was standing halfway open, but we didn't think anything about it. The house was old and the door was bad for sticking." Her fingers crept to her mouth. "Excuse me a minute."

She climbed out of the car and paced around it a few times. Clouds crawled in front of the moon, so Peter strained to see her. Leaning through his window, she said, "There's a bottle of pop in my cup holder. Will you get it for me?"

Retrieving the bottle, he got out of the car and handed

it to her. She swished soda around her mouth and spit it out. They returned to the car, but this time Peter climbed in the driver's seat. "You don't have to finish this now," he said.

"No, I want to." She wiped her mouth before she continued. "We walked into the kitchen and set the food on the counter. I started through the house to tell Bailey and Becky that we were back with dinner. The living room was dark. That's when I knew. That was always the last light in the house to go out before we went to bed. As long as somebody was up, that light was on. But not this time."

Peter looked across the hood of the car at Coeburn. Some of the lights had winked out since they had parked. He wondered if the residents down there ever looked up at the mountain and thought of people watching them from on high. Feeling like he was seeing Wren's life unravel from far away, he ached to knot it up again, safe and tight.

"I should have screamed. I know that now. But I didn't. Instead, I headed for the stairs. Shuffling through the dark, my heart beat so hard I thought it would explode. Just as I passed the couch, Don popped up and pulled me down across the back of it."

Her voice broke as she spoke and she fanned her face. When she regained her composure, she finished. "He never said a word. I don't know if he was trying to keep Thomas from hearing us or what. I know this sounds crazy, but I wish he'd said something. *Anything*. All that silent groping and breathing against my neck." She shuddered.

"He had his hand over my mouth, so I couldn't scream then. He wasn't as strong as he used to be, though, and I managed to roll us off the couch. I landed on top of him and it took his breath away for a few seconds. While he was struggling to sit up, I ran my hand under the couch cushions."

"Thomas had a gun there?"

"Bailey did. A Ruger handgun. I got my hand around it and started to crawl away, but by then Don had gotten his second wind. He grabbed my leg and I tried to kick him, but he wouldn't let go. He knocked the coffee table over and the crash was really loud. When he jerked me on my stomach, I dropped the gun and it flew across the floor. Then it seems like everything happened all at the same time."

Even in the dark, Peter could see her eyes glaze and he knew she was in the moment. "Bailey and Becky come running along the upstairs hallway. Thomas runs into the living room and bangs his knee on the curio cabinet. He's always running into that cabinet. 'Shit,' he says. It's the only thing anybody says the whole time. And that about sums it up, too.

"I feel Don raise up, grabbing for his gun. About the time Don gets on his knees, Becky clicks on the living room light from the upstairs hallway."

Peter squeezed her thigh.

"He aims the gun at Thomas, then turns it toward me, then back to Thomas. It's like he can't make up his mind which one of us he hates more."

Wren reached up and caressed Peter's face. "People always say things like that seem to happen in slow motion. It's not true. Even replaying it in my mind, it happens so fast.

"Bailey's gun is right there at Thomas's feet. He looks down like he can't even believe it's right there. As he bends down to pick it up, Don shoots at him, but he misses. His eye's bad, you see, where Thomas beat him before.

"I scoot on my belly, trying to get away, but Don falls on top of me, grabs my hair, and raises my head. I hear a second shot and wonder if that's normal, to hear the shot that's being fired into your brain. But Don hasn't shot me. I feel something warm rain across my arms. It's blood, so much blood. It smells like--"

Wren found a napkin in the glove compartment and pressed it to her mouth. Composing herself, she said,

"He looked like he had roses sprouting out of his neck. Blooming roses . . . a damned bloody rose garden."

"What happened then?"

"He bled out fast. Believe it or not, we tried to help him. We really did. But we couldn't get the blood to stop. Thomas had hit his carotid artery. He died in less than four minutes. Later on the EMT crew said they wouldn't have been able to get to him in time anyway. He just lost too much blood too fast."

Peter shivered. "Whose idea was it to say Bailey did it?"

"Bailey's." She shook her head. "Bailey and Thomas are best friends, more like brothers, really. Thomas was going to take the blame for it, but Bailey said his prior record might make them think twice about a self-defense story." She blew her nose on the napkin.

"Bailey and Thomas were like machines. Becky was standing over the body crying her head off. Thomas sat her and me down on the steps and told us to shut up. Bailey took Thomas to the bathroom and scrubbed his hands and arms with hot, soapy water. When we came back to the living room, he stood where Thomas had been, wiped off the gun, and fired off another shot into the wall. They made me and Becky repeat the story they contrived over and over. Then they called 911."

"Good Lord."

"I know it was wrong. Believe me, Peter, we all knew it was wrong. But Bailey kept saying he wasn't going to let Don ruin the rest of our lives. He kept saying everything would be better from now on." She looked at Peter. "It *was* self-defense. Don would have killed me. He would have killed Thomas. Becky and Bailey, too."

"The cops didn't question the scenario?"

"No. I think they were shell-shocked by the stuff happening in New York and that plane crash in Shanksville. Or maybe we were all just good liars."

"Weren't you afraid Bailey might really go to jail?"

"Terrified. But I was even more afraid of Thomas going to jail again. I love my brother, Peter. He's been through a lot. He has scars from Don's belt buckle. And Bailey . . . he seemed so calm about it all. He just kept saying everything would be okay."

Peter looked down at Coeburn again. Now most of the town was in darkness. *I wonder what time it is. I must be dreaming. I'm going to wake up any second now and laugh at this stupid dream.* But it wasn't a dream, and he was shocked to feel sorrow trying to climb out of his chest as a sob. He coughed to cover it. "Can I drive while we talk?"

She nodded. Peter started the car and pulled off the roadside. He felt sick to his stomach as the car crawled from curve to curve.

"When they let Bailey go, we all agreed not to talk about it. We agreed not to tell anyone. And we didn't. Until now. You're the only other person in the world who knows what went on in the house."

Peter bit his lip. "And you and Bailey?"

"What he did for Thomas, I can't explain what it means to me. I just wanted to make him happy." She rolled up the window and leaned her head against it. "But he's not happy now."

They didn't speak again until they reached Peter's house. The car's clock read 2:37. He hoped Caroline hadn't wakened and found him gone. The seat squeaked as Peter turned to face Wren.

"Where are they now?"

"They both went back to Pittsburgh. Bailey's upset and Thomas's mad at me for hurting his best friend. And here I am pouring all my troubles out on your head. Seems like old times, huh?" She bared her teeth in a joyless smile.

Peter scratched his head. "I don't know what to think, Wren."

"I'm not asking you for anything. Not forgiveness. Not understanding. I'm not even asking you to keep it a secret.

271

I wanted you to know the truth. If I had known you'd been to Bristol, maybe things would have turned out different. Maybe not."

He bounced his knuckles against the steering wheel. "It's a lot to take in all at once."

A light came on in the house. Wren opened the passenger door. "Go on inside. Caroline might need you."

He got out and waited for her to take the driver's seat. Closing the door behind her, Peter bent down and rubbed her earlobe between his thumb and forefinger. "Give me some time, okay?"

She nodded. "Good night, Peter."

~~~

He didn't call Wren Monday, nor the next day. He walked around in a daze, answering his mother only when she nudged him, hugging Caroline without seeing her. At work, he leaned back in his chair and stared at a water spot on the ceiling. It was brown and reminded him of an old bloodstain.

Would I have done any different? He tried to picture someone holding a gun to Wren's head. To Rachel or Theresa's head. To Caroline's head. His heart skipped a beat.

He opened a lower drawer, retrieved a bottle of Maker's Mark, and set it on his desk. Purchased the day his divorce became official, it had never been opened. He picked at the red seal with his fingernail. His head started to ache, so he laid his cheek against his desk and curled his arm around the bourbon bottle. After a moment, he returned the bottle to the drawer. Leaving the office early, he drove home and crawled in bed. Caroline tried to climb onto the bed, but Ginny scolded her. "He's got a sick headache. Leave him alone."

Peter's sleep was restless. He dreamed of angels tending rose gardens. An angel with silver webbed wings hoisted a sword over the roses. She lopped off a bloom and red liquid oozed from the stem. When she turned to Peter and raised her sword, he awoke with a yelp.

He crept downstairs and found Caroline and his parents in the kitchen eating ice cream. "Daddy! Do you feel better?" She jumped from her chair and wrapped her arms around his waist.

"A little bit." He eased himself into a chair and heaved her onto his lap. "Finish eating your ice cream."

Watching her stir the cold treat into a gushy soup, Peter smiled and kissed the top of her head. She looked up at him with chocolate eyes and he felt his heart swell with compassion.

You do whatever it takes for the people you love. *Whatever it takes.*

~~~

He called Wren before he left work Wednesday. The phone rang so many times he started to think she was avoiding his call, but she finally picked up, sounding out of breath. "Hello?"

"Did I catch you at a bad time?"

"No. I was just cleaning the bathroom. Hold on a second." When she returned to the line, she sounded more at ease. "I thought maybe you had given up on me."

"Been doing a lot of thinking."

"And?"

"And I think . . . I think you should go to the fair with me and Caroline. She wants to go Friday night."

Wren exhaled a loud breath into the phone. She laughed, but her voice quivered when she spoke. "What time will you pick me up?"

~~~

He pulled into her driveway at seven Friday evening. When he sounded the horn, Wren popped her head out the door and yelled, "Be there in a sec!"

She was stuffing money in her back pocket as she walked out on to the porch. She climbed into the truck and greeted Caroline. "I hear you like the fair."

"I'm going to ride all the rides and I want to watch the horse show and I want to pet the baby chicks and I want to eat cotton candy and a candy apple and a funnel cake!"

Wren laughed. "Wow, you may have to go back tomorrow night to do all that!"

Peter shook his head as they pulled out of the driveway. "One night will be plenty. She'll be worn out by the time the night's over."

When they turned onto Route 58, they could see the fair in the distance, a halo of light hovering over it. By the time they parked in the fairground's dusty field, all the rides were in motion. Metal monsters spun and twirled, twisted and turned; the fair was a whirling dervish of painted light bulbs and neon. Caroline skipped between Peter and Wren as they passed through the entrance.

They walked through the farm animal exhibit so Caroline could pet the animals, then they pulled her into the building that displayed food and crafts. Rows of jars sparkled like jewels, a treasure trove of apple butter, raspberry jelly, peaches, pickled beets, corn, beans, and tomatoes. Wren leaned down and whispered in Caroline's ear. "I don't know about you, but all this food is making me hungry. I think we need a funnel cake."

"Yeah! Come on, Daddy." She grabbed Peter's hand and dragged him toward a metal kiosk with crude pictures of funnel cakes painted on it.

They sat at a scarred picnic table and picked greasy morsels of cake from paper plates. Powdered sugar dusted Caroline's face and fingers. Peter gave her a cat bath with spit and a paper napkin. "You'll have to have two baths tonight just to get the sticky off," he exclaimed.

"What are you fussing about now?" Rachel, Matt, and Abigail gathered around them. "Hi, Wren." Rachel smiled at them.

"I didn't know you guys were coming tonight," Peter said. "Where's Martin?"

"Matt's mom is babysitting for us. He was cranky and I didn't want to haul him all over the fairgrounds crying and screaming."

Matt tousled Caroline's hair. "We're going to the carousel. You wanna come?"

Caroline peered up at Peter. "Can I go with Abigail?"

"Are you going to mind Rachel and do what she says?"

"Yes."

"You better." He pulled tickets and money out of his pocket and handed them to his sister. "You sure, Sis?"

"Yeah." She looked from him to Wren. "As a matter of fact, Caroline's welcome to spend the night with us. She's got clean clothes at our house."

Peter hesitated. "I don't know."

"Please, Daddy? I'll be good. I promise!" She grinned up at her father and he laughed.

"You've really got me pegged for a sucker, don't you?"

Peter kissed Caroline's forehead and watched her walk away with his family. He turned to Wren. "Well, I've been deserted. How about a spin on the Ferris wheel?"

At the ride, Wren grimaced. "You know I'm full of funnel cake. If I throw up, it's your fault," she told Peter, as the ride operator pulled the safety bar across their laps.

Peter laughed. "I take full responsibility." The chair rocked as they rose in the air. "Just don't throw up in my direction."

Wren squealed as they descended, the warm air whipping their faces. As the wheel ascended again, Peter turned and kissed her. They rose and fell and rocked through the kiss. Then it seemed to him that they were spellbound, frozen in the air with the world spinning around them. She clutched his shirt and he laughed, breaking the spell.

They stumbled from the Ferris wheel and wandered from shadow to shadow, embracing in way stations of partial darkness. Sugar hung heavy in the air and each sweet breath they took intoxicated them.

They made their way to the horse show and leaned on the fence. Peter propped his foot on a rail and put his arm around her. He nuzzled her neck and she scooted close to him. They kissed again, and dust clung to their skin as horses pranced around the ring kicking up dirt.

An announcer gave details about each horse, rider, and trainer through a P.A. system. The loudspeaker lived up to its name, and Peter's head started to throb again. Seeing him rub his temple, Wren suggested they depart. He agreed and they left the bright lights behind them.

~~~

"Come inside," she said. "I'll see if I can find something for your headache."

Peter leaned against the kitchen counter and rested his head on his arms. Wren popped the cap off a bottle of medicine and handed him two capsules and a glass of water. "You used to get those headaches when you were stressed. Are you stressed now?"

He laughed before throwing his head back to swallow the pills. She disappeared into the bedroom, and when she returned to the living room, she was barefoot. She had changed into a white sleeveless blouse and a flounced skirt. She poured two glasses of tea and asked Peter to join her on the back porch.

They sat on the back steps sipping tea and watching moths singe their wings on the naked light bulb. Peter's head continued to pound. He squeezed his eyes shut and a single tear leaked from the corner of his left eye.

Wren scooted up one step and put her legs around him. She pulled him back against her chest and he realized she had discarded her bra. She massaged his temples with a gentle circular motion and he let his head fall back until it rested on her collarbone. Her skirt rode up her thighs and he saw her legs were pale and smooth, but well-defined. He let his elbows rest on the outside of her ginger-freckled knees.

She picked up her glass and placed it against his temple. The cold container soothed the pain and he felt himself relax. Rivulets of cold water trickled down his face and dropped onto her toes. She bent forward and her cheek grazed his. "Come inside," she whispered.

His legs wobbled as he followed her to the bedroom. It was dark and cool there. Placing her hands on his shoulders, she pushed him down on the edge of the bed. She removed his shoes and socks, and he shivered when his feet touched the floor. She peeled his shirt over his head and dropped it, then she did the same with her blouse.

Peter unzipped his pants and kicked them across the floor. Wren let her skirt fall around her ankles. Her skin was milky in the shadows. She stood in front of him and he ran his hands up her hips to her breasts. He laid his head against her stomach and she ran her hands through his thick hair.

Her voice was softer than her touch. "I love you."

Those simple words, words he had waited thirteen years to hear, kindled a fire in his heart. He pulled her down onto the crisp, clean sheets, feeling as if he had finally returned home from a long journey.

~~~

The phone jerked them from sleep. Wren fumbled with the phone and dropped it. She scooped it up, yawning before she spoke. "Hello?"

Peter rubbed his eyes and looked over at the clock on the nightstand. He rubbed his eyes again. Ten-thirty? He tilted his head back and caught a glimpse of bright blue sky behind the curtains. When he sat up, Wren laid her hand against his chest.

"He's right here. Hold on." She handed him the phone. "It's your mother."

"Mom. Anything wrong?"

"Caroline's been worried to death about you. Rachel

dropped her off early and she wants to know where you are. She's been pure meanness this morning too. She and Abigail put a dead snake in my clean water barrel. I'm gonna wear her out one of these days! Don't you think you'd better get your tail home?"

"I'll be there in a few minutes. Time got away from me. I'll be right there." He clicked off the phone and tossed it on the bed. "Oops."

Wren drew the sheet up to her neck. Pulling on his clothes, Peter paused when he realized she was studying him. "I'm sorry. Are you okay?"

"I don't want you to go. Please stay." Her tone of voice was odd. She didn't sound mad. Or sad. Peter couldn't figure her mood.

Leaning across the bed, he kissed her. "I don't want to leave you, but Caroline comes first, Wren."

She smiled then and he realized he had passed some kind of test. Popping little kisses all across his face, she laughed. "Go."

Sixteen

St. Paul/Castlewood, Summer 2004

After Peter left, Wren called Thomas. They hadn't spoken since he and Bailey returned to Pittsburgh. Becky answered the phone.

"Hi, Sis. How's the lump?"

"Heavy. I hope I can hold out three more weeks. My blood pressure's been acting up again, and the doctor said he may take the baby early if it gets worse."

"Oh, Lord, I hope not. Where's Thomas?"

"Hang on." Wren pictured her holding the phone away from her face. "Thomas! Phone!" She came back on the line. "He'll be here in a minute. He and Bailey were a mess when they came back home last week."

"A mess?"

"Thomas was drunk. I could have killed him! Drinking and riding a motorcycle. I really wonder about him sometimes."

"And Bailey?"

Becky sighed. "I won't sugarcoat it, Wrennie. You've broken his heart."

Wren dropped her head and closed her eyes. "I couldn't go through with it, Becky. We'd be living a lie."

"Oh, I didn't say you were wrong for doing it. I never

thought you should have got engaged in the first place. Oh, here's Thomas. Love ya!"

"Hello." Thomas's voice sounded gruff, but Wren knew he was more hurt than mad.

"Hi, big brother."

"Hi."

"What are you up to?"

"Nothing."

"How is everything?"

"Fine."

Wren clenched her jaw. "Thomas, I'm not paying these rates so you can grunt at me."

"In case you didn't notice, Sis, I'm pissed off at you."

"What do you want me to do, Thomas?"

"Well you could start by fixing things with Bailey." Becky said something in the background and Thomas growled at her.

"If by fixing things you mean take back his ring, I can't do that." Her heart raced and she realized she was mad too.

"Would you have married him if you and Peter hadn't crossed paths again?"

Wren didn't answer him.

Thomas's voice rose. "You've spent a decade pining for a guy you barely know." He cleared his throat, but lowered his voice. "You've always been too much of a dreamer, Sis. Dreamers fall in love with ideas. You're in love with the idea of him. You're in love with the idea of home. You need to live in the real world."

"And that means marrying someone I don't love so we can both be miserable for the rest of our lives?"

"Bailey would do anything for you, Wren."

She sighed. "I know that. Where is he, anyway? I need to talk to him."

"He's on the computer trying to get cheap plane tickets."

"Plane tickets? Where's he going?"

"He's going to Japan for a few months."

"So he's just going to run away?"

"You ought to know all about that." Thomas hung up on her before she could respond. She slammed the phone on the kitchen counter.

~~~

If she could have measured her emotions that week, she thought the tape might look like a spiky EKG. She was high with Peter and low alone. He came to her house a couple of nights, but didn't stay until morning. She had dinner at his house Thursday night and Caroline amused them with a constant stream of chatter. Washing the dishes, they stole a moment to embrace.

Peter stood behind her and nuzzled her neck. She caressed his cheek and left a trail of suds on his skin. Laughing, he grabbed a dish towel and dried his face. "We're having a cookout this weekend for Labor Day and I want you to come."

"I don't think that's such a good idea. Anastasia will be here this weekend, won't she?"

"Everybody's gonna have to get used to the fact that we're together, including Ana and Caroline." He rinsed a glass, held it to the light, and set it in the dish drainer.

"I just remember how it felt to have someone intrude on my time with Daddy. It was scary."

"Well, I'm going to set Caroline down before she leaves for D.C. and talk to her about you. It'll be okay." Kissing her, he backed her against the refrigerator. The enamel was cold against her neck and she shivered.

They jerked apart when Ginny brought more plates from the dining room. She stacked them on the counter. "Y'all doing alright? Need any help?"

"We're fine, Mom. Tell Caroline we'll be done in a minute and then I'll play ball with her."

Ginny raised her eyebrows at Wren before leaving the kitchen.

"Your mother doesn't like me."

Peter set the dirty plates in a pan of soapy water. "She loves you."

"I wonder what I'd feel like if she hated me?"

"Ask Ana."

~~~

"Where are you?" The phone crackled behind Peter's voice.

"I thought it would be better for me to stay home. It'll be awkward with me and Ana both there." Wren stared out the window. Clouds, dark as plums, piled on top of each other in the grey sky. "Besides, it looks like it's going to rain."

"It's not going to rain. Mom's putting the food out right now. My family's expecting you. Please come."

She sighed and said, "Okay. I'll be there in a few minutes. Bye."

Wren grabbed a casserole and a pan of brownies she'd made the previous night and headed out the door. She kept looking up as she drove to Peter's house. The clouds had ripened and burst; they stained the sky. *I don't care what you say, Peter. It's going to rain.*

She parked the car and retrieved her food from the passenger seat. Walking across the yard, she felt electricity stir the thick air until it snapped around her. The family was gathered around a cedar picnic table in the backyard. Wren lifted her laden hands in greeting. Matt and Murphy took the food from her and set it on the table.

She saw a young woman sitting at the table. Ana. She wore a sea foam green crocheted tank top and skirt; a matching ribbon held her ponytail in place. Her eyes were icy blue and her expression was equally frosty when Caroline and Abigail ran across the yard to greet Wren. *I knew I should've stayed home,* she thought as she hugged the girls.

"Look what Mommy brought me," Caroline said. She held up a purple teddy bear.

"Oh, he's sweet," Wren replied. "Better not get him dirty."

"I won't." Caroline and Abigail ran up on the porch and jumped in the swing. They giggled each time it hit the wall with a whack.

"If y'all don't stop that, your Granddad's gonna tan your hides!" Shaking his head at the girls, Peter kissed Wren on the cheek.

She exhaled and spoke to him through clenched teeth and a wide smile. "I have a feeling this was a bad idea. If looks could kill, I wouldn't have made it across the yard."

"Good thing they don't, huh?" Peter hugged her tight.

"You're not helping matters!" She pulled away and straightened her T-shirt. "You'd better introduce me."

She squeezed his hand as they walked to the picnic table. Ginny and Theresa shuffled bowls and pans back and forth across the tablecloth, fussing at the men for not helping. Rachel bounced Martin on her knee as she fed him pieces of banana. She laughed when he reached for Wren. "Who is that, baby? Is that Wren?" He babbled and clapped.

They sat down across from Ana. "Ana, this is Wren. Wren, this is Caroline's mom, Ana."

Wren extended her hand and Ana gripped it for one quick shake. "Hello. Caroline's talked nonstop about you today. You've made quite an impression on her."

Heat spread across Wren's face. "She talks about you a lot, too. She's a real sweetheart."

Ana nodded and turned to speak to Meade. Wren used the moment to study her. She knew they were the same age, but she thought Ana seemed older. Her skin was smooth and clear, but her bearing matured her. She's like a diamond, Wren decided. Beautiful, but hard.

Eating was a noisy affair. The children giggled and screamed while everyone else discussed the neighbors, the garden, and the weather.

"You hear about Johnny Norton's boy? No? Lord, have mercy, listen to this . . ."

"I reckon Connie Hill died. You know, Matt's brother's wife's cousin."

"Your garden looked awful puny this year, Meade."

"Ahh, Lord, I had to plant my corn three times for the crows. Got some good tomatoes, though."

Wren couldn't keep up with the many strands of conversation being knit together around her. She leaned her elbows on the table and listened. Ana did the same.

"I can smell rain. It's fixing to come a gully washer," Matt said.

Peter agreed. "Mom, we ought to get this food in the house before we get caught out here."

"Well, you boys get cracking then. We cooked all this mess. Y'all can carry it back in the house." She cackled at the unified male groan that rose around the table. Thunder rumbled above them and everyone jumped to their feet.

They made several trips from the yard to the house while lightning scratched the sky. "I left my windows down," Peter said. He started out the door and Ana yelled for him to check her car, too.

Ginny looked around the living room. "Where'd them girls get to?"

"Probably still playing. I'll go get them," Wren said. She walked out into the backyard, but she didn't see the children. "Abigail! Caroline! You'd better get inside!"

When they didn't come, she started around the corner of the house. Abigail crashed into her and screamed. Wren steadied her by placing her hands on her shoulders. "Where's Caroline? You two need to get inside."

Abigail started to cry. "Caroline fell in the rain barrel. I can't get her out!"

"Oh my God. Go get Peter!" She pushed past the little girl and ran to the side of the house. Water streamed down the sides of the metal barrel. When Wren reached it, she saw the bottoms of Caroline's sneakers floating just below the water's surface.

"Oh God-Oh God-Oh God!" She reached into the cold water and pulled Caroline up by her ankles. She grunted when her arms scraped the rusty edge of the barrel. When the water sucked at Caroline's body, Wren dug her heels into the mud and heaved the limp child out of the barrel.

She was the color of a bruise, her face grey, her lips garish blue. Blood streamed with water down her face. She had stopped breathing, so Wren began mouth-to-mouth resuscitation. Tears dripped from her eyes onto Caroline's blank face. Please God. Don't let her die. Don't do this to Peter and Ana. Breathe, Caroline!

The little girl gurgled and took a rasping breath. Wren turned her on her side and rusty water gushed from her mouth and nose. "Caroline? Sweetheart, open your eyes. Come on now!"

She didn't respond. A hand pushed Wren back and Peter cradled Caroline in his arms. He ran his hand across her head and they saw a gaping cut in her scalp. Ana rounded the corner of the house and screamed when she saw her daughter. The rest of the family trailed her.

"Somebody call 911!" Peter barked. Ana fell to her knees and laid her trembling hands against Caroline's face. Her skin was pink again, behind its mask of blood.

"She wasn't breathing when I pulled her out," Wren said. She started to weep. "I did mouth-to-mouth, but her head--"

"She must have hit the bottom when she fell in," Peter said. He removed his shirt and pressed it against her head to stanch the wound. "Caroline," he crooned. "Wake up, honey. Talk to me, baby."

She didn't stir. Wailing, Ana rocked back and forth on her knees. She laid her hands on her head and yanked on her ponytail until she was staring at the black sky. Her cries grew so loud that Peter bawled at her. "Shut up!"

Wren gripped Caroline's wrist. "Her pulse is pretty weak."

Abigail pushed through the adults and stared at Caroline. "I'm sorry, Uncle Peter. I helped her climb to the edge of the barrel. It's my fault she fell in." She sobbed and clung to Meade's leg.

"I've told y'all about playing around that water barrel." Ginny's voice shook.

"She dropped her teddy bear in the water. We were trying to get it out and we couldn't reach it." Abigail dropped to the ground, crawled to Caroline, and patted her wet shoe.

Theresa turned and stared at the road. "I think I hear the rescue squad." Everyone stood still and listened to the wail of the siren grow loud, then soft, then loud again, as it crawled up the mountain. Matt ran to the road to make sure they didn't miss them.

The ambulance skidded to a stop and the EMTs followed him to the side of the house. They spoke in soothing tones as they worked on Caroline, but she didn't respond. They moved her to the ambulance. Peter and Ana jumped in his truck and followed them as they transported Caroline to the hospital.

The rest of the family grabbed car keys and purses and headed to their vehicles. Wren climbed in her car and gripped the steering wheel with ice-cold hands. The sky ruptured just as she started the engine and an explosion of rain pounded the roof. The world grew dim and she peered out the window as the car crawled down the mountain.

The rhythmic *swish-swoosh swish-swoosh* of the windshield wipers mesmerized her and she found her head growing heavy. She rolled the window down for a second, but water streamed inside and pelted her arm. She leaned forward and pulled at the seatbelt digging into her chest. Squinting at the orange numbers on the dashboard clock, she prayed. Let her be okay, Lord. Please. Just let her be okay.

Arriving at the hospital behind everyone else, she ran across the parking lot and reached the emergency room sopping wet. She shivered when she walked into the air-conditioned waiting room.

Peter and Ana were filling out forms on a clipboard. Abigail sat on her grandmother's lap and sucked her thumb. Ginny didn't try to correct her. Wren sat down next to Rachel.

"How is she?"

"They won't tell us anything except that they're still examining her." Rachel hugged Martin to her chest and rocked him.

Wren watched Peter and Ana whisper to each other as she wrote on the forms. He pulled a card from his wallet and gave it to Ana. She left him crouched in a hard plastic chair while she returned the forms to the intake nurse. He leaned his elbows on his thighs and rested his palms against his forehead.

Wren wanted to wrap her arms around him, but his ex-wife walked back and sat down beside him. Ana whispered in his ear and he shook his head without looking at her. She laid her arm across his back and rested her head on his shoulder. Wren looked down at the floor.

Nobody spoke and the only noise was the hiss of the emergency room's double doors sliding open and closed as people entered the hospital. Wren picked up a magazine from an empty seat. Opening it, she stared down at the colorful pages without seeing them.

She remembered the feeling of water closing around her. Twice. It explored every opening, seeking a way in, promising a deep, sweet sleep. It was easy to let go. So simple to drift into darkness. The magazine dropped from her fingers and she jolted out of her trance. She bent to retrieve the magazine and when she sat up, Peter stood before her.

He sat down and gazed at her with eyes as black as widow's crepe. When Wren folded her arms around him and laid her palm against the nape of his neck, he shuddered and groaned. "She'll be okay, Peter. She will," Wren told him.

The doctor walked into the waiting room. "I'm looking for Caroline Sullivan's parents."

Peter jumped up and hurried to Ana's side. The rest of the family gathered behind them, but Wren hung back.

"Well, she has a concussion, but she is awake. She's going to have a nice scar on her head, but she'll be fine."

The family cheered, but Ana burst into tears. Peter squeezed her; they rocked back and forth, and covered each other with kisses. Wren hugged herself and tried to smile.

"She's asking for you both," the doctor said. "Come with me." Peter and Ana disappeared behind a heavy door.

Rachel turned to Wren and patted her arm. She looked up at the ceiling and exclaimed, "Thank you, Jesus!" The family echoed her thanks, its muffled murmur filling the room like soft cotton.

Wren tapped Meade's shoulder. "I'm going to go home now. Tell Peter to call me if he needs anything."

"Why don't you stay, Wren? They'll be out in a few minutes."

"I don't want to intrude on them. He and Ana need some time together to deal with this."

Meade looked puzzled. "Well, whatever you think is best. Be careful driving home. And listen, thank you. You saved my grandbaby's life."

~~~

The rain set in for the night. It drummed the roof of her house, drowning out the sounds of silverware clanking against plates and glasses when Wren washed dishes. The wind blew rain sideways until water puddled on the porch and dripped off the porch swing. Restless, she paced from the front door to the back door and back again.

She called the hospital to check on Caroline. "Are you family?" the nurse asked.

I don't have a family, she thought. "Uh, no. I'm a friend of the family. Katherine Johnson."

"I'm sorry. All I can tell you is she was admitted to the hospital from the emergency room."

"Thank you anyway."

Wren called Peter's house, but the answering machine picked up. She hung up on Ginny's tinny voice. Why don't you just go back to the hospital? You know they're all still there and you can see Caroline for yourself.

She lay down on the couch. No, I can't do that. For all I know, this may be a second chance for Peter and Ana. I don't want to screw it up for him. For once, I've got to think about someone else besides myself.

She clicked on the television and watched news images of fiery explosions in Iraq. But we're in the middle of our second chance. It's not fair!

Thunder boomed across Castlewood and the walls of her house shook. She ran to the window and saw the earth standing out in sharp relief with each flash of lightning. It blazed across the sky. A ragged streak seemed to rise from the ground. Purple lightning struck a pine tree at the edge of the road and the tree crashed across the utility lines that hung in lazy Ws across the fields. Seconds later the electricity went off and darkness collapsed around her.

She fumbled through the living room and knocked against a table. Something fell to the floor and shattered. Great. What was that? She stood on her toes, wary of glass, and tiptoed toward the kitchen. Running her hands along the wall, she found the flashlight plugged into its recharging mount. Wren detached it from its base and clicked the rubber button on the handle.

A yellow beam sliced the night. She gathered candles from around the house and placed them on the coffee table and kitchen counter. All the metal and glass in the rooms glimmered in the shimmering candlelight. She saw shards in the floor and realized what she had broken: her angel. She wept as she swept it into the dustpan and dumped it in the trash.

She stretched out on the couch again, closed her eyes, and listened to the rain. Its steady beat lulled her to sleep and she fell into the old dream. She walked through a spongy yard, fleeing flood waters that dogged her heels. Brown water rose and roiled around her ankles. Frantic, she spun around, but the water surrounded her. Thunder rumbled. It banged the heavens. It banged again.

Wren sat up with a gasp. *Bang. Bang. Bang-bang-bang.* Someone was pounding her door. She pressed her hand against her chest and took a deep breath to slow her heartbeat. "Hold on! I'm coming!"

She yanked open the door and found Peter standing on the porch. The rain had soaked him and he had the sleek look of a seal. He's beautiful, she thought.

"I've been trying to call you for the last two hours!" He pointed to the downed tree. "Now I see why you didn't answer. Are you okay?"

Wren pulled him inside and shut the door. "Yes. I fell asleep on the couch. I called the hospital earlier, but they wouldn't tell me anything about Caroline. How is she?"

"She's okay. The doctor's keeping her in the hospital overnight just to be on the safe side."

"Then what are you doing here?" Wren crossed her arms. "You should be at the hospital with her." And her mother.

"I'm going right back, here in a minute. I just wanted to check on you first. I was worried about you. Why did you leave?"

"I didn't want to intrude on your family. It wasn't my place."

"Wren, anywhere I am is your place. What's really wrong?"

She shook her head. "I thought-- the way you and Ana kissed each other, maybe you might be having second thoughts about your divorce. I didn't want to get in the way."

Peter stared at Wren without responding. He stood in a puddle in front of the door. The only sound was the *tappity-patter* of water dripping from his clothes onto the floor. Wren was shocked when he burst out laughing. "That's not going to happen. As a matter of fact, we already had a fight tonight."

Reaching out, he pulled Wren to his chest and caressed her face. "I want you. I need you. I love you." He kissed her. "Remember the night you asked me why I saved you?"

Her laughter sounded like the bleating of a lamb. "Yeah. You said you couldn't think of a reason not to."

"Well, now I know why. I saved you so you could save Caroline. It was meant to be. *We* were meant to be."

She tilted her head back and searched his face. "You really believe that?"

"I have to believe that. Everything happens for a reason, even the bad stuff. Otherwise, life would be unbearable."

"Life has been unbearable," she said.

Peter kissed her forehead. "But not now."

Smiling, Wren reached up and wiped raindrops from his face. "No, not now."

Seventeen

Pawpaw Ridge, July 2005

"Are you excited about seeing the fireworks?" Peter asked Caroline.

"Yes. I love the ones that go like this." She demonstrated with a curlicue motion of her hands. She ran ahead a few yards, and then stopped to wait for Peter and Wren. "Hurry up, you two!"

"No, you slow down," Peter said. He put his arm around Wren. "You sure this was such a good idea, Mrs. Sullivan?"

She laughed and patted her swollen belly. "Our little guy's slowing me down a bit, but I'm okay."

Peter grinned at her. She wore an orange sundress and he thought she looked like an overripe peach. He laid his hand against her abdomen and spoke to the baby. "Son, don't let us get up here on top of the mountain and decide you want to come out."

"Daddy, you're silly." Caroline giggled and flapped her hands at them. "Come on!"

Wren looked down into the valley below them and smiled at the house still under construction. "Our house looks so tiny from up here. I can't wait for Thomas to see it." She spread her arms wide. "Thomas told me once that home isn't a place on a map. Home is being where people love you."

Peter grinned. "I guess that makes you doubly blessed. When will they be here?"

"Next week. I told Becky that Caroline can't wait to play with Eddie again."

"Play? She worried the poor kid to death last time, dragging him around the yard." Peter laughed and rubbed her shoulders. "Have they heard anything from Bailey lately?"

"Actually, he called me this morning. You know that tattoo apprentice he met in Japan? She's working in the States now. They're dating. From the way he described her, she sounds sweet."

"That's great, Wren. I hope he's happy."

"Me, too." Tears welled in her eyes and she brushed them away with her fingertips.

"Come on, Momma." Peter pulled her to her puffy feet. They reached the top of the ridge and Peter spread a blanket on the ground. Stretching out on the blanket, they stared at the sky. Caroline rested between the adults, laid her hands on her stomach, and twiddled her thumbs. "I hate waiting."

"Waiting builds character," Peter told her.

"I don't want character. I want fireworks!"

Wren laughed. "Okay, I've got a game you can play while we're waiting."

Caroline sat up on one elbow. "What?"

Wren waved her arm in a sweeping motion. "Look up there at all those stars. How many can you count?"

The little girl leaned back and counted out loud. She gave up at one hundred. "There's more stars than I can count!"

"You know those stars are really angels," Wren said. "As many stars as there are in the sky, that's how many angels are looking out for you."

Caroline linked hands with Wren and Peter. "What are

they doing up there?" she asked in a quiet voice.

Wren whispered into her ear. "They're taking soft steps across the sky."

Peter shushed them. "Look," he said. "It's beginning."

Acknowledgements

I extend my heartfelt gratitude to Sharyn Martin for reviewing the initial version of *St. Peter's Monsters*. I also thank Frank Kilgore for your time and advice during the research stage of the book. Jesse Steele of The Editorial Department provided outstanding editing assistance.

I express my appreciation to the many people who have encouraged me and supported my writing: Jane Hicks, James and Sara Combs, Charlie Engle and the staff of the J. Fred Matthews Memorial Library, Ann Gregory, the writers and staff at the Appalachian Writers Workshop, and all my friends and coworkers.

Rita Quillen — poet, mentor, and friend — you have encouraged and challenged me more than you can imagine.

My mother and my aunts have been my biggest fans. Thank you for everything you do for me.

I thank God . . . for Your works are wonderful.

Neva Bryan's poetry and short fiction have appeared in several literary magazines, including *Appalachian Heritage* and *Appalachian Journal*. She has received a dozen writing prizes, including a James Still Award for Poetry. Neva is a native of southwest Virginia. This is her first novel.

Readers and book clubs may contact the author via e-mail at neva_bryan@yahoo.com or through www.nevabryan.com.

Printed in the United States
140951LV00001B/2/P

9 780615 263915